Also by James Aitcheson

The Conquest Series

Sworn Sword
The Splintered Kingdom
Knights of the Hawk

James Aitcheson

HERON
BOOKS

First published in Great Britain in 2016 by
Heron Books, an imprint of

Quercus Publishing Ltd
Carmelite House
50 Victoria Embankment
London EC4Y 0DZ

An Hachette UK company

A CIP catalogue record for this book is available
from the British Library

HB ISBN 978 1 78429 730 5
TPB ISBN 978 1 78429 731 2
EBOOK ISBN 978 1 78429 732 9

10 9 8 7 6 5 4 3 2 1

Typeset by CC Book Production

Printed and bound in Great Britain by Clays Ltd, St Ives plc

For Liesbeth

LIST OF PLACE NAMES

In *The Harrowing*, as in my previous novels, I've chosen to refer to the various locations mentioned in the novel by their contemporary names, as recorded in charters, chronicles and in Domesday Book (1086). My main sources have been *A Dictionary of British Place-Names*, edited by A. D. Mills (OUP: Oxford, 2003) and *The Cambridge Dictionary of English Place-Names*, edited by Victor Watts (CUP: Cambridge, 2004). Locations in this list marked by an asterisk (*) are fictional.

Ascebi	Ashby-de-la-Zouch, Leicestershire
Bebbanburh	Bamburgh, Northumberland
Cantwaraburg	Canterbury, Kent
Catrice	Catterick, North Yorkshire
Deorbi	Derby
Dunholm	Durham
Dyflin	Dublin, Republic of Ireland
Eoferwic	York
Fuleford	Fulford, North Yorkshire
Griseby	Girsby, North Yorkshire
Hæstinges	Hastings, East Sussex
Hagustaldesham	Hexham, Northumberland

Heldeby*	near Rosedale Abbey, North Yorkshire
Heldernesse	Holderness, East Riding of Yorkshire
Humbre	Humber Estuary
Ledecestre	Leicester
Licedfeld	Lichfield, Staffordshire
Lincolne	Lincoln
Lincolnescir	Lincolnshire
Lindisfarena	Lindisfarne, Northumberland
Lucteburne	Loughborough, Leicestershire
Lundene	London
Mann	Isle of Man
Miklagard	Istanbul, Turkey
Orkaneya	Orkney
Rypum	Ripon, North Yorkshire
Skardaborg	Scarborough, North Yorkshire
Snotingeham	Nottingham
Stanford Brycg	Stamford Bridge, East Riding of Yorkshire
Stedehamm*	near Bardon Hill, Leicestershire
Sumorsæte	Somerset
Suthperetune	South Petherton, Somerset
Suthreyjar	Hebrides
Swalwe	River Swale
Tine	River Tyne
Wærwic	Warwick
Yrland	Ireland
Ysland	Iceland

Northern England
c. 1070

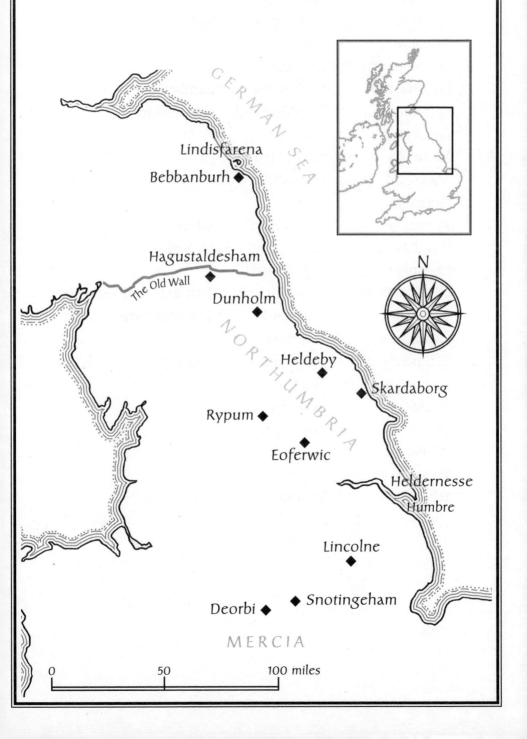

GERMAN SEA

Lindisfarena
Bebbanburh ◆

Hagustaldesham
The Old Wall ◆
Dunholm ◆

NORTHUMBRIA

Heldeby ◆
Skardaborg ◆

Rypum ◆

Eoferwic ◆

Heldernesse
Humbre

Lincolne ◆

Deorbi ◆ ◆ Snotingeham

MERCIA

N

0   50   100 miles

The horsemen start down the slope towards her. All four of them, kicking up thick swirls of snow dust that the wind takes and scatters. Their spear points shining coldly in the light.

She sheds her gloves, curls her numb fingers around the hilt of her knife. Not the one he gave her. Her own. The one she brought with her all the way from home. The one she practised with, which he showed her how to use. Smaller, more easily concealed. She pulls it from its sheath and draws it inside her sleeve where they won't see it. Not, she hopes, until it's too late. If she is to die, then she might as well try to kill one or more of them first.

Stay strong, she tells herself.

She fixes her gaze upon the horsemen. Tries to, anyway. Everything is blurred. White stars creeping in at the corners of her sight. She blinks to try to get rid of them, but they won't go away.

Closer the riders come, and closer still. Her lungs are burning. Her cheeks are burning.

Attack, don't defend, she remembers. Be quick. Strike first. Kill quickly.

She grips the knife hilt as tightly as she can as they loom larger. It won't be long now.

FIRST DAY

Not much further, Tova pleads. She doesn't know how much longer she can go on. She can hardly place one foot before the other any more, but she doesn't want to be left behind and find herself alone on these hills, with night's shadow falling all around her. She presses on up the path, leading Winter, clenching her teeth as she struggles against the wind. It grasps at her clothes as if determined to tear them from her, fierce but clumsy, like the fingers of an unwanted admirer.

Her lady, Merewyn, strides on in front, leading her own palfrey, fifty paces ahead. Almost at the crest already.

She'll kill us, Tova thinks. She'll kill us both. She's brought this upon us, and now we'll probably die out here, in this wilderness. Either they'll catch us or else the cold will do for us. Because of what she's done.

Of course Tova didn't have to come. If she'd been strong enough, she could have refused, could have stayed behind, where it's safe and warm, where there's no one pursuing her. That's what she tells herself. But she knows it's not true. How could she have forgiven herself if she'd abandoned her lady in her hour of need, after everything Merewyn has done for her?

That's why she's here. That's why she came. And whatever happens now, she knows there's no turning back.

The wind whips once, twice, then dies away. A moment's respite. And that's when she hears it. Blasting out across the hillside, each time louder than the last: a sound she recognises. A sound that makes her stomach lurch and her skin turn to ice.

The sound of the horn. She turns, ready to cry out—

But there's no one. Only a goat with an injured foreleg, bleating forlornly as it negotiates a rocky outcrop and limps on down the hill. Her tiredness is catching up with her, and now her ears are playing tricks. She takes a deep breath, trying to still her nerves and her pounding heart. She glances down the path, back along the valley. Fields and hedges glisten white with frost that the day's small warmth has failed to melt. Between them winds the swollen stream: tumbling, frothing, bright with the dying sun's fire.

She shivers, and not just from the cold. If she stays in one place too long, her feet will freeze and won't want to move again. Her dress is wet at the hem, and she wishes she'd had time to gather some thicker clothes, ones better suited to the road, rather than these thin things. Gloves, too. Her hands are dry and beginning to crack at the knuckles. Her fingers might as well belong to someone else, for all that she can feel them. Sharp as steel, the wind pierces fur and wool and linen, biting into flesh: ice-burning, wounding deep. In all her fifteen years she can't remember a winter as bitter as this.

Keep going, she tells herself.

She pulls her borrowed cloak closer around her shoulders and belts it more tightly to try to stop it flapping. Someone back home will be missing it, she thinks, and for a moment she feels sorry for him. It must be a man, she decides, not just because of its size but also because of the hole in one armpit, which any woman would have made sure to mend. Was it Skalpi's once?

6

Probably not; Merewyn would surely have seen to it if it were. It's heavy and the sleeves are too long, but it's all she has and better than nothing. In the darkness and in their rush to leave, she couldn't find her own anywhere, and this was the best her lady was able to lay hands on. Theft, to add to everything else.

This will end up being my burial shroud, she thinks.

At last she manages to drag herself and Winter, her faithful mare, to the top of the hill. Merewyn is waiting. Her fine woollen cloak, with its ermine trim and paired silver brooches, is wrapped tightly around her shoulders. Her fair hair has come loose from its braid and flies in the wind; her cheeks are flushed pink, and her face is drawn in a stern look.

'Keep up,' she tells Tova. 'We can't stop. If they find us . . .'

She doesn't finish. She doesn't have to.

And the fact that Tova's here, helping Merewyn: will that make her just as guilty in their eyes? Maybe they'll show her mercy. As for her lady, though, she's less sure. Not after what she's done.

Tova knows, even without being told. She has seen the spots of blood on Merewyn's sleeve, at the wrist where she's tried to conceal them underneath her bracelet. Small and dark, they could be easily mistaken for spatters of dirt, like those now decorating her skirt after a day's hard riding across the moors.

But they aren't dirt. They were there at the beginning.

She remembers hearing Cene's barking, although it seemed somehow distant. She remembers Merewyn's hand on her shoulder, jolting her from her dreams.

They needed to go, she said. Straight away.

Tova didn't understand, not at first, but then in the lantern light and through blurry eyes she saw those crimson spots. And straight away she knew.

The desperation in her lady's hushed voice. The whiteness

7

of her face. The quickness with which her eyes darted about the room, as if she expected to be discovered at any moment. How Tova's own heart wouldn't stop thumping as she tugged on clothes and at the same time shoved what she needed into her pack. She didn't hesitate, didn't question. Instead she kept her fears bound up as tightly as she could while she concentrated on doing what she needed to do, as quickly and as quietly as possible. And so under cover of night she and her lady slipped away from the hall, from the manor. From Heldeby. From home. By the time the first sliver of sun crept above the eastern hills, they were already long gone.

It was only a few hours ago, and yet it feels like an age. She has no idea how many miles they've travelled, but she doesn't think it's very far. Which is why Tova thinks that sooner or later, Ælfric will find them. Him and Ketil and whatever band of men they've managed to gather. They'll have dogs with them to sniff out the trail; they'll have swift horses beneath them—

'Come on,' Merewyn says. 'Just a little farther, before dark.'

'Wait,' Tova says.

'We can't stop. You know we can't. If we're to have any hope of losing them, we have to keep going.'

'Going where? Do you even know where we are?'

Tova doesn't know this land, and she's beginning to doubt that her lady does too. They've been keeping off the main tracks and droveways, staying well away from any manor or vill, since two young women travelling on a harsh winter's day like this and in such uncertain times as these, are highly conspicuous and easily remembered. What they don't want is to meet anyone who can say later that, yes, they did indeed spy a lady and her maid upon the road, and strange it seemed for them to be out by themselves, and that they came through not an hour ago, and they were riding in that direction, and that if you go after them quickly you should catch them before the day is out.

She has been trusting Merewyn. Trusting that she knows what she is doing and knows her way. But now Tova sees her hesitation. And she realises the truth.

They're lost.

Lost and chilled to the bone and starving too. Tova is no stranger to hunger: she remembers that year after the dry summer when the barley wilted in the fields, when they had to boil roots they'd dug up in the woods so that they could make what grain they had stretch through the cold months. But it's not just a question of food. They have no tent, nor kindling for a fire, nor so much as a winter blanket between them on which to bed down. Already it's growing late; the river mist is starting to settle over the meadows below. The first stars are appearing. Clear skies. A frosty night to come.

'The old road is this way,' Merewyn says, but she's only repeating what she has already said several times, and the words have grown stale. 'If we can find it, we can reach my brother's manor. We'll be safe there, I promise. He'll take us in, he'll protect us.'

'And what if they've sent word ahead? Don't you think that if Ælfric has any sense, he'll guess that's where we might go? What if they're already waiting for us when we arrive? How is Eadmer going to protect us then?'

Merewyn is silent for a while as if contemplating, but there's nothing to contemplate. Tova knows she's right.

Her lady asks, 'What would you have us do, then?'

Tova glances towards the west, where the tiniest gleam of sun is still visible. It won't be for much longer.

'We need shelter. Some place where there's fodder and food

and a fire, where we can rest until we work out what to do next. We can't keep travelling through the night. We don't know the paths. What if one of the horses loses its footing and goes lame? What if one of us falls and breaks an ankle?'

Merewyn bites her lip. It's fear above all else that has kept them going all day without food or water, with hardly any pause. That same fear is what drives her still. But for the first time since this morning Tova sees doubt in her eyes: a sign that reason is at last beginning to win through.

'I thought I saw a hall about a mile back, maybe a bit more than that,' Tova says. 'We could ask the people there if they could spare—'

Merewyn presses her hands against her forehead as though an ache has been building for some time and won't go away.

'It's all right,' Tova says. She puts her arm around Merewyn as she turns and buries her head in Tova's shoulder.

'I never meant to do it,' Merewyn says, sobbing. 'You know that, don't you?'

'I know.'

But she doesn't know. Still all these hours later Merewyn hasn't told her the whole story of what happened, and Tova doesn't feel it's her place to ask. So she's guessing, filling in the details as best she can, piecing the story together from what she already knows.

'This is all my fault,' says Merewyn.

'Don't say that.'

To the west, the sun has at last vanished below the hills. If they're going to find somewhere to spend the night, they need to do so quickly. Tova doesn't want to be stumbling across these hills in the moonlight.

'Look,' she says. 'It's not far back to this hall. If we try, we can probably still make it before dark.'

Merewyn wipes her eyes with the back of her hand. 'All right,' she says as she pulls away, breathing deeply, trying to regain her composure. To reassert herself. 'But we tell no one who we really are. Do you understand? No one. We're travellers – pilgrims who have lost the road and are looking for somewhere to spend the night.'

Tova nods. As if she needed to be told. She understands they need to be careful. She only hopes that the folk are friendly, that they have food and ale to spare, and a bench by the wall or a mattress of straw set aside where guests can bed down.

And then tomorrow, she thinks, we'll do this all over again.

She knows something isn't right long before they reach the hall. Night has fallen. Only the faintest ribbon of orange above the woods to the west. The wind has eased, at least, and for that small mercy she thanks God. Her hunger has gone too; her stomach seems to have given up any hope of food. All she wants is to sit in front of the hearth fire, to dry these damp clothes of hers, to warm her ice-bitten hands and to feel the glow upon her cheeks.

Except as she gazes across the vale she sees no smoke rising from the thatch, nor from any of the field labourers' cottages and laithes that surround it. Not a wisp anywhere. And no smoke means no fire. Yet it isn't that long since dusk. Surely it can't be that everyone is already in their beds.

It's quiet. Not a bleat nor a whinny from byre or stables; no goatherd calling out as he rounds up the last of his lord's flock, nor the sound of a child crying, nor gentle music carrying softly from the hall. Only the owls calling to one another across the valley.

'What's wrong now?' Merewyn asks.

'Listen,' Tova says, surprising herself with her own forcefulness.

'For what?' Merewyn asks, her frown darkening. 'I don't hear anything.'

'That's what I mean.'

It's as if everyone who lived here has simply disappeared: flown away on the wind to join the swallows wherever it is they go for the winter, leaving their homes and all their possessions behind them.

'Do you think we should go on?' Tova asks. Her feet won't carry her much further, certainly not as far as the next nearest village or manor, wherever that might be.

Her lady doesn't seem to hear. She glances about, suddenly anxious. But everything is still: no sign of movement anywhere.

Tova asks, 'What?'

'I don't know,' Merewyn says. 'Stay close to me.'

There's an unwelcome feeling in the pit of Tova's stomach, the same as the one she had when Merewyn woke her in the night. She can't help but feel that someone, somewhere, is watching them.

She remembers the stories the grown-ups used to tell when she was young. Stories of the shadow-walkers, creatures that stalk the night, which were said to come when the moon is new, as it is tonight, to steal away children and livestock to eat or sometimes to sacrifice to the Devil. Tova never paid much heed to those tales; it didn't take her long to work out that they had been made up only to frighten children into behaving. The closer they get to the hall, though, past the churchyard and the empty sheepfold, the surer she becomes. Something's out there. A shadow-walker, in one form or another.

Enough, she tells herself. You're letting your imagination get the better of you.

She keeps a tight hold of Winter's reins as they approach the hall, which is built in the old style, like a boat turned upside down, wider amidships than at bow and stern, the keel arching towards the sky. Like the one at home, until it burned down five years ago and Skalpi had the new one built. Nowhere near as grand, though. It seems a poorer place than Heldeby; at most a dozen families must live here. Or lived. The roof of one of the barns has collapsed in on itself, while the cob is crumbling away, exposing the wattle. Hoes and shovels have been left propped up against walls. Pails stand half-full of murky water.

They come to the yard, which is bounded on one side by the hall and on two others by squat timber-and-thatch buildings that might be storehouses or kitchens or stables. Tova thought that maybe someone might have come out to greet them, if not from the cottages then from the hall itself. But no one does.

'Where is everyone?' she whispers as they near the well in the middle of the yard. She feels the need to be quiet, in case whatever it is that's watching them should also be listening. The wind has died to nothing. Silence hangs everywhere like a shroud.

'Stay here with the horses,' Merewyn says.

'Where are you going?' Tova calls after her, but Merewyn is already making her way across the yard to the hall door. Taking charge. Her skirt trails in the mud, but she's too preoccupied to notice or care. She hammers with pale fists upon the oak, calling to whoever's inside, asking if they'll offer respite to two weary travellers. When there's no answer, she shakes the handle, but it won't budge.

Tova glances around, searching the shadows. Whatever happened here, she decides, it can't be good. As desperate as she is for food and warmth and rest, suddenly she wants nothing more than to leave, and as soon as possible. Out here in the yard they're too exposed. Whatever was watching them before is still out there, and she doesn't like it.

She's about to call out to Merewyn, to ask if they can go, when she hears the laughter.

Laughter, and voices.

She stands as still as ice, hardly daring to breathe. There are people here after all. Not just one or two, but more like four or five or six. All men by the sound of it, somewhere beyond the outbuildings that ring the yard.

Ælfric and Ketil, Tova thinks. They've been tracking us all day, and now they've found us.

Then she realises the voices are coming from the other direction: from the north and west. So it can't be them. Then who? Some of the villagers whose home this is returning from wherever they've been?

They're coming closer. She can hear them muttering to one another and sniggering, as if sharing a joke. She can make out the jangle of harnesses, faint but unmistakable. That, and the clink of mail.

Not just any men. Warriors.

She looks about for her lady. Merewyn's nowhere in sight, but Tova doesn't dare call out.

They need to hide, and quickly. If they're discovered, they'll be entirely at the mercy of these men, whoever they are.

Taking hold of the horses' reins, she tries to lead them away from the well. Behind the hall, she thinks; they'll be out of sight there. Winter follows without complaining, but Merewyn's palfrey is as wilful as her owner and won't move an inch.

Please, Tova beseeches the creature as it tosses its head and shies away. Don't play these games with me. Not now.

The more she fights with it, the more determined it grows. It has travelled far enough already, it's decided, and will go no further.

'Tova!'

She glances across the yard, sees Merewyn's face pale in the moonlight, peering out from behind the door of one of the many sheds and storehouses. Her eyes are wide, frantic, as she beckons Tova.

But the horses, she thinks.

At any moment the men will appear; she can hear them just beyond the low barn opposite the hall. She doesn't have much time. One lets out a guffaw that splits the night like a roll of thunder. Her throat is dry, her breath sticks in her chest and her feet are rooted where she stands.

'Tova!'

Abandoning the animals, she pelts, heart pounding, across the yard as fast as her feet will carry her, the fear that was holding her stiff now driving her on. Her ankle sinks into a puddle that's deeper than it looks, and she stumbles, the mud sucking at her shoe. She claws at the air, trying to keep her balance, but it's no use. She meets the yard face first: mud in her hair and on her cheeks, on her hands and sleeves and the front of her dress. She scrambles to her feet, struggling against the weight of the dirt plastering her clothes, and hurls herself through the doorway into the arms of the waiting Merewyn, nearly knocking her from her feet. The blood is pounding so hard inside her skull that she thinks her head must burst.

'Quiet,' Merewyn whispers. 'Not a sound.'

Tova nods, unable to speak even if she wanted to. Merewyn pulls the door to. Darkness enfolds them.

Not a moment too soon, either. One of the men shouts out, and the laughter and talking cease.

They've spied the horses, she thinks.

She holds her breath as she huddles down between her lady

and a pile of unsplit logs. Small ones for the hearth fire or the kitchens. Bigger ones for fencing and staving. There's no bolt on the door and so it hangs ajar. Not by much – a finger's breadth, maybe – but enough to let in a sliver of moonlight. In the walls are cracks where the daub has crumbled away from the wattle: some needle-fine, others large enough to poke her thumb through.

'Five,' Merewyn says. 'I saw them.'

'Did they see you?'

Merewyn doesn't answer. Maybe she doesn't know. Her eyes are shut tight; her breath comes quickly and lightly and her lips move silently.

She's praying, Tova thinks. As well she might. They're trapped. If they try to leave, they'll surely be seen. And where would they go? Across the fields towards the woods? Their packs are with the horses; everything they own is inside them.

One of the men calls out, although whether for their benefit or to his companions, Tova isn't sure. Whatever he's saying, she can't make sense of it. It isn't English, and she doesn't think it's Danish, either.

Which can only mean—

A chill runs through her, deeper even than when they were up on the high hills, and the wind was battering her and screaming in her ear.

It can't be.

Moving as quietly as she can, she edges towards the wall that faces the yard.

'What are you doing?'

Tova peers through the cracks, trying to catch a glimpse of them. She has to know. At first she sees nothing except shadows. Then she makes out the well, and the figures next to it.

Five of them, just as her lady said.

One is still mounted; the others are on foot, standing beside their horses. Each one clad from head to knees in steel. Their byrnies and spurs glint in the moonlight as if newly polished. Slung across their backs are tall shields of a sort she has never seen before, wide at the top and tapering to a rounded point. Gold-inlaid sword hilts protrude from garnet-studded scabbards.

One of those on foot has taken off his helmet. She notices his hair, cut close on top and shaved at the back. Not like any Englishman.

And she knows.

'Normans,' she breathes. 'They're Normans.'

'Are you sure?'

No, she isn't. Tova has never seen one before, even though it's more than three years since they first came to England. They've never come this far north.

Like everyone, though, she has heard the stories. In her imagination she has always pictured them clearly enough. Dark featured, built like bulls, with eyes as cold as the steel in their scabbards.

Just like these men.

'We know you're there,' barks the helmet-less one in clumsy English, as if he can't quite get his tongue around the words.

Through the crack she sees him stride forward. He must be their leader, she thinks: he looks like he's used to giving orders. Long-limbed, he stands tall, his thin face in shadow.

'Show yourselves,' he says. 'We won't harm you!'

He flashes a grin at his friends. Two of them rest their hands on the pommels of their swords.

They know no honour; they are the Devil's creatures, craving only pillage and ruin. She has heard how they have ravaged the south, how they have built towering strongholds everywhere from which to keep watch over the land. But people always said they were too frightened to venture this far, that they feared to go up against the proud people of Northumbria. Even once the rebellion was defeated, still they hadn't come. The weeks had passed, Christmas had been and gone. Tova, like everyone else, had begun to believe they were safe.

But not any more.

Have mercy upon us, Lord, Tova prays silently, sitting with her back against the wall, hardly daring to breathe. As if that will make them go away. God didn't stop them crossing the Narrow Sea that fateful autumn. He didn't lend his aid when it was most needed: in the great battle at Hæstinges, or in the rebellion that everyone hoped would drive them from this land.

Her heart thumps in her chest so loudly that she fears they're going to hear.

This is how we die, she thinks.

She wishes this day had never begun. She wishes more than ever that she'd never come.

How long it is until she realises she can no longer hear the men's footsteps, or their mail or the harnesses on their horses, she isn't sure. No longer is there laughter, nor murmuring in a foreign tongue. All is still. She exchanges a glance with Merewyn.

Merewyn whispers, 'Have they gone?'

No, Tova thinks. They can't have. They're only listening, waiting for us to make some sound, some movement that will give us away. They know we can't hide for ever.

And then, on the other side of the thin wattle work, there's the soft chink-chink of mail. Slowly, deliberately, one pace at a time, a shadow breaks the tiny moonbeams that shine through

18

the cracks. Tova can't breathe, can't do anything but watch as the shadow passes gradually along the wall, towards the door.

It halts. Darkness fills the finger's breadth between the door and the jamb. The small sliver of light is blotted out. He knows. He's noticed the door standing ajar, and he knows!

Make it quick, she thinks as the door flies open.

One moment she's huddled on the floor by the logs, shrinking away from the giant towering above her, the next his rough hands are upon her, dragging her to her feet. Shrieking, she flails wildly with fists and feet, trying to escape his grasp and his hot, putrid breath.

Eyes and groin, she thinks. Eyes and groin.

She lashes out towards his face, but his fingers clamp about her wrist before she can land the blow. He twists her arm behind her back as easily as he might bend a withy, and plants his other hand firmly on her shoulder. Merewyn flings herself at him, clutching at his arm, but he brushes her aside before shoving Tova out the door faster than her feet can carry her. She falls forward, landing awkwardly on her shoulder.

A chorus of cheers. She scrambles on to her back and sees the rest of them, and then the giant emerges from the woodshed, ducking beneath the lintel, all six feet of him and more. The one she took for their leader. Dark, hard eyes gaze out from beneath his helmet rim, probing her, stripping her to her bare skin. She's seen that look before.

Grinning like a fisherman pleased with his day's catch, he advances. She edges away, crab-wise. One of her shoes has slipped off. Her skirts are bunched up around her thighs. Her palms and one of her knees are stinging.

Nowhere to go. The giant and two of his friends encircle her.

Hungry looks in their eyes. One more still in the saddle, but that only makes four. Then she sees the fifth, squat and bearded, dragging Merewyn backwards from the woodshed, his arm around her neck and shoulders.

'Please,' Tova says, though it's probably in vain. Even if they understand, what chance they'll listen?

Merewyn's captor gives a yell as he shakes his wrist free from between her teeth. She twists away but doesn't get far before his other hand catches hold of her arm. He spins her to face him, then slaps her across the cheek and pushes her into the middle of the circle; she wails as she slips on the mud. Eyes wide, arms outstretched, she tumbles towards Tova, who's still trying to back away when her lady collapses on top of her.

Tangle of limbs, of clothes, of hair. The breath is knocked from Tova's chest as the heel of Merewyn's hand slams into her ribs. As they try to separate themselves, Tova finds her face somehow caught in her lady's cloak. She can't see, but she can hear the howls of laughter ringing out. She feel tears welling, like a cauldron about to boil over.

And then it happens. A sound like nothing Tova has ever heard before. A sharp whistle, like the very air is being torn apart.

All at once the men are yelling, their horses shrieking. Tova prises herself away from Merewyn. She shakes her head free from her lady's cloak and sees one of the animals rearing up, teetering on its hind hooves, the whites of its eyes gleaming. Its rider is on the ground, yelling as he struggles to free his foot from the stirrup where it's lodged.

Again that sound. And again, and again. Shouting to one another, the men unsling their shields from across their backs and draw their swords. No longer interested in her and Merewyn, they face the darkness, turning first this way and then that.

Something silver flashes through the air, ringing off a helmet. Another strikes the bearded man square in the back. He staggers towards Tova and Merewyn, before crashing to the ground inches from their feet. White feathers adorn the shaft protruding from his byrnie. His eyes are glazed. He doesn't move.

Tova would scream but all the breath has been stolen from her. Merewyn squirms away, as if afraid that his corpse could still hurt them. Her lips move, but above the thunder of blood inside her skull and the shouts of the men, Tova can't hear what she's saying. Fear has her in its grip and won't let go.

Another arrow. And another. And another. The Normans duck behind their shields, still yelling. Their horses are bolting back the way they came, down the track.

Merewyn clings to Tova's arm. 'What's happening?'

The one on the ground has freed his trapped leg; he scrambles away from where his mount writhes on its side in the mud: a flurry of flailing hooves kicking up stones and clods of mud and turf. The giant who laid his hands upon Tova is in the centre of the yard, pointing, waving his sword as he bellows orders. And then they're charging towards the long barn on the other side of the yard.

Towards the barn, where stands a figure. A shadow among shadows. He tosses his bow aside; in his hand instead is an axe.

The first of the Normans hurls himself at the newcomer. The axe blade whirls, gleaming silver in the moon's light. It crashes into the foreigner's mailed stomach, sending him sprawling, and the stranger is spinning away, ducking beneath a sword swing as he heaves his axe around, into the shin of the next man.

A crack. The blade sinks through flesh into bone. The Norman gives an unholy scream as he falls.

'Run!' the stranger barks. With the barn to his rear, he sets

21

himself to face those who are left. Dark hair trails over shoulders as broad as an ox's. He wears no byrnie, no helmet. 'Run!'

It takes Tova a moment to understand what he's saying: first that he's speaking English, and then that he means herself and Merewyn.

Rising, she extends an arm to help her lady up. Merewyn clasps it and is halfway to her feet before she falls back down again, crying out. She must have injured herself when she fell. Once more Tova tries, this time with both hands. She's strong for her size, or so she has often been told, but it's a struggle all the same. She grits her teeth as she places one arm under Merewyn's shoulder.

A ring of steel. A roar of anger. A howl of pain.

Tova glances up as the stranger's blade strikes a Norman's cheek, slitting his face open from ear to chin. Blood and teeth fly; he goes down heavily, limply, like a sack of grain, and the stranger is twisting away, teeth bared, roaring as he does so.

Two still standing.

Two, when moments ago there were five.

One is bent over, clutching at his stomach with his shield hand. He staggers forward, but he is slow, unsteady on his feet. The stranger is on him before he can raise his shield or get out of the way. He buries his axe in his foe's neck. The Norman falls and doesn't get up. The stranger snatches up his shield from where it lies.

Leaving just one.

'Behind you!' Tova screams. The giant is coming at him again, sword in hand.

She doesn't know if the stranger hears her, or if he has already sensed the danger. He turns just in time to meet the giant's sword strike upon his shield, and another and another and another still.

Scraps of hide flail loose from the wood as the stranger is forced back under the hail of blows towards the barn.

One pace. Two, three, four. Nearly stumbling. He's struggling. Tiring. And if he falls then the giant will come after them next.

She has to do something. That's the only thought going through her mind as she glances about for the corpse of the bearded man, the one who was arrow-shot.

There, close by the well.

Ignoring Merewyn's shouts, she runs towards the body. His sword arm is outstretched, his weapon still in hand. Clumsily, trying not to retch, she prises his limp, still-warm fingers away from the hilt and snatches it up. It's lighter than she's expecting, but even so she needs both hands to lift it.

The Norman hasn't yet noticed what she's doing, but the stranger has.

'No,' he yells above the crash of steel. 'While you can, run!'

He can't hold out for ever, she sees. His shield droops, exposing his face. Into that opening the giant lunges. The stranger ducks again, and the blade misses by a hair's breadth. But the Norman hasn't finished yet. He throws himself at the stranger, hammering upon his shield, hacking splinters from the boards.

And Tova sees that the stranger won't last much longer. One leg slips out from beneath him as his foot loses purchase on the mud. He falls to one knee—

'No!' Tova cries out.

Reason gives way to instinct. Before she knows it she's rushing forward, wielding the sword in both hands, breathing hard, feet pounding the dirt, her eyes stinging and blurred with the sweat running into them. Summoning all her strength, she raises the blade as high as she can, fixing her gaze on the giant's mailed back, picturing in her mind how she'll bring it crashing down, and again and again, until he lies prone and she can ram the steel through his mail and his flesh, through his ribs and into his heart—

He hears her coming; his head whips round. Her heart all but stops as he starts to turn. It's too late to change her mind. She heaves the blade, screaming without words.

The point tears through his sleeve below the mail, biting into flesh. A glancing blow. He howls and staggers back. Tova yelps as the weight of the weapon pulls her through the stroke, off balance. She staggers sideways, almost tripping over her own feet, somehow manages to stay upright. The giant turns to face her again, and she sees the promise of death in his eyes.

This is it, she thinks. Her feet have taken root. The sword lies heavy in her hands. She knows that she has to lift it, has to try somehow to defend herself, but she can't.

Unable to fight and unable to run.

He steps towards her, raising his sword for the blow that she knows will pierce her neck or crack her skull, slice her open or run her through—

And he stops.

His mouth hangs open as if in surprise. Wide eyes gaze without seeing. His lips tremble but make no sound. Then his sword falls from his grasp; his legs give way, and he sinks first to his knees before finally crashing to the mud.

Tova backs away slowly. At any moment she expects him to rise. But he doesn't. A broad gash decorates his neck. Blood trickles down his back, pooling on the ground, where it mixes with the dirt and the water.

Dead.

And not just him. All five of them. Every single one, in little longer than it would have taken Father Thorvald to intone the Paternoster.

The stranger stands, his fingers still curled around his axe's handle. Even in the darkness she can see the blood spattered across his tunic and his face.

Five men dead by his hand, and not a scratch upon him. Five knights of Normandy. Warriors whose skill at arms she has heard so many tales about.

His brow gleams with sweat. Beneath it, his eyes are hollow pits. Like a wolf's, Tova thinks, and she knows because she happened to see one prowling in the dusk not that long ago, a week before Christmas. Except that these eyes are less friendly. Her mother often used to tell her that you could glimpse a person's soul by meeting their gaze, but if that's true then it seems to her that his has already fled.

Tangled hair hangs in lank strands, clinging to his forehead and to his cheeks. His clothes are threadbare, torn in places and frayed at the hems. On his arms, countless scratches and grazes, as if he has been dragged through a briar patch.

A wild man, she thinks. One of those outlaws who are said to dwell in the marshes and the hills and the woods, who prey upon travellers, who waylay messengers, purse bearers and reeves. She has heard the rumours.

'Put it down, girl,' he says. 'You don't want to fight me.'

At first she doesn't know what he means. She stares back at him, too frightened to do anything else. There's a scar on his lip that she guesses he has carried for some time. Another beneath his right eye that looks more recent. Crooked nose. Gaunt face.

That's when she realises she's still clasping the sword. The cord of the grip digs into her grazed palms, and her arms are tiring under its weight.

'I'm not going to hurt you,' he says as he lets his axe fall to the ground. He raises his hands, his palms facing outwards.

25

Slowly she lowers the blade, then drops it. Her heart is still pounding; she can barely feel her feet.

Then suddenly Merewyn is at her side, throwing her arms around her, asking if she's hurt, if she's all right. Tova nods and tries to speak but she can't find the words. She's shaking, and doesn't know how to stop.

But for this stranger she'd be dead. That Norman would have run her through, cut her apart. How close she came, she realises suddenly.

She glances at the still bodies of the enemy, then swallows to moisten her throat.

She can hardly believe she's still alive. 'You killed them.'

'I didn't have any choice,' he says. 'They'd have killed you otherwise.'

'Who are you?' Merewyn asks, her voice trembling.

He keeps his distance, like he's afraid of something. Like he's wary of getting too close.

'No one,' he says. 'Just someone trying to survive.'

'Do you have a name?'

'Beorn.'

'Just Beorn?'

Not Beorn of someplace, Tova thinks. Or Beorn somebodysson.

'As I said,' he answers. 'What about you? What do I call you?'

'Tova,' says Tova.

He nods appreciatively. 'A good name. My mother's sister's name.'

She catches her lady glaring at her, and at first she doesn't know why, but then she remembers. They were supposed to be keeping their names secret.

Beorn turns to Merewyn. 'And you?'

She's still moving gingerly, Tova sees. She must have hurt her ankle when she fell.

'Merewyn,' she replies reluctantly.

'You shouldn't be out wandering these hills on your own. There are enemy raiding parties everywhere, swarming these hills, hunting for folk like you. You need to find somewhere to hide, and quickly, until they've gone back south.'

'Raiding parties?' Tova asks, feeling a chill run through her body. 'There are others out there? More Normans?'

'You mean you haven't heard?'

She exchanges a glance with Merewyn. What is he talking about? 'Heard what?'

'Listen, girl. I don't know where the two of you have come from, or where you've been these past few days, but it's not safe for you here.'

'The Normans are coming?' Merewyn asks. 'You know this for sure?'

'I know,' he insists. 'Not just a few of them, either. Hundreds. Thousands, even. King Wilelm is on the march, and his entire host with him. The biggest army ever seen north of the Humbre, the likes of which you've never even imagined. They're laying waste everything they can find, slaughtering every living thing: every man, woman, child or beast whose path crosses theirs. No one is safe. If you had any sense you'd already be long gone. I thought everyone had already fled. Haven't you seen the fires? The hall burnings?'

Tova stares at him. Hall burnings? King Wilelm marching?

'I don't understand,' she says.

'Because they're the enemy,' Beorn replies. 'Because that's what they do. I've seen it happening with my own eyes, so believe me when I tell you.'

'Oh God,' Merewyn says in a small voice. She raises a hand to her mouth. 'The smoke. It was them. The Normans. It was their doing. It must have been.'

27

'Smoke?' Tova asks, frowning. 'What are you talking about?'

'Yesterday. Ælfric saw it yesterday evening, just before dark. When he came back, he told us. He spotted it while he was out riding the manor bounds. To the south, some miles away, he said. Thick black smoke, like a whole village had gone up in flames. He came back as soon as he saw.'

'You never said anything.'

'Because we didn't know what it meant. We didn't want to make people afraid for no reason, so we agreed to keep it to ourselves. Ælfric, Orm, Ketil, Thorvald and I. We were the only ones who knew. Oh God. We shouldn't have waited. We should have warned everyone straight away. We should have started making ready to leave, just like Thorvald said. And now what if it's too late? Tova, what if the Normans have been? We need to go back. We have to.'

Tova clasps Merewyn's trembling hand in her own. 'We can't. You know we can't.'

Her eyes are wide. 'Do you think they got away? What if they didn't?'

'They will have. They must have. I'm sure of it.'

'How can you be sure?'

Desperately Tova glances around, but Beorn has gone. He's walking away, down the track.

'Beorn, wait!'

On hearing his name he stops and turns.

Tova runs after him. 'Where are you going?'

'To find their horses and search their packs. To see if they have anything I might use. Then I'm heading north.'

Tova's heart sinks. 'You're leaving us?'

'You don't want to come with me. Believe me, you don't.'

'Where are you headed?'

'A place called Hagustaldesham, near the old wall, the one built by the Romans that runs from sea to sea. A long way from here, in St Cuthbert's land.'

She's never heard of it. 'Why? What's there?'

'It's where all those who still oppose King Wilelm are making their stand. He didn't crush the rebellion, only scattered it. Some have given up the fight; others have submitted to him, but not all. Those who are left, who still believe we have a chance of defeating the foreigners, they're gathering there. Our last stronghold.'

The rebellion. She hasn't heard anyone speak of it in months. Not since their menfolk came back in the weeks between harvest and Christmas. The great rising, led by the ætheling Eadgar, which was supposed to drive the invaders from the kingdom and back across the Narrow Sea. The war that promised victory and ended in ruin.

She asks, 'You fought in the rebellion?'

'Girl, I don't have time to stand here all night talking.'

'You can't just abandon us,' she protests. 'Not if there are more of them out there.'

'Hagustaldesham is where I need to be.'

'Then take us with you.'

'No,' Merewyn says hurriedly as she joins them, limping on her injured ankle. 'We just have to get to Eadmer's manor. He'll know what to do. We'll be safe there. My brother,' she adds for Beorn's benefit.

'And where does your brother live?' he asks her.

'Not far from Catrice. An hour's ride upstream from where the old road crosses the River Swalwe.'

He shakes his head. 'You'll want to stay away from the old road. The Normans will be watching it. They're heading north

29

as well. Unless your brother has a small army guarding his gates, chances are that by the time you get there they'll already have taken his hall, burned it to the ground. You won't find safety there, I promise you.'

Merewyn stares at him with wide eyes. 'What are you saying?'

'I'm saying that, if he has any sense, he'll have left as soon as he heard the news.'

'Then where are we supposed to go?'

'Up into the high hills, or deep into the woods where the enemy won't be able to come at you.'

'In the middle of winter? What are we to do about food or shelter?'

'Then go back to wherever's home for you and hope that the Normans haven't been there already. Hope that they don't come, and if they do, hide.'

Tova blurts, 'We can't go back home.'

'Why not?'

'Because . . .'

She stops herself before she can go on, glancing at her lady, who has turned pale. What can she say? If he were to learn the reason they're out here on their own, he's hardly likely to help them.

But Beorn has found something more deserving of his attention. He crouches down beside the corpse of the bearded Norman, removes his helmet, turns it over in his hands as he inspects it, then tries it on his own head before casting it aside.

'Look,' he says as he stands. 'It's a long way to Hagustaldesham. A long, long way. I go much faster on my own.'

'How far?' Tova asks.

'A hundred miles, maybe more. A week's travel at your pace, probably.'

A hundred miles? She can't even imagine how far that is. Last spring, when the roads were still safe to travel, she went with Merewyn to the market by the sea at Skardaborg, which was two days' ride. In all her life she's never been further from home than that. Hagustaldesham, by comparison, seems a world away.

She asks, 'Is it safe there?'

'No safer than anywhere else. But there are warriors gathering there. All that's left of the ætheling's army.'

'So let us come with you,' she says.

'It's dangerous. The Normans are scouring this land, razing and killing as they go. They're everywhere. If they catch up with us, I can't promise that I'll be able to protect you again.'

'We understand. Don't we?'

She turns to Merewyn, who looks unsure. She's thinking about Eadmer, Tova guesses. She has never met her lady's brother, but she knows that they're close; they were always writing letters to one another. Until the war came, and the letters stopped.

'You don't want to come with me,' Beorn says. 'You really don't.'

Tova says, 'So you're going to leave us to our fates, then.'

He glares at her, but there's a troubled look in his wolf eyes.

'We're not afraid,' she says. 'And we won't slow you down, either.'

The truth is that she is afraid. But she's not about to let him see that.

'All right,' he says after a while. 'Wait here. I'll go and fetch your horses. If you want to make yourselves useful, you can gather up my arrows. Those that aren't broken, anyway. Good ones are hard to find.'

He sets off again down the track. Tova watches him go. She still can't quite believe that what he says is true. That the Normans are coming. Here, to Northumbria. For so long there were rumours, but no one believed that it would ever happen.

And now it has.

Merewyn clutches at her sleeve. 'Now. This is our chance. Come on.'

'What?' Tova asks. 'Run?'

Her lady is still hobbling, Tova notices. How far, and how fast, does she expect she can go on that ankle?

'Anywhere. It doesn't matter. Before he comes back. Quickly.'

'But he can help us. He'll take us to Hagustaldesham.'

'I don't want to go to Hagustaldesham.'

Neither does Tova, not really, but that's where he's going, and she doesn't have any better ideas. They've seen with their own eyes what he can do. She doesn't know much about the ways of war, except for what she's overheard in the feasting hall and what she's glimpsed of Ælfric and Orm and sometimes Skalpi sparring in the training yard. But none of them ever moved like he does. None were ever as light on their feet or as quick to strike. They never made it look as easy.

'Don't you think we'll be safer if we stay with him?' she asks.

'He's no different from the others,' Merewyn protests. 'He's a killer.'

And so are you, Tova almost says, but holds her tongue. Surely Merewyn of all people realises that blood on a person's hands isn't necessarily a mark of evil?

'So what if he is?' she asks. 'He saved our lives.'

'We don't know the slightest thing about him.'

'He's on our side,' Tova insists.

'You'd have us entrust our lives to a stranger.'

'What choice do we have?'

Merewyn bites her lip. She must see that Tova speaks sense,

even if, like so many times before, she won't admit it. 'If you're wrong about him . . .'

Then God help us both, Tova thinks, and she prays silently for both their sakes.

They sit on fleeces laid upon the damp floor, around the lantern that is their only light, listening to the rustling of mice in the thatch, eating in silence. Nuts and mouldy cheese and stale ends of bread, which Beorn has given them from his own pack. He's elsewhere: finding more provisions, she thinks. He didn't say where he was going or what he was doing. Wherever it is, it can't be far, since he's left his bow and his pack here with them.

They huddle in their cloaks, she and Merewyn, in this rough hovel with the crumbling walls, a far cry from the hall at home, with its fire and its benches and its embroidered many-coloured wall hangings that keep out the draughts. The night is cold, but Beorn has forbidden any fire. He says the smoke will draw unwanted attention, and he's probably right. The last thing they want is for another horde of Normans to descend upon them. Or indeed the folk whose home this is. If they were to find them sitting here, Tova doesn't think they would be pleased.

'What if they come back?' she asked Beorn earlier, when he brought them here. He'd chosen this place because it was hidden halfway up a hillside in the lee of some woods, an arrow's flight with a good wind from the hall and the village, and because it offered a good view across the dale so they'd be able to spy anyone approaching.

'They won't come back,' he said.

'Why not?'

'Because they're probably dead already.'

'Dead?'

33

'How many families were there living in this valley, do you think? A dozen? More? There aren't many places you can hide that many people. Not when they have all their sheep and their cattle with them as well. No, believe me, they won't be coming back.'

Maybe he's right, Tova thinks. But we're still intruders here. We've stolen into someone else's home. Now we're making use of their blankets and oil and lantern. Even if it's true that they're dead, and so don't have any more use for them, that doesn't mean we can just take whatever we want. That doesn't make it right. Does it?

Perhaps when they go, they can leave behind some token of their gratitude, although she isn't quite sure what. They left this morning in such a hurry. Aside from their clothes and the horses, what do they have that they could offer?

She glances towards her lady, sitting opposite, her knees drawn up in front of her as she rubs at the ankle she hurt earlier. That ermine cloak, maybe, or the ivory comb she always carries with her wherever she goes, or the brooch of interlaced silver that Skalpi gave her before he went away all those months ago. She'll never part with those things, Tova thinks, not because they're precious in their own right. Not just because of that, anyway, but because without them how is anyone to know she's a woman of means, of noble stock, someone worthy of respect? They're all she has left to prove who she is. All she has left of her pride.

Not that Tova blames her. She fingers the ribbon tied around her left wrist, one of the few belongings she had time to gather before they left. The green silk glimmers softly in the firelight. She supposes Merewyn feels the same way about her cloak and comb and brooch.

Footsteps outside; a screech of iron hinges as the door swings

34

open. Tova's breath catches in her chest. A shadow appears in the entrance.

But it's only Beorn. With his shoulder he nudges the door closed behind him to keep in the warmth. There's no lock, presumably because whoever lived here reckoned they had nothing worth stealing. Under each arm he carries a roll of folded cloth that he lays down between them, next to the lantern. He opens them out, revealing a collection of smaller bundles that he unwraps to reveal a clutch of candles, some clay pots, leather flasks, wooden bowls and spoons, three drinking cups, a handful of shrivelled apples, half a dozen small loaves, bunches of parsnips and leeks, and four round cheeses wrapped and tied with string.

'Some for tonight,' he says. 'The rest for the journey. There should be enough to keep us fed for a few days at least.' He glances at Merewyn's ankle. 'Is it swollen? Can you walk on it?'

'I twisted it when I fell, that's all,' she says as she rubs at it. 'I'll be fine.'

'If you want, I can look at it for you.'

'No,' she says sharply, scowling. One of her favourite expressions. Tova has often thought that if she does it too much, her face will become stuck that way. 'I don't need your help. I told you. I'll be fine.'

He shrugs, then sits down on the floor, snatches up one of the apples that he has brought and sinks his teeth into it, more like an animal than a man.

Tova clears her throat. Straight away Beorn looks up.

'Why are the Normans doing this?' she asks. 'For three years they've left us alone. Why are they coming now?'

'Because they're Hell creatures, bent on spreading suffering wherever they go,' he says, spitting the words as if he cannot stand the taste of them. 'They know no kindness or pity. All they know is how to kill. They want to scour us from the face of this earth once and for all, to make sure we can never again take up arms against them. So that we'll never again threaten King Wilelm's grip upon his kingdom.'

'But the rebellion was defeated. He crushed it.'

She remembers all too well when the men came back after the war. Weary, hobbling. Broken inside as well as out. Their dreams shattered. Missing friends and brothers. The hope gone from their eyes. Everyone knew then that their best chance was gone.

'The rebellion isn't defeated. Not as long as there are some of us still willing to fight. The war isn't over, and don't listen to anyone who tells you that it is.'

'But so many have died at their hands already,' Merewyn says. 'Eadgar has fled back to Scotland, hasn't he? What more does King Wilelm want from us?'

Beorn sighs. 'What do I have to say before you understand? He doesn't want anything that you or I or anyone can give him. He doesn't want our surrender, our silver or our homes. He doesn't want to bargain with us. He isn't coming to take possession of this land. He's coming to lay it waste.'

His eyes bore into her, as if daring her to say that he speaks false. But Tova's throat is dry. It's like something out of one of her darkest fear-dreams.

He's wrong. He has to be. He must be confused in his head or else simply mad. Has he really seen all these things happening?

He can't be right, she tells herself. He can't be. It isn't possible.

And yet what if he is?

He turns away from them and goes back to his apple. Who is he? Where has he come from? Men like him don't often travel alone, do they? If he's a warrior, then where's the rest of his band? Did they die in the rebellion?

The way he moves, the way he fights: they mark him out as still a young man, although he has to be older than Merewyn, who has only twenty winters behind her. How much older, she's not sure. The scars that decorate his cheeks, his weather-worn appearance, his curt manner, the haunted look in his eyes: these are things that she has usually seen only in men Skalpi's age. Men who have known loss, who have known hardship, who have known all the ills that the world has to throw at them and are tired of it all. And there's an aloofness to him that she can't account for. Hearing him speak and watching him sitting hunched over as he is now, lost in his own thoughts, she sees someone who has travelled and who has loved, who has lived but who at the same time has also died a little inside himself.

His eyes are open again. Open and fixed upon her. 'What?'

She asks, 'How long have you been on your own?'

He frowns. She imagines he is asking himself what sort of a question that is.

'Longer than I would have liked,' he says.

'Were there others? Like you, I mean. Fighting men.'

He nods.

'What happened to them?'

'I don't want to talk about it.'

'Were they killed by the Normans, the ones we met tonight? Were you lying in wait for them?'

'Tova,' Merewyn says warningly.

But he was. Of course he was. It makes sense now. Otherwise, was it mere coincidence that he was there just when they needed him?

He snatches up one of the ale flasks and gets to his feet. 'I said I don't want to talk about it.'

'Where are you going now?' Merewyn asks.

37

'To keep watch.' He slings his bow and arrow bag over his shoulder, slides the haft of his axe inside his belt loop and makes for the door. 'Eat what you can, then get some sleep. It's late and we have many miles ahead of us. I don't want to spend any longer here than we have to.'

He wrenches open the door and ventures outside. Frigid air sweeps in once more, disturbing the rushes and causing the lantern flame briefly to flicker.

And then he's gone, and they're alone again.

'Are you still awake?' she hears Merewyn whisper later. How much later, Tova doesn't know. The lantern has burned itself out. Somewhere out in the night the *kew-wick* of an owl out hunting. Otherwise, silence.

They lie back to back, huddled together on the wooden boards and bundles of straw that pass for a bed, rolled up in layers of wool and linen to guard against the cold that creeps in through the cracks in the walls and seeps up from the ground.

'I'm awake,' Tova replies, though she wishes she weren't. She could hardly eat and now she can't sleep either. Every time she closes her eyes she is back in that woodshed with the tall Norman standing over her. She feels his rough hands on her as he tries to haul her to her feet, and she feels the panic rising, the sickness brewing in her gut.

'Tova?'

Merewyn must have been dozing; her words sound slurred. At least one of them has been able to get some sleep.

Tova asks, 'Yes?'

'Do you think he's telling the truth?'

'About what?'

'About the Normans. About what they're doing.'

What can she say? She knows only what Merewyn knows, after all: no more and no less. She doesn't want to believe it, but that's not the same thing.

Instead she says, 'Why would he lie to us?'

If it's all true, she supposes, it might explain one thing. It would explain how they've been able to get this far, and why nobody from Heldeby has come after them.

A numbness spreads through her. If the enemy arrived in force this morning, not long after she and her lady fled . . .

Then what?

She can hardly bear to let the thought form in her mind. She never cared for Ælfric, or for Ceolred or Hæsta or Saba either for that matter, but what about everyone else? What about red-faced Ulf the cook, or Leofric the swineherd's son, who always had a smile for her, with whom she shared a drunken kiss beneath the willows after the Christmas feast and who was too shy to even speak to her for a week afterwards? What about timid Eda the alewife, more gentle a soul than anyone else she has known, or hoary-haired Thorvald the priest, reckoned by everyone to be easily a hundred in years? Are they all dead as well?

She's already accepted they can't go back, but what if there's nothing now to go back to, even if they wanted? Everyone she knew, everyone with whom she once lived and worked and feasted and fasted—

No. She mustn't think that way. She doesn't want to believe it. They'll have got away, she decides, fled up on to the moors, high up the valleys, where the enemy won't find them.

'Merewyn?' she whispers, wondering if the same thought has occurred to her too, but all she hears is the sound of her lady's breathing, soft and slow. 'Merewyn?'

Her lady stirs but doesn't wake. Tova doesn't have the heart to

39

disturb her. She shifts, trying to make herself more comfortable on the hard boards.

Will Beorn be as good as his word? Will he still be here, she wonders, when dawn comes, to take us to Hagustaldesham? Or will he take the chance while we're sleeping to slip away unnoticed?

She doesn't know, and the longer she lies there asking herself such questions, the less sure she is what exactly she's hoping for.

SECOND DAY

'Girl.'

She wakes with a start. Still dark. A figure looming over her – a creature of the night, a shadow-walker, come to claim her. To carry her off. Her heart leaps and her stomach sinks and she's about to let out a scream when something clamps across her mouth. A leathery hand that smells of horse dung and something sharper that can only be blood. She struggles, trying to free herself, but she can't.

'It's me, girl,' the shadow says. Insistent, impatient. 'It's me. Beorn.'

She recognises the name but doesn't know how. For a moment she can't work out where she is or what she's doing here, why she isn't in her usual bed at home, with Cene curled at her feet, and why her bones feel so chilled.

The moment passes quickly. She remembers. How they came to be here. Why they're running. The Normans. Everything.

Beorn.

She blinks to clear her watery eyes. The scars on his face, those deep-set eyes. Tentatively, as if afraid she might still let out a cry, he lifts his hand away.

'What?' she asks between breaths. She sits up, trying to escape sleep's clutches. 'Are they here?'

He shakes his head. 'It's time for us to go. Wake your lady. I'll gather what we need. Eat what you can; once we're on our way I don't intend to stop. We leave as soon as it's light.'

With that he is gone again, as swiftly as he arrived. Tova blinks as she sits up. Morning can't be far off; a faint half-light glimmers through the finger's gap beneath the door where the passage of feet has worn a groove in the earth. Everything has taken on a grey hue.

How she managed to sleep with so many thoughts dancing inside her head, she isn't sure. She doesn't feel well rested. Her limbs are stiff from lying on the hard boards and the old, flattened straw; her neck is paining her, and there's a pounding in her head and she doesn't know why. Beside her, Merewyn continues to sleep, as serene as ever, curled in a ball with the blankets drawn up around her face, murmuring something that Tova can't understand. Gently she lays a hand on her lady's shoulder to rouse her. She wakes with a start, her expression putting Tova in mind of a deer that has just heard the sound of the hunting horn.

They find some hard bread on which to break their fast and have just finished washing that down with the remains of the ale when Beorn returns. He's saddled their palfreys, which spent the night in a shed behind the hovel together with his own grey, snorting stallion. Although maybe not his own. Maybe he stole it from the Normans.

Tied to panniers across the two palfreys' backs are bundles of kindling, a coil of rope, leather flasks, small iron cooking pots, thick winter blankets. Fastened on either side of his saddle is a roll of linen and what look like wolf pelts. He unbuckles the leather straps holding them in place and tosses one to Merewyn and another to Tova.

44

It's heavier than it looks, and Tova almost fumbles hers.

'What's this?' Merewyn asks.

'A gift,' he says in a way that makes it hard to know whether or not he's joking.

'A gift?'

'Dry clothes. I thought you might appreciate them.'

'Where did you get them?'

'Where do you think?'

'They aren't ours to take. They don't belong to us.'

'They do now. Whoever they belonged to would have wanted us to have them. Now, put them on and be quick about it. Or leave them here if you prefer, but in that case don't complain to me later if you're shivering and there's snot dripping from your nose.'

Tova can't remember the last time anyone dared speak to Merewyn in such a manner. Her husband, of course, but only rarely and, besides, that's different.

Merewyn stands there, open-mouthed, clearly not knowing quite what to do or how to respond. She isn't happy, that much is sure, and she's even less happy once they're inside and unwrapping the rolls to see what Beorn has found for them. Rough-spun dresses of grey wool cloth, thick but plain. Linen undershifts, frayed a little at the hems and worn thin in places but serviceable. Wolf-pelt cloaks, with cord for belts, and gloves as well. Gloves! Tova tugs them on over her pink knuckles, her chilled, cracked hands, delighting in the feeling of the wool against her fingertips, then takes a closer look at the rest of the clothes, turning them over in her hands. Dry, free from holes and, as far as she can tell from a quick inspection, no lice either. She sheds her damp, slept-in overgown and is about to peel off her old much-worn shift when she sees Merewyn marching outside, her dress clutched in one hand.

'You expect me to wear this?' She flings it at Beorn, who is checking over the panniers, tightening knots and straps. It falls to the ground long before it reaches him.

'If you'd prefer to keep those mud-stained things you're wearing, that's your choice,' he says, without looking up.

'Are these the best you could find? These rags, these penitents' sacks?'

He snatches up the garment from where it lies and thrusts it at her, but she won't take it.

'Listen to me,' he says darkly. 'This land is being torn asunder, is overrun with men who would kill us the moment they see us, and you're complaining because the clothes I've done my best to find for you aren't fine enough for your high-born tastes?'

'You will not insult me in this way,' she snaps back at him. 'You will not treat us like we're your servants.'

He steps closer, so that their faces are almost touching. But still Merewyn won't take it from him, nor will she budge.

'Do you think I care who you are? I've said I'll do my best to protect you, to keep you both from harm, and that's what I mean to do. If you're determined to catch your death from cold, that's your choice.'

Merewyn eyes him for a moment longer, then snatches the dress from him and stalks past Tova without a word, back inside.

When at last she does emerge again, she's wearing the clothes Beorn found: all except for the wolfskin cloak, which she has passed over in favour of her own, the one she brought from home with the ermine trim, even though it's thinner and not really suited for winter's travelling.

Beorn doesn't argue. They haven't gone anywhere yet but Tova hopes he isn't tiring of them already.

*

For an hour and more they ride without exchanging a word. The day is strangely quiet, or maybe it's always like this in the hour after dawn on a winter's morning, and it's just that Tova is always too busy fetching water and lighting the fires in the kitchen and the chamber to notice. It's colder even than yesterday, and the hovel is hardly out of sight when she's feeling glad of her new cloak. Her breath makes clouds before her face and leaves a trail behind her as she rides. Beorn leads the way. He alone has any idea where they're supposed to be going. Fog hangs like a shroud over everything. Over the waterlogged ings. Over the slopes and the woods. So thickly that in places Tova can barely see more than fifty paces ahead.

On narrow, crumbling tracks and rutted droveways he leads them, past fields recently ploughed, around dense thickets. She thinks they're travelling west, or possibly north, but since the sun is hidden it's hard to tell. She can tell he's impatient. He's always a short way ahead, stopping every so often to check that they're keeping up. They can't go much faster; the frost has made the earth hard and a thin layer of ice clings to exposed stones, so they have to tread cautiously.

All the while Beorn keeps his bow in hand. The arrow bag at his side hangs open. A feathered shaft waits to be drawn. Is he nervous? If so, he doesn't look it.

Tova is, though. At the slightest sound she glances about, expecting someone to come charging out of the swirling murk and strike them down. But no one does, and every moment that passes when they don't feels like a gift.

They descend into a wide valley where the air is cold, the ground hard with frost. The mist hangs thickly, even though by now it must be mid-morning. They edge their way down the steeply winding track. They're halfway to the bottom when, a short way off the path, she glimpses a dark heap upon the frosty ground. Unmoving.

Her heart stops.

'Look,' she says, pointing. The other two stop and turn at once. She wonders that they haven't already noticed, but maybe they're distracted or else their eyes aren't quite as good as hers.

She doesn't need to ask what it is. Even as they leave the path and ride towards it, she knows. And it isn't long before she makes out a head, a pair of legs, a hand splayed out in front of her as if reaching for help that didn't come, nor ever will. It's a woman, not much older than herself, lying sprawled on her front with her head to one side. Sixteen, maybe seventeen winters; no more than that, Tova thinks. Frost clings to her lips. Her blue eyes are wide, and her mouth hangs agape, as if death caught her suddenly. The back of her skull is decorated with a deep gash, dark and crusted. Her hair, copper-brown and fine like Tova's own, has come loose from her braid and is matted against her cheek.

Tova sits, frozen to the saddle, her hand clamped to her mouth as she tries to resist the urge to spew. Beorn squats down by the woman's side. Gently he touches the back of his hand to her cheek, as if she might just be sleeping and he doesn't want to wake her.

'Cold,' he says after a moment. 'Dead several hours already. Since yesterday, I'd say.'

Nor is she the only one. Behind Tova, Merewyn gives a stifled cry; she's spotted another, and another still close by, and a second pair not ten paces beyond them. Two young men with wounds to their chests that suggest they at least had the chance to see their killers before the light passed from their eyes. A woman Merewyn's age, and next to her a fair, round-cheeked boy who

48

can barely have been beyond crawling and was probably her son. They lie contorted, their limbs at angles that make no sense. The woman's jaw is smashed, her face a mask of blood. The child's neck is twisted, his chest crushed.

'Trampled to death,' Beorn says as he gazes, unblinking, down upon their broken bodies. 'They rode them down from behind.'

'They do that?' Tova asks. 'They use their horses as weapons?'

'Believe me,' Beorn says. 'Whatever tales you've heard about their cruelties, the truth is much worse.'

She doesn't need to see it to believe. She can imagine it all too clearly. Here, mailed men upon their snorting beasts, kicking up dirt as they gallop; there, folk fleeing the naked swords of the foreigners. The very earth trembling; the pounding of hooves at their backs, relentless, with every heartbeat growing louder and closer, closer and louder. Screaming, willing their feet faster. Then nothing.

At least it would have been quick.

Bile churns in her stomach. Even though she's trying not to get too close, death's odour fills her nose. Like the slaughter yard back home in the weeks before winter, when the pigs and cattle they can't afford to feed through the cold months have to be killed so that their meat can be salted. And yet not like that at all.

That's not all that she can smell, either. There's something else. It clings to her throat and to the back of her mouth, sharp and bitter and dry.

Smoke.

With the mist all around she can't see where it's coming from, but there's no mistaking it. And if there's smoke, there must be something burning. She'd like to believe it's a hearth fire, but she knows that's only wishful thinking. She glances at the others; they've smelt it too.

49

Beorn climbs back into the saddle. 'Stay close to me,' he warns, hefting his bow and nocking a feathered shaft to the string.

'We shouldn't be here,' Merewyn says. 'We should go back the way we came.'

'Quiet,' he says while he looks about, watching the mist for signs of movement. 'They should be long gone by now, but in case they aren't, let's not take any chances.'

They ride on, the scent of smoke growing ever stronger. Through the swirling, all-enshrouding gloom rise the sharp lines of a hall. Or what used to be a hall. Only one corner still stands. Of the rest, nothing but two rows of stunted, blackened timbers, collapsed roof beams and ash. Beyond, the remains of several other houses and outbuildings, laithes and pens. From one, a smell like that of roasted pork, but which Tova knows isn't. Feeble wisps rise where the wreckage still smoulders.

And there are the rest of them: too many to count, even if Tova wanted to, which she doesn't, but at the same time she can't tear her eyes away. Men and women alike, some with spears and hayforks and hoes in hand or close to, their features blackened by fire, disfigured by the sword, missing eyes and noses and hands and feet, with wounds to their faces and their backs and their chests. Pink tendrils spill out from gashes in their bellies; carrion birds flock about them, picking at the shining kets. Eyes black as jet stare back accusingly, suspicious of the newcomers who have arrived uninvited to their feast. Strings of flesh trail from their beaks.

That's the last thing she needed to see. Her stomach lurches again, and this time she knows she can't keep it down. She lets the reins slip from her grasp as she bends over, and then it comes, sharp-burning, rushing up her throat, spewing from her mouth in a long stream that dribbles down her chin. Again it comes, and again, and again. Each heave worse than the first. She wipes a sleeve across her mouth and spits once, twice, three times, trying to get rid of the taste, but it won't go.

A hand on her back. She looks up to see Merewyn.

'I'm sorry,' Tova says, although she's not sure why. She never imagined this, even after what Beorn told them. She didn't believe him, but then how could she? It sounded like something from one of those poems that Skalpi sometimes asked Ælfswith to sing. Those songs of ruin, the ones that tell of long-gone times, of fallen wonders, of tarnished glories, of warriors bereft of kin and companionship, whom fate has abandoned. Tales of loss, of guilt without redemption. Tales of darkness. She doesn't remember much of the words but she remembers how they made her feel, those few times when she was invited to sit by the hearth with the rest of household and listen. Alone and afraid. Shorn of hope.

That's exactly how she feels now.

It's true, she thinks. What Beorn said. Everything he told them. It's all true.

No pigs snorting and squealing as they run wild in the fields and the hedges and the woods. No horses or heifers or sheep grazing in the fields. No chickens left scratching in the dirt. They're alone, the three of them. And the Normans are out there somewhere, in their dozens, their scores, their hundreds, their thousands. Their raiding-armies scouring this land, crushing every living thing.

'Better to have it out than in,' Beorn says. 'Are you all right?'

The way he speaks, it's like he knows it's something he ought to ask, rather than having any genuine concern for her well-being, but Tova nods anyway. A numbness spreads through her as she stares at the smouldering wreckage. Her world, everything she knew, is crumbling around her, and she feels herself crumbling with it.

He asks, 'Do you believe me now?'

They pick their way carefully through the scorched ruins, their eyes and ears open for some sign of life, but there's none.

'We should bury them,' Tova says. 'We can't just leave them as fodder for the beasts. We should lay them to rest properly.'

'We don't have time,' Beorn says. 'Do you have any idea how long it'd take to dig graves for them all? We'd be here for days.'

She shakes her head. 'They deserve better than this.'

He turns to face her, and suddenly it's a different Beorn she sees. His shoulders hang low. His eyes are watery. Those eyes, which she thought were empty, which she thought betrayed no feeling.

'Of course they deserve better,' he says. 'But we can't undo what has already been done, can we? We can't give them back the life that's been taken from them. Whether we lay them in the ground or leave them in the open, it doesn't make any difference. It's all the same in the end, isn't it?'

They make their way slowly by drovers' tracks and winding woodland paths. Beorn reckons the men who came this way are long gone, but he'd prefer not to take the risk.

They skirt the bounds of half a dozen more manors to which the torch has been put. Even from several miles away they spy the fires. Smoke rises in great plumes, twisting and coiling, blacker and thicker than before, a sign that the enemy have been here recently. Nothing moves, save for the birds circling overhead and those gathered down in the fields: angry clusters of black feathers, squabbling and shrieking at one another over the flesh of some unlucky person or animal. They never come close enough for Tova to see which. She'd rather not know.

And still no survivors.

She keeps praying they'll come across some. Even just one person who has somehow managed to escape, or who might perhaps have been spared. She has heard that sometimes raiding bands will let one person escape. Just one, so that he or she will go and tell others elsewhere of what has happened. All day long she guards that small hope, in the same way she might cup her hands around a candle flame to keep it from blowing out. But as the hours pass and still there is no sign of anyone, the harder it is to keep that hope aglow. The flame grows ever colder, ever dimmer, while the darkness enveloping her only deepens.

She trails behind the other two, following in their hoofprints, her head bowed, hardly daring to look up in case she should happen to catch a glimpse of another smoke-spire or yet more bodies. Beorn calls to her, urging her on, but his voice seems far away and she hardly hears him.

A flicker of movement amid distant ruins. Too small to be a person, she thinks, although it was gone before she could say exactly what it was. An animal of some kind. Maybe just a deer.

She halts anyway and squints, trying to make it out through the fog, hoping it will show itself again. But she knows that the longer she waits, the further ahead Merewyn and Beorn will be. She doesn't want to be left behind, on her own.

She's just about to give up when she spots it padding out from behind a smoking heap of timbers, its head low, sniffing the ground. Bigger than Cene, Skalpi's running-hound back at home, his favourite and hers too. This one is longer-legged and thinner in the waist. Its coat black all over. Searching forlornly for some trace of its lost master.

It stops. Turns its head. Sees her.

For a moment it just stands there. Its eyes meet hers – as stunned to see another living being as she is, probably. Unsure whether what its eyes are telling it is true. Bewildered, wondering where everyone has gone. Why there is no one to feed it and take it out running.

Then it's hurtling across the furrowed field, barking and barking and barking some more, in relief and in joy. As she would if she were it.

She gets down from the saddle. It bounds towards her, jumping up at her, tongue lolling out of its mouth. She kneels down and lets it lick her face, laughing as it jumps up at her and she's nearly toppled over. Laughing at the rough feel of its tongue and the warm stickiness it leaves on her cheek. Its tail wags vigorously as she fusses over it.

As playful as Cene. She wishes they hadn't left him behind.

She digs in her saddlebag for some treat she can offer, and finds a parcel of cloth containing thick slices of dried bacon. She unfolds it and tosses a slice on to the ground. It's gone at once, swallowed in a single gulp.

'Girl,' Beorn calls. 'Leave that thing alone. We don't have any time to waste. Don't be giving it any more of our food, either. We don't have much as it is.'

She crouches down and hugs the animal to her while it licks eagerly at her greasy, salty fingers, and sniffs at the roll of cloth in which the rest of the meat is wrapped. It looks up at Beorn then wriggles free and turns to her, gazing plaintively with wide eyes, letting out a little whine at the same time.

She asks, 'Can't we bring it with us?'

'You know we can't.'

'It could keep watch at night, guard our camp, warn us of any—'

'No,' he says. 'I'm not having that thing trailing us, getting under our feet, growling and barking and giving us away to our enemies.'

She looks hopefully up at her lady, who keeps her distance, gazing at the hound with a mixture of pity and disdain.

'He's right, Tova,' Merewyn says. 'I'm sorry.'

So is she. She hugs it closer for a while longer, rubbing its neck and murmuring soothing noises, before at last she's able to tear herself away. It runs around her feet and leaps up at her.

'Sit,' she says, and she keeps on saying it until it obeys, while she replaces what's left of the bacon in her saddlebag. She climbs back into the saddle. At once it's up, coming after her, its tail still wagging.

'Stay,' she tells it, and once more to be sure: 'Stay.'

It gives a whimper but does as she says. As they ride away it barks once, twice, three times in protest. But she doesn't look back, and it doesn't follow.

The day is growing old, the shadows lengthening. They lead their horses down into a hollow where ash and beech and hazel and birch grow close and tangled, where the musky scents of damp leaf-mulch and decaying tree flesh fill the air. This path is ill travelled; they go in single file. In places it's so overgrown that Beorn has to lay about with his axe to clear a path.

Above, a branch creaks in the wind. Somewhere amid the low holly bushes a twig snaps. Is there someone there?

'I don't like this, Beorn,' Tova says. 'Are you sure we're going the right way?'

'We'll be through these woods soon enough. Just keep up.'

A rustle of leaves, a light drumming upon the earth, a flash of mottled brown. For a moment her breath catches in her chest. But it's only a deer, bounding through the trees.

Stop it, she tells herself. Or else it won't be the Normans that kill you. You'll end up worrying yourself to death.

From above, a chorus of jeers. She looks up, sees perhaps a dozen crows, flapping excitedly as they peer down at her from their perches along the gnarled, twisted limbs of a broad-bellied oak. She makes the sign of the cross to ward off the evil they carry. Are they the same birds as those corpse eaters they saw earlier? Are they following them, waiting, waiting, waiting for one of them to drop? Hoping for fresh meat to claw and rend and tear to shreds and gorge themselves upon? As if they hadn't already had their fill.

She glares at them as she passes beneath. They settle back down, hunched within their feathers, and watch back with cold, jet-glistening eyes. The Devil's messengers, her mother used to tell her when she was younger. She remembers how she was scolded when once she brought home a chick that had fallen from its nest, so small that its feathers were still downy, not yet black but charcoal-grey. Creatures of evil, her mother said. She'd made Tova, who was no more than seven years old at the time, hold it underwater in the rain barrel behind the kitchen until it stopped moving, all the while standing over her, watching to make sure it was done.

Tova shudders, and not because of the cold. How long is it since last she thought about her mother? How many years now since she died? Five? Six? She doesn't remember any more.

Two broad-bellied oaks stand like sentinels on either side of the path, their stout limbs outstretched, branching into fingers that reach out to form an arch. She doesn't have to look too hard at the knots and cankers to make out noses, eyes, ears.

Behind her, another rustle, another crack. She spins, searching in the direction of the sound.

Nothing.

She stares back up the path, past the twisted trunks and the fallen boughs, past the holly and the brambles, into the shadows. Breathing as shallowly as she can, she listens.

Nothing.

Show yourself, she thinks. If you're there, show yourself.

But of course no one does. It's her imagination again. Her lady is calling, telling her to hurry up, and she turns and follows.

Almost dark. Another day gone. Another day survived.

The woods are behind them, the moors even further. These gently sloping plains could belong to another kingdom entirely; they're nothing like the high, craggy hills that Tova has grown up beneath. She has never felt so far from home in all her life.

Beorn says that, come the morning, they'll need to start looking for the Tees river. There's a place called Griseby, which is the lowest fording point and ought to be no more than a few hours' ride from here. If they're lucky they'll be able to reach it before the Normans do, although the foreigners are fast riders, some of them almost born in the saddle.

'And if we don't?' asks Merewyn.

'Then we'll have to follow the river upstream until we find a ford.'

'And if they're all guarded? What's your plan then?'

'Then I don't know. We'll find some other way, I suppose, even if it means . . .'

He trails off as he stops in his tracks, a frown on his face.

'What is it?' Tova asks. Earlier, she barely had the strength to keep going, but now that it's nearly night-time and the rain is returning, she doesn't want to stop. Not until they've found shelter. If they keep still for too long then she thinks she'll freeze stiff, and not be able to move again.

But then she follows Beorn's gaze towards a half-collapsed barn at the bottom of a hollow some way off the track ahead. And she sees what he sees.

An orange glimmer, so tiny as to be barely visible. A lantern? A campfire?

It might be a hundred paces away, or more like half a mile; in the gloom it's hard to tell. A shadow moves briefly in front of the light. There's someone there.

'Is it them, do you think?' she says, keeping her voice low.

His hand reaches to the loop in his belt from which his axe hangs. 'Unlikely. The fire looks too small for it to be one of their raiding bands.'

It's quiet. The rain is fine, more like a mist, and it makes not a sound as it falls. She remembers the laughter, the singing, the raised voices of the Normans last night. She doesn't hear any of that. Maybe they're just too far away.

He says, 'I'm going to get closer. Stay here.'

He starts to move, but Merewyn grabs at his arm. 'You're not leaving us on our own. Not if the enemy are nearby. We're coming with you.'

'All right. But stay close to me, and don't do anything unless I tell you to.'

Leaving the horses and their packs, they descend the track towards the source of the light, speaking not a word, moving slowly so as to make as little noise as possible, with Beorn leading the way.

The barn stands by a beck, under some alders, with the fire in front of it. Of whoever started it, there's no sign.

'Where did they go?' Merewyn asks as they duck behind a bramble hedge.

Beorn glares at her, puts a finger to his lips and signals for them to keep low to the ground. They're close now, so close that the slightest sound might give them away.

A man emerges from the barn. He stands between the fire and them, so Tova can't easily make out his features, but he moves stiffly, with a slight limp and a weary look about him. Wispy hair straggles past his shoulders. To her eyes he seems old, although that doesn't mean much. He must be about the same age as Skalpi, she thinks. Not for the first time, she wishes he were there with them. He would keep them safe. He would know what to do.

This man isn't Skalpi. He's not exactly fat but he's wide around the middle, with a rounded face and pudgy-looking fingers. He's no warrior. He lacks the stature: the broad shoulders, the sturdy arms. Neither, though, does he have the look of someone who has spent his years labouring in the fields and toiling at the plough.

'He doesn't look like one of them,' she whispers. She means the Normans, of course.

Beorn nods but doesn't say anything. His gaze is fixed upon the man. They've gone the whole day without seeing another soul, and now here at last, maybe, is someone like them. The flame she holds inside her warms, just a little. They aren't the only ones, after all.

He carries a scrap of timber, which he tosses on to the flames, throwing up a cloud of sparks. He stands by the fire, staring at it, hardly moving, his arms folded tight against his chest. His lips are moving; he seems to be muttering something. To himself, though. There doesn't seem to be anyone else about. Not that she can see, anyway.

Without warning he falls to his knees. His hands clasped tight, he bends forward, his chin pressed against his chest.

'Forgive me, Lord,' he cries into the night, loud enough that even from fifty paces away they can hear him, and he's sobbing. 'Forgive me, I beg you!'

Tova looks at her lady, and then they both look at Beorn.

'What now?' Merewyn asks.

But he has already made up his mind. Hefting his axe, he rises and, as silent as the night itself, darts out from their hiding place, towards the barn and the campfire and the kneeling, whimpering figure.

'Beorn,' Merewyn says. Too late: he's already beyond earshot. Then, because she's too scared to look for herself, she asks Tova, 'What's he doing?'

The fire is between Beorn and the other man as, keeping low to the ground, he approaches. Only when he's less than twenty paces away does he slow. The man is still lost in prayer and hasn't noticed him yet. No one else rushes out from the barn to challenge Beorn. Whoever this person is, he's travelling alone.

Beorn's waving to them, signalling something. He's beckoning them over.

'It's safe,' Tova says as she takes hold of Merewyn's hand and helps her up. 'Come on.'

They hurry after Beorn, stumbling across the ridges and furrows, Tova's feet sinking into the soft earth. He's nearly at the fire already. His axe remains in his hand. Just in case, she supposes. Still the older man's head is bowed. He's muttering to himself.

Beorn stops. He clears his throat.

The man breaks from his prayers and looks up. He sees Beorn, standing in front of him. His eyes widen in panic and his mouth opens, but no words come out. He tries to rise, but his feet find no purchase on the damp grass and he scrabbles on all fours as he backs towards the barn, trying to get away.

Beorn slides his axe back into his belt loop as he steps around the fire. 'It's all right,' he says. 'We're English. We're running from the Normans, just like you.'

The man is on his feet now, fumbling at his side for his knife. Gripping it in both hands, he holds it out in front of him warningly. His face is lit and Tova can see the wildness in his eyes.

'No,' he says, backing away. 'You're not taking it. I won't let you. I won't. I haven't come this far to give it up just like that.'

'We don't want anything from you,' Beorn says. 'I told you, we're English. We're not the enemy.'

A golden cross studded with precious stones the colour of blood hangs from a chain around the man's neck. It looks heavy. Maybe that's why he walks with that stoop.

He looks askance at Beorn. 'Who's "we"? How many of you are there?'

Beorn glances over his shoulder, sees Tova and Merewyn, and beckons them out from the shadows. Nervously Tova steps forward, staying close to her lady. The heat of the fire is overpowering after the seeping cold of the fog and the wind and the rain.

The old man stares at them for a long time, and then slowly he lowers the knife, although he doesn't put it away. He looks anxious and yet at the same time relieved.

'Just the three of you?'

'That's right,' Beorn replies and gives him their names. 'What do we call you?'

'Guthred.'

'Are you alone, Guthred?'

61

'Yes, I'm alone. I'm sorry. I don't normally pull knives on folk. I thought you— You surprised me, that's all. You're the first souls I've seen in three whole days. Apart from the Normans, I mean. Every time I look over my shoulder, I expect to see my death coming. So far God has chosen to take pity on me, though he alone knows why.'

'Would you mind if we shared your fire?' Merewyn asks. 'We've been travelling all day. We're hungry and we're cold.'

'The fire you're welcome to. I'm afraid I don't have any food to offer, though. I haven't eaten since, well, not since I fled.'

'We can help, can't we?' Tova says brightly, turning to the others. 'We have food. Not much, but some. Enough, anyway. We could trade.'

'No,' the warrior says and turns to Guthred. 'We can't spend the night here. It's too exposed. We saw your fire from half a mile off, which means that others will too.'

Guthred shakes his head as he slides his blade back into its sheath. 'The Normans have already been this way; they won't be returning. I've seen them with my own eyes. A whole army. A thousand men, maybe, riding under a lion banner. I caught one glimpse of them riding along the valley bottom, and I turned tail, riding as hard as I knew how, knowing that if I didn't and they were to spot me . . . Well, anyway, I got away, as you can see. Only a few hours after that I happened across the trail they'd left behind them. Nothing but ashes. I've seen some terrible things in my time, but never anything like this.'

'The lion banner,' Beorn mutters.

'That's King Wilelm's emblem, isn't it?' Tova asks, and he nods. She has never seen it herself; she only knows because she has heard others mention it in their stories. It was the banner he fought under when he slew his rival Harold, the true king, at Hæstinges.

Beorn asks Guthred, 'Where did they go?'

'North, I think. Following the course of the old Roman road. I don't know any more than that. When I saw them they were riding hard. They seemed in a hurry, and I didn't stay to watch what they were doing. Please, if you do have any food that you can spare—'

'How long ago was this?'

'Yesterday. Truly, if I knew anything more, then I'd tell you. I can only say what I've seen.'

'It's nearly dark, Beorn,' Merewyn points out. 'We're going to need to find shelter somewhere soon anyway. This is as good a place as any we're going to come across.'

Tova folds her arms tight across her chest. Now that they've stopped moving, she's beginning to feel the cold again. Like Merewyn, she doesn't want to carry on riding through the drizzle for another hour or more.

'There's space enough for all of you,' Guthred says, gesturing towards the barn. 'It doesn't look like much, I know. It's the best I could find. At the moment it's just me and Whitefoot.'

Tova asks, 'Whitefoot?'

'My horse. My one true friend in all the world. The only one I have left, anyway. But enough of my woes. You don't need to hear about that. Please, come. You must be freezing.'

'Our packs,' Merewyn says suddenly. 'We left them with the horses.'

'I'll go,' Tova offers. She doesn't feel so nervous now.

The animals haven't wandered far; in fact they're more or less exactly where they left them, chewing contentedly on what meagre grass there is beside the track.

'Just a little further now,' she says to them as she rubs Winter's flank. 'Then we can rest.'

She notices that one of her saddlebags is hanging open at one end. She goes to tighten the strap, but that's not the problem. It's the buckle itself that's bent. She curses but knows it's her own fault. She shouldn't have tried to cram so much into it this morning.

There's nothing she can do about it now. She takes hold of the reins and turns—

And stops still. And screams.

A figure blocks her path, its features in darkness. A night-stalker, a shadow-wight. As tall as a man. Taller.

Tova backs away as quickly as she dares. She can't feel her feet. She can't breathe.

'No, no, no, no,' it says hurriedly as it follows her. 'I didn't mean to startle you. I thought you heard me.'

It speaks. Not a wight, then. A man.

'Stay away from me,' she says, for all the good it'll do.

A weapon is what I need, she thinks. But he's hardly five paces away. If she so much as reaches for her knife, he could be upon her in an eyeblink. And even if she had it in her hand now, what would she do with it?

'I'm not going to hurt you, I swear.'

She keeps backing away but he keeps on coming at her. Where can she go? She could turn and run but he'll surely be faster. The horses have run off down the track, startled by the noise.

Another time, in another place, it started just like this. Herself and him alone: she helpless, trapped, with nowhere to go . . .

'It's all right. I'm not what you think. I'm not one of them. My name is Oslac. I came across your horses and saw the fire. I saw you talking to the old man. I didn't know that there were any other friendly folk left alive until I saw you all. I thought the Normans had done for everybody. Please, don't be frightened. Don't run away. I'm on your side, really I am.'

The words come tumbling out, like water from a burst weir. His voice is young, with a drawl that makes her think he isn't from these parts. His features are in shadow so it's hard to say what he looks like, but he doesn't sound much older than her. Certainly he can't be any older than Merewyn.

He's no longer advancing. This is her chance, she knows, if she wants to take it.

But she doesn't. He sounds earnest, and, in a way, as lost and as desperate and as afraid as she is.

Then she remembers. The sounds she heard, back in the woods.

'You lie,' she says.

'What?'

Now that her heart's no longer beating quite as fast, she sees him properly for the first time. He wears a cloth cap, cone-shaped with the point drooping forward. Flaps covering his ears. Tufts of curly hair springing out from underneath.

'You were following us, weren't you? It was you earlier, I know it was, so don't try to pretend otherwise.'

'So what if I was?'

'Why?' she asks. 'Why were you following us?'

'Tova!'

She turns. Merewyn is running towards her, limbs flailing. Behind her is the old man, Guthred. In front of them both, charging with his axe in his hand, is Beorn.

Oslac spreads his arms wide to show he means no harm, but Beorn doesn't care. He seizes the newcomer by his collar, nearly lifting him off his feet as he forces him back against the nearest tree. Oslac yells a protest, but the warrior isn't listening. He brings his knife up to the other man's face, so that he can see just how wicked is its edge.

'If I hear you've harmed her,' he says, 'your death will come so quickly you won't even have time to scream. And don't think I won't do it. When you've killed as many men as I have, one more is nothing.' He calls over his shoulder: 'Are you all right?'

This last is directed at her, Tova guesses.

She swallows and says, 'I'm all right.'

'Who are you?' Beorn growls at the younger man. 'Speak!'

Wide-eyed, he opens his mouth but can't seem to find the words. For all his height, he looks small beside Beorn.

'His name is Oslac,' Tova offers. 'He's been following us.'

'He has a tongue of his own, so let him use it,' Beorn says, and then to his captive, 'Well? Is what she says true?'

Oslac's mouth opens again and closes. And opens. And closes.

Beorn pulls harder on the younger man's collar, shaking him so hard that his cap falls from his head. 'Answer me!'

'It's true,' he says quickly. 'Yes, it's true.'

'You were following us? Why?'

'Because I thought you might be friendly.'

He says it without any hint of irony. Just as well, Tova thinks. Anyone who dares joke when there's a knife at his throat would have to be brave indeed.

'Yet you waited until now to show yourself?'

Oslac's eyes flick down towards the blade at his throat, then back to Beorn. 'I wanted to make sure, that's all. Please, don't kill me. I haven't done anything wrong.'

Tova can't help but feel a little sorry for him, but it's his own fault really. He shouldn't have crept up on her like he did. What did he expect?

'Let him go, Beorn,' Merewyn calls. 'You've made your point. He doesn't mean any harm.'

Beorn gazes hard at him for a few moments longer, before

finally he releases his grip on the other man's collar, returns his knife to its sheath and steps away. 'So your name is Oslac?'

'Oslac, son of Osferth, son of Oswald—'

'I don't need to hear your whole family line. Where did you come from?'

'Everywhere. Nowhere.'

'I'm in no mood for riddles,' Beorn snaps.

'It's not a riddle,' Oslac says. 'It's the truth. I'm a traveller. A poet. A wordsmith. I wander from place to place, gathering tales to weave into songs that I sing at feasts. I used to, anyway. I don't suppose there'll be any more of those now. I play them on my harp. I can show you, if you want. Look, I have it with me. It's in my pack. You'll see that I'm telling the truth.'

'It's all right,' says Merewyn, before Beorn has a chance to answer. 'You don't have to show us. We believe you, don't we?'

He doesn't look much like a poet, Tova thinks, which is to say he doesn't look much like the ones who used to come to Heldeby. Skalpi and his first wife, Ælfswith, loved nothing more than an evening of singing and storytelling. Whenever one happened to arrive at the hall on a winter's evening, drenched from the rain and mud-spattered from the road but bearing lyre or flute or reed pipe, they would invite him in with open arms, hustling him into the hall, where they'd lavish on him mead and the finest food that Ulf the cook knew how to make. And of course he'd savour all of it – every morsel, every gulp, every word of praise – and that was even before he'd played a note or sung a line, tested his audience with a riddle or told them anything of the places he'd been and the marvels he'd seen.

None of those men were ever as young as Oslac, though. Yes, some of them came accompanied by students, who would watch and listen and sometimes, if they were lucky, be allowed to try a few stories, a few verses of their own. But she was told that it takes many years to master the poet's art. No youth, no matter how deft his fingerwork might be or how talented he is at crafting words, has ever seen enough of the world, its glories and its ills to be able to speak with true wisdom.

'I can't tell you how glad I am to find you,' Oslac says. 'Everywhere I went— Well, you've seen, haven't you? I was beginning to think that there was no one left alive, except for me and the robbers.'

Guthred fingers the gold cross at his breast. 'Robbers?'

Oslac nods. 'I've seen them roaming the hills. Like carrion beasts, they are. They live off whatever the Normans leave behind. I've tried to keep well away from them, but a couple of times all I could do was hide and pray that they didn't find me. That's why I had to follow you for a while first. I needed to be sure.'

As if we didn't already have enough to worry about, Tova thinks. Now we have thieves as well.

'You thought we were robbers?' Merewyn asks him. 'Us?'

'I didn't know if there were more of you nearby. More of him,' he says, gesturing at Beorn. 'It's hard to know who you can trust.'

Tova sneezes. The rain is turning to sleet. It's going to be another harsh night.

'Let's go back to the barn,' says Guthred quickly. 'It's dry in there, more or less. The roof leaks a little but it keeps most of the rain out. We'll all end up catching a chill if we stand out here much longer.'

It isn't long before they have the fire blazing. Tova for one is glad of its warmth. She can't stop shivering, despite the blankets wrapped around her shoulders. She hopes that sneeze wasn't the first of many. There's a tickling at the back of her throat that's been there for a while, and she's already starting to worry. The last thing she needs right now is to fall ill. If ever there was a time for that, this isn't it.

It can happen so quickly. A sniffle that becomes a sneeze, a tickle that becomes a cough, a shiver that becomes a sweat. Soon a fever, and after that? The rest is in God's hands.

That was how it went with her mother. She was still young at the time, not yet even thirty, and easily as strong as any man. All that counted for nothing, though. Christmas hadn't long passed, Tova remembers, when she woke that morning to find her mother groaning as she lay in her bed, her throat so dry and swollen that it was painful to swallow, and barely able to stand because all her limbs were aching and because, when she tried, it made her dizzy. At once Tova went to fetch Eda, who as well as ale also knew how to prepare remedies to treat all manner of illnesses. She came with her herbs and her poultices, and spent many hours mixing up ointments and pastes and rubbing them into the places where it hurt the most. When none of those things eased her suffering, Eda even sent word to the next village, where her sister lived, asking her to come and help if she could, which she did that very same day, though none of her preparations did any good either.

Every day after that, her mother grew weaker. Along with the fever came bouts of sickness and the skitters. She couldn't take any proper food; the only thing she could keep down was a watered-down broth of mashed carrot and barley, and sometimes not even that.

Tova realised then that the end was close, although that didn't stop her praying, hoping, wishing, pleading for a miracle to be sent. Eventually, after four days and nights, an hour or so before first light on the eve of the Epiphany, her mother breathed her last breath and left this world.

Left Tova, alone.

Enough, she tells herself. She has seen enough sadness and suffering already today. If she dwells any longer on such things she'll only become lost in her own grief. Besides, it was all so long ago. What's past is past. Some day she'll see her mother again. For now, though, she has to put those memories from her head.

She shifts closer to the fire. It isn't anything like the kind they used to have in the great hearth back at home, the logs stacked so deep that the flames would burn yellow-bright, that its heat could be felt even from the far end of the hall, that even in the morning when she came in to clear out the hearth and sweep up the ashes, they'd still be hot. But it's better than nothing. Merewyn kneels beside it, keeping it fed with wood, while Guthred idly stirs the iron pot hanging from a spit over the flames, to which they've added a few thin parsnips and beans and pieces of bread.

Her stomach growls. It feels like weeks since she last had hot food inside her, even though it's only been two days.

Gunnhild, who was like a mother to Tova after hers died that winter, always did say she was too thin. She was forever trying to get her to eat more. You never knew how long God's bounty would last, she said; it was important to have your fill when you could, since leaner times were rarely far away.

Where are Gunnhild and Ase now? Are they even still alive? It's been a long time since she thought about them too. Now that she has, she wishes she hasn't.

Stop it, she chides herself. You have to try to keep your spirits up.

She closes her eyes and remembers sitting with Ase, Gunnhild's daughter, by the hearth in the kitchen where they sometimes come to sleep because it's always warm there.

It's long after dark, and the embers are darkening as she and

Ase, the same age as her and the closest thing she has to a sister, play with the tæfl pieces by candlelight. They know they're supposed to be in bed, not spending the night hours on games when they should be sleeping, but that's part of the fun. They don't know the rules since it's only ever the men who play, and so they make up their own, taking it in turns to move the carved antler and jet counters across the board, each trying to be the one who gets all their counters to the other side first. To each piece they give a name, usually of someone they know.

That one's Lord Skalpi, says Ase, because he's bigger and rounder than the rest.

Then this one must be Lady Merewyn, says Tova, because she's thin and pale, and they fall about giggling and shushing each other. They know if anyone hears them they'll be for it.

Tova can't help herself, though, and when Ase starts talking about the sow that escaped its pen, which Leofric spent an hour this morning chasing around the yard, that sets her off again, and once she's started she can't stop, and Ase is telling her to keep quiet but at the same time is laughing too, until they hear footsteps outside in the yard and suddenly things are no longer funny. Hurriedly they shove the tæfl board with its pieces under their mattress. The set doesn't belong to them; they found it on the table in the hall, left out by Orm and Ælfric when they went to bed, and Tova knows they'll have to return it quickly in the morning before anyone notices it's missing. No sooner is it out of the way than they blow out the candle and leap under the blankets and then they lie as still as stone, not even daring to whisper to one another, their hearts pounding as they do their best to still their breathing, until the footsteps go away and they know they're safe.

How long ago it all seems now, Tova thinks, although it was

only last spring. Of course it can't have been long after that night when—

She's doing it again. Stop it, stop it, stop it.

'How's the stew?' she asks Guthred, to distract herself more than anything. She can't smell it yet, but she can see wisps of steam rising. 'It must be nearly ready by now.'

The old man doesn't answer. He's staring into the fire, his eyes glazed.

'Guthred?'

At the sound of his name he turns around, blinking. 'I'm sorry. I was thinking.'

'What about?'

He smiles gently, sadly. 'I was thinking how only a few hours ago I was wondering whether I was going to die without ever seeing another friendly face again. Now here you are. Here we are.'

'None of us is going to die,' Merewyn says, in that stern way that she has. 'We're going to survive this, somehow. All of us. I know it. We're going to get to Hagustaldesham, and everything will be all right.'

'Where?' Oslac asks.

'Hagustaldesham. It's somewhere to the north of here. About a week's ride, Beorn says, or maybe a little less. I'd barely heard of it before, either, but he tells us we'll be safe there. It's where the rest of the rebels are mustering, apparently. The ones who are left.'

'The rebels? But I thought the war was over.'

'We did too,' Tova says. 'But Beorn says otherwise, so that's where we're going.'

'And you don't think that if that's where they're rallying, King Wilelm will be on his way there as well soon enough, to crush them once and for all?'

'He wouldn't dare,' says a voice from out of the darkness of the barn. It's Beorn, returned from feeding the horses. 'Not that far north, so far from his castles. Certainly not in the middle of winter like this.'

'How do you know? What's to stop him? He's already come this far, hasn't he?'

'Into a land where he met no resistance, where his foes have already scattered. Beyond the River Tine, things are different. Gospatric, earl of Bebbanburh, rules there. He was one of the rebellion's leaders, one of the last to give up the struggle, even after half our army had abandoned the cause.'

'You fought in the rebellion?' Guthred asks.

'I did,' Beorn says. 'Much good though it did.'

Oslac says, 'What brings you here, then? Did you desert?'

'You take me for a coward, do you?'

'No—'

'Then keep your mouth shut.'

A hush falls.

'I think you underestimate the king,' Oslac says after a while, softly but firmly, speaking as he might to an ill-tempered child, which sounds strange coming from him, young as he is.

'Oh, you do, do you? And what would you know?'

'Only what I've seen and heard on my travels. He's single-minded in everything he does. Once he has made up his mind, he doesn't change it. He'll stop at nothing to destroy those who oppose him, even if that means marching the length and breadth of Britain.'

Beorn folds his arms across his chest. 'So tell me, then. Where should we go instead?'

'I don't know. Across the sea, maybe. That was my plan. If we make for the coast, we might be able to find a boat that will take us far enough away that we won't have to worry about the Normans. To Yrland, or across the German Sea. Away from England entirely.'

'Away from England?' Tova echoes, her heart sinking. She has barely left the manor in all her life; now already they're talking about distant shores.

'No,' says Beorn. 'The Danes are prowling in their ships all the way from the Humber to the Tine, doing what they do best. Taking everything they can. Food, slaves, silver – whatever they can lay their hands on.'

'The Danes?' Merewyn asks. 'I thought they were your allies against the Normans.'

'They were. But then they made a pact with King Wilelm. He bribed them with gold and agreed that they could raid for supplies along the coast, if they broke off their alliance with us and returned back across the sea in the spring.'

Guthred shakes his head in disbelief. 'So the Danes are doing the Normans' work for them?'

'That's right.'

Oslac frowns. 'If not the coast, then where?'

'Well,' says Beorn, 'you could flee into the high hills to the west, where the Normans won't come at you, as many have already done. There's precious little up there to live on, though, and I certainly wouldn't want to be up there when the snows come.'

'Lindisfarena,' Guthred says abruptly.

'What?'

'We should go to Lindisfarena. The monks there will take us in. They'll shelter us. The Danes won't be roaming that far north, surely?'

'The Holy Isle?' Oslac asks. 'But that's easily a hundred miles from here.'

'All the more reason to go. We'll be safe from the Normans there, won't we? And from the Danes, too.'

'I'm not going all the way to Lindisfarena,' Beorn says. 'I'm going to Hagustaldesham.'

'Whatever we do, we should stay together,' Tova puts in, her voice small. No one has asked for her opinion, she realises, but she feels she has as much right to speak as anyone. 'Especially if Oslac's right and there are robbers around. We'll be much safer together, won't we?'

Beorn glares warningly at her. Wondering why he ever agreed to let them join him, probably. He never wanted to take the two of them under his protection in the first place. Now she's offering his help to strangers.

'She's right,' Merewyn says, and it isn't often that Tova has heard those words from her lips. 'There's no sense in us going our separate ways.'

'You'd let me come with you?' Guthred asks hopefully.

'Why not?' Tova asks.

Beorn says, 'Girl—'

'You agreed to help us. Why not them as well?'

He doesn't answer, but fixes her with a stern look.

Guthred's head is bowed as he plays with the cross at his breast. 'For so long I haven't had a friend or ally worth the name. No one except Whitefoot to talk to and share my fears with. I was losing my wits. The last thing I want is to be alone again. I'd greatly appreciate the company, if you'd let me join you.'

'Of course,' says Tova quickly, before Beorn can say otherwise.

Merewyn turns to Oslac. 'What about you?'

The poet sighs. 'If you ask me, I think that making for Hagustaldesham is a mistake. On the other hand, if what you say about the Danes is right, then I don't know where else we can go.

Whatever we do and wherever we go, it's going to be dangerous. So if Hagustaldesham is where you're going, and if you'll accept me, then yes. I'll come with you.'

It's settled, then. Five of them against the might of King Wilelm's army.

Tova's eyes meet Beorn's. He stares at her without speaking, just shaking his head, before at last he turns and stalks away.

The flames have begun to dim and the pot has been scraped out so many times it's a wonder there isn't a hole in the bottom. Beans and parsnips and bread don't make much of a meal, but for now it's enough. She sits with her legs crossed, leaning against Merewyn, her head resting upon her lady's shoulder, her eyelids drooping. Another long day, and there'll be more like this ahead of them.

Beorn sits inside the entrance to the barn, checking the fletchings on his arrows. From the other side of the fire floats the soft sound of strings being plucked: Oslac on his harp. The same careful passage, over and over: first hurrying and then drawn out. Not mournful, exactly, but somehow wistful. Every time the notes climb the scale, she wills them to reach the top and find some sort of perfection, but they never do. Just as they approach the summit, they waver, once, twice, before despondently tumbling back down again. Never content; instead always struggling, striving for purity that never arrives.

The song isn't one Tova recognises, but it reminds her of those she'd sometimes hear at night coming from Skalpi's chamber. Sometimes when his old injuries pained him or he found himself in one of his darker moods, he'd have Ælfswith sing the old laments: songs that were in every way the opposite of the bawdy airs those poets who visited used to perform in the hall.

Tova never liked them then and she likes them even less now. She closes her eyes, trying to shut out the sound, but then he begins to sing, in a voice more sweet and true than she could have imagined a man ever possessing.

A once-bright hall with hearth aglow
Cast into shadow by the foe.
Voices of men made silent by sword;
Spear wives cry sorrows for their lords.
That passed away. This also may.

The exile on the whale road toils;
Back bending, cursing, dreaming of native soils,
Of home and kin, of mead cup and cheer.
O wretched fate that has brought him here.
That passed away. This also may.

Dark the night and cold the embers
In hardest winter that folk remember.
To hunger, sickness and frost no end;
They brought the death of many a good friend.
That passed away. This also may.

Eormenhild in years gone by
When 'twas foretold her man would die,
In vain entreated him to stay.
To fight he went—

'That's enough,' Merewyn snaps in that sharp tone that Tova has heard many times. She raises her head and sits up abruptly. 'I didn't think it was possible to feel worse than I already did.'

Silence. Oslac's fingers pause over the strings.

'I didn't know anyone was listening,' he says. 'I didn't mean to offend.'

'Well, we were and you did.'

'It's meant to be a song of hope, not sadness. You know that, don't you?'

'Hope?'

'Even the deepest grief, the worst hardships, they all pass in time. No matter how terrible things seem, things always heal. What matters is that we stay strong and don't give in to despair.'

Beorn snorts. 'And what would you know of such things, whelp? You look barely weaned from your mother's teat. What hardships have you known?'

'I've seen my share. You think that just because I'm young that means I haven't known difficult times? I know what it means to lose loved ones. But I also know that there will come a time when all suffering will end, and we'll be reunited with them. That's right, isn't it, Father?'

Guthred glances up abruptly from the stew pot. 'What?'

Oslac points at the gold cross at the old man's breast. 'You're a priest, aren't you?'

'This?' Guthred asks and looks away as if embarrassed. 'Yes, well, I used to be. Now, I don't know what I am, to tell the truth. I lost my way. Now I suppose I'm trying to find it again, in the hope that I might return to God's favour.'

'Why?' Tova asks. 'What happened?'

'Oh, it's not important. You wouldn't be interested, anyway.'

'I wouldn't ask if I wasn't.'

Merewyn says, 'When we found you, you were praying. You were begging God's forgiveness.'

'I was,' says Guthred, taking a deep breath. 'I've been doing a lot of that lately. Trying to make up for lost time, I suppose. Before it's too late, you understand. I turned my back on him; I only hope that after all this time he hasn't turned his back on me and that he'll still listen to my prayers.'

'Why wouldn't he?' Tova asks. 'And what do you mean, before it's too late?'

'Too late for salvation. Don't you see, child? All this suffering is God's way of punishing us for our wickedness.'

From the shadows of the barn, Beorn gives a curt laugh.

'You don't believe me?' Guthred asks. 'After everything you must have seen, you don't think this is God's vengeance upon our people?'

The warrior steps forward. 'And why doesn't he punish the Normans? Don't tell me you think they're the instruments of God's will, come to cleanse this land of our sins.'

'Why else would he allow these things to happen? We have sinned, every single one of us. We refused to heed the warnings—'

'What warnings?'

'You remember, don't you, the hairy star that appeared in the night sky four years ago? That was a sign. A sign from God.'

Tova remembers. 'That's what Thorvald said,' she says eagerly. 'Our priest. He said it was a sign too. We didn't listen, though. We didn't believe it. No one did.'

Thorvald claimed to have seen the same star the last time it had appeared in the sky, some seventy years and more before, when he had been but a boy. Then, he said, it had portended the coming of the heathens from across the sea to wreak fire and slaughter and ruin upon England.

It had happened then and so, he said, it would happen again.

'No one believed it,' Guthred says. 'To tell the truth, I didn't believe it either. Like other folk, I thought at the time it was foolish superstition. It was only later, much later, that I saw it for what it was. It was God's last warning that we should change our ways. We didn't heed it. Now we pay the price.'

Beorn spits upon the ground. 'I don't have to listen to this. Signs from God? Don't be foolish. Yes, we've all done bad things in our time, every one of us. Things we're not proud of, that we'd undo if we could. Things we'd rather forget. But that has nothing to do with what's happening here. This isn't God's judgement upon us. This is war, nothing more than that. You just don't know it because you've never witnessed it before.'

'I wish I could believe that were true,' Guthred says sadly.

'What are you doing here, then? What makes you so special, that your god should spare you when so many others have died?'

'I don't know,' Guthred admits. 'I don't pretend to understand his plan. If I were to guess, though, I'd say that he's offering me one last chance to atone. To make things right, as best as I can.'

'Atone how, and for what?' asks Merewyn impatiently.

'It's a long story. A long, long story.'

'Well, we have time, don't we? We're not going to be travelling any further tonight.'

Beorn fixes Guthred with a hard look. 'What did you do?'

The priest swallows. 'May I show you something?'

Without waiting for an answer he stands, stiffly, and ventures inside the barn, where he fumbles amid his bundled blankets and returns moments later carrying what looks like a pilgrim's scrip.

'This is the reason I mentioned Lindisfarena,' he says. 'That's where I'm trying to get to, if I can. Everything in here belongs rightfully to the Church. I can't take it back to the place it came from because the Normans have overrun the land, so I thought to take it north instead, beyond their reach.'

He sits back down, cross-legged, by the fire. From the scrip he draws a cloth bag the size of Tova's two fists placed together, which makes a clinking sound as he sets it down in front of him; there must be coins inside. Next comes a pair of silver candlesticks, followed by a jewelled cross, larger than the one he wears around his neck, which looks like it belongs on an altar; then an ivory æstel for pointing out passages when reading, like the one Thorvald uses on account of his failing eyesight, only much more elaborate. Its handle is gold, in the shape of a bird's head, with tiny shining jewels for eyes.

'Where did all this come from, exactly?' Oslac asks.

'From the minster at Rypum. Most of it, anyway. Look, there's more.'

He draws out a bundle the length nearly of his forearm and as thick as his fist, wrapped in linen. Whatever it is, it's heavy, for he cradles it in both hands, handling it with the same care he might give a small child. Slowly he unwinds the cloth, revealing glistening panels of sun-bright gold, in between which are set garnets and other precious stones, mounted on the front of a rectangular object.

A book.

Tova has seen books before, but never one like this. Thorvald had one – a psalter, he called it – which he kept in a locked box in his house. Skalpi used to own one too, until he sold it to pay for new helmets shortly before he went to fight the Normans. He couldn't read, as far as she knows, so how he came by it and why he kept it she isn't sure. She only glimpsed it a few times, when he brought it out to show to his guests. She always thought it was a thing of beauty, small though it was. This, though, is something else.

She shrugs off her blankets and kneels down beside the priest, peering over his shoulder as with light fingers he opens the cover.

A figure that she guesses must be Christ stares back at her from the page, enrobed in flowing garments with a halo of gold behind his head. And there are letters, row upon row of thick ink curls. She has no idea what they mean, but there are lots of them: little ones in long rows, and larger ones too, intertwined with vines and whorls and flowers in bright colours. Reds, like splashes of blood. Greens, as dark as the leaves of the yew outside the church at home. Blues, thick and murky, like the sky just before dawn.

'What does it say?' she asks.

'Well, this part here is only the dedication and the preface. The rest of it, though, is Scripture: the first six books of the Holy Bible. They tell of the world's beginning and the law that God laid down for his people, and of the journey to the Promised Land.'

He turns the leaves slowly, each one filled with writing, neatly laid out, with even spaces between each line, like the ridges and furrows in a field. She can't imagine how long it must have taken for a scribe to copy out all those letters. There are pages and pages of them: a stack, thicker than her fist, of crinkled, yellowed vellum.

Merewyn asks, 'How much is it worth?'

'Oh, more than you could imagine.'

'So,' Beorn says, 'you stole it and now you feel remorse. Is that it?'

'Beorn!' Merewyn scolds. 'How can you accuse him of such a thing? He's a man of God.'

'What does that have to do with it?'

Guthred says, 'How it came into my possession is a shameful tale.'

'So you admit it. You're a thief.'

'No, I'm not. Well, I was, but all that's behind me now. It's complicated.'

'Which is it? Yes or no?'

'Look,' the priest says angrily, almost in tears. 'I saved it. I, Guthred. If it weren't for me, this book and everything else would be in the hands of soulless fiends, enemies of God. I couldn't let them have it, I couldn't.'

Hurriedly he closes the covers and sets about wrapping the tome back inside the linen sheet.

'It's all right,' says Merewyn, placing a hand upon his knee, trying to calm him.

Oslac scratches his forehead. 'So you rescued these treasures from the Normans, is that what you're saying?'

'Not the Normans. Others.'

'Who?'

'Hateful people, whose hearts were hard and whose minds were filled with evil. Wretches for whom the sanctity of the Church meant nothing. Outlaws. Reavers.'

Beorn is watching him carefully. 'You make it sound as if you knew them.'

Guthred doesn't say anything for a long time. He raises a hand to his forehead, as if he has an ache there.

'I did. Yes, I did. I knew them. I was one of them.'

Tova isn't sure what she was expecting to hear, but it wasn't that. 'You, a reaver?'

'For a while, yes, I was, although my sins go back further than that. I'm a bad person, you see. A bad, bad person. But it's a long story, as I said. I wouldn't want to burden you with my woes. The last thing you want to hear is my sorry tale.'

'I'd rather listen to your tale than hear any more of his singing,' Beorn says as he glares at Oslac, who glowers back at him. 'It can't be any more depressing than that.'

'If he doesn't want to speak, he shouldn't have to,' Merewyn says. 'What gives us the right to pry? It's not any of our business. Like you said, Beorn, we've all done bad things. We all have our secret shames – things we're not proud of. Shouldn't we be allowed to keep those things to ourselves if we want to?'

'Speak for yourself,' Oslac mutters. 'My slate is clean.'

Tova glances anxiously at her lady. If any of the others only knew the truth about them, knew what they're running from . . .

'It's all right,' says Guthred. 'If we're going to be travelling together, you deserve to know the truth about me. It's been far too long since I made confession. Maybe I'll never get the chance to do so again. So this might as well be it. That is, if you'll indulge a broken old fool.'

He glances around the fire. Oslac waits patiently for him to start. Of course, there's probably nothing a storyteller like him relishes more than spending an evening exchanging tales. Whether they're joyous or grim probably doesn't even matter to him. Beorn shrugs, as if he couldn't much care either way, but Tova can see from the frown on his face that he too is intrigued by this man. This was-but-is-no-longer-priest.

As is she.

'We're listening,' Merewyn says.

He nods. 'Very well.'

And he begins.

GUTHRED

As I said, it's a long story, but I'll try to make the telling of it as quick as I can. For my own sake, and for yours.

Like everyone else, you probably see this grey-haired figure, wrinkled and decaying in body, wearing this cross, and you say to yourselves, he must be a good man. Well, I'm not. I'm no more holy or worthy of respect than any of you. How many times have I done penance? How many times have I prostrated myself at my bishop's feet, begging his forgiveness and vowing to do better in future?

Words. That's all they were. All those promises, as empty as the sky. I can't run from the truth any longer. After all that I've done, Hell is no more than I deserve.

For I've sinned. Sinned worse than you can imagine.

No, it's true. I don't say this because I want your pity. I say it because I don't want you to think I'm something that I'm not. Lord knows how many people over the years have sought my guidance, have come to me for comfort and wisdom and hope. They looked to me as an example of how they should live and give praise to God. An example of goodness and honesty and virtue.

If they only knew how wrong they were.

I'm no priest, nor should I ever have been. I was never meant for the holy life, not really. The truth is I'd probably have died long ago in the village where I grew up, worn out through years of toil, had it not been for a lie.

That's how it started, you see.

I was the youngest of six. Three brothers, two sisters. They were all much older than me and were forever tormenting me. Sometimes they let me join in their games, but more often I was the victim, the one who was always blamed for everything that went wrong. Every pot that was broken, everything that went missing: it was always my fault. I hated them. All of them. I hated my father too. This was so long ago now that I don't remember much about him any more, except for his face, which was gaunt and sharp-featured. Sharp, like his tongue. Like his eyes too, which were ever alert and missed little.

He cared nothing for me. Indeed he resented me from the start. He never saw me as someone to nurture and teach the ways of the world. No, instead he regarded me with a sort of cold indifference, as if I were a stray dog my mother had brought in from the cold and to which she'd developed some inexplicable attachment. To him I was nothing more than another hungry mouth foisted upon him without his permission, who nonetheless had to be fed and clothed and sheltered and given space to sleep on his floor. That said, food was never something we found ourselves short of. Even during the worst winters or following a poor harvest, when others struggled to get by, there always seemed to be plenty on our table. Salted sea fish, spices from distant lands, ale of the finest quality and even, sometimes, mead. Meats of various kinds, even during Lent when it was forbidden, although at the time I was too young to know this or to appreciate what luxuries these were.

I suppose I learned my ways from him. He was no one of any great account: the miller on a small estate owned by Bishop Leofgar of Licedfeld. Still, he did more than well enough for himself. It wasn't until I was a little older that I understood how this was so, that I learned the first of the few lessons he ever did teach me.

There were two ways of living, I discovered. One was by honest labour, the way of all God-fearing men. The other was my father's way.

He wasn't a good man either. I sometimes wonder what he would make of me if he could see me now. If he could see what I've become.

For every sack of grain the village folk brought for him to grind, he was entitled to keep one sixteenth of the resulting flour, which he could then sell or use for himself. That was his privilege as the miller. Sometimes, though, he would measure out more than his due, mixing chalk dust or grit in with what he gave back so as to make up the weight. He didn't do it often, lest anyone should guess what he was up to, and only took a little at a time. He claimed that was the mistake people often made and why they got caught in the end: because they were too greedy. Not that he told me any of this directly, you understand. He hardly spoke to me the whole time I lived under his roof. It was my mother who found out. Exactly how she did, I don't know, but I overheard her confronting him one night when I was supposed to be asleep. He told her not to utter a word to anybody if she knew what was good for her, and maybe that was why he often beat her – to remind her of that warning.

From the very beginning, you see, I grew up surrounded by wickedness and deceit. I was born into it; it ran in my veins. Exactly when I began stealing, I don't remember any more, but it couldn't have been long after that. Deep down I knew it was wrong, of course, but the idea of it filled me with excitement, and I suppose I must have thought that if he could do it, then why shouldn't I?

I began taking things, small things at first, when no one was looking. Pots of ointment from shelves, spoons and knives, a handful of nails from the forge, keys that happened to be left lying about – that sort of thing. I became adept at concealing objects in my palm or up my sleeve or in the folds of my tunic. No one showed me how; these were tricks I taught myself, with practice and some narrow escapes when I came within an eye-blink of being found out. I never dared to sell the things I took, and in any case I didn't know who'd want them. What I'd do instead was either climb the great gnarled oak that stood by the edge of the meadow and cram my prizes into its crevices and hollows, or else bury them all together deep in the woods: dig a hole and cover them over with earth and bracken and hope that no one noticed. Sometimes, when my help wasn't needed at home, I'd go and make sure that no one had disturbed my hoards. I'd sit on the ground with everything laid out in front of me and feel like a king counting out his gold. Of course I was always terrified someone would discover me, especially once I learned that the penalty for theft was flogging, but at the same time it gave me a thrill like nothing else, and I couldn't stop myself.

And it paid, in the end. The summer I was eleven, Bishop Leofgar himself came to visit the manor where we lived. He held lands in three shires, and would tour them all from time to time, although apparently he hadn't been to ours since before I was born, so it was considered a great honour when the reeve received the news and announced it before everyone. A great celebration was arranged for the bishop's arrival, and after that there was a procession in which he and all his under-priests entered the church in their fine robes and bestowed blessings and gifts upon the manor. The whole village came to hear the Mass. I'd never seen the like before. All my life had been lived in browns and greens and greys, but suddenly a different world was revealed to me. A glimpse of Heaven. At the head of the procession was carried a silver cross the length of one's forearm, studded with sparkling stones. On a bier two monks in robes carried a gilded box shaped like a house that shone like the sun. A reliquary, it was, though at the time I didn't know that. The other churchmen wore richly woven chasubles over their robes, and in the middle of them came the bishop himself.

In my memory I picture him as being almost as old as I am now, and maybe he was, although to a child's eyes everyone seems ancient, so probably he wasn't quite as frail as I thought at the time. He came dressed all in white, I remember, like a saint. In one hand he held a staff, while his fingers were decorated with silver rings engraved with tiny letters, which he took off later on, when it came to the feast that had been prepared in his honour. He obviously didn't want to get them dirty, and so he laid them out on the long table in front of him, in plain view. Four of them, all in a row from left to right.

I was there, and my sisters too; the reeve had chosen us along with some of the other children to attend on the bishop and his retinue in the hall where he was being entertained. We were to carry food from the kitchens and take away empty bowls, fetch pitchers of water and ale, see that they had everything they needed and otherwise make ourselves useful. It was a summer's evening, still hot, and so the hearth fire hadn't been lit; I remember the great doors had been opened to let in the light, but even so it was dim, and noisy too. There were dozens of people all talking over one another, dogs yapping as they scurried around the table in search of scraps, while in the corner a harpist struggled to make himself heard above it all, and amid all that commotion and with so many people going to and fro, I thought to myself how easy it would be to snatch up one of those rings from the table when no one was looking.

It was reckless, thinking about it now. If I'd been spotted, that would probably have been it for me, no matter that I was young. The only thing worse than stealing from a bishop is probably stealing from the king himself. I could easily have lost my hand, or worse.

But I was thinking about the challenge, not the consequences. That was why I did it, you understand. Not because the things I took were necessarily valuable, although in this case they were, but just to see whether I could. Only later did I seek to profit from it. Back then it was little more than a game, that was all. The more I played, the better I grew, and so I always had to set myself harder and harder tests. And this was a challenge if ever there was one. The silver lay there, inviting me, taunting me to take it if I dared.

And I couldn't resist.

'What does this have to do with your friends the outlaws?' Beorn asks. 'I thought you were going to tell us about them, not about some bishop and his rings.'

'Please,' Guthred says. 'If this is to be my confession, then I want you to hear everything.'

'Let him speak,' says Oslac. 'Some tales need time to tell.'

Beorn doesn't look happy, but he waves a grudging hand in acquiescence, too tired, it seems, to argue.

I waited until there was a distraction, a moment when the bishop and those around him were engaged in deep conversation. About the nature of angels, I seem to remember it was. They were gesturing wildly, and one of the older priests was thumping his fist upon the table, either excited by the debate or in objection to something that had been said, causing knives to jump and bowls to rattle.

Anyway, they paid me no attention as I refilled their ale cups, nor as I set the jug down in front of them, nor as I lifted away their greasy plates. Nor did they notice as with the same hand I slipped one of those silver rings into my palm and walked away.

I ought to have known I wouldn't get far.

In fact I'd barely managed five paces when the bishop cried out in his scratchy voice, 'My ring! Where is it? Where is it?'

I thought that was it. I thought they were about to catch me.

Stools scraped against the floor and there was a shuffle of feet; I turned and saw the bishop's attendants shouting and waving for silence. One with a deep voice called for the doors to be closed. The harpist had stopped playing; the laughing and singing had ceased, but there was a muttering and murmuring as people heard what was happening. The bishop himself had turned white as a cloud, seemingly frozen to his seat, his eyes filled with horror, while all around him was commotion.

'Everyone stay where you are,' the reeve bellowed. 'No one leaves this hall!'

Of course I was panicking when he said this. Every instinct told me to run, to drop the ring without anyone noticing and get out of there as soon as possible. But I didn't do that.

Instead I said, 'I see it!'

While everyone turned to look but before they had any idea what was happening, I let the wooden dishes I was carrying fall and hurled myself under the table. I scrambled past the legs of the assembled churchmen, ignoring their shouts of protest, towards one of the reeve's hounds, which was sniffing at a morsel that had fallen amid the straw and the rushes and the sawdust. It yelped in surprise when it saw me coming, then darted away. For an instant I pretended to fumble in the straw and the sawdust before rough hands grabbed my shoulders and dragged me out from beneath the table and on to my feet. Men were demanding to know what I was doing, and my heart was pounding as I unfurled my fist, and in open palm held the missing ring out towards the bishop, who was sitting across the table.

'Here, Lord Bishop,' I said, and swallowed because my throat was dry. I hoped no one noticed how I was trembling. 'It was on the floor. It must have rolled off the table. I saw the dog go near it. You're lucky he didn't swallow it.'

A hush fell across the hall; the hands on my shoulders were withdrawn. The bishop rose from his stool, his look of confusion turning to one of relief.

'My dear boy, bless you,' he said as one of the other priests plucked it from my palm and laid it before him. 'These rings were a gift left to me by my predecessor in his will, and to him by his predecessor in turn. If I'd lost one, I'd never have forgiven myself. Truly you are Heaven-sent. What is your name?'

I told him and said earnestly that I was the miller's son, the youngest of six, in my eleventh summer, and that I was honoured to serve at his table and humbled to meet him, and that his grace and kindness were well known to everyone.

'And so well spoken,' he said, smiling gently. 'We must see that you are rewarded handsomely for your help. Are you a good Christian?'

To tell the truth, I didn't understand really what he meant by that. At that age all I knew was that a thousand years ago there'd been a man called Jesus Christ who was killed by the Romans, and that he was the son of the one God, and that we should pray to them and live according to their rules, because if we did those things and forswore all other spirits and superstitions then we would live for ever in their heaven.

I didn't say any of that, though. Instead I replied simply that I thought I was, that I tried to be, although it wasn't easy, and I hoped that answer would please him.

Bishop Leofgar smiled. 'Alas, when is it ever easy? Tell me, do you go to church often? Do you receive the sacrament?'

When I could, I said, although I told him that a priest only came to us once every three months, and sometimes less often than that if the weather had been bad and the roads were impassable.

He nodded sagely. 'Perhaps there is something I can do. A youth of such virtue and honesty as yourself should be better placed to receive God's grace. Where is your father? May I speak with him?'

I said I would fetch him, and he bade me do so. Of course my father, when I found him back at the house, didn't believe me when I said breathlessly that Bishop Leofgar wanted to see him and that he wanted to reward me, but when I wouldn't stop harassing him he gave in and let me take him to the feasting hall, where he was surprised to find that I was telling the truth.

The reeve sent me to the storehouse to bring in another large cheese for the table so I wasn't there to hear what exactly passed between the two of them, but the substance of it was this: the bishop wanted to provide me with a place in his household, where I would receive schooling in letters and the other arts and one day learn to deliver the sermon. My father must have thought he was joking at first, that a son of his should be considered worthy by someone so exalted, but I think he was glad to be rid of me, for when the bishop and his travelling party took to the road again after their stay three days later, I went with them. No one asked me whether I wanted to go or not; it had been agreed and that was that.

And so it was that a thief and a liar came to be a priest.

'He took you with him, just like that?' Merewyn asks. 'For no other reason than because he thought you'd found his ring?'

'Why not? He was a generous man, and kind-hearted too, a great giver of alms.' Guthred sighs. 'I ought to have learned from his example. Maybe if I had, then things would have turned out differently.'

*

In some ways life at the church school in Licedfeld was not so unlike life at home. The other children all came from noble families; their fathers were lords or priests or deacons. I was the exception. The outsider, the country boy. The bishop's favourite, they whispered behind my back, and sniggered and made snide remarks.

I won't bore you with the details of my first years there, but suffice to say I made few friends. I didn't miss home, my father or my brothers, but I did miss my mother. Years later, when I did happen to return, I discovered that she'd died only a few months after I'd gone away.

I was lonely, but I managed to survive. I concentrated on my studies and, at least to begin with, tried not to draw too much attention to myself. For three years I managed to resist the temptation to steal or do anything that might bring me trouble. The last time had been too close. Now that I'd been granted a chance to better myself, it was only right that I made the most of it.

After three years at the school my perseverance was rewarded and I was made an ostiary, which is to say a doorkeeper, holder of the keys to the church. I was responsible for opening the doors before Mass and for ringing the bell, and for tidying away the incense and the candles and the altar cloth and locking the building again when I left, which meant that over the months I spent many hours in there by myself.

Alone, with no one watching over me save for the Lord himself.

That was when I succumbed.

My master in those years was a priest named Æthelbald, a humourless man who must have been a little younger than I am now. He was all of six feet tall and maybe more. Thin in the face. Quick to anger. I saw him once tear the wax tablet from a pupil's hands and strike him around the head when he thought he wasn't trying hard enough. That said, he was a pious man, eager for us not just to study God's word in the schoolroom but also to witness how his work was practised in the wider world. Each month he would take his older students with him out from the minster into the shire to help him spread the holy truth and deliver Mass to the folk of the surrounding villages. Everywhere we went there'd always be wise women and superstitious folk looking to obtain pieces of the consecrated Host for their own ends: to ward off evil, or to use in magic rituals or in remedies for ailments of various sorts, because of the power they were convinced it possessed. People would often ask if they could have additional wafers to take away with them – for their small children who were too sick to come, they said, or for their cousins in the next village – and when Master Æthelbald refused they'd try to bargain with him, offering all manner of favours in return. His patience thinning, he would try to explain that to employ Christ's body and blood for such heathen practices was not only foolish and misguided, but sacrilege too. But they didn't understand.

And so I had my idea.

As ostiary I was one of only a few with access to the strongboxes where the communion bread and wine were kept. All I had to do, if I wanted any of those things, was take them. And that's what I did. Before each journey I'd make sure to slip half a dozen or so wafers – never so many that they'd be missed – into my coin pouch, and sell them quietly once the Mass was over to those who seemed most desperate, in exchange for a silver coin if they had one, or else for trinkets: a beaded necklace, a clutch of coloured stones, a bone flute, some fishhooks, a pewter brooch – whatever they had to offer. Within a few months I'd acquired more things than I knew what to do with, most of which I had no use for. But I held on to them nonetheless.

95

Why did I do it? Out of frustration, I suppose, more than anything.

For three years I'd worked patiently and without complaint, learning my Latin and the psalter and then the teachings of the Church Fathers, but there was little joy in any of it. Certainly not how Master Æthelbald taught it, anyway. After all that time, I felt I deserved more. We weren't supposed to have many possessions save for what we needed for our studies; our clothes were simple and the food was always plain: barley bread, cheese, stewed cabbage and boiled carrots, with fish or salted bacon if we were lucky. To have all those things I'd come by, then, made me feel like a lord. Some could be traded at the market, or else they made useful gifts if there was a girl in the congregation who caught my eye.

I'd be lying, though, if I said I didn't take a thrill from it as well. It was the joy of doing something I wasn't supposed to, the danger each time that I might be caught.

And they did catch me eventually, though it took them many months. The problem was that there were few good hiding places to be found around the church precincts – few, at least, that I could easily reach but which no one else was likely to stumble upon. The more things I acquired, the harder it became to hide them all. The only place I found that was really large enough was the space underneath a loose floorboard in the dormitory, and that was the hoard that Master Æthelbald found. How he did so, I never learned; probably one of the other boys happened to spy me as I was depositing my latest gains, and reported me. I thought I'd been careful, but obviously not careful enough.

Æthelbald confiscated everything and demanded to know where it had all come from.

I'd stolen them, I said, which wasn't far from the truth and yet was much better than telling the truth. Thieving from the

Church, selling the Host, knowing full well it would be used for profane purposes: these things were an affront to the Almighty. I didn't like to imagine what my punishment would be if I admitted all that, and that's why I lied.

As it was, they stripped me of my duties, taking away the robes that as ostiary I'd been entitled to wear. For forty days they made me take my lessons and eat my meals alone. They even moved me to a separate dormitory away from the other boys. They made me wear a grey penitent's smock so that all who saw me would know of my wrongdoing. They forbade me from speaking to anyone unless so instructed by my master or another priest. During that time my daily sustenance consisted of nothing more than bread and weak ale and a single cup of goat's milk.

Those forty days were the longest of my life. How I endured them, I don't know, but I did, though I've never been able to stomach goat's milk since. When it was over and I was allowed to rejoin my peers it was like stumbling out of doors into sunlight after being bedridden with some long illness. Certainly I was thinner at the end of that time than I'd been at the beginning, but there was one other outcome I hadn't been expecting, which was that I suddenly had more friends than before. The more pious ones continued to hate me, of course, and took pains to avoid me, in case whatever had caused my soul to become stained should rub off on them. But others who'd previously thought me a simple country lad – pure and diligent, who kept himself to himself – saw me differently. To them I had become a dissenter, a breaker of strictures, a defier of elders, a troublemaker, and in a strange way they revered me for that.

By and large I enjoyed my newfound reputation and the friends it brought me. There was one, though, whose attention I'd rather have escaped. Wulfnoth, his name was. He was a couple of years younger than me, which I suppose would make him thirteen at the time. He looked up to me in the same way he might an elder brother, although in my eyes he was never anything more than a nuisance. He was quietly spoken but keen-witted and silver-tongued too. He trailed me like a hound, so much so that I came to detest his pox-scarred face with its thick brows and his ridiculous ears protruding like two great serving dishes stuck to the side of his head.

Had he tried, he could have been a good student, I think. He was clever enough, but easily bored, which meant he often turned his attention to other things. Usually these were small matters, such as hiding our master's quill and stylus before a class, but not always. One summer's morning he took some two dozen pots of honey from the storehouse and smeared their contents underneath the benches where we sat in the schoolroom. As the sun climbed higher and the day grew warmer, we were besieged by wasps, and Æthelbald was stung several times on the arm and was in too much pain to continue, which meant we had no more lessons that day.

How did I know it was him? Because he came and told me afterwards.

'I did it,' he said, beaming proudly as if he'd done us all a favour. He wasn't the bragging sort, so I can only guess he was looking for approval and thought I might be the one to give it.

Instead I said he'd been foolish, and that nothing good would come of what he'd done. Sure enough one of the deacons quickly discovered what had caused the sudden plague of insects. He demanded to know who the culprit was, and when no one confessed his gaze turned upon me. I knew then that I was for it. I protested, of course, but he wouldn't listen. He subjected me to ten strokes of the birch rod and then, straight afterwards, set me to work. He found me a pail and brush and cloth and made me clean the schoolroom from top to bottom while the stingers and the flies buzzed around my head.

'You should have told him it was me,' Wulfnoth said later that day, when I returned to the dormitory and gingerly sat down upon my bed. My arse was still hurting; my arms felt about to drop from my shoulders, and I was ready to collapse from the heat.

'I did,' I replied.

I was expecting him to apologise, but he didn't. There was no glimmer of remorse, no sign of gratitude in his eyes. Instead he merely nodded, his usual smile gone.

'I owe you,' he said simply, as if it were merely a mark on his tally stick, a weight needing to be balanced on his scales. And then he went without saying how he meant to repay his debt.

I wanted nothing more to do with him for a long time after that, and avoided him whenever I could. He'd brought me enough trouble as it was. Master Æthelbald returned a few days later, once the swelling and the pain had diminished. While the redness on his arm had gone, though, the redness in his face was deeper than ever. Every time I misremembered a passage or forgot my grammar he would instruct me to hold out both my hands and he'd strike me hard across the palms with his birch rod. Meanwhile Wulfnoth sat on the bench opposite me, his face impassive.

It was many weeks before he dared speak to me again. The leaves had fallen by then and the river mist hung over the church precinct as we made our way to our first lesson of the morning.

'I have a favour to ask of you,' he said as he scurried up along-side me.

He was mistaken if he thought he was getting any favours from me. I pretended not to hear him and quickened my pace, but he wasn't about to give up so readily.

'I know you don't want to speak to me,' he went on as he fell into step with me. 'But find me after class, by the tree behind the bakehouse, and I'll explain.'

There was an earnestness about him, a desire to please, that I found unnerving, and yet at the same time I was intrigued. And so as soon as the morning's teaching was done I went to see what he had to say. I told myself that I was really going so that I could dissuade him from whatever folly he had in mind, but that was a lie.

He was waiting for me as he said he would be. He was clutching a leather pouch, which he thrust towards me as soon as I approached. I took it, more in surprise than anything. It felt like there were coins inside, and quite a number of them too, to judge by the heft.

'I need you to get something for me,' Wulfnoth said.

I asked him, 'How did you come by this? Did you steal it?'

'My father sent it to me.'

'I thought your father hated you.'

That was why he'd sent him away to the cathedral school – to be rid of him. So Wulfnoth had told us when first he arrived.

'My uncle, then,' he replied flatly. 'My uncle sent it to me.'

'You took it, didn't you?'

'Listen,' he said impatiently. 'I haven't told you yet what it is I want you to get.'

'I don't care.'

He gazed back at me, tight-lipped. He was hoping to appeal to my baser instincts, I knew, and I was sorely tempted, but his earnestness made me suspicious. Whatever he had planned, I wanted no part of it.

'I'm paying my debt to you,' he said. 'But first I need you to do this one thing for me.'

'Why can't you do it yourself?'

'Because you're the one who has the keys.'

So it was something from the church that he was after. I reminded him they'd taken the keys from me after they found my hoard. Besides, if he reckoned I was going to risk punishment again on his behalf, he could think again.

He didn't answer.

'Anyway,' I said, 'what do you think will happen when they find me with this silver?'

They kept a close eye on me now, and I had little chance of being able to hide it from them. Besides, I wasn't about to become a playing piece in his game. That's what these things were to him. It was about seeing how clever he could be, and how much he could get away with, while making sure that others paid the penalty.

I thrust the pouch back at him. 'Find someone else to do your work for you. Better yet, take that back to wherever you got it from.'

He took it from me and I walked away without looking back. Still, that wasn't the last time he tried to solicit my help. I suppose he saw me as something of a kindred spirit, and that was why he confided in me and tried hard to win me over. Certainly I never encouraged him. It's true that we were alike in some ways, but there was much more that set us apart. Yes, the school's strictures could be harsh, and they grated upon me too. And yes, there was always that urge to rebel. But the difference between us was that, deep down, I wanted to be good. I'd come to believe what the deacons and Master Æthelbald said, which was that the temptations that plagued me were a sickness that needed to be cured.

Wulfnoth wasn't like me. He didn't have a pious bone in his body. He had no desire to learn, no instinct for hard work or understanding for its value; he didn't see why it might be useful to know one's letters or to be able to engage in the art of rhetoric. Everything we did was to him a waste of time. Why his father had thought he should be schooled at the cathedral and train as a priest, I could never work out. Maybe he was hoping that the masters would instil some discipline in his boy. But there was no disciplining Wulfnoth. He was restless and forever in need of something to do, something to occupy his mind.

Many things went missing around the cathedral quarter over the next few months, as the old year went out and the new one began, from candles to gold-spun altar cloths and even the embroidered cushion from the bishop's throne. None of those thefts were my doing, but I could guess who was behind them.

That never stopped them from blaming me, though.

It was after the cushion disappeared that I was called before the bishop himself. Brihtmær, it was by then, kindly Leofgar having died the year before. He was a much sterner man, thin like a withy but not nearly as old or as frail as his predecessor. He demanded to know why I continued to defile God's house with my sins, but when I tried to defend myself, he shouted me down. Leofgar had been too lenient, he said; if it had been his choice he would never have taken on a wretch like me in the first place. A miller's son, no less. But that was what Leofgar had done, and so Brihtmær owed it to his predecessor to try to cleanse my soul and rid it of evil. He lectured me for the better part of an hour, warning me that my obsession with worldly goods would condemn me to eternity in Hell if I didn't mend my ways. He told me that if anything else went missing, I would be expelled from the school and barred from receiving communion.

I tried to explain that it wasn't I who had taken his cushion, or the candles or the altar cloth, and that if I knew where they were I would say. He was deaf to my protests. I knew then that I had

102

to do something. I couldn't allow them to send me away, back to work under my father's eye, assuming he still lived. The cathedral school was all I'd known for so long, and it was still preferable to labouring with my hands out of doors, hefting sacks of grain and flour from storehouse to mill and from mill to kitchen, bending my back to the plough under the blistering sun and the driving rain. That was not the life I wanted. At least in the Church I could live in some comfort.

Which meant that Wulfnoth had to go.

I knew I couldn't wait long. If I didn't get rid of him soon then it would be too late. And so almost from the moment Bishop Brihtmær dismissed me I started plotting.

It had to be something truly terrible, some act for which there could be no forgiveness. The masters never liked to give up on a student, you understand. No matter how wayward he was, they always made their best efforts to bring him back within the fold, as they did with me. It was almost unheard of for any boy to be sent away. They preferred instead to impose penance and to pray fervently for the salvation of the souls in their care.

Remember I said I used to be a keen climber when I was young? Mostly it was trees that I climbed – that oak was my favourite – but sometimes it was buildings too. Often, back when I was living with my father and wanted some time alone with my thoughts, I used to climb the mill itself, just so that I could watch the stream glistening in the sun, the wheel turning.

Anyway, I decided to put those skills to good use. Two nights after I'd been called before Bishop Brihtmær, long after everyone else had gone to sleep, I rose from my bed. Barefoot and stepping as lightly as I could, I slipped out the dormitory door, the satchel that usually contained my tablet and stylus slung across my shoulder. The moon was full and the skies were clear, which meant I was better able to see what I was doing, although I suppose had anyone been about it would also have made it easier for them to spot me. Fortunately, there was no one. I hurried through the shadows towards the small stone church and proceeded to scale the outside, working my hands and my toes into the cracks and the crevices, one limb and then the next, as quickly as possible until I was able to swing myself on to the roof of the nave, which had been rethatched the previous summer, so I knew I could trust it with my weight. I scrambled up so that I was sitting astride the roof and then, taking from my bag one of several blocks of chalk that I'd taken from the schoolroom earlier, I set to work.

It was after Easter by then, but it was a chill night, and I was glad of the long winter cloak draped across my shoulders. Not my own cloak, you understand; I had no intention of getting all that dust on my own clothes and so giving myself away. That would have been foolish of me. But it wasn't long before my hands, my face, my hair was caked in the stuff.

I worked as quickly as I could. By the time I'd finished, the first glimmer of grey was already beginning to show in the east. My eyes were sore from lack of sleep and my backside was hurting from sitting so long in the same position. Before anybody else woke and noticed I wasn't in my bed, I stuffed the chalk back into my satchel, climbed down and stole back through the shadows to the dormitory, pausing first to shed my borrowed cloak and to rinse my face and hands and hair as thoroughly as I could in the brook that ran behind the dormitory, knowing I had to be quick. Then, folding it into a bundle so that none of the dust came off on my person, I carried the cloak back inside, opening the door carefully so that it didn't creak on its worn hinges. None of the other boys stirred, for which I thanked God as I made my way to where Wulfnoth was curled up underneath his blankets, eyes closed and with a frowning expression on his face, breathing softly and steadily. Hardly daring to breathe, I knelt down by the chest at the foot of his bed, lifted open the lid and laid his dusty cloak back inside, together with what was left of the chalk from my satchel, before hastening back to my own bed.

Sleep must have claimed me not long afterwards, although how I was able to settle, I don't know. I remember waking to the sound of shouting as daylight flooded in through the doorway, paining my eyes. Master Æthelbald stood in the middle of the room, roaring at us all to get up, while the deacons marched from bed to bed, pulling the sheets back from those who were too slow, forcibly dragging them from their mattresses.

'Out,' Æthelbald roared. 'All of you, out!'

I remember catching Wulfnoth's eyes as we filed, one by one, out of the dormitory and were made to wait in the yard outside. He had a puzzled look on his face, as did the rest of them, but when he asked me what I thought was happening I merely shrugged. The sky was light, but the sun was barely up and there was a keen breeze, and we stood in our shirts and our bare feet.

'Which one of you is responsible?' Æthelbald asked us.

'For what?' one of the younger boys asked. Of course no one had any idea what he was talking about.

No one but me. I hoped Æthelbald didn't look in my direction, thinking that I would surely give myself away.

Our master thrust out his arm, pointing above our heads. 'For that!'

We all turned as one, looking up in the direction of his out-stretched finger, towards the church, and specifically the bell tower, where my handiwork was clearly visible. It looked even better in the light of day, and I smiled with pride despite myself as howls of laughter rang out from the assembled students.

'This isn't funny,' Æthelbald screeched, and his cheeks were bright red. 'Whoever did this will be sorely punished!'

In bright chalk across the southern face of the belfry was what I'd spent a full hour last night working on. Two male figures, crudely drawn and yet clear enough. Both naked save for the crosses hanging around their necks. Both with members erect: members almost as long as their arms, I remember. Balls as big as platters. I was especially proud of those details. One of the figures was bent forward, his rear exposed, resting upon his bishop's staff, while the other approached him from behind. Above the standing one I'd written, in tall majuscules so that they could be easily read from a distance, 'ÆTHEL', while below the one bent over I'd scrawled 'BRIHT'. It wasn't the most clever thing I could have attempted, but I was never much good at drawing.

I know, I know. It shames me to think back on it, on what I did. At the time, though, I couldn't stop grinning. I didn't have much time to enjoy the moment, though.

Æthelbald rounded upon me. 'This was your doing, wasn't it, Guthred?'

'Me?' I asked, looking up because he was tall, and hoping that my performance was convincing enough. 'No, master, I swear it wasn't.'

He fixed me with his darkest frown. He didn't believe me, I know he didn't, because he never did, and I remember starting to panic, thinking that if this didn't work then it would be on my head, when just at that moment one of the deacons emerged from the dormitory and called Æthelbald over to see something.

I knew then that they'd found it.

Our master went to see what the deacon had discovered, and shortly called us all back inside. The blankets and sheets had been torn from the beds, some of which had been overturned. The contents of our chests, where we kept our spare clothes and the few possessions we were allowed, had been spilt on to the floor.

'Who sleeps here?' Æthelbald asked as he pointed to where an acolyte stood at the foot of one of the beds.

At first none of us said anything. We all knew it belonged to Wulfnoth, but no one dared be the one to tell, and I certainly wasn't about to, since that would only invite suspicion.

'Someone speak quickly,' Æthelbald said, 'or else you'll all be facing the rod. Five lashes for every one of you until I have an answer. Well?'

Wulfnoth stepped forward, looking confused. 'It's mine, master.'

Æthelbald beckoned the deacon across, who held up Wulfnoth's cloak for all to see. White marks everywhere, as clear as if one of the bishop's precious doves had defiled it.

'And this?'

There was a look of such bewilderment on the boy's face that I almost wished I hadn't done it. Almost. He looked at the cloak, then back at Master Æthelbald, not yet comprehending, and then his eyes widened as he began to realise.

'I don't know how—'

'And yet you don't deny that it's yours.'

'Yes, but—'

'What about these?' Æthelbald said, hefting two of the lumps of chalk. 'They're yours too, aren't they?'

Wulfnoth shook his head. 'N-no.'

'You thought you wouldn't get caught, didn't you?'

'I swear I don't know where they came from,' he said.

'Liar,' said the deacon.

'Sacrilege,' said Æthelbald and spat.

He towered over Wulfnoth, who was short for his age, and not the strongest either, with some of the scrawniest arms and legs you've ever seen. If Æthelbald or any of the deacons had asked themselves how he'd managed to climb all the way up the side of the tower, by himself and without a ladder, then they might have worked out he was telling the truth. If they'd paused for even a moment to ask why he hadn't simply rid himself of the chalk once he'd finished with it, they might have seen through my deception.

But Æthelbald was red with fury and in no mood to ask questions, so they did none of those things. And so Wulfnoth's fate was sealed.

'Bishop Brihtmær will hear about this,' Æthelbald said as he seized the boy's arm.

Wulfnoth yelped, but his protests were ignored. I made sure to avoid his gaze as he was led away, for I couldn't afford to let him see the smile I could feel breaking out across my face. It wouldn't take him long to realise what had happened; maybe he already had.

As it was, the rest of us didn't escape unpunished. Æthelbald came back soon afterwards and sent four of us with ladders and rags and pails of water to scrub those disgraceful pictures from the stonework. It was supposed to be a market day in the town but there wasn't much trading taking place. Instead men and women were gathering outside the church, pointing up at the tower, some laughing and others nudging one another knowingly, much to our master's displeasure. At first he tried shouting at them to go away, and some did, but they only went and told others, and so he turned his anger upon us, yelling at us to scrub more vigorously, to remove the chalk marks all the sooner.

'Harder, faster!' he cried, which of course the crowds thought even funnier.

Poor Æthelbald. I didn't feel all that sorry for him at the time, but I do now. I hope he managed to live the rest of his years in peace. He deserved that much, especially after everything he had to put up with.

As for Wulfnoth, once the bishop learned the nature of the images that had desecrated his church, there was no reprieve, no chance to make amends. That same day a letter was sent to his father by the fastest rider Brihtmær could find, informing him of what had taken place and that his son would be returning to him. Wulfnoth's belongings and clothes were all cleared from the dormitory by midday, and by mid-afternoon he was on his way, escorted from the church precinct by two of the bishop's retainers while my fellow students and I watched on. He didn't say anything or even look at us, but kept his eyes fixed on the road ahead so that I couldn't see if he was angry or upset or even relieved.

I'd done it, I thought, as I watched them disappear down the road. I'd finally rid myself of him.

Did I ever regret what I'd done? Not at all. After all the trouble he'd brought me? No, he deserved everything that came to him. And I would never have to suffer him again.

Or so I thought, until three months ago.

'Why?' Merewyn asks. 'What happened three months ago?'

But Tova is one step ahead of her. 'That was when you joined the reavers, wasn't it?'

The priest nods. He presses his fingertips hard to his brow, as if the very act of remembering is painful.

'You mean Wulfnoth was one of them?' Merewyn says.

'Not just one of them,' Guthred replies. 'He was their leader.'

'Their leader?'

'It was fate, I suppose. God's will. It's often said that he works in ways that are difficult for men to understand. But I understand now. This was another test, perhaps the greatest of them all. He wanted to see whether or not I was worthy of his grace. And I failed.'

Beorn is frowning. 'So in all that time your paths never crossed, but then suddenly this Wulfnoth appeared again, from nowhere, for no reason at all?'

'It was no coincidence, Beorn. This was the divine hand at work; I know it was.'

It happened like this.

It was about a month after Michaelmas, not long before the feast of All Saints. The first frost had just been and everywhere the leaves were falling. I was travelling from Rypum, which for seven years had been my home, out to the surrounding villages and manors to spread the Lord's word among the country folk, just like my master, Æthelbald, used to do all those years ago. And, like him, I had with me students of my own: three wide-eyed youths, the sons of nobles all, who knew little of the world beyond Rypum's minster school. Hedda with the spotty face. Wiglaf the fat one, whose nose was forever bleeding. Plegmund the abbot's nephew, so God-fearing and self-righteous that he would make the saints themselves spew.

That's what I thought. Imagine that. Me, a priest, despising a child for his piety. A child. God help me, but I did. I resented all of them.

Why? Because after all the years I'd spent serving God's glory, traipsing from village to village, across hill and fen, saying Mass and listening to countless hundreds unburden themselves as they made confession, I thought I deserved better than looking after a crowd of snotty children and wasting my days in a dank school-room teaching them the rudiments of Latin grammar.

I understand now how Master Æthelbald must have felt.

I resented them, but not as much as I resented myself. Because the truth is I could have had more, if only I'd tried harder. I could have had a church of my own, if only I hadn't strayed from the path, hadn't succumbed so readily to temptation and sin.

I've said it already, but I'll say it again. The Church was not the place for me. What I hated most was all the rules we had to follow. These days we're supposed to live like monks. That's what the bishops want. It started years ago, long before the Normans came to these shores, but things have only been growing worse since. These foreigners the new king has been bringing across from France, arriving with their instructions that they say come from the pope himself in Rome. We should all take the tonsure, they tell us, and must dress sombrely at all times and eat as plainly as possible, and only by doing these things can we hope to reach salvation.

So many rules, and so many different penances to be undertaken should you break any of them. And I was always breaking them. It used to be that priests could marry and take whoever they chose to their beds; now they tell us that if we even so much as glance at a woman in a certain way we're entering into sin. They say we must be purer than pure. So when they found me with a whore, I was made to wear a hair shirt for a whole month in penitence. The second time, it was two months. When it got out that men and women had been coming to me, offering coin if I'd divine their future from swirls of wine in the baptismal font, I was accused of daring to determine the mind of God. They didn't care that those folk had given their silver willingly, or that I'd correctly seen that the blacksmith's child would be a girl, and that the harvest would be poor because it was going to rain all summer. They said what I was doing was sacrilege, and imposed a fast upon me, and for nine months made me recite the Paternoster in church fifty times each day.

Things like that only made me hate them more, and soon enough

I turned that anger upon myself. I drank more than I should, more than God would have wished. Many were the dawns when I woke with head aching and stomach churning, cursing the rising sun. I lost count of the number of times I missed morning Mass because I was insensible from too much mead the night before. The more I drank, the more I hated myself, and the more I hated myself, the more I drank. I'd swear at my students and shout at them and beat them whenever I thought they weren't trying hard enough. They deserved better than me, they really did. Meanwhile I kept on stealing whenever I thought I could get away with it. A few coins from the alms box; a candle here; a loaf of bread there; an antler comb, a copper spoon, a jar of honey or spices from the storehouse. Not for the challenge, or because I sought to profit from it. No, I did it to keep myself amused. Each one was a trophy, a small victory in my struggle against the world, and against God.

For a long while I was convinced he hated me. In my darkest hours, to my shame, I wondered if anything of what we preached was true. If God existed at all, and if he did, whether or not he cared about what we did on this earth or who or what we worshipped. Or maybe, I sometimes wondered, just maybe the heathens had it right after all. Maybe ours was but one god among many, and had no control over the lives of men, and our fates instead were governed by the whims of the three spinners, sitting at the foot of the world tree, weaving the threads of our fates. Maybe I would do as well to pray to Odin and Thor and Frigg as to our Christian god.

It pains me to admit these things, to confess such things to you, but it's true. I regret all of it now. I see how selfish I've been. But at the time I didn't. For years all I yearned for was simply to be free.

I suppose that's why I joined them, really. To be free.

*

'Why didn't you just leave, if you hated it that much?' Tova asks. At the start she felt sorry for him, but now she's not so sure. 'What was stopping you?'

'I could have, it's true,' Guthred says. 'I suppose it was fear that stopped me. Fear of the world outside the Church. You have to understand that I had no trade or craft, no skill with my hands that I could rely on, nothing except what I'd learned in books. What else what I supposed to do? So I was trapped. Realising that only made things worse, because I knew there was no escape, and that I was doomed to live the rest of my days in misery.'

Where was I?

Yes, that's right. We'd been warned when leaving Rypum to take care on the roads. Word had reached us that the rebellion had failed, and there were all sorts of rumours about what might happen, and whether King Wilelm would come north and seek revenge. Armed men, and I don't mean Frenchmen, were said to be roving the land; we heard tales of night raids, of pigs and sheep and cattle being stolen. Of robbers and bandits waylaying travellers, demanding payment and threatening with violence anyone who tried to resist them. Everywhere we went, folk were living in fear. The laws of the land were being forgotten; there was no justice to be found anywhere. Many thegns and reeves had failed to return from the fighting, and so there was no one to maintain order. Killings were going unpunished, we were told, while thievery was rife, and men who knew those parts well said we ought to hire warriors for protection, just in case.

Like a fool, though, I didn't listen. I thought my robes and my cross would protect me. I thought that no one would dare attack a priest and his followers.

I was wrong.

It was still early in the afternoon when it happened. We were on the old Roman road, heading north. An icy wind was gusting in our faces and so we didn't hear the hooves behind us until it was too late.

It was Hedda who noticed first. 'Robbers!' he shouted, and we all turned.

There were horsemen, a half-dozen of them, riding towards us with spears and clubs in hand, whooping and yelling.

My students fled, or tried to; they were pursued by some of the riders. I stood as if frozen, my knees shaking. I didn't know what to do. We were helpless. Outnumbered. We had no weapons, and even if we had, none of us would have known what to do with them.

So I did the only thing I could. I fell to my knees, closed my eyes and started praying. I prayed to God, prayed that he would keep me safe from harm. Not that I expected him to hear my pleas.

The sound of hooves grew closer, and I looked up to find our attackers forming a circle around me and Whitefoot. They were a strange lot, of all ages: one or two youngsters, not much older than my students, but most of them in their middle years. Their faces were dirty, and almost every one of them had leaves and bits of twigs in his hair, but despite that they were dressed like kings: decked out in gold chains and silver arm rings; robed in ermine and otter fur, beaver pelts and wolfskins and good wool cloth. I confess I didn't know what to make of them.

'He's just a priest,' said one scornfully, and I blinked in surprise as I realised that it was in fact a woman, dressed in a man's clothes, her fair hair cut short. 'He won't have anything worth stealing.'

'We should search him anyway,' one of the men said, a hulking fellow as big as an ox. He dismounted and strode towards me. Sihtric, I later learned his name was. He was missing his left hand, but with his other one he grabbed me by the collar and lifted me to my feet. 'Show us your treasure, priest.'

I didn't know what to say. We didn't have any treasure and we weren't carrying any coin either. There was no need, when every village and manor we came to would gladly feed and shelter us for as long as we needed.

'Speak,' he said, his breath foul upon my face, but I was too frightened and couldn't find my voice. Some way away, I could hear Hedda and Plegmund and Wiglaf. Had they been caught?

The fiend shoved me hard. I landed on my backside, and they all laughed.

That's when he arrived, shouldering his way past the others: this grey-haired man with sharp eyes. He walked with a limp and yet with purpose. From the way the others moved aside to let him pass I guessed he must be their leader. Belted around his waist was a sheath for a long knife or short sword. He stared at me for a long time, and I wondered if he planned to kill me. But he didn't draw his blade. Instead he stood still as stone. A quizzical look came across his face.

He said, 'Guthred?'

'It was him, wasn't it?' Merewyn says.

'Yes, it was him. Not that I recognised him. Not at first, anyway. But then it had been nearly forty years. We were little more than children when we last knew one another. I'd forgotten he even existed. After his expulsion, that was it. I never heard any more about him, and I didn't care.'

'He recognised you, though,' Oslac says.

Yes, he did. How he did, I don't know. For the longest time I said nothing but gawped at him. I still had no idea who this stranger was.

'I'm right, aren't I?' he asked. He was grinning by then. 'After all these years, who would have believed it?'

Eventually I found my voice, and asked him how he knew my name.

'It's me,' he said. 'Wulfnoth.'

I hadn't heard that name in so long. It took me a moment to remember where I knew it from. My memory isn't what it used to be, you see. But I quickly saw the resemblance.

The years had changed him, of course. His hair was thinner, longer, greyer; half his teeth were either missing or broken, and there was a bearing about him that was different. But then I noticed those ears sticking out, those thick brows, that pock-marked face overlaid with scars small and large.

It was him.

He turned to the others, laughing. 'It's all right. He's an old friend of mine.'

'What do you mean, a friend?' the woman asked as Wulfnoth extended a hand.

Still numb with surprise, I took it as he helped me to my feet. He was as short as I remembered, which was to say about half a head shorter than me, although he was no longer the scrawny soul he'd been back then. His hand was rough, his grip crushingly strong.

He grinned, gap-toothed, at me and threw an arm around my shoulder. 'We know each other from long ago. A different life, eh?'

I nodded but didn't answer. I was still so confused. I saw Pleg-mund and Wiglaf, and spotty-faced Hedda being held firm by the others, and I met their fear-filled eyes.

He looked me up and down. 'After all this time, who'd have thought our paths would cross again? And you a priest! What brings you here? Who are these others?'

I could have asked him the same things, but I wasn't sure I wanted to know the answers. Whoever these people were, they were dangerous.

I replied that these were my students, and that we had left Rypum that morning, and that we didn't have any treasure to give them. I was babbling, I realised, but I still didn't know what to make of these people and whether or not we could trust them, or what they planned to do with us.

He laughed again, told me not to worry and that he had no intention of robbing an old friend.

'If we're not going to rob them,' said the foul-smelling one who'd threatened me, 'then what are we going to do with them?'

'We're going to let them go,' Wulfnoth said to a chorus of groans and protests from the others. 'Yes, that's what we're going to do. But first Guthred and I have much catching-up to do. Isn't that right?'

He tossed me a leather flask from his pack and asked me how it was I came to be in these parts. I didn't know what to say. I still couldn't quite believe somehow that this was the same Wulfnoth I'd known all those years ago. I knew he was almost the same age as me, yet whereas a few hours in the saddle these days often leaves me stiff and creaking, he moved with the ease of someone half as old.

He introduced me to his companions, all five of them. To Sihtric the One-Handed, he of the bad breath, and to the fierce woman, whose name was Gytha. She was Wulfnoth's lover. Then there was Halfdan, whose life he'd apparently saved many years before, though I never learned how, and also two dark-haired brothers: Cudda, short and round; and Cuffa, tall and thin. I got to know them well over the following weeks.

Of course Wulfnoth had much he wanted to tell me about what

117

had happened in the nearly forty years since we'd last seen one another. It was as if we were children again: the way he spoke, it was like he wanted to impress me, wanted my approval just as before. Not that I was really listening; I was still a little bit in shock. My nerves aren't what they once were. Wulfnoth bade us all sit and had the two brothers fetch some wine and bread from their packs for us all to share. I remember wondering whether we were their guests now or their prisoners. My students were just as fearful as I was. Their faces were white and they exchanged anxious glances.

They deserved better than me as their teacher. That's no excuse for what I did, you understand, but it's the truth. I was ill tempered and impatient, and often spoke harshly. I was no good for them.

I suppose Wulfnoth must have sensed my mind was elsewhere, for he gave me a nudge and then assaulted me with all manner of questions about how the years had treated me, and what had happened to the other boys with whom we'd shared lessons.

'What are you?' I asked him back. 'Thieves?'

He frowned as if hurt. 'Is that any way to speak to an old friend?'

Old friend. He kept saying that, as if doing so it would make it true. Obviously he remembered things very differently.

'What, then?' I asked.

He shrugged. 'We live off the land, do what we can to survive. We take things sometimes, when we have to, or when folk are foolish enough to leave them undefended. When they travel the roads without armed men for protection. Whose wise idea was that, anyway?'

I ignored his question, because he wasn't answering mine. 'These horses, these fine clothes, they aren't yours.'

'Of course they're ours. And so they'll remain until the day when someone else takes them from us. That's the way it works.'

'So you did steal them.'

He didn't try to deny it, but merely laughed. 'This from the man who once sold pieces of the consecrated Host! Sold it to foolish country folk who knew no better, who'd hand over coins they'd taken years to scrape together. Is what we do any worse?'

I hadn't expected him to remember that. My cheeks burned hot. My students, sitting ten paces away, turned their heads but I refused to meet their eyes.

'Master?' one of them asked. Plegmund, I think it must have been. I could sense him judging me, as so often he seemed to be, from beneath his thick dark eyebrows.

'That was a long time ago,' I muttered to Wulfnoth, keeping my voice low. He didn't know, of course, about all my other transgressions over the years. About all the penances I'd had to undertake for my sins. Selling the Host had just been the beginning.

He was right, though. I was no better than them.

'Anyway,' he said, 'tell me about yourself. You must have some stories of your own.'

I replied that there wasn't much to tell. Certainly there was nothing I was very proud of, although of course I didn't say that.

'I'd have thought you might be a bishop by now,' he said with a smile.

At that I gave a bitter laugh. There was no point telling him that it was only ever the sons of nobles who secured such offices. A country priest – a miller's son, no less – had as much chance of becoming a bishop as a fish did of growing legs and walking on land, although miracles were known to happen.

'With all that cunning of yours, I'd have thought that if anyone was going to climb to the top of the Church, it would be you.'

119

At once I froze. Climb to the top of the church. I tell you: those were his exact words. Had he guessed, I wondered, that I was the one who had chalked those pictures on the tower? Did he know that I had got him cast out from the school?

My mouth was dry and I couldn't speak as I stared at him. But he didn't look angry, not at all.

'I'm joking,' he said and laid a reassuring hand upon my shoulder as he chuckled. 'Don't look so ashamed. You shouldn't feel bad that you haven't got your hands on a bishop's pallium yet, even if it means you're still one step behind me.'

'What do you mean?'

'Well, I did get my hands on his cushion, didn't I? Do you remember that?'

Somehow I forced a smile. So he didn't know. I could breathe easily again. I'd no idea whether or not he might harbour a grudge after all this time, but I knew that I didn't want to find out.

'How little things have changed,' he said. 'Even after all these years, we talk and share jokes just like before. We had fun, didn't we?'

When he said that, it did cross my mind that perhaps he had me confused with someone else. As I said, I never liked him from the beginning. I was forever trying to stop him from following me around. Certainly I didn't recall having ever shared jokes with him.

'Those were the days,' he said wistfully. 'I suppose I never realised how lucky I was to have such schooling until it was taken away from me. Not that I enjoyed it much at the time. I was glad to get away from the deacons and the masters. All those passages we had to memorise, all those saints and their feast days. I hated that. Grammar, rhetoric, poetry. I hated it all. I could barely put together a Latin sentence, let alone remember how to say the words for Mass. Can you imagine what a terrible priest I would have made?'

No worse than myself, I thought. For I had completely squandered the chances that had been given me. All those hours spent in the classroom learning my letters, copying out passages of the Bible. All that work, all that effort, and what for? What had I made of myself? What use had all that learning been? I was no good as a priest, no good as a teacher, no good to anyone.

'Patience always was one of your virtues,' he went on. 'I wanted everything straight away. I would never have been content to do what you do. I would have been too eager for riches and rewards. The lure of gold and silver has always been too strong for me to resist. One way or another, I would have ended up where I am now.'

That was the moment, I think, when I realised what I had to do.

Ever since I was young I'd known that I was a sinner, a slave to temptation. I'd tried to be honest and pure in deeds and in spirit, had tried my best to resist errant urges, but it was no use. I'd tried to make up for everything I'd done. Again and again I'd admitted the error of my ways and sworn to be a better person in future, only to break those pledges.

For years I'd been fooling myself, drawing a veil over my eyes so that I didn't have to face the truth. All I had to do was recognise who I really was, and I would be free.

Maybe, I thought, I was more like Wulfnoth than I'd ever wanted to admit.

Softly, so that my students wouldn't hear, I said, 'Let me join you.'

He almost choked on his ale. 'What?'

'Why not? We're old friends, aren't we?'

'You'd join us? You, a priest?'

To his ears it must have sounded ridiculous. A man of God saying that he wanted to give up everything he knew and become an outlaw.

What I saw, though, was a way out. A way to escape the life I'd grown to despise. A way to save me from myself.

'So you gave up the life you'd led for forty years, just like that?' Oslac asks. 'On a whim?'

'No, not on a whim. I knew what I was doing. It was what I wanted, or thought I did, anyway. I always was good at telling myself the very things I wanted to hear. At the time it seemed like a chance had been offered to me, and that if I didn't take it, I would regret it.'

Tova just stares at him. She hears what he's saying, but she still can't believe he would turn his back so easily on God. He is nothing like kindly Thorvald, their priest at Heldeby. He's nothing like she thought he would be.

'And Wulfnoth agreed?' Oslac asks.

Not at first. No, to begin with he just laughed at me, as if it were the funniest thing he'd ever heard. When he realised I was serious, though, he changed his tone.

He said to me, 'If you knew some of the things we've done, you wouldn't be asking to join us.'

I'd done things too in my time, I replied. Things at which my confessors blushed when I told them. I wasn't the saint he thought I was. And then I told him everything: the years of drinking, the stealing, the lies, the fornication, the swindling, my forswearing of God. And the strange thing was, I didn't feel ashamed to be saying those things. I felt proud, as if each one were a mark of honour.

'I don't belong in the Church,' I whispered and gestured towards my students. 'I'm not like them. I never have been. For years I tried to deny it; for years I tried to be the person they wanted me to be, and I'm tired of it. Let me come with you.'

He shook his head, disbelieving. 'You must know that what we do is more than the kind of petty theft you're used to. You're a good man, Guthred. Not like me. Believe me, you don't want to become involved with us.'

That was when I grew angry. I knew what I was, I said, and what I wanted. This was what I wanted.

He shook his head. 'We move around a lot; we have to. I have no room in my band for those who can't keep up, who can't do their fair share.'

What he was saying was that he didn't need someone like me slowing them down. I replied that I was used to spending long days in the saddle, and that Whitefoot and I had travelled countless leagues together.

'There's danger,' he said.

These were uncertain times we lived in, I said.

He sat for a long time, chewing his lip, contemplating. 'It's been a long time since we had anyone new,' he said eventually. 'Let me speak to the others.'

He stood and then left me alone. At once my students came over to sit beside me.

'What's happening, Master?' asked Wiglaf, wide-eyed. He wiped his nose with the back of his hand, which came away smeared with blood and snot. It always bled when he was nervous. 'What are they talking about? When are they going to let us go?'

'Soon, I think,' I said, but I wasn't really paying him or the others any attention. I kept glancing towards Wulfnoth and his band. The one called Sihtric was shaking his head.

'He's old,' I heard someone mutter.

The woman glanced up and saw me staring. She gave me an evil look and spat upon the ground, and I looked away.

Plegmund's head was bowed, his eyes were closed and he was whispering a prayer that God might deliver us from our enemies. Hedda was trembling; his face was ashen. I think he still expected them to kill us at any moment.

'Do you really know that man, Master?' he asked, his voice small.

'I used to. Many, many years ago. When I was as young as you.'

'We heard you laughing. What were you talking about?'

I didn't know how best to answer that, but fortunately I didn't have to, for just then I looked over my shoulder and saw Wulf-noth marching towards us, and Gytha beside him, a stony look in her eyes. I rose to my feet hurriedly, not knowing what to expect. My palms were sweaty, and I could feel my heart thumping as I turned to face them.

All I saw was a fist hurtling towards my head, and the next thing I knew I was on the ground, with my face in a puddle. Pain blossomed in my cheek, and I could taste blood and mud and rainwater. Someone's foot was pressed down on my back, and it felt like all the breath was being squeezed from my chest.

'Master Guthred!' one of my students was shouting, but I couldn't tell which one. My cheek was throbbing; there was a ringing in my ears, and I still didn't know what had happened.

'The three of you can go,' I heard Wulfnoth say. 'You're worth nothing to us. Your master is, though. He's our hostage now.'

'If you want to see him alive, come back here in a week's time with one thousand shillings in silver,' the woman added, and I reckoned it was her foot on my back, for her voice seemed closer. 'Any less and you'll be taking back a corpse.'

My mind was racing, my heart too, as I wondered what I'd got myself into.

'Now, go,' Wulfnoth said. 'That is, unless you want him to suffer. Do you hear me?'

I'd made a terrible mistake, I thought. Now I was about to pay, probably with my life. Why had I thought I could trust such scoundrels? My breath came in starts, and I felt suddenly faint. I heard my students shouting to one another in alarm, followed by hoofbeats on the track, which gradually grew more distant. They were leaving me, I thought; they really were leaving me. I wanted to shout out to them, but fear kept the words from reaching my tongue.

The weight pressing upon my back suddenly lifted; Wulfnoth began laughing, and then the woman as well. I didn't know if I dared move, but I looked up, and there he was, beaming at me, his hand outstretched.

'I think they were convinced,' he said. 'You can get up now.'

I took his hand cautiously. I still wasn't quite sure what was supposed to have happened. My cheek stung, and I winced as I put a hand to it.

'You hit him too hard, Gytha,' Wulfnoth admonished her.

'I hit him like I hit everyone,' she replied tartly.

He helped me to my feet, apologising on her behalf, and said that of course I wasn't their captive. I didn't see why the pretence was necessary, but he seemed to think it was and I didn't feel like arguing.

'No need to look so scared,' Wulfnoth said. He wrapped his arm around my shoulders and grinned. 'You're one of us now.'

And so it was that things came full circle, and the priest became a thief.

*

He won't even look at them as he speaks, Tova notices. That's how ashamed he is. And so he should be. She tries to imagine Thorvald doing the things Guthred says he has done, but she can't. How can they both wear the cross and yet be so different?

She wishes Thorvald were here with them now. He'd know what to say, how to give them comfort, how to assure them that things would be all right. Of everyone at Heldeby, he's the one she misses most. Kindly, patient, white-haired Thorvald, who hardly raised his voice nor uttered a harsh word nor spoke ill of anyone, who was always willing to give his time to listen and offer his wisdom and advice to anyone who asked it, even though, as he often said, his own time was growing short.

He'd never have consorted with robbers. The mere thought would have sickened him. He'd never have lied to and cheated humble country folk, full knowing what he was doing, for the sake of a few coins. He'd never have drunk so much that he couldn't rise the next morning. Even at Christmas, when there was barrel upon barrel of mead and wine – enough for every cottar and slave to drink his fill – barely half a cup passed his lips. A delicate stomach was the reason, he said, though she always suspected it was more than that.

But then there are few in the world like Thorvald. And who is she to be passing judgement, anyway? It's not like she is a model of virtue, given some of the things she has done. Things she would rather forget. Is she any better than Guthred, really? Will God see her any differently, when the time comes?

He's supposed to be better than that, though. He's supposed to be an example to others.

But he hasn't finished yet, and she senses there's worse to come.

*

Would it have made any difference if they'd come back with my ransom? Would I have changed my mind? Maybe. I don't know.

But the fact is they didn't. Was I surprised? Not really. I think my students were probably almost as glad to see the back of me as I was of them. Who knows what they told the dean and his canons when they arrived back at Rypum? Maybe they decided it would be easier to say we'd been ambushed and I'd been killed. Or maybe they told the dean exactly what happened, but he simply didn't think my life was worth wasting any silver on.

Either way, it was clear they didn't want me back. They didn't care what happened to me. They would rather I was martyred than see my safe return. They'd washed their hands of me, and so I washed my hands of them in return. I burned my robes, broke the arms off my wooden cross and snapped the shaft in two and tossed the pieces in a river.

This one? Stolen. Like almost everything else, it doesn't belong to me. But I'm coming to that.

God have mercy on me. I turned my back on him completely, renounced everything I'd ever been taught, everything I was supposed to uphold. It was like a madness had come over me, a thick fog that descended over my mind, darkening my thoughts and making it impossible to see the light.

It seems now like some terrible dream. I only wish it were.

Why they ever accepted me into their band, I'll never know. I think Wulfnoth came to some agreement with them that, provided I dirtied my hands like everyone else, they'd tolerate me, but that if I ever caused any problems they'd get rid of me the first chance they got. That wouldn't surprise me. My only ally at first was Wulfnoth himself; it wasn't until a couple of weeks had passed that the others started speaking to me. Like you, they found it hard to believe that a churchman would abandon his faith so readily. They didn't understand, and because they didn't understand they didn't trust me. Eventually they did, but it took some time.

We moved around a lot in those first few weeks, as winter set in. We had to, for there were other bands like us prowling the hills, most of them more numerous and better armed than us, Wulfnoth said, which meant we had to be always on our guard. The others, they all slept with one hand on their knife hilts, although I hardly ever saw them use their blades. They weren't warriors, you understand, only wretched folk whom life had ill treated. There was Sihtric, whose lord had thrown him off his land when he lost his hand and could no longer work as hard. There was the she-wolf, Gytha, who had fled the beatings and worse delivered by her husband. There were the brothers Cudda and Cuffa, former slaves who had run away, and Halfdan, who was deaf and dumb and communicated with the others by way of complicated hand signals that I never did understand.

And there was Wulfnoth. I wondered how a man of thegnly birth like him had ended up as a brigand and a common thief. One evening after a successful day's scavenging he told me. We'd brought back ale, lots of it, so his tongue was loose and the story came spilling out. His father was so disappointed in him for being expelled from the school that he all but disowned him. When the old man died of a fever the following winter, he left nothing in his will for Wulfnoth. All the land the boy should have received was divided up instead between his two elder half-brothers. They let him stay because he had nowhere else to go, and gave him a house and a scrap of pasture, but made him pay rent as if he were a lowly ceorl – rent that only grew more onerous when, years later, they in their turn died and their sons inherited the land, until it was more than he could pay and they threw him out.

That was ten years ago, he told me. After that he became an outcast, wandering from place to place, living on what he could scrounge and steal, all the while cursing God for having failed him. Eventually his path crossed with others to whom fate had been similarly unkind: Halfdan and Sihtric and a couple more who had since perished. They banded together, with Wulfnoth as their leader, and that was that.

'The Lord never cared anything for us,' he said bitterly. 'He's never looked after us, so we've had to look after ourselves.'

As I listened I couldn't help but think that all his misfortunes, all his troubles, had begun when I got him thrown out of the cathedral school.

It was my fault, all of it.

My face must have turned as pale as snow, and it was a good thing that it was dark and he was drunk, for otherwise he would surely have noticed.

Anyway, I don't want you to think that I'm making excuses for what they did . . . what I did—

'It sounds like you are,' Oslac says, interrupting.

'Well, I'm not. Yes, they could be cold-hearted and pitiless, but they were also in their way a sorry lot, who felt they deserved better. That's all. As I told you, they weren't warriors. Doubtless they could handle themselves in a scrap, but they rarely went looking for one. They carried weapons to intimidate, not for killing. If danger threatened they would rather run than fight.'

Beorn says, 'And yet they attacked you, didn't they?'

'Because we were easy prey, as I've said. All the time I was with them, we only attacked anyone if we thought they were unlikely to fight back, and even then only if we thought they might be carrying something valuable. There was no sense in taking risks if we didn't have to. Most of the time we didn't even go that far. We'd lurk on the edges of manors and steadings, taking a pig here, a few chickens or ducks there; we'd raid a storehouse for cheese and eggs and salted fish and fresh bread, or cloaks and blankets and firewood and pots and pans that we could use. If we could get away with it, we might try stealing a horse to take to market and sell on. It was wrong, I know, but the things we took were rarely worth that much and so it wasn't harming anyone. That's what I told myself, anyway.

'Yes, I did make excuses then. But not now.'

From those pickings we were able to live. Not well, I should say, but we survived. We had enough to keep ourselves warm and our stomachs full, and we always had dry clothes and were never short of shoes. We were comfortable, but I don't want you to imagine that we dined every night like kings, or that we had a great hoard of gold buried in the woods, like the robber lords you sometimes hear stories about. It wasn't like that.

Christmas came and went. We heard the bells ringing out from some faraway church and so we knew folk were celebrating Our Lord's birth, but we didn't mark it, except to share out some bottles of mead that we'd pilfered on one of our recent raids. We needed it to warm us, for it was a particularly bitter day, and the frost lay thick that morning, I remember giving a thought to Rypum and the festivities that would be happening there. They'd be laying out the feast and lighting a great fire in the dean's hall; there'd be wine aplenty, and sweetmeats spiced with pepper and ginger and cinnamon. I felt a pang of regret for having left all that behind, but I pushed it away quickly, before it could grow.

It was after Christmas that things changed. For several weeks we'd been hearing rumours that the king was sending bands into the marshes of Heldernesse and the wolds around Eoferwic to stamp out the final embers of the rebellion. Then for a while things went quiet. About two weeks after the holy day was when we realised that something was wrong. We always kept a lookout over the road, in case any easy targets came our way. It was Halfdan who was on watch that morning; towards midday he came running back to camp, flustered and red-faced and waving his arms. It was some while before he calmed down and Wulfnoth could get any sense out of him. Using his signs, which the others translated for my benefit, Halfdan told us that there were dozens of travellers on the road: many, many more than there would normally be on a cold winter's morning. And all of them, every single one, going north. One group he'd seen numbered more than thirty: it looked like an entire village, he said.

It sounded unlikely, but he was right. We followed him to where he'd been keeping watch, on a ridge overlooking the road, and we saw for ourselves. Scores of men, women and children of all ages, lords and common folk, on horse and on foot, swathed in thick winter clothes. Some with crooks in hand and dogs running at their feet were driving sheep. Others were leading oxen and carts laden with goods along the bumpy track.

I'd never seen anything like it. I had such a feeling in the pit of my stomach, a pang of dread; I knew something had to be wrong for all those people to be on the move all at once.

Straight away Wulfnoth sent the brothers to see what they could learn. They came back with the news that a great army was on the march from Eoferwic; the Normans were riding in their hundreds and thousands, with steel and fire and fury. All sensible folk were leaving their homes without delay, gathering what possessions they could and abandoning the rest to the enemy. Some of them were making for the hills, where they hoped to find protection within the great ringworks that the old ones had built in ages long gone, while others were just trying to get as far away as they could.

'What do we do?' asked Cuffa, while Sihtric made hand signals for Halfdan's benefit, so that he knew what we were all talking about.

'I don't see that we have any choice,' Gytha said. 'We go north, like everyone else.'

'No,' Wulfnoth said. 'We do have a choice.'

We all turned to look at him, surprised, but he was quite serious. Gytha spoke for the rest of us, I think, when she asked what he meant.

'I mean we go south. Think about all those halls left empty. Spoils for the taking, and no one to guard them. Spoils that could be ours.'

'If the foreigners haven't seized them first,' Gytha pointed out. 'And who's to say those folk will have left anything valuable behind, anyway?'

'There's always something. They can't have taken everything. What they couldn't carry they'll have hidden, or buried. We just have to find it.'

'Before the Normans do,' Gytha muttered.

'Better we claim it than they do, don't you think?'

'For all we know they could already be overrunning the country-side.'

'Then we'll just have to keep our eyes open and our wits about us, won't we?' Wulfnoth said, with that same cheeky grin that I remembered.

Gytha didn't look sure, but the mere thought of so much easy plunder had got the others excited, I could see.

'What do you think, Guthred?' Wulfnoth asked. 'You haven't said anything.'

If I'm honest I thought Gytha was right. It seemed far too reckless for my liking; a risk we didn't need to take. But it was clear we were going to be outvoted, and I didn't want to dampen the others' enthusiasm, so I agreed.

And so we rode south. While everyone else was fleeing, we ventured into what for all we knew was the very heart of the storm. It almost sounds noble, doesn't it? If only it had been.

It wasn't long before we came across our first deserted vill, although that's probably too grand a word for three crumbling cottages and a cattle byre that had seen better days. It didn't look as though we'd find much there and so we ignored it. After another hour we spied a hall in the distance, which we thought more promising, but as we got closer we saw there were still lots of panicked folk running to and fro, loading carts and wagons, while a man on horseback who I guessed was their reeve shouted orders and pointed. We kept our distance, lying low and watching for a while, but there was no telling how long we might have to wait until they left, so we decided not to waste any more time there.

We rode on, through dales that with every mile looked more and more familiar. After another hour or so, it seemed to me that I must have travelled some of these paths before. I recognised, or thought I did, the way an oak overhung the track where it dipped, and how a certain hill formed a sharp ridge against the sky, how particular trees appeared to huddle together in a hollow. That's when I realised that of course we couldn't be far from Rypum.

Wulfnoth, who was riding ahead of me, called back to ask what was wrong, and I became aware that I'd stopped. I said that if memory served me well, we could follow this track for another few miles, ford the river and climb the next rise, and then we would see the minster in the valley below.

133

'The minster,' he said, and began laughing. 'Of course.'

At first I didn't know what was so funny; I thought maybe he was having some kind of jest at my expense. He glanced at the others, and they all grinned back at him. All except Gytha, whose lips were set firm. That's when I understood.

He meant to raid it.

I know. That should have been the moment when I paused to question what in the Lord's name I was doing. But it wasn't, and I didn't. That was how far I'd fallen from God's grace.

'The Normans could be here by day's end,' Gytha said. 'We'd do better to turn back and see if those folk have left that manor yet. There'll be spoils enough for the taking there. More than we can carry. Why risk our skins?'

'Not as much as there'll be at Rypum,' Sihtric pointed out, which was probably true. I knew how much the canons loved their silver platters, their bejewelled wine cups, their gold brooches.

But I knew this wasn't about plunder for Wulfnoth. This was about revenge. Raiding the minster was his way of getting back at the Church for the wrong it had done him all those years ago. My eyes met his, and I glimpsed in them that same glint, that same hunger for mischief that I remembered from all those years ago. Except it wasn't quite the same. Behind those eyes of his there was a coldness, a festering hatred that I hadn't seen before.

Until then I hadn't appreciated just how deeply those wounds ran within him, or how powerful was the grudge he held. Right then I felt afraid like never before. Afraid for my safety in this little band of his. Afraid for my life.

What would he do, I wondered, if he ever found out that all the hardships he'd suffered in his life had begun with me?

'It's settled, then,' he said, even though it wasn't. He often did that: challenging anyone to defy him. And it worked, because none of us would.

The deeper we travelled into those debatable lands, though, the more I began to think that Gytha was right. The enemy were close, I could feel it somehow, and must surely be growing closer with each hour that passed. I was as eager to lay my hands on silver as the rest of them, and moreover I felt something of what Wulfnoth felt: that the Church owed me something for all those years of service I'd given it, patiently, without reward. But not if it cost me my life.

I voiced none of those concerns, though, gutless as I was. I could have. I should have. Maybe the others would have sided with me. But he had such a look of determination about him that I knew nothing would sway him. Now that he'd got the idea in his head, he wasn't about to give it up.

If I'd only known what was going to happen . . . If I'd had even the faintest inkling, I swear I'd never have . . .

But the fact is I didn't know.

It's because of what happened that I have to keep this book and these treasures from him. That's why I have to get to Lindisfarena.

That's why, in the end, I fled.

I'm getting ahead of myself.

We arrived at Rypum late that afternoon, just as the sun was setting. I hadn't been there in, well, three months. With everything that had happened, though, it seemed like longer. Much longer. The minster church, in the shadow of which I'd spent many a winter, rose from the valley as if from some half-remembered dream. Familiar and yet unfamiliar.

I suppose you'd call it a town, although it isn't a big place, or rather it wasn't. I doubt there's anyone left there now. Then, it was home to some forty cottager families who paid rent to the Church, and to twelve priests known as canons, who lived in a closed community a bit like a monastery, with the church at its centre. I wasn't one of them; I was just the humble travelling preacher who did the hard work of spreading the Lord's word across dale and moor, in all weathers, while they lived comfortably in their new houses, discussing matters of theology. I was already there before they came, at the archbishop's behest, with their quills and their books and their servants. It was they who decided I should be in charge of the students in the school they established. The canons foisted those duties upon me, so that they could spend more time speculating on the nature of the dog-headed men and the monopods and the blemmyae and other creatures that supposedly inhabit the distant east, and because they had the support of the archbishop, there was nothing I could do about it.

I hated the canons and their dean more than anyone.

I mention this only because all these thoughts were running through my mind as we approached Rypum. It was quiet. That far south, it seemed that everyone had already left their homes; not a single thread of smoke wove skywards from any of those houses and halls. The light was fading, shadows were falling, the wind was sweeping along the valley, gusting in our faces, but Wulfnoth didn't seem to care. He spurred his horse headlong down the rutted road, making straight for the church, which was where I'd told him the best treasures were likely to be found, and we followed.

'It was strange to see that place again after so long,' Guthred says. His face takes on a troubled expression. 'To see it so empty as well. That was the strangest thing. All those houses, simply abandoned. Everything as still as death. Not a soul around. Or so we thought.'

'What about the Normans?' Tova asks. 'Had you seen any sign of them?'

'No, and that only made Wulfnoth even more confident. We didn't spy a soul anywhere in the gathering gloom as we approached. We weren't expecting to find anyone, either. Probably that's why we failed to realise that we weren't the only people there.'

What should have made us wary was the fact that the minster's great door wasn't locked. Instead we just took it for a piece of good fortune and assumed the canons must have forgotten to secure it in their haste to get away.

Although they'd only recently established themselves at Rypum, the church there belonged to an earlier time. The plaster was crumbling away from its cracked walls; its roof was missing several tiles. And, because it was old, it was dark, with a row of narrow scraped-horn slits high up along each side that even on a sunny day failed to let in much light. Halfdan dug out the oil lantern from his pack and set about lighting it. He always had one, since he needed light to be able to talk to the rest of us, reliant on his signs as he was.

He went first. Barely had he taken three paces inside when he stopped. We soon saw why. The light the lantern gave was feeble, but it was enough. In front of us, laid out on a sheet on the floor, were gilded candlesticks and serving platters, silver chalices, pyxes, spoons and knives all engraved with the christogram. By the wall stood a great ironbound chest upon which rested a bundle of embroidered vestments and wall hangings and altar cloths, some woven with threads of gold. On the altar was a jewel-studded relic house like the one Bishop Leofgar had brought with him on his visit to our manor all those years ago, only not quite as large.

And a great golden-panelled book. Yes, this one, here.

It was so much treasure that I knew at a glance we would struggle to carry it all. But all laid out, there for the taking – it was that easy. We were so astounded we just stood there for long moments, not saying anything; we didn't know even where to begin. Even I'd never seen more than a fraction of it, and I'd been inside that church so many times. I could only guess the dean, sanctimonious miser that he was, had kept it locked up somewhere out of sight, but that didn't explain what it was all doing here.

To be frank I didn't care. All I could think was that it must be God's wish that we should have all this, so that we might save it from the Normans. After all my doubts, here was proof that he existed and was watching over us. It sounds ridiculous, doesn't it? Why would he leave it to us? To me? But that's the first thing that came to my mind.

Sihtric whooped with delight. Gytha's eyes were wide, her mouth agape. Wulfnoth was grinning from ear to ear, his teeth flashing in the lantern light. He told Cuffa and Cudda to find something to put it all in, and they went out to our horses at the back of the church where it nearly abutted the dean's hall. They came back shortly with four large sacks and straight away we started filling them, armfuls at a time, clattering and clinking and making a din loud enough to wake the dead.

We were so busy and so noisy that we didn't hear the voices approaching. Not until it was too late, until they were right out-side the church door.

At once we froze.

'Is someone there?' we heard one of them say, and I thought I recognised his voice. 'Father Osbert? We brought the cart, just like you asked—'

The door swung open. A boy holding a torch entered, sol-emn-looking, as he always was. Plegmund the Pious. Behind him was another boy, short and round, and behind him another with a square face that even in the flickering light I could see was a mass of blotches. Hedda. Wiglaf.

They couldn't have recognised me; I was near the back of the church, in the shadows by the altar, with a candlestick in one hand and a sack in the other. The boys stood as still as stone, staring at us, and we stared back.

Wiglaf was the first to find his voice. 'It's you,' he said, almost breathless. 'You're the ones who attacked us. You're the ones who took our master hostage.'

At once he began backing away. So did Hedda.

Plegmund, though, stood his ground. He fixed his gaze on Wulfnoth. 'You killed him. You killed Master Guthred.'

The other two were calling to him, but he ignored them. Even I was silently willing him to leave. And this was Plegmund. The one I'd despised for so long.

Don't stand up to them, you fool, I was thinking. Run, just run. You don't know what they'll do.

Wulfnoth just laughed, and then the others were laughing too, and I shrank back as deep as I could into the shadows because I realised that the truth was about to come out.

'Killed him?' he asked Plegmund, and he was still laughing, as if it were the funniest thing he'd ever heard. 'You think that's what we did? Do you?'

'But the ransom. They said that we couldn't, that we mustn't—'

'We didn't kill him. Look. He's one of us now.'

'What?'

'He's right there,' Wulfnoth said. He pointed at me, his outstretched finger like an arrow, nocked and drawn and directed at my head. 'See for yourself.'

Would you believe that I tried to duck behind the altar? Still holding the candlestick and the sack, I bent over like some wretched half-man, as if that way I'd escape his notice.

Of course it was no use. He could see it was me, and he could see exactly what I'd been doing.

Plegmund's eyes met mine. 'M-Master?'

I didn't know what to say. I saw the confusion in his expression, and how quickly it turned to hurt and feelings of betrayal, as he looked me up and down. I can only imagine what he must have thought when he saw me. How the last months had changed me. My hair was unkempt, my clothes were ragged, my face was smeared with dirt, and those were only the visible signs.

Plegmund didn't speak. He didn't need to. Neither did Hedda and Wiglaf, who'd stopped in the doorway, caught halfway between curiosity and fear. Judging me.

And they were right to. This time they were right. For finally I saw myself for what I was. I saw myself as they saw me.

And I realised what I'd been reduced to. What a base creature I'd become. Looting the Church, which for forty years had sheltered me and schooled me and fed me and clothed me, which had tolerated and forgiven my transgressions. My many, many transgressions.

'Alas,' said Wulfnoth, 'as touching as this reunion is, we have more important things at hand.'

Hedda stepped forward. 'You can't take these things,' he said. 'They belong to—'

He broke off as Sihtric with his one hand seized him by the collar and lifted him off his feet.

'They belong to us, whelp,' he said as the boy gave a yell and kicked his feet and struggled against the big man's grasp. He had to be twice the size of the poor lad.

'Let him go,' I said. 'He doesn't mean you any harm.'

Sihtric grunted but, to my surprise, did as I instructed, dropping Hedda to the floor, where he fell in a heap.

'You should go,' I said to the three boys as Hedda, his teeth clenched, rubbing his elbow, got to his feet. 'All of you. Now.'

They didn't move.

'Didn't you hear your master?' Wulfnoth asked as he tossed a bronze censer into his sack. 'Get gone!'

That's when Father Osbert appeared in the doorway. I recognised him at once. A frowning, studious type who looked older than his years, he walked with a stoop due to the hours he spent hunched copying out passages from his books, and he had trouble seeing very far.

'What are you doing?' he asked the boys, blinking rapidly. 'Why are you just standing here? We don't have much time. They'll be here soon!'

He peered into the darkness towards us. When he saw me his mouth fell wide open.

'You?' he said. 'What are you doing here?'

After that everything happened so quickly that it's all a haze in my memory. I'm not even sure in what order it took place. I remember Wulfnoth nodding to Sihtric, who slid his seax from its sheath and advanced upon Osbert and the students. I let go of the sack I was carrying and started forward in protest. I thought he was going to hurt them, and maybe he had every mind to. Meanwhile Gytha and Halfdan and the others were snatching up what they could of the rest of the treasure and stuffing it into their belt loops, into their packs, up their sleeves, wherever it would go.

Then Hedda hurled himself at Sihtric. I'm not sure why he did it or what he was thinking, but he did, fists flailing, yelling something I couldn't make out.

Sihtric was faster. He lashed out with his seax, catching Hedda below the shoulder, ripping through his tunic, carving a gash down his arm. Blood spilt in God's house, defiling what was supposed to be a place of sanctuary. The boy screamed in pain and Sihtric gave a savage grin, but not for long. Plegmund rushed at his flank, thrusting the torch towards his head before the big man could turn. The flames caught Sihtric full in the face. He yelled, dropped his weapon and stumbled back, blinded by the heat and the light, knocking over the lantern, which Halfdan had set down in the middle of the tiled floor. His hair was on fire and he was waving his hands like a madman, and still Plegmund came at him.

Gytha was rushing to her companion's aid, trying to wrest the torch from the boy's hands. Wiglaf had picked up the fallen seax and was swinging it wildly to fend off Cuffa and Cudda. Father Osbert had fled.

I should have done something. I don't know what, but I should have done *something*. Instead I just stood there. Coward that I am, I just stood there.

Hedda and Sihtric were both writhing on the floor, one clutching at his arm and the other at his face, and I did nothing but gawp. Then Wulfnoth was clutching at my arm and saying we had to go quickly, and the brothers were trying to drag the big man outside, and that's when I noticed that Wiglaf and Plegmund were no longer there. Were they dead? If they were, I didn't see their bodies. Had they run away? I didn't know.

Wulfnoth thrust a sack into my hands and told me to hold on to it, while he snatched up the torch from where it lay, guttering dimly, on the floor. He led us out into the cold of dusk, where Gytha was waiting for us. There was blood all across her cheek, and somewhere people were shouting and she was shouting too, screaming in my face, except that I couldn't work out what she was saying, but she seemed to be angry, and I felt a tug on my arm and then I was running as best I could, still clutching the loot that Wulfnoth had given me, because I wasn't thinking properly, and because I didn't know what else I was supposed to do.

Smoke was billowing around us; the roofs of the dean's hall and the surrounding buildings were all burning, and I couldn't work out why, until I heard the horns blaring out close by, and war cries and hooves thundering. Through the swirling blackness, I caught a glimpse of men in helmets and byrnies, with fire and steel in hand.

Choking, fighting the smoke and the falling ashes, we managed to find the horses, still tethered to the post where we'd left them behind the church. They were panicking, the whites of their eyes bright in the fireglow. I made my way to Whitefoot, climbed quickly into the saddle and then fled, following the others' shadows as they galloped away.

I don't tell it very well, I know. Forgive me. It doesn't make much sense, but then it didn't at the time, either. I'm sure if you'd been there, Oslac, if you'd seen what I saw, you'd be able to give a better account of it than I have. But the way I've described it, that's how it felt.

Shock must have numbed me after that, because that's the last I remember, until after many miles' hard riding we stopped. I realised then that Sihtric wasn't with us, and neither was Cudda. We'd left them behind.

I wished I'd been left behind. That's where I deserved to be.

Gytha's bruised eye had closed up and blood was crusted across half her face. Wulfnoth was hurt too, his hand and wrist burned, the skin white and tender, and he hobbled when he moved. Tall, bony Cuffa wasn't wounded, but he kept wailing like a child for his brother, begging Wulfnoth to let us go back to look for him, until Gytha struck him across the face and told him to shut up or else she would keep on hitting him until he did. Halfdan as always was quiet; he lay on the ground and stared up at the sky for the longest time. He didn't use his signs to try to talk to us. Sihtric had been his closest friend, and now he was probably dead.

The plunder? We had one sackful. That was all we had to show for it. The one Wulfnoth had thrust upon me, which somehow I'd held on to through everything. And it wasn't even full, either; all there was is what you see here. As for the rest, I don't know what happened to it. Maybe in the rush to get away it got left behind. Maybe my students and Osbert and the other canons managed to recover it in the end, before they fled.

If they still live, that is.

'So now you know everything,' Guthred says, wringing his hands, his head bowed. 'Now that you do, I wouldn't blame you if you decided to leave me here and go your own way. It would probably be for the best. Everyone I've ever crossed paths with, I've only ended up failing, disappointing, hurting in some way. Yes, better that you just go. Leave me. Let me do what I have to do. Let me go to Lindisfarena alone.'

For a few moments everyone is silent. No one wants to be the first to speak, Tova realises.

She knows what she'd like to say. She'd like to tell him to his face that he is a bad man, but he already knows that. She'd like to tell him that he'll get no sympathy from them, but he's made it clear that he isn't looking for any.

Maybe we should just do what he says, she thinks. After what he's done, he deserves nothing less.

But then another part of her says, at least he's trying. He's doing what he can to make amends, though it may be too late. Is what he's done so bad that it can't be forgiven? Doesn't everyone deserve a second chance?

What Merewyn did was far, far worse. And Tova hasn't forsaken her.

'We're not going to abandon you,' she says and glances around at the others. 'Are we?'

Beorn says, 'You heard what he said. He doesn't want our help.'

'We can't just leave him. We can't.'

'I've made it this far by myself,' Guthred says. 'I can go the rest of the way on my own if I have to. I'd understand.'

'No,' says Merewyn firmly. 'We stay together, like we agreed. We made that decision together, and we're going to keep to it. Isn't that right, Beorn? What matters is that we trust one another. We have to, if we're to survive.'

'Trust has nothing to do with it,' Beorn retorts.

He stands abruptly and marches over towards Guthred, who looks up at the warrior towering over him.

'Listen, priest. I couldn't care less about the things that you've done. I'm not interested in whatever guilt burdens you, or in your search for redemption. As I said before, I'm not going to Lindisfarena. I'm going to Hagustaldesham, and nothing is going to make me change my mind. Not you. Not anyone. Understand?'

Guthred nods, carefully. His eyes are dark and hollow. How hard it must have been, Tova realises, for him to say all these things, and in front of strangers besides.

Except that he hasn't told them everything yet. He hasn't said how the story ends.

She clears her throat to get his and everyone else's attention. 'After Rypum, what happened? Where did you go? How did you escape?'

'I'd been wondering that myself,' says Oslac.

145

Guthred rubs at his eyes, trying to stave off sleep or possibly tears. 'I suppose it's only right that you should hear the rest. It's about the only part of it that gives me any pride, after all.'

You ask how I got away. Well, this is how.

We sheltered that night in an old hall on a deserted manor – so recently deserted, in fact, that the rushes were still fresh, still dry. There was a frost that night and I wondered if it might even snow. I tried to settle underneath my many blankets, but they weren't enough; my teeth wouldn't stop chattering and I couldn't sleep. None of us could. Not far away I could hear Cuffa whimpering softly, still worried for his brother, while Wulfnoth groaned as he turned. His hand was paining him. Gytha refused to be near him; she was sitting in one corner of the barn by herself, her knees drawn up in front of her chest, mumbling curses and from time to time sniffing back tears.

None of that, though, was what kept me awake. It was that every time I shut my eyes and tried to give myself up to sleep I kept seeing Plegmund's plaintive, questioning face. The disbelief in his eyes. The inability to comprehend. What he was asking me with that look was the simple question: why?

And even all those hours later I had no answer. There was nothing I could have said, no reason or explanation or excuse I could have given that would possibly have been enough.

I'd failed him. I'd failed all of them. My students, my fellow priests. The masters who taught me all those years ago. Saintly old Bishop Leofgar, who had first chosen me for the holy life. God himself. I felt him looking down upon me, and I felt the crushing weight of his disappointment.

My whole life serving God, and yet it took all of that to happen before I finally found him. Before I finally sought out his grace. Before I finally believed, and saw clearly for the first time.

I'd sinned worse than I'd ever imagined possible. I'd long realised that I was no paragon of virtue, nor had I ever been, nor was I going to be. But what I'd done that night – what I'd been a part of – was far worse than any misdeed I'd ever committed before. My soul would surely be condemned to the fiery depths, I knew, unless I did something. This was my last chance.

You might think I would have been too afraid, too cowardly, to run away from Wulfnoth and his band, just like I'd been too scared to act back in the minster at Rypum. But I tell you it was fear that drove me to it. Fear of ending up in Hell.

That same fear is what drives me now.

One by one I think the others must have fallen asleep; after a while I realised the whimpering and the groaning and the cursing were no longer to be heard. I was still lying there, wrapped in my grubby blankets. There was a gale blowing, but I could barely hear it for all the thoughts clamouring like a thousand voices in my ear. I tried to shut them out, to fix my mind on other things so that they would go away, but every time I tried to settle they kept coming back, stronger and louder than before, until I could bear it no longer.

I threw off the blankets covering me and got to my feet. Our packs were in a pile in the middle of the barn. As silently as I could, I crept towards them, limping a little as I went. My ankle was paining me; I vaguely remember stumbling and twisting it when we were fleeing Rypum. Anyway, I found my own tattered pack and threw it over my shoulder. That's when I saw the sack containing the plunder from the church.

I couldn't let them have it. It wasn't theirs. It wasn't mine either, but I was the one who'd led them to it, and so it was up to me to do the right thing. I had to take it. Somehow I had to return it, to make sure it went back to its rightful owners.

147

Yet I couldn't go back to Rypum. There was only one place I could think of where I could take the treasures so that they would be safe, and that was the Holy Isle. What I also knew was that it was up to me. I, Guthred the liar, the robber, the sinner. I had a chance to redeem myself in the eyes of the Lord, and I couldn't afford not to take it.

A voice behind me said, 'What are you doing?'

I turned. It was Wulfnoth. All I could see of him was the fox-like gleam of his eyes. His breath was laboured and he sounded in pain as he hobbled towards me, his injured foot disturbing the rushes as he dragged it along the ground.

'I'm leaving,' I told him as I backed away, gripping the sack tightly in one hand while keeping the other free, just in case. 'And I'm taking the treasure. Everything we stole from the church, I'm taking it. And you're not going to stop me.'

He snorted. 'Listen to yourself.'

I said that's exactly what I was doing, and he asked me what in the world I was babbling about. All the while he kept coming closer, and I was edging towards the door, still holding on to the sack. At any moment I expected the others to wake, and then that would be it. But they didn't.

Still keeping my voice low, I said, 'I'm going to return all this to its rightful owners. I'm taking it to Lindisfarena, where it'll be safe.'

'You pious fool,' he hissed. 'I thought you'd put all that behind you. I thought you'd finally seen their lies for what they were.'

I told him I'd been wrong, and that this was wrong: everything they – we – had been doing. The raiding, stealing, extortion, blackmail. I should never have succumbed to temptation. I'd given in to my own selfish desires, and now I would pay the price, unless I redeemed myself, and that's why I was going.

He said, 'You can't leave.'

I asked him why not, and that's when I saw the soft glimmer of steel appear in front of him. Too small to be a seax. A knife.

He said, 'Because I'm going to kill you first.'

I'd never seen him take anyone's life before. I'd hardly ever seen him spill blood. As I said, that wasn't his way. That was how he defended what he did. It allowed him to pretend that they weren't so bad really. It made him feel better.

And yet despite all that, at that moment I had no doubt that he meant what he said.

'Aren't you going to run?' he asked me.

I wanted to, but I couldn't feel my feet; they were numb with fear, and I thought if I tried to run, I would only stumble and he would plunge that knife into my heart. Before I could answer, he lunged at me, thrusting me back against the wall with one hand around my throat, the other holding the tip of his blade up towards my eye.

'I hate them,' he said. 'I hate them all. Men of God, they make me sick. But I thought you were different. I thought you were like me.'

And then suddenly I was in that place beyond fear. It didn't matter now what I said, it seemed; in my mind I was about to die and so it all came flooding out.

I replied that I was nothing like him. That I never had been and never would be.

'I took pity on you because I thought you were my friend,' he said, 'and this is how you repay me?'

We'd never been friends, I said. He was wrong. Maybe something was broken inside that head of his, I suggested. Maybe all those years of being trampled underfoot by his own kin, then cast out to fend for himself, had caused him to remember things differently to how they really had been.

To speak like that while he had a knife to my face was foolish beyond imagination, I know, but until the moment when he silenced me I thought that I might as well keep going.

I said, 'You always thought you were so clever. Then, as now. But you weren't clever at all. You remember, don't you, that day when they sent you away from the school, back to your father?'

He said that of course he did, that it had destroyed his life, and that things had never been the same since then.

'It was me. Your friend, Guthred. I was the one who drew those pictures on the church tower, who put the chalk in your chest so that they would find it. I did it. Me.'

He stared at me, wide-eyed. The knife point trembled.

'What's going on?' came a tired voice from out of the darkness. Gytha's voice. She stood and started towards us. 'Wulfnoth?'

He gave a quick glance behind him, and I saw my chance. I ducked low and barrelled shoulder first into his chest. I wasn't as strong as he was, not by a long way, but with his injured foot it didn't take much to send him sprawling.

I heard him fall and shout out, but I didn't stop to look behind me. The treasure still in hand, I made for the door, threw it open and ran outside. Whitefoot was with the rest of the horses in a larger barn across the yard. I didn't have time to saddle him; I just heaved myself up on to his back and started riding. As I galloped away, I heard Gytha and Cuffa shouting as they emerged from the hall, and I think Halfdan was with them too. As soon as they saw me they ran in my direction, but I was already gone, tearing down the track, disappearing into the night.

If they followed me, I never knew of it. I didn't see them or hear them, but I didn't stop until I was sure I'd left them long behind me.

And that's how it happened.

And now you know.

After the last couple of nights Tova hoped sleep would come easily. It must be hours since the priest finished his tale; the others are all soundly slumbering but still she can't settle. She lies under her blankets, eyes tight shut, but it's no use. All that talk of sin and repentance, she can't shake it from her head.

Will God forgive her for the things she has done in her life? Will he forgive Merewyn for hers?

And what if Guthred is right? What if everything that's happening is God's punishment for the evils of this land and its people? If that's his will, what's the point in trying to flee? How long will it be before fate catches up with them?

Her mind is too filled with thoughts. She needs to clear it if she's to get any rest tonight. Often when she found it hard to sleep in those months after her mother died, Gunnhild would take her out to show her the stars and point out to her the different patterns that they made – of beasts and heroes from long ago that she'd only heard of in songs – and she would tell Tova stories about each of them, some that she'd learned herself as a child and others that she made up especially that night.

That's what she needs, she decides. She shrugs off the blankets and rises, bracing herself for the cold. Then, taking care to tread lightly so as not to wake the others, she makes for the door, opens it and steps out.

She's not alone. Guthred sits in front of the fire, or what's left of it, blowing gently on the ashes in an effort to coax some life back into them. The last person she wanted to talk to. She wants comfort, not to be swallowed up in his self-pity.

He looks up as she approaches, the soft glow of the low flames lighting up one side of his face while making a shadow of the other.

'You couldn't sleep either, I suppose,' he says and attempts a smile, but it's a sad smile.

'I didn't realise anyone else was still awake.'

'Come, child.' He places his hand on the ground next to him. 'I'd appreciate the company.'

She hesitates, but she doesn't want to offend him and so she sits, though keeping her distance. She knows in her heart that Merewyn was speaking good sense when she said earlier they all have to trust one another, but she isn't sure that she can. Not yet.

He pokes at the ashes with a piece of twig, then tosses it on top of the pile and watches closely, eyes glazed, as it catches fire. It's not conversation that he's after. Maybe, like her, he just doesn't want to feel alone.

'Do you really believe what you said earlier?' she asks. 'About this being God's vengeance upon us?'

'Yes, I do. That and more.'

'More?'

'The signs are clear enough. To me they are, anyway, if to no one else.'

'What signs?'

He clears his throat. '"And I looked, and there before me was a white horse. And its rider held a bow, and a crown was given to him. And he rode out as a conqueror, bent on annihilation."'

Tova shakes her head. 'I don't understand.'

'It's coming to pass, child, just as it has been written. The world is hastening towards its end, and very soon it may be no more. I fear that we're living through the last days.'

She feels the hairs on her arms stand on end as a chill creeps across her skin. 'The end of the world?'

She almost can't get the words out. This is exactly why she didn't want to speak to him. He is too full of woe, of darkness and gloom. He is supposed to be a beacon of light, a bearer of good tidings, telling of God's grace and promising a better life to come. Instead he is everything but.

'I remember one of the texts we had to learn as students,' he says. 'It was a sermon Bishop Leofgar had heard preached by his superior, the archbishop of Eoferwic, some time around the year I was born, I think, when this land was being overrun by the heathens. He had a copy of the sermon sent to him. We were made to recite it from memory. Even now I can recall it word for word; that's how deeply it's etched in my mind. The archbishop wrote of the failings of the English people; he castigated them for the many injustices that prevailed across the kingdom, for allowing laws to be flouted without regard and evils to go unpunished, for the bad faith that existed between kinsmen, for the feuding and betrayals, for the kinslaying and breaking of oaths, for the ill treatment of the Church and of God's servants. He warned that things would only worsen in time, and that it wouldn't be long before the coming of the Antichrist.'

'But the world didn't end,' Tova says irritably. She shouldn't need to point that out to him.

'No,' Guthred admits. 'No, it didn't. We were spared. But now I see those same things happening again, and I fear that everything the archbishop foresaw all those years ago may finally be happening. I didn't say it earlier, because your friend Beorn was mocking me, but that's the other reason I feel I must make the pilgrimage to Lindisfarena as soon as I can, because there may never be another chance. Each day that passes is bringing us closer to the end. Each day that passes may be the last.'

Tova stares at him. 'You don't really believe that, do you?'

He nods sadly. 'I do, child. Believe one who has lived long enough to see all the cruelties this world can bring to bear. I've seen drought and hunger, floods and sickness: so much misery, and every year it only grows worse. Everything is falling into ruin. It has been so for a long time, though we've become blind to it. Everything that we see happening around us now, this is the last chapter. Soon the book will close and we must prepare our souls for when it does.'

The book, Tova thinks. That's it. She's been desperate to find a different subject; she can't take all this doomsaying. If she doesn't divert him from this path, he will start talking about seas boiling and skies burning, and she isn't sure she'll be able to remain patient with him if he does.

She asks, 'Does Wulfnoth know how much the book is worth?'

'Wulfnoth?' he echoes, sounding confused. She's caught him off guard, broken his line of thought at last. 'I should think he does. He must have some idea. Maybe only in the sense of gold and precious stones and how much he might sell it for. To him, that's all it would mean. But he would know, yes. And there's the rest of the loot too, of course.'

'He won't try to come after it, will he?'

Guthred wrings his hands. 'I don't know. But it's been five days already. I'd have thought if he was coming for it, he'd have caught up with me by now.'

She supposes it depends just how desperate he is. What if he feels he has nothing more to lose?

THIRD DAY

Hard, icy, sharp. It strikes her cheek. And again. And again.

Drowsily, Tova opens her eyes to unfamiliar walls. A place she doesn't recognise. A bed not her own.

Where is she?

It comes back to her, of course, just as it did the day before. But she hates that helpless, panicked feeling. If every morning were to be like this from now on, she'd never want to sleep for fear of waking.

Another drop hits her face and rolls down the side of her nose. She wipes it away and, blinking, turns over to find herself staring at a circle of grey-white sky through a hole in the thatch.

Already it's light. Time to be on their way.

They roll up their blankets and gather their things, then cover the ashes of the campfire with leaves and clumps of sodden turf, and lastly bury the horse dung using a rusted spade that Guthred found propped up against the back wall.

They have only four horses between the five of them, it turns out; Oslac came on foot. She has noticed how he keeps a watchful distance between himself and the animals. How he made sure to sleep at the other end of the barn from them too.

'What happened to yours?' Beorn asks him as they're saddling up. 'Did someone steal it?'

'Nothing happened to it. I can't ride. I don't know how.'

'You can't ride?' Tova asks, surprised, although perhaps she shouldn't be. Most ordinary folk can't. She couldn't either, until Merewyn taught her, and only then because she wanted some female companionship when she went out riding.

'I'm afraid of them,' he says.

After a moment Merewyn laughs. It's been a long time since Tova heard that sound. 'You're scared of horses?'

'It probably sounds foolish to you—'

'Are you telling us that you walk everywhere you go?' Guthred asks. 'You traipse from hall to hall on foot? Even in winter?'

'Is it so difficult to believe?' Oslac asks, red-faced.

'I find it strange, that's all.'

'Well, that's how it is. So don't expect me to help feed them or brush them down or anything like that.'

Tova rubs Winter's flank. 'How can you be scared of such lovely creatures? What's there to be frightened of?'

'Everything. They're too big. Too strong. I don't like their eyes. You know the way they look at you sometimes, with the whites showing? You can't tell what they're thinking. You don't know what they're about to do next. I don't trust them. I never have.'

'Why not?'

'You want to know? My sister, Dunne, she was killed when she was only nine winters old. I saw it happen; I was seven at the time. We were in the yard, brushing down the horses one evening after our father and his lord's retainers had returned from town, when something spooked them, I don't remember what. It all happened so quickly. They bolted; she was kicked in the head and fell under their hooves. She died at once. I didn't even hear her

158

scream. Afterwards, my mother refused to let me near them. Said they were dangerous, vicious creatures. She blamed my father for Dunne's death, and forbade me from having anything to do with them. I suppose that, over time, hearing all those things and always being warned away from the stables, I grew frightened of them. You probably think I'm being foolish. I wouldn't blame you if you did.'

'I'm sorry,' Merewyn says after a moment. 'I didn't mean—'

'It's all right. You didn't know.'

'If you want,' Tova says, 'I'll ride with Merewyn and you can have Winter. She won't harm you, I promise. She's as docile a creature as any I've ever known.'

'Thank you, but no. I know you mean well, but you won't ever see me riding one of those things, no matter how peaceable it might be, or how friendly towards strangers you tell me it is.'

'In that case you'd better keep up,' Beorn says. 'Because we won't be waiting for you if you fall behind. Do you hear me?'

He doesn't even wait for Oslac's answer. Instead, as if to make his point, he turns and at once rides off.

'Don't worry about me,' the poet mutters under his breath, so quietly that Tova's sure he didn't mean anyone else to hear.

All morning the rain continues to fall. Hard then soft then hard again, it drives at Tova's side.

The going is slow, and not because of Oslac. Most of the drove-ways are in poor repair, and the rain has turned the tracks into muddy streams that hurry down the slopes, pooling in every dip and every hollow to form lakes that they have to work their way around. Some of the tracks are too overgrown even for Beorn and his axe, and they have to turn back and find another way. Every time they halt even for a moment, he glances about, his hand reaching up towards his bow, as if expecting the enemy to be lurking. But they've seen no other living person since they set out this morning. They spy sheep roaming on the hill pastures, but no one herding them; houses still standing, but no hearth smoke. Tova wonders why the Normans didn't burn these villages like they did the ones they saw yesterday, why they didn't slaughter the livestock.

'Maybe they were in a hurry,' Guthred suggests. 'Maybe they didn't have time.'

'Maybe,' Beorn agrees.

All the same, they don't venture too close. Beorn rides on ahead, scouting out the way, returning from time to time to tell them what he's seen and in which direction he thinks they ought to go next. Each time he disappears, making for the next ridge or tump where he can get a better view of the valley ahead, Tova grows a little more anxious. It isn't that she doesn't feel safe with Oslac and Guthred, she tells herself, strangers though they are, or that she doesn't trust them. It's just that she trusts Beorn more.

She's noticed how he's always moving: how he never lets himself settle for long. He always needs to have some purpose, to feel useful. Trying to make up for lost time, perhaps. Or to stave off madness. If he didn't need to sleep or eat, she feels sure he'd never stop.

'Who is he?' Oslac asks the next time Beorn's out of earshot.

They've stopped by a stream while the warrior goes on ahead so that the horses have a chance to drink and graze, and so that they can wolf down some bread and hard cheese. They save the bacon for later; although Tova thinks she could manage an entire pig all by herself, she knows they have to make what they have last, especially now that there are five of them rather than three. Oslac has already shared out what he had, though it wasn't much. A few handfuls of nuts. Some shrivelled pears.

160

'What do you mean, who is he?' asks Merewyn in between mouthfuls. 'He's Beorn.'

'A friend of yours, is he?'

'A friend? I don't know. Can you call someone a friend who you only met two days ago?'

'Oh,' says Guthred, looking sheepish. 'I assumed . . . I'm sorry.'

'For what?'

'Well, I assumed he'd come with you from wherever's home for you. To tell the truth, I thought at first he was your husband.'

'My husband?'

Oslac asks, 'How did the two of you end up with him, then?'

'He saved us from a Norman raiding party,' Tova says. 'There were five of them. He killed every single one.'

The poet looks askance at her, as if she might be joking but he isn't sure. 'Five men? By himself?'

There's something about those eyes she doesn't like, she decides. Those grey, changeable eyes. How they can darken like thunderclouds just like that: one moment patient, respectful, friendly; the next guarded and accusing.

She nods. 'By himself.'

Oslac turns to Merewyn. 'Is this true?'

So he won't believe her, but he'll believe Merewyn? She might be young but she's not stupid. She knows what she saw. She was there, wasn't she?

Merewyn says, 'It's true. All five of them. One after another. It all happened so quickly. There was no stopping him. There was just anger, raw hatred. It all came out, all at once, and at the end of it they were all dead. You wouldn't believe it unless you saw it.'

That isn't quite how Tova remembers it. She doesn't recall hatred; what comes to mind is the calmness with which, one by one, he sent them to their deaths.

'We were looking for somewhere to spend the night when they

came upon us,' Merewyn goes on. 'That's when he appeared. If he hadn't— Well, I don't want to even think about it.'

'He appeared, just like that? Where did he come from?'

'He hasn't said. He's hardly told us anything besides his name.'

'Peace, Oslac,' Guthred says. 'Why all these questions? If you want to know, surely he'll tell you himself. Ask him when he comes back, if it's so important.'

He won't, though, Tova thinks. That's why he's asking the two of them instead. He doesn't want to talk to Beorn. He fears him.

Oslac promptly shuts up and they pass the rest of their meal in silence. He's in a dark mood today, for no good reason that she can work out. Is he still angry after what Beorn said to him earlier?

The priest, too, doesn't seem the same man, somehow, as the one she was speaking with last night. Until now he has hardly said a word all morning, but his silence seems more contemplative than brooding. Certainly he doesn't have the same hunched look about him; he walks taller, sits straighter in the saddle. In the light of day he no longer looks as world-weary, or as old. Relieved of the load that was weighing him down, now that he's shared his burden. Maybe that's what it is.

Beorn returns not long afterwards. He followed the path for another half-mile, he says, and found the river, but it's broken its banks, swollen by the recent rains, so they'll have to go upstream in search of a better crossing place.

'How much further, do you think?' Tova asks him.

'It could be as little as another hour, or we might not find one until tomorrow. We won't know until we get there, so let's not stand here talking.'

'What about you?' Tova asks Oslac a little later, while they wait for the priest, who's busy relieving himself behind a thorn hedge. 'You aren't from these parts, are you?'

He smiles. 'My voice gives me away, doesn't it?' he asks. 'No, you're right. I'm not. I grew up in a place far from here. A long way to the south, in Wessex. The shire of Sumorsæte, not that you're likely to have heard of it.'

Tova shakes her head. She probably has at some time, and has simply forgotten. There are so many shires that make up England; she could never remember all of them, especially since their names mean nothing to her. Sumorsæte might as well lie in another kingdom entirely, for all that she knows about it.

'I have,' Merewyn says. 'That's where King Ælfred took refuge from the heathens. When they were overrunning the land. Years ago, I mean. My tutor, Leofa, once taught me about how he fled to the marshes where they couldn't come at him, then sent out secret messages to his allies, urging them to rally to his banner when he marched again.'

Oslac says, 'So I've heard.'

'Where in Sumorsæte?' Beorn asks abruptly.

'A place called Suthperetune. I don't suppose you know of it.'

'Why did you leave?' Tova asks. She isn't interested in hearing about kings from far away and long ago; she wants to know about him. 'What brings you here?'

'Our home, the manor where I grew up, was burned one night,' Oslac says with a sigh. 'My father was killed. He taught me most of the songs I carry in my head. It had been just the two of us. My sister was dead, as I told you. My mother too. After he was gone, well, there was nothing left for me there. I decided instead to make of myself what I could, on my own. And that's what I've been doing these past couple of years: wandering the kingdom, only I've had to keep travelling ahead of the foreigners as they've moved ever northwards, seizing the land. They have their own storytellers, you see. Their own verses. They don't want to hear mine. So that's why you find me here, north of the Humbre.'

'And people really pay to hear you sing, do they?' Beorn asks. 'They pay good silver?'

The poet shrugs. 'Sometimes. But just as often I'll settle for a hot meal, a jug of ale and a bed of straw in the hall of whoever is lord. I'll stay a day or two, and then I'll move on to the next place, wherever there's a feast taking place.'

But now there are no halls, Tova thinks. No halls. No lords. No feasts. And what use are stories then?

The wind's changing. It gusts in her face; she keeps her hood up and her head down to try to keep the worst of the rain off, but it's not enough. Icy darts prick her cheeks.

North and west they ride, following the course of the river valley. Deserted strip-fields stretch out under a wide sky. It's too open, too exposed. To the rain and the wind. To the eyes of the enemy.

They move cautiously, keeping to the cover of woodland wherever they can. To the north, to the south, to the west, to the east, smoke rises in thin coils. More hall burnings. Some of the larger fires still glowing. Every so often Beorn pauses to glance over his shoulder, scanning the distant hills. When he goes on ahead, he doesn't venture as far. It's the first time he has betrayed any sign of disquiet. The fact that he's worried makes Tova worried too.

This isn't the way he would have chosen, she knows. It's taking them closer to the old road, the one that the Romans built in years gone by. And closer to the old road means closer to the Normans.

They'll be watching it, he says. Watching for folk fleeing towards Dunholm, into St Cuthbert's land, seeking sanctuary. Folk like them.

They have no other choice, though. And so they carry on, mile by mile, as the skies ahead of them grow heavier.

They lead their horses one at a time. Branches overhang the path, crossing over one another. Oak and hornbeam. Beech and birch. It's not long after midday but it feels closer to dusk. A strange half-light falls over everything.

A half-light upon a half-world, slipping into a shadow from which it might never emerge.

'Wait,' Beorn says. He stops in his tracks, his arm raised.

'What is it?' asks Merewyn, who's behind him. 'What have you seen?'

Tova cranes her neck to see what's happening. It's not the first time they've halted this afternoon, and it probably won't be the last either.

'Why are we stopping?' Oslac calls. He's bringing up the rear, keeping a lookout behind.

Tova leaves Winter momentarily and ducks under the low branches as she makes her way forward to join Merewyn. And she sees what they're looking at.

Horse dung.

'We aren't the only ones going this way,' says Beorn as he crouches down and takes a pinch of it, rubbing it between his fingers.

Tova feels a prickling all over her body. They could be close. They might be watching them right now. She searches amid the trees, past the tangle of brambles, the hollow lichen-matted trunks and the thick holly bushes that the birds have picked clean of berries.

Beorn sniffs at his fingertips. 'A few hours old, I'd say. Not warm, but not cold either.'

A few hours ago. She breathes more easily as the prickling feeling subsides. She was worried it was more recent.

'Maybe we should turn back,' Oslac suggests. 'Maybe coming this way wasn't such a good idea.'

Absently he fingers what looks like a gold chain hanging around his neck. Some keepsake or charm? He catches her looking at him and immediately tucks it back out of sight, under the collar of his tunic. He fixes her with a warning glare, his cheeks blossoming red, then turns abruptly away as if embarrassed.

Beorn is already marching back to his horse. 'We go on,' he calls over his shoulder. 'But keep your eyes and your ears open.'

She can tell when Winter is tired. Her head is low; she won't go when told to, and when she moves she won't obey commands, but picks and chooses which ones she thinks sensible and which ones not. She isn't used to long journeys, or to being made to carry such heavy packs.

Three days it's been now since they fled Heldeby. Almost, anyway. Once this day is out, it will be. No wonder Tova can hardly feel her feet any more.

Because Winter isn't the only one who's struggling. Not for the first time she finds herself trailing behind as they climb through the woods. The rain keeps falling and her nose is running and it won't stop, no matter how many times she wipes it. She hears her lady calling to her, urging her on. She knows she has to keep up. But she can only see so many burned-out halls, so many animal carcasses with limbs missing and eyes picked out, so many broken corpses lying cold and ashen in the fields. If she'd had any idea it would be like this, she'd never have come.

She has to stop for a moment. Her head is spinning; she can't feel her feet.

Through the trees to the north she spies the river, or thinks she does. Its banks are shrouded by tall spindly trees. No sign yet of a bridge. Beorn would say, wouldn't he, if he thought they were near?

She turns to look back the way they've come, towards the crossroads at the bottom of the vale, where the droveway and their own muddy track met. So many miles behind them already. So many still to go. It doesn't matter in which direction she turns, it's all the same. Hills upon hills, as far as her eyes can make out. Dense copses of birch and elm. Empty fields, recently ploughed. Green meadows where the grass grows long. Everything so still, caught in winter's grip.

Black specks flutter up to the east, from one of the far thickets close to the droveway. Dozens, scores, hundreds. Spiralling up, swooping, diving. Too far away to hear their chatter above the wind. A quarter of a mile? Less than that?

She knows she ought to be riding on, trying to catch up with the others. But she doesn't. Instead, leaving Winter, she ventures off the track, tramping through the undergrowth, brambles catching at her cloak and her dress, towards the edge of the trees, trying to get a better look.

Something must have scared them, she thinks. Those crows, or jackdaws or rooks or whatever they are, they wouldn't just take flight for no reason. She wouldn't, if she were them. It's too cold. Better to stay still and conserve warmth. Stay close. Huddle together.

She fixes her gaze on the distant thicket and the birds circling high above. Just for a moment, she tells herself. Then she'll go.

The moment passes. Still nothing. A deer bounds across the hillside. Nothing else moves. No other sign of life. She hears her lady calling from further up the track, sounding alarmed.

She should go, she knows. She's about to call back to say she's all right when she sees them. A cluster of figures on foot. Three of them. No, four, bursting out from the cover of the trees. Shields slung across their backs, brightly daubed in red and green and yellow. Pelting across the open ground, across the harrowed earth. Scrambling over a hedge, over ridge and furrow. Falling and then picking themselves up. Running along the valley, across the open pasture. Running as if their lives depended on it.

Running from what?

'Girl,' Beorn calls from behind her. 'Are you listening to me? Come on. You shouldn't be wandering on your own.'

She glances over her shoulder, sees him fighting the bracken as he comes towards her.

'Look,' she says, beckoning him closer. 'Look!'

Pursuing them, charging from out of the thicket, comes a band of mounted men. Three at first, then another two behind them, and another two, then three more. Ten in all. Pennons flying. Their shouts carry faintly across the ploughed fields. The blast of a war horn. And this time she isn't hearing things.

It's them.

Galloping after the four men on foot, skirting field edges, rounding hedges. Closing on them. Closing fast. Hooves pounding the dirt. Helmets glinting, spear points gleaming wickedly in the grey afternoon light.

The Normans.

Beorn asks, 'What is it, girl?'

He stands beside her, following the line of her outstretched finger. And he sees.

'Get down,' he says.

She doesn't move. She can't. She's forgotten how.

His hand on her arm. Clutching so tight that it hurts. Before she knows what's happening he's pulling her down. Hard. To the ground. She lands on her elbow and wants to let out a yelp but he clamps his hand across her mouth.

'Quiet,' he says. 'Stay still.'

He crouches low behind the brambles and peers over. Tova joins him, rubbing her arm where she fell.

'Will they have seen us?'

'I don't know. Let's not take any chances.'

They can't have done, Tova thinks. Surely they can't. They're too intent on their prey.

The men on foot are no longer together, but strung out. Each man for himself. They fling aside their spears, their shields, their packs, cloaks, everything, so that they can flee all the faster. But where? She can hear them calling to one another, the panic in their voices, faint though they are. Those ahead shouting to the stragglers. The enemy not far behind. Only a couple of hundred paces away now. Getting closer and closer to the crossroads.

One of the Englishmen trips, falls face first on to the earth, struggles to get up. Looks over his shoulder as he does so, sees the horde bearing down upon him. And yells out something that Tova can't make out.

'Don't watch,' Beorn says.

But she does. She can't help it.

A lance head strikes the man's shoulder, spinning him around. Another glances off his side and he staggers back. A sword across the back of his neck. He falls, disappearing amid the long grass.

'No,' she says under her breath. 'No, no, no.'

'What did I tell you, girl?'

She wants to stop, she really does, but she can't tear her eyes away.

The rest of the Normans, they're fanning out, riding after the Englishman's three companions. The first is cut down from behind.

The second hears them coming, turns and draws his sword. Too late. A spear finds the middle of his chest and he goes down.

The third hears their screams and glances over his shoulder. He knows what's about to happen. He stops; he turns to face them, sinking to his knees. He lifts his eyes to the heavens and moves his hand rapidly across his chest. Crossing himself, Tova realises.

No sooner has he finished than they're on him. One blow is all it takes.

A flash of steel. A shower of blood. His face a crimson mess.

'Oh God,' Tova says. She wants to be sick. She feels it welling up inside, burning her throat.

A whoop of joy. Laughter. A cry goes up in their barbarous tongue. She looks up, sees one of them holding something aloft. It doesn't take her long to work out what it is. Severed, dripping, smeared red.

A head.

Holding it by its long hair, the Norman whirls it about him and, letting out a roar, tosses it far into the field, where it rolls and settles in a furrow.

'Stay down,' Beorn hisses. 'Stay down and keep quiet.'

She feels dizzy. It's going to come. She knows it.

He pulls her back down behind the bramble bush. 'It's all right. Look at me. You're all right. Deep breaths now.'

She realises she's been holding her breath. She takes a gulp of the cold air. The queasiness subsides.

More whooping, more laughter, but steadily receding. Heading back the way they came, she thinks. Along the droveway, towards the east.

'That could have been us,' she says when at last she can speak again. 'If they'd spotted us, if they'd come this way . . .'

'I know.'

170

'They were right there!'

'I know.'

Her heart hammering, not quite daring to believe how close they came, she closes her eyes. The laughter and the shouting grow ever quieter. Then, after a while, nothing but the wind. The creaking of branches.

The long quiet.

'I want you to teach me,' Tova says to Beorn that evening when the two of them are out gathering wood.

They've made their camp at the bottom of a narrow dell, far enough away from the track that their fire shouldn't be seen and their voices are unlikely to be heard. The cold has settled in the shadow of the hill, but the light hasn't gone yet.

'Teach you what?'

'How to fight.'

He laughs. 'You?'

'Why not?'

She's been thinking about it ever since this afternoon. Every time there's danger, she feels so helpless. Hiding, fleeing: it's all they seem to do, and she's tired of it.

Beorn looks askance at her, then bends down to pick up a fallen branch, which he snaps in two across his thigh.

'Think about it,' she says. 'What if the enemy come and you're not here?'

'Then you run.'

'What if we can't run? What if they have horses, or if they just have longer legs than us? We won't have any choice then, will we?'

'Don't try to face a man on horseback. Not until you've had years of practice.'

'You don't believe women should fight, do you?'

171

'I believe that, if you draw a weapon in anger, then you have to be ready to die.'

'I know that. I'm not stupid.'

He stops, turns to her, looks her up and down. She holds her head high, folds her arms, meets his stare. He has to know that she means what she says.

'All right,' he says, with a smile so slight and fleeting that she isn't sure if she imagined it. 'I'll teach you.'

When they return to camp they set down the firewood they've gathered. Straight away Beorn marks out a wide circle with stones and some of the larger branches.

Oslac asks, 'What's that for?'

Beorn tells him he'll see soon enough. He lays down his bow and his axe outside the ring, and a leather scabbard hanging at his side that looks like it belongs to a seax or a short sword.

'Priest,' he says. 'I need to borrow your knife.'

Guthred looks puzzled. 'My knife?'

'Only for a short while. I'll give it back, you have my word.'

The priest hesitates but draws it and hands it to the warrior, who marches into the middle of the circle. He beckons Tova towards him. Nervous but at the same time excited, she steps forward.

'What's going on?' her lady asks. 'What are you doing?'

'I'm showing her how she can defend herself,' Beorn says. 'I'll show you too, if you want.'

She doesn't, Tova thinks. Not after what happened the other night. No doubt Merewyn would be happy if she never had to see another blade in her life.

'Well?' Beorn asks her, when she doesn't answer.

Merewyn looks suddenly very pale, but no one else seems to notice, so maybe it's just Tova's imagination.

'It's your choice,' Beorn tells her. 'It makes no difference to me.'

She shakes her head. Slowly but decisively. Her eyes fixed on the steel in his hand.

'Very well,' he says with a shrug. He stands beside Tova. 'This is a knife. A simple weapon. The simplest. But it's no less deadly than a sword or spear or axe. It can be just as good, if you know how to use it properly. Show me yours. Show me how you hold it.'

Hesitantly, she draws the blade from the sheath at her left side, placing her thumb along the side of the handle, like she would when cutting her food. That's what it's for; she has no idea if it's sharp enough to do anyone any real harm. She's never thought about it before. She glances across at Beorn's hand, to see how he holds his, and is reassured to find he has the same grip.

'Good.' He turns to face her. 'The first thing you have to know is that a knife's no weapon for defending with. At best you can ward an attacker off for a while. You can't block or parry. Your best chance if someone comes at you is to make sure you strike first. Now, you're small, but that's no bad thing, because it means you can be quick. Quicker than anyone will expect. And quickness is what matters. Be one move ahead of your attacker. Kill him before he kills you. Stay off your heels and keep your weight forward. Not all the way forward so that you're on your toes, but so that you can easily step in whichever direction you need to go.'

Attack, don't defend, she repeats silently. Be quick. Stay forward. Strike first. Kill quickly.

Beorn shows her how to stand when facing her foe, her right foot in front of the left, one shoulder back, offering him a narrower target while also presenting her blade edge. How to use her feet to back away when an attacker comes at her. How to cut circles through the air in front of her to ward him off and make him keep his distance. He gets her to try these things while he advances upon her. At first she doesn't want to, thinking she might injure him by accident, but he laughs off her worries and tells her he'll be fine.

'Small movements,' he urges. 'Keep your elbows in, or else you leave yourself open. Little circles, like this.'

Over and over they practise it. She protests that she doesn't need to keep repeating the same thing, that she understands, but he refuses to teach her anything else until he's satisfied that she really does.

Their shadows in the firelight deepen as dusk quickly fades into night. Out of the corner of her eye she sees the others watching her: Guthred and Oslac in bemusement, her lady with her hand over her mouth in concern. Tova does her best to ignore them, but it isn't easy. Every time she stumbles she feels her cheeks burning. She expects them to laugh at her, but they don't. She expects Merewyn sooner or later to try to put a stop to things, but she doesn't.

'All right,' says Beorn eventually. 'Now you're ready to try something harder.'

Instead of getting her to back away when an attacker comes at her, this time he wants her to move to one side, so that she gets her body out of the path of his blade. He talks her through it, slowly to begin with, like showing her the steps of a dance: he comes at her, lunging forward, thrusting his knife point towards her chest; she moves neatly outside the line of his outstretched arm. Again they go through the same motions, and again, and again, gradually getting faster.

Then he shows her how, as she moves to his flank, she can slice her blade down across the back of his wrist and use her free hand to force his weapon arm out of the way, leaving his chest exposed, ready for her to stab straight at his heart.

'That's how you make a killing blow,' he says. 'If you only wound your foe, he's still dangerous. But if you strike him there, he won't be getting up. You have to be quick, though, and you have to be sure of yourself. If you aren't, you're dead.'

They keep on practising for the better part of an hour, until her brow is slick with sweat and her limbs are aching and her fingers can barely grip the hilt of her blade any longer. Her arms are tiring, her feet hurting, but she clenches her teeth and vows to keep going. She wanted this, she reminds herself. She mustn't show weakness.

Before long though she's tripping over her own feet. He sees she's struggling and says that's enough for one night.

He sheathes his borrowed knife, then throws his arm around her shoulder and tousles her hair. She squirms away, protesting as she brushes it out of her face, annoyed and yet at the same time quietly pleased because she knows he's proud.

'They say you saved them from the Normans,' Guthred says to Beorn when they're sitting around the fire later.

Beorn has tied a rope between two trees, and over it draped a large sheet made from hides stitched together, which he secures with pegs at each of the four corners to make a shelter. It's open to the wind but at least it'll keep the rain off.

'They were alone,' Beorn says. 'Up on the moors. No one to protect them. The enemy had found them and so I did what I had to do.'

'Five of them, all by yourself?'

He doesn't seem to hear, or else he doesn't want to answer. Most men would relish the chance to brag about something like that. Orm certainly would, Tova thinks, had he ever managed such a feat. They'd never have heard the end of it.

Oslac flicks his gaze between Tova and Merewyn. 'Why were

you alone, anyway? What happened to everyone else where you came from? Was there no one else left after the Normans came?'

'We were on pilgrimage,' Tova says quickly, glancing at her lady. She's been quietly rehearsing their story, ready for when it's needed. 'We were on our way to Dunholm. To see St Cuthbert's relics. We didn't know the Normans were marching. We didn't know anything until they came upon us that evening. Until Beorn told us what was happening.'

Careful, she thinks. Don't talk too much or too quickly, or they'll be suspicious.

'On pilgrimage alone?' Oslac asks. 'Wandering the moors in the middle of winter? Hadn't you heard how dangerous it was?'

'We'd heard rumours. But that was all. Nothing certain. We were lucky, I suppose. God was with us.'

She looks again towards Merewyn, whose eyes are cast down towards her lap as she wrings her hands.

Say something, Tova thinks desperately. I can't be the one doing all the talking. If you don't speak, they're going to suspect something's wrong. And then they'll want to know.

Too late.

It's the priest who notices first. 'What's going on? Why do you keep looking at her like that?'

Tova opens her mouth, then closes it again when she realises she doesn't know how to answer.

'What is it?' Oslac asks. Those eyes again, hard like granite. 'What aren't you telling us?'

'Nothing,' Tova says, feigning indignation as best she can. 'It's just as I said. There's nothing more to it.'

'It's all right, Tova,' Merewyn says. 'They might as well know.'

Oslac frowns. 'Know what?'

She takes a deep breath and then says, 'I too have a story to tell. Something I'm ashamed of. Something that, if I keep to myself any longer, will only eat away at me from the inside, as it has been for days already.'

She mustn't, thinks Tova. She can't. She won't. Will she?

The look on the priest's face is somewhere between puzzlement and concern. 'Why? What did you do?'

She's trembling, Tova sees. Actually trembling. Suddenly Merewyn seems much younger than her twenty years, like she was when she first came to Heldeby. No longer as innocent but still as vulnerable.

'We're not pilgrims,' her lady says. 'When Beorn found us that evening, we were fleeing. Not from the Normans, though. From something else. Like you, Father, I've sinned, and I'm sorry.'

'Whatever it is,' Guthred assures her, 'you can tell us.'

Don't do it, Tova implores her silently.

But the others are waiting. Expecting. She can hardly refuse.

Oslac mutters, 'It must be something terrible.'

'Hold your tongue or I'll make sure you never speak again,' Beorn says sharply.

'I'll tell you,' Merewyn says. 'On one condition. Don't judge me. Not, at least, until I've finished. That's all I ask. Can you promise me that?'

She's going to do it. She's going to tell them. When they hear what she's done, God preserve us.

'So,' Merewyn says, with a deep sigh. 'How much do you want to know?'

'Everything,' says Oslac. 'You might as well. I don't suppose we're going any further tonight.'

'Everything?' she echoes. 'I don't know how to start. Or where.'

'How about at the beginning?' Guthred suggests gently. 'That's often a good place.'

meɲepyn

MEREWYN

From the beginning, then.

The best place to start, I suppose, is when I first came to Heldeby. That's where we're from, Tova and myself, not that you're likely to have ever heard of it. Until that summer I hadn't either. A modest manor on the northern slopes of a wide valley on the other side of the high moors, where the hills meet the river plain. A mile or so upstream from the fording place where the three streams come together. Nowhere especially rich, although it was prosperous enough as long as I lived there. It was home, odd though that seems when I think about it now, given that until about a year and a half ago I'd never even set eyes on it. But it's true. Like a sapling torn from the earth where it sprouted, at first you yearn for what you know, what you can never go back to, but then you're planted in new soil, given new skies under which to spread your limbs, and before you realise it you've taken root again and new shoots are beginning to emerge.

That's how it was with me. I didn't know then how it was all going to end.

Don't look at me like that, Oslac. You wanted to hear our story, didn't you? Well, this is it, and I'll tell it just as I promised. Maybe I'm not as good at this as you are, but I'm going to do it my way.

I was already in my nineteenth summer when I arrived at Heldeby, not that I wanted to go. My mother was the one who made the arrangements, or rather it was Eadmer really, since he was lord, but she was behind it all. I think he would have been content to let me live out my days however I chose. He was my only surviving sibling. Our elder brothers had both died when we were still young, one in a hunting accident and the other in a fall. Eadmer was five years younger than me, but we'd always been close, maybe because we had both survived when the others hadn't. He enjoyed my company and my conversation, and I enjoyed his. But he was still coming to terms with what it meant to be a thegn and a master of men, a giver of silver and a receiver of oaths, and he was easily swayed. Our father had taken ill during the snows only a few months earlier, you see, and fallen into a fever so terrible that no one could do anything for him: not the wise woman nor the priest nor the pedlar who came with his mule and cart bearing ointments made from herbs and spices from distant lands to the east. None of us was expecting it; he'd always been strong, both in body and in spirit, and it was painful to see him laid so low. But day by day, hour by hour, his strength left him, until eventually during that night when the millpond froze he died, leaving Eadmer, fourteen and only just a man, to become lord in his place.

The burden was too heavy for him, young as he was and weighed down with grief at our father's passing. Our father, who had always been kind, who had always provided, who had vowed to do whatever was necessary to keep us safe from the Frenchmen and their so-called king, Wilelm. All those duties were now Eadmer's. He had to learn to be a lord even as he was still learning to be a man, and the only person he could turn to for counsel and help was our mother. She'd hear the monthly pleas in the manor court and administer justice; she understood when to be firm and when it was better to show clemency. She knew how much grain we could expect to reap if the weather stayed fine throughout the summer and how much if it was wet, and how much we would have left over and how much we might sell that for at market, and which fields should be set aside next year. She was more than fifty in years by then, but had lost none of her vigour and was still as wilful as she had ever been. She was the one who made the decisions in those early months after our father's death, and Eadmer was happy to let her.

One of those decisions was that I should be married. Our father had indulged me too much, she said. By resisting her pleas to find me a husband and allowing me to remain unwed, she claimed he'd done me a disservice, making me lose sight of a woman's place in the world. He'd always laughed off such remarks, and I knew this irked her. It was his wish that I should marry only when I felt I was ready and even then to a man I myself had chosen.

Of course I realise now that she was only trying to do what she thought was best for me. She was thinking that so many young thegns had already lost their lives fighting against the Normans in the wars in the south of the kingdom; she was worried that if I waited much longer there might not be anyone left for me. She herself had been lucky, so she would tell me often, for she was past twenty-five when my father took her to their marriage bed. Almost turning grey, I remember he'd once joked, or maybe it wasn't a joke, because even in my earliest memories I remember noticing in her hair a few strands behind her ear that were paler than the rest. I don't suppose it could have mattered to him, because he always used to tell me that when he first laid eyes upon her he thought her as beautiful as any girl ten years younger, and he said that if I turned out anything like her then I needn't worry about finding a good husband even if I was thirty before I decided I was ready. In the meantime he encouraged me to practise my letters and to read the teachings of the Church

Fathers and to learn the different tongues of these isles. He found me a tutor, a young priest named Leofa who had travelled widely across Britain and had even been as far as Rome, and who was well known for the breadth of his learning.

But then he died that winter – my father, I mean, not Leofa. He died and everything changed. My mother took it upon herself to find me a man, and Eadmer didn't stop her. I think he was reluctant to get involved, in case he ended up upsetting either one of us. He had no wish to foist upon me a husband I didn't want, but at the same time he needed our mother's guidance. The last thing he wanted was to drive a wedge between them. In the end it was easier for him to give his consent and to let events take their course.

I don't blame him, I really don't. I don't blame my mother either, before you start thinking otherwise. Not any longer, anyway. It hurt at the time, but I forgive her now. As I said, she only wanted what she thought was right and proper.

And I could have refused. It would have been easy. They couldn't make me do anything against my will. But I didn't want to make things harder than they already were or to be yet another burden on Eadmer, who had more important concerns than having to intervene in the squabble between myself and our mother, which only grew more bitter the longer it went on. I was tired too. I didn't want to be arguing over my fate each and every day, and I didn't want to keep on living there if it meant having to suffer her voice in my ear.

And the truth was I could have done worse than Skalpi. He was the man my mother found for me, a thegn and the son of a thegn. A warrior too, who'd led men in the two great battles at Fuleford and Stanford Brycg, when the other Harold came to these shores a few years ago, but of course you know all about that.

181

I was lucky, she kept telling me, because there weren't many who wanted to marry a woman of nineteen whose best years were already behind her. The lord of Heldeby, he was a little older than me, or so I gathered, and had been married before. He wasn't rich, although he did better than most. Better than us, at any rate. The bride price he'd offered was more than double what any other man had promised. From that alone I realised, even before I'd met him, that he could give me a life better than I'd find with anyone else. That was why my mother chose him over the others, and that was why, much to her surprise and her delight, after months of arguing and shouting and cursing, I gave in and agreed to marry him.

'Wait,' says Beorn. 'Your husband's name was Skalpi?'

'That's right,' Merewyn replies. 'Why?'

'Skalpi Guthfrithsson?'

Her frown softens into surprise. 'How did you—?'

'It isn't a common name, is it?'

'You knew him?'

'Knew him? Not exactly, although our paths did cross a handful of times when we were marching under Eadgar's banner. Not a bad swordsman, I thought, the one time I saw him fight. Good with a spear and seax too. Quicker on his feet than you'd expect for someone his size, and his age. Always had a solemn look about him, I remember. He kept himself to himself.'

That sounds like Skalpi, thinks Tova.

'Do you know what happened to him?' Merewyn asks, her eyes wide.

'As I said, I only met him a few times, and only in passing. The last time I saw him was at Eoferwic during the battle. After that, I don't know.'

182

'Oh.'

No sooner does hope begin to kindle in Merewyn's eyes than it's pinched out.

Oslac says to her, 'I thought you were about to tell us that you'd poisoned your husband, or something like that.'

'Skalpi? You thought I killed him?'

He shrugs. 'It was a guess, that's all.'

'Well, you're wrong.'

'What, then?'

'Let her speak, Oslac,' says the priest. 'That way you might find out.' He gestures for Merewyn to continue.

Where was I? Oh, yes.

You're all probably thinking that it was a bad match. That a marriage should never be made in haste or to please others. But I suppose I was relieved more than anything. Relieved to be leaving my mother's house at last. I'd grown up there, and it was a place of happy memories, but there was sadness as well because I knew those times had now passed and wouldn't be returning. As it was, I didn't really understand what I'd committed myself to until it was too late.

A date was settled upon. We exchanged betrothal gifts with the messengers who came on Skalpi's behalf. The bride price was paid. A contract was drawn up in which we declared what property we each would bring to the marriage and what rights we held over that property.

And so, on a bright July morning – the feast of St Swithun it was – he came to our manor with his retinue. I was standing in the yard, watching the track that led down from the wolds, while around me preparations were being made for the feast. A long table had been carried out from the hall, and benches and stools set around it and two great carved wooden chairs like thrones placed in the middle, and there were ale cups and wooden bowls and clay pitchers and ewers filled with water, and a canopy was being erected over everything so that we'd be protected from the sun. Close by, stones had been laid to make a hearth, with a spit suspended over it. Elsewhere, a wide ring had been marked out with wooden stakes where later there would be games. Streamers of cloth in red and green and ivory-white were nailed to fence posts; from all the cottages and barns and workshops hung bright banners and bunches of foxgloves and poppies and forget-me-nots and other field flowers. Skylarks warbled somewhere in the blue above and a gentle breeze played across the meadows where the sheep grazed, making waves in the tall grass.

I spied the first of them coming, a column of mounted figures with a cloud of dust rising at their rear, and a banner unfurled and fluttering in the breeze. I leaped up and cried out, and that was when my mother called me inside. It wasn't right, she said, that a man should see his bride before the ceremony, for it would only bring misfortune. And so while Eadmer and Thurkil the reeve and Father Leofa, my tutor whom I'd invited to give holy blessing to our union, rode out to greet Skalpi and his retinue, my mother went with me to my chambers to help me get ready. As she combed out my hair and fretted over the tangles I kept being distracted by the sounds of conversation in the yard outside. I was trying to guess which of the voices belonged to my husband-to-be, but they were too far away for me to make much out, and my mother kept fussing and eventually I gave up as they moved away.

I couldn't stop pacing, I was so restless. My mother was explaining what I should do at each part of the proceedings, as if she hadn't told me a dozen times already. She kept giving me instructions as to how I should carry myself as I entered the hall

– how I shouldn't look up but should instead concentrate on my feet and make sure that I took only small, careful steps, because that way I wouldn't trip over the hem of my dress, and because men expected their brides to appear timid, not bold. She kept on asking if I was listening to her at all, and I said half-truthfully that I was. Those are just the things I remember; there was more but I was too nervous to take it all in.

It felt like hours later when Eadmer came knocking on the door of my chamber, saying that everything was ready, and that it was time. I made my way across the yard to the long mead hall, where the ceremony was to take place. It was only then, standing before its great oak doors, waiting for them to open, dressed in my finest gown of yellow wool, which my mother had ordered sewn for me especially for the day, with my hair uncovered and falling loose over my shoulders, and a crown of buttercups resting upon my head, with Eadmer and my mother beside me, that I realised this was truly happening. All the worries I'd been trying to quell over the last few days and weeks burst out from the place inside where I'd kept them bound up.

What if I didn't like him? What if he didn't like me, or if he thought me too plump or too slender? What if he preferred a woman who was dark-haired rather than fair? What if I couldn't please him in the ways he was used to, in the ways his first wife had done? I didn't know much about that sort of thing; I knew only what everyone knew, and of course my mother had told me what to expect, but being told isn't the same as doing it yourself.

And then I thought just how little I knew about him, apart from his name. I had no idea what he looked like, or whether he was fierce or kind, cultured or boorish.

Whether it was because of all those thoughts running through my head all at once or because of the heat of the morning, I'm

185

not sure, and probably it was both, but suddenly it felt as though my throat was narrowing, for I couldn't breathe, and my cheeks were burning and my eyes too, and my head felt light, and my heart was beating like this, this, this, this, and my knees were weak and I couldn't feel my feet.

Eadmer thumped his fist upon the oak, and a moment later there was a creak and the doors began to part, like the jaws of some monstrous creature opening up to swallow me. This was it, I thought.

Inside it was so dark, or at least it seemed that way because the day was so bright. All was silent. Men and women and children were gathered on either side of the hall, awaiting my entrance, forming a path from the doorway to the dais at the far end, where, surrounded by candles, stood my husband-to-be.

Skalpi Guthfrithsson.

And I took one look at him and burst into tears.

'Why?' asks Guthred.

'Because she was happy, you fool,' says Oslac.

Merewyn shakes her head.

'He was ugly, then?' the poet asks. 'Missing half his face? Did he have a battle scar?'

'It wasn't anything like that. It's just that no one had told me. I suppose it's my own fault. I never thought to ask. I simply assumed. Remember this was the first time I'd ever met him.'

'I don't understand that,' Beorn says. 'How can you decide to marry someone without even knowing what he looks like?'

'I didn't think it was unusual,' Merewyn replies. 'No one did. Maybe it's different where you come from.'

'But then how could you know that you wanted to marry him? And how could he know that he wanted to marry you?'

'For all the reasons I've just told you. I never for a moment thought when I was growing up that my marriage, whenever it happened, would have anything to do with love. As far as I and Eadmer and our mother were concerned, this was a contract between Skalpi and our family, nothing more than that. This was about land and wealth and rank. If friendship or love blossomed, then so much the better, but also I knew that it would be wrong to hold out too much hope.'

'And did you love him?' the priest asks.

She reddens. 'I don't know. Maybe. I think so. Not straight away, though. Only later, when I came to know him better. Even then it was a different love to the kind I hoped for.'

Guthred frowns. 'How do you mean?'

'Maybe if you all stop asking her these questions and give her a chance to speak, she'll be able to tell you,' Tova snaps.

They all turn to look at her, as surprised as she is by her forcefulness. She feels her cheeks growing hot and hopes that it doesn't show.

'Besides,' Tova says, more softly now that she has their attention, 'if you carry on, you'll only spoil the story. Do you want that?'

No one says anything. Maybe she's stunned them all into silence. After a moment, Merewyn takes a deep breath and begins again.

I don't know what I was expecting. Should I have tried to find out more about him beforehand? Should I have paid more attention to the things they were telling me and the things they weren't? Probably. The truth is that, for all that my mother and I had argued, I still trusted her to do her best for me. Maybe that's what she thought she was doing.

At the time, though, it didn't seem that way. At the time, I felt tricked. Betrayed. Because the man standing before me looked older than my father.

His hair, which was tied back with a leather thong, was grey and turning white, as were his beard and his moustache. His face was creased and cracked like old parchment, and his skin looked as dry. I'd known he was older than me, but not by how much. In time I'd find the courage to ask him, and he would say he didn't know exactly, but he reckoned he must have seen at least forty-five winters and possibly more.

He remembered growing up in the days of King Cnut, when just as now England had been ruled by an invader from across the sea, only this one had come not from France but from Denmark, and so Skalpi's family, being in a way distant kinsfolk of his, had prospered. He told me how as a boy he had dreamed of one day joining the royal war band and taking up arms, and he remembered the struggles after Cnut's death as the king's two sons squabbled over who should succeed him. These were things of which I'd heard stories from my father and uncles and their friends, but to me they were so distant they might as well have come from one of those ancient poems that they were always so fond of reciting.

That was later, though. Then I knew only that I was giving myself to a man twice my age and more. Yes, I could have changed my mind. I could have fled across the yard and back to my chamber, or taken horse and ridden far away where no one could find me. All these things crossed my mind. But, if I did that, I'd bring shame not just upon Skalpi and his kin, but also upon myself and my own family. Upon my mother and upon Eadmer, and I knew they would never forgive me. Word would spread of the woman who had broken her betrothal promise, who had broken her oath, and what man would ever want me after that? I would grow old without ever finding a husband, without ever knowing love, and I would die childless and alone.

So you see I was trapped. I had no choice.

At first I think everyone in the hall assumed that the tears spilling down my cheeks were ones of joy, or else that's what they preferred to tell themselves. But as I was led, trembling, towards the dais, head bowed like a slave being taken to market, and when my sobs didn't stop but went on and on, I think they began to realise. People fidgeted and grew uncomfortable. Smiles turned to frowns. A whisper passed around the hall, like a breeze stirring the rushes. Someone coughed, then another, and another. One of the younger children began to cry.

Skalpi knew, of course. Right from the start, he knew. I remember so clearly the heartbroken look in his eyes. For he'd tried his best. He might have been more than forty-five winters in age, but he still looked every bit the warrior. Later, when the ceremony was over, my tears had subsided and he led me out from the silent hall into the glare of the day, I saw him more clearly. He was tall, by which I mean he stood probably a head and a half over me, and he was powerfully built too, without much of a belly. Yes, he had his fair share of scars, but he had taken care over his appearance. He'd combed his beard and per-fumed his tunic, which was plain and unembroidered, the colour of holly leaves. His sleeves were bunched where he wore his arm rings, which were fashioned from rods of gold twisted around one another. I supposed they must have been old family treas-ures because no one wears such garish things nowadays, but he prized them greatly.

He was a proud man, and I don't just mean in his appearance. I could tell straight away that I'd wounded him, and deeply. His weather-worn face was flushed with embarrassment, which only made me feel worse. We weren't even wed and already I had failed him.

Thurkil the reeve, who was in charge of the ceremony, asked me quietly whether I was well, and if I wished to go on. Skalpi was looking anxiously at me, and I said with a sniff that yes I did. But I was sobbing as we knelt before each other, sobbing through the vows and sobbing as, afterwards, Leofa the priest led the hall in prayer and wished us a long and fruitful life, and asked that our marriage be blessed with many children in the years to come.

For the sake of everyone watching, I tried to swallow my tears as Thurkil bade us rise and proclaimed us man and wife, and as Skalpi gently, uncertainly, took my hand in his, which was leathery and had to be twice the size of my own. I could hardly feel my feet, and at any moment I thought I would fall. Together we began what felt like the longest walk of my life: from the dais, past all those folk, who shuffled their feet and averted their gaze, through the open doors and into bright sunlight, where we were greeted with cheers and showers of petals from those waiting outside, and bright peals from the bell tower. As we took our places at the feasting table I caught my brother's glance, and on his face there was a look as if he couldn't believe what he had done. I wanted to tell him that it wasn't his fault, but then my mother sat down beside me, her head raised proud and her chin jutting out. She didn't speak to me or even look at me.

That night was my last under the roof where I'd grown up. I managed somehow to stifle my sorrow through the feasting and the games and the music and the dancing, but I was dreading what was to come. I had hardly eaten all day, I felt so sick. All too soon the sun fell below the gable of the hall. The skies turned the colour of fire as the day blazed its last, and then the stars began to emerge.

Evening fell.

I'd witnessed enough marriages to know what would happen next. Someone would blow a horn; at once the cavorting and the swilling would cease; a cry would go up, and then all the men would chase after the bride, ripping her garments from her as tokens of good luck until eventually she stood in just her under-gown or what was left of it, and then everyone would cheer as the newly married man stepped forward and scooped her up in his arms and carried her off to his chamber, and there would be jokes about his manhood and her chastity, and much laughter, and ale cups raised and lewd songs and raucous cheers.

All the time, as we joined in the dancing, and the men passed between the women around the circle, laying a kiss on each one's cheek before moving on in time with the sound of the flute, I was waiting for that to happen. First Eadmer took me by the hand, and he was smiling but there was sadness in his eyes at the same time. I did my best to smile back before we changed partners, and then it was Leofa's turn, and after that one of Skalpi's retainers, a dark-haired man whose name I didn't know but whose face seemed fixed in a perpetual smirk, and it was almost a relief when the music changed and he moved on and I found myself once again looking into Skalpi's blue eyes, as clear as crystal.

'Come with me,' he said in my ear, gently, although there was a rasp to his voice, like a saw grinding against timber. 'Quickly, before anyone notices.'

He took my hand, and I didn't know what else to do except go with him. My heart was pounding as I bunched my skirts in my other hand to stop them trailing. Like everyone we had left our shoes by the table while we danced, and so we ran barefoot

191

across the yard, away from the revellers and the fire, the earth still warm from the day. For a man whose hair was grey and who had probably seen many battles in his years, Skalpi was nevertheless quick on his feet. Quicker than me, anyway, and I struggled to keep up. The flute-player carried on but we slipped away into the darkness, across the yard, towards the house. Behind us the music grew softer and softer.

At least I was spared the rest of it, I thought. The jokes and the cheers. The tearing of clothes.

He hustled me inside, shut the door and set the bolt so that no one else could get in, and then without a word he led me carefully up the stairs to the bedchamber, holding my hand all the way so that I didn't miss a step. It was difficult to see anything at all; we had no candle and the darkness was like tar in the way it clung to everything. The air was hot and heavy, and I felt as though I would drown, for it was so hard to breathe.

'I'm sorry,' he said, a shadow among shadows, when we reached the top. He took both my hands in his, caressing the backs of them softly with his thumbs. His palms were warm, greasy from the feast, and I wanted to snatch my hands away, but I knew it wouldn't be right. All was still, save for the sound of our breathing and the far-off trills of the flute. We were closer to one another than you are to me now and still I couldn't see him, not even his arm rings gleaming, it was that dark.

This was how it began, I thought. My throat was dry and I had to swallow to moisten it.

'Sorry for what?' I asked.

'For not being what you were expecting. What you were hoping for.'

I was trembling. In the darkness I couldn't see his face. From the sound of his voice alone I couldn't tell if he was angry at me.

I said hurriedly, 'No, Lord—'

But he cut me off. 'It's all right. I know. You don't have to say anything. Or do anything. Not tonight.'

Outside, a horn blast. The music stopped. A cheer went up, and people were whooping with laughter, but it wasn't long before the whoops turned into cries of confusion as they realised we were nowhere to be found.

'When you're ready, then we will,' Skalpi said. 'Not before.'

I felt his warm breath on my face and flinched as he laid a kiss upon my forehead, and he must have felt me shaking, felt my apprehension, because he didn't linger but broke away quickly. He let go of my hands and then he was gone. I heard his feet on the stairs, heard the door open as he went out back into the night to join the revellers. Exactly what he told them, he never said, but I imagine it was nothing that caused him to lose face. As I lay down on what would have been our marriage bed and closed my eyes and breathed deeply and tried to work out what had just happened, I could make out what sounded like his voice as he rejoined those celebrating, and then there was more laughter and the singing began again.

All I could think about was how relieved I was.

The next morning, under heavy skies that promised a downpour later, we left for Heldeby, which was two days' ride away. What I had decided to bring with me to furnish my new home was already packed in chests and trunks and saddlebags: everything from clothes and shoes to a tæfl set made from chestnut and walrus ivory, a gift from Eadmer to Skalpi in recognition of the new bond between our two kindreds, and an embroidery of a hunting scene that my mother had given me, which she herself had helped to make and which she hoped we might hang somewhere in our hall.

Not that I felt in the beginning that it was ever my hall to hang things in, or that I had much share in Heldeby, apart from the land he gave me as my morning gift. For weeks I felt like a stranger. At first I was greeted with wonder, their lord's new wife, but in time that faded and what remained were barbed tongues and cold eyes. For what no one told me until I arrived, one of many things, was that he had two sons from his first marriage: Orm, who wasn't much older than Eadmer and whose face from his brow to his neck was a welter of red blotches, which he had a habit of picking at, a habit that only made them worse; and Ketil, who had seen only ten winters and was a sickly thing, always too thin, and who never ate as much as he should. Skalpi was devoted to them and lavished on them gifts of horses and hawks and bows and arrows, but for all that they were forever scowling, or at least they always were in my presence. They both resented me for taking their mother's place, which I could well understand, but they also resented their father for reasons I couldn't work out at first.

What happened to his first wife? At first I thought she'd died, because that's what my mother had told me and because no one at Heldeby would utter a single word about her, even when I asked them directly. I thought they were just being respectful, and so it wasn't until later, when Tova and I became friends, that I learned Skalpi had discovered her in bed with another man, a former love from years earlier who'd disguised himself as a travelling monk so that he could meet her and gain access to her chamber without arousing suspicion.

Skalpi had killed him on the spot and cast her out, never to return, with nothing more than the clothes she was wearing. It was said she had gone into a nunnery somewhere, although no one knew for sure and most preferred to keep their thoughts to themselves, in case word ever got back to Skalpi and he cast them out too.

Why he chose to marry again, I don't know. Not because he needed another heir. Companionship, maybe, although he had plenty of that from the slave girls who often warmed his bed. The only other reason I can think of is pride. He'd been wronged, and felt ashamed. Taking another wife was the only way he could think of to rid himself of that shame, I suppose, and to escape the humiliation he had endured. By pretending in a way that it had never happened. By refusing to ever speak of his first wife, either in private or in company. By walking from the table without a word and taking his food in his chamber whenever his sons spoke of her during the evening meal, whether they did it in passing or deliberately, to provoke him.

He cared for them deeply, which is why he didn't send them away with their mother after her betrayal. Ties of blood are the hardest to sever. But they didn't thank him for it, and probably that was why he was so desperate to win their affection, though they rarely showed any sign of returning it. They were a strange pair. They kept to themselves most of the time, and didn't speak much except with each other. The younger one, Ketil, I didn't mind, but Orm I never liked from the moment I first met him. The way he looked at me, the mixture of loathing and desire that I saw in his eyes, made my skin turn to ice. He had a sullen manner and a sharp tongue when he cared to use it, and I took pains to avoid him. It wasn't that I was scared of him, not exactly; what could he do to me? But all the same I never liked being in the same place as him if I could help it.

I didn't have many friends in those early days, but it was bearable, I suppose. Skalpi kept hoping that I would come to love him in time. Whenever he came back from the markets at

Eoferwic or Skardaborg he would bring me a fine cloak or a new dress trimmed with silk that came all the way from Miklagard, or silver rings and necklaces of amber and jet, all in an effort to win me over. He never pressed me and was always patient. Outwardly he seemed a man in control of his feelings, lacking in passion, but inside the scars must have run deep; he remained heart-stricken, and was doing his best to heal that hurt. After a while, whenever he had to go away he'd leave me in charge not just of the household, but also of collecting rents and even of hearing pleas in the manor court, the same things that at home my mother often took care of on Eadmer's behalf. Orm didn't like that because he felt those responsibilities should be his, and at sixteen he was certainly old enough. Skalpi didn't trust him, though, whereas he trusted me, because I was lettered and had a kind way with people. Not like Orm, who could hardly open his mouth without causing offence. So that gave him yet another reason to hate me. As if he didn't have enough already.

As far as I could tell, Orm had one true ally at Heldeby apart from his brother, and that was the smirking man who had danced with me that night after the marriage feast. His name was Ælfric and he was Skalpi's reeve, a weasel-faced creature for whom nothing was ever enough. He was forever arguing that we could squeeze higher rents out of the cottars who lived on our lands, or that we could get better prices on the fleeces if we sold them across the sea rather than at the markets nearby, or that the slaves, the few that we owned, should be made to work harder for their keep, and when he didn't get his way he would hold it as a slight against his person and spend the rest of that day lashing out at whoever happened to cross his path. He had a quick temper and was no man's friend.

Skalpi himself was no great supporter of his but instead

tolerated him, and only kept him on because in spite of everything else he was a good overseer. Ælfric took a liking to Orm, though, I think because they were similar in character. He would spar with him in the training yard and ruffle his hair when he did well, and they would go on hunts together, and drink and joke long into the night, often laughing so loudly that they would wake me in my chamber, which was next to the hall. The reeve wasn't married and had no sons of his own, and so he saw Orm almost as a fosterling: someone whom he could teach and whom he could fashion as he chose.

They were each intimidating enough by themselves, but together they were worse. They took confidence from one another, inflicting cruel words that neither one alone would dare deliver. I quickly noticed how the house servants and the stable hands and the kitchen girls all took care to avoid them, especially when they were together.

That's how I met Tova.

Hearing Merewyn speak, Tova feels a pricking in her eyes. Her cheeks burn and she bows her head before her lady notices.

To hear these things from someone else's lips, as they saw it, is strange. Uncomfortable. It's like looking down a well and seeing oneself reflected in the flat water below. All the details are there, but they're dimmer and more distant and harder to recognise.

This was around the same time as the business with the silver. I'd been counting out some coins from Skalpi's money kist, the one he kept locked in the floor space underneath his chamber, so that I could buy a few lengths of linen at market, when I noticed that we were a few shillings short. I checked again to see how much there was supposed to be, and tried to think if there was anything I'd paid for lately that I might have forgotten to note down. But the numbers were the same, and I couldn't think of anything, which meant that somebody must have taken it, and recently too, because nothing had been missing three days before, which was when we'd last had the kist out, to give the geld we owed to the shire reeve.

Of course I went to Skalpi. At once he ordered all the cottars and the slaves out of their houses so that they could be searched, and Ælfric went in with Orm and Penda the smith, to protests from the men and weeping from the women. Knives were drawn and mattresses were slashed open and the straw emptied out; thatch was torn in clumps from the roofs; cooking pots were overturned and the heaps of dung that stood outside every toft were raked over as the men looked for the telltale glint.

Eventually we found it, in the slave quarters close to the kitchen, hidden beneath the bed of one of the women, whose name I think was Gundrada, who had a daughter. She pleaded ignorance, saying that she didn't know how it had got there, but then one of the male slaves remembered that not a few days before she had been complaining about how hard they were being made to work, and he said that maybe she thought she deserved it and that was why she had taken it. Anyway, Gundrada—

'Gunnhild,' Tova murmurs under her breath.

'What?' asks Merewyn.

'It was Gunnhild,' she says. She remembers only too well. 'Not Gundrada.'

'Is it important?'

'It was her name, that's all.'

*

198

Gunnhild, then. She said that he was lying, and no, she hadn't taken the silver, and if she had she would never have hidden it in so obvious a place. But that only made people think that if nothing else she must have considered stealing it, which made her guilty in mind if not in deed.

What did I think? That she was guilty, of course, although I pleaded with Skalpi not to be too harsh. But it was his decision and his alone, and eventually he made up his mind. An example needed to be made, he announced, so that no one else would ever think about doing the same thing again. And so he sent her away, and not just her but her daughter too, who must have been around the same age as Tova. What happened to them? Well, they were slaves so they were sold on, of course, to a merchant who would take them across the sea. To Dyflin, I think, where he said he could get a good price for them.

Anyway, it was around that time, as I was saying, that I met Tova for the first time. I already knew who she was, in the same way that everyone knew everyone on the manor: the slight girl with the wavy hair who during the day worked in the dairy and sometimes in the evenings attended table, where she'd stand behind Skalpi with his cup in one hand and in the other a jug of ale or wine or water depending on his mood. I knew her name but not much more than that.

Not until the day when I overheard what sounded like a cry coming from the kitchen. It was cut short and quickly followed by what sounded like Orm's voice, although I couldn't make out what was being said. A chill rose through me and I quickened my pace, then something made me stop. I'd noticed how Orm and Ælfric had been treating the slaves lately – waiting for one to spill a pail or break a pot, or for the harvest team out reaping the barley to overlook one corner of a field, when they'd set

199

upon them with insults and cuffs around the back of the head and sometimes worse – but I'd never had the courage to face up to them both at the same time.

For once, though, I didn't hear the reeve's voice. If ever there was a time to stand up to Orm, I thought, this was it. It was the middle of the afternoon and everyone else was at their tasks: the smith at his forge, the cowherd moving his animals to new pasture, the swineherd out foraging with the pigs in the woods, the others cleaning the pens and helping to lay new thatch on one of the barns. Skalpi was away, as he often was, visiting one of his other manors. And so it had to be me.

What I found when I threw open the door was Orm, with the sleeves of his tunic rolled to his elbows and his hand raised, standing over Tova, who was on the floor in front of him, her back against the wall, her head turned, her eyes closed and face screwed up tight in anticipation. He struck her, hard across the cheek, and was lifting his arm to strike her again when I shouted out.

At once he turned. And saw me. He stopped mid-movement.

'What are you doing?' I asked.

He should have apologised or made himself scarce. But he didn't. Instead he stood where he was and scowled at me, as if I was the one in the wrong. He was tall for his age, taller than me at any rate, broad-shouldered and thickset as well, with arms like a smith's from all the time he spent in the training yard. Even though the reeve wasn't with him, and I was in my own house with a dozen people within earshot if I shouted out, I was still more than a little afraid of him, but I tried not to let it show.

'She broke a pitcher,' he said flatly.

'Get away from her now,' I told him.

He asked, 'What's she to you?'

Trying not to let my voice tremble, I said that I needed her to run an errand for me. He replied that I could have her, but first she needed to be punished for her clumsiness.

'You don't get to decide that,' I told him. 'Only your father does, and he won't be pleased when I tell him you struck one of his cup-bearers.'

He glared at me with those small eyes of his. The surprise on his face was gone and in its place was that loathing look I'd grown used to.

'He won't care,' he said. 'She's nothing to him. Just a slave. A worthless, stinking slave who deserves to be beaten.'

'Maybe so,' I said, 'but she's your father's slave, and if you hurt her so that she can't work he won't thank you. He'll still have to feed and clothe and shelter her regardless.'

'You don't tell me what to do,' he said as he advanced on me. 'This is my home, not yours. I'll do what I like.'

I backed away towards what I thought was the door, but instead I found the wall. He pressed close, his breath warm upon my face. At first I thought he might be drunk, even though it was still early in the day. But I didn't smell any ale on him, and that only scared me more. I didn't know what he had in mind, except that I didn't like it. I tried to twist away but he thrust out an arm to stop me. There was nowhere I could go.

'When your father returns, he'll hear about this,' I said, but even to my ears it sounded like a feeble threat.

He raised his hand towards my face and I flinched, thinking that he was about to hit me too. Instead he brushed my cheek with the tips of his dirt-stained fingers, running them softly, almost in wonderment, down the side of my neck towards my collarbone, his broken nails lightly scratching my skin. At any moment, I thought, he was going to pull me towards him and plant his lips upon mine. I could hardly breathe; I wanted to be sick.

'It's your word against mine,' he said. 'Which one of us do you think he's going to believe?'

Outside I heard Ælfric shouting, for what reason or at whom I didn't know, but it was probably one of the other slaves, as it always was. Orm glanced towards the door. He must have come to his senses then, realising that someone else could walk in at any moment, and that if they did it would look bad for him. Because he didn't wait for an answer. Instead he drew his hand away and without a backward glance stalked out of the kitchen. But I could still feel his fingers lingering, sliding across my cheek, as I heard him greeting the reeve.

Their voices grew further and further away, leaving me and Tova alone.

I remember you were rubbing your face as you got to your feet, and I asked if you were all right. You told me you were, but I noticed that you didn't look at me as you said it, and I put my arms around you and told you I'd see to it that Orm stayed away in future. I wasn't sure how I'd do that, but I swore it anyway, and an oath is an oath.

Of course nothing was done. I told Skalpi what I'd seen when he came back from his travels, although I left out the part about the threats Orm had made towards me. Why? Because I felt embarrassed, I suppose, and dirty too, for letting him touch me. And because I wasn't sure there was anything to tell. He hadn't done anything except to frighten me, but then he had always frightened me. He hadn't hurt me, and in any case he was right: it was only my word against his.

Anyway, Skalpi listened. He was patient and didn't interrupt, but he let me say what I would, and all the time there was a solemn expression on his face that I found hard to read. He believed I spoke the truth, I think. He even called for Tova so that he could hear for himself what she had to say and see the marks on her face. I pleaded with him to do something about his son, and said that if he didn't act to curb his unruliness things would only grow worse. In the end, though, feeling won out over reason. As much as he hoped to please me, and as much as he saw I was affected by what had happened, he craved his son's love and couldn't bring himself to punish him. He warned Orm that next time there would be consequences, but they both knew it wasn't true.

Thankfully Ælfric stopped having much to do with Orm after that. Maybe Skalpi spoke to him and told him what he'd heard, or maybe the reeve realised on his own that things had gone too far. At any rate, from then on he and Orm were rarely seen together. They would no longer sit drinking by hearth-light late into the night. While occasionally they still took to the training yard to practise spear work and sword craft, there was never quite the same warmth between them.

For a while, then, things got better. Tova said that although Orm would still spit in her direction and hurl curses at her from across the yard if there was no one around to hear, he didn't come near her any more. The slaves weren't forced to work quite as hard either, for which they were grateful. Not that the work was easy, but at least it was tolerable. I understood that Skalpi had instructed that, rather than being threatened with punishment if they didn't produce enough butter or cheese, they should be promised rewards for doing well. A cup each of the better ale to drink with their morning and evening meals, and a further cup of beans and another of grain on top of what they were already owed by custom and by right.

Still, those were difficult times. Many were the nights that Skalpi retired early to his chamber, sometimes in the middle of our evening meal, after barely touching his plate or his cup. He would stand from the table and leave without a word, and later I would find him lying on his bed in the darkness, without even a single candle lit. Without taking off his tunic or his shoes. Without sleeping. Without any of the girls I knew he sometimes shared his bed with. Just lying there, by himself, in silence.

The first time I thought he must be ill. He let me hold his hand when I knelt by his bedside, but he wouldn't tell me what was ailing him. His skin wasn't clammy, his brow wasn't running with sweat, he didn't have a fever, he wasn't coughing or sneezing or finding it hard to breathe, but in spite of all that he looked in some sort of pain. I feared he might be dying and wondered whether I should call the wise woman or the priest, but when I asked him he said they could do nothing for him. I asked him whether I could bring him anything, whether I could recite for him some of the poetry that he liked, which I'd learned at the hearth in my father's hall, and whether that might help. He said he wanted only to be alone and that I needn't worry about him. But I did worry, especially when the same thing happened a few nights later, and a third time the night after that. I might not have loved him the way he had hoped, but over time I'd grown to care for him. The last thing I wanted was for him to die, because where would that leave me then?

Nothing I could say, though, would stir him, so I had no choice but to do as he asked and leave him alone with his thoughts. The first couple of times a night's rest was enough to see him right, and the next day he would rise with the cock's first crow and be smiling and laughing once more. The third time, however, he failed to appear at dawn. At the second hour I went up to his chamber with what was left of the previous day's bread and some slices of sausage and a jug of well water, to find him not sleeping but beneath the blankets, lying on his side in the same position he had been the night before, hollow-eyed as he stared at the wall. He didn't look up as I came in, nor as I set down the victuals by his bedside and drew up a stool.

I must have sat with him for an hour or more, not saying anything because it was impossible to get any sort of reply from him. He would talk if he wanted, and if he didn't he wouldn't. And so I stroked his wiry hair and noticed for the first time how there was a bald patch at the back of his head where the skin was discoloured, and I wondered whether that was a war scar from his younger days, and realised how much he had yet to tell me about his life. Was it because he simply didn't want to bring those memories to mind, or because he thought I wasn't interested? Either way it made me sad. And I ate some of the bread and poured myself a cup of water, and I closed my eyes and listened to the birdsong outside and the *clink-clink-clink* of the smith at his forge.

He said, 'They hate me.'

He spoke quietly, but even so he startled me. It took me a while to find my voice. I asked him what he meant, but of course I already knew the answer.

'Orm and Ketil,' he said. 'Ælfric too, but it's my sons I care most about. They despise me. Orm especially.'

'They don't hate you,' I said, trying to soothe him, and it was partly true. I was fairly sure that Ketil bore no grudge against his father, and if he sometimes appeared to it was only because, being younger, he tended to follow Orm's example in everything.

Skalpi, though, told me not to be foolish. He knew well what was happening, he said, and if I didn't see it then I was either blind or lying, and that if I had taken to lying to him then that meant I hated him too.

'No, Lord,' I protested. 'That's not true.'

'Then you resent me at least. I know you do, before you try to deny it.'

I supposed I did, in a small way, but not for anything he had done. He'd always been kind to me, after all, and had given me freedoms I'd never enjoyed at home, even while my father still lived. If there was anything I resented him for, it was for not being the husband I had hoped for, and there was nothing he could do about that.

He knew from my silence that he was right.

He said, 'At least you're honest with me. Not like the others.'

And he told me everything. About his first wife, Ælfswith, and her faithlessness towards him. How he longed for the companionship that she had given him. Not the sort that his bed-warmers gave him, that wasn't what he meant, before you say anything. He wanted a woman who was learned, who knew her letters and could read to him in the long winter evenings, whom he could engage in conversation and in the table games he liked to play, who shared his love of poetry and of music and perhaps had some skill with harp or flute. A wife who was pleasing to the eye and whom he could proudly show off. Yes, he wanted that too, of course he did, because every man does. But he had no desire for more children, not at his age, and besides he doubted that he could any more. If he lived another ten years he would be lucky, he told me. His health was not what it had once been; each winter was harder than the last. It was his intention to spend whatever time God allowed him in peace. He had enough woes with the two children he had, and wouldn't want Orm and Ketil to think that he was trying to rob them of their inheritance.

And as I listened I couldn't help but feel guilty. All these weeks and months he had tried to please me and to show me his affection, and what had I done for him in return? No wonder he thought everyone was against him. He felt alone, he said, in a way he'd not felt since he was nine winters old and his father sent him to be fostered in the house of his uncle across the sea, where they spoke a tongue he didn't properly understand and they laughed at him for his English ways.

But it wasn't just that which was troubling him. There was more, something that had been pressing on his mind and he was reluctant to tell anyone, even though we would probably have learned it soon enough.

'What is it?' I asked.

The foreigners were marching, he said. King Wilelm was coming north, and he didn't know what was going to happen.

'He's coming north?'

'He took Eoferwic,' Skalpi explained, 'a week ago. The townsmen didn't even put up a struggle. They knew things would only go badly for them if they tried.'

I didn't know what to say. I could hardly believe it. All through that summer we'd been hearing how the foreigners were advancing through the midland shires, overrunning the country, crushing without mercy any who dared to stand in their path. Everywhere they went they built those strongholds they call castles to terrify the people and cow them into surrendering. Every week it seemed another town fell to their swords. Wærwic. Ledecestre. Deorbi. Snotingeham. Lincolne.

'But we're safe here,' I said, 'aren't we?'

That was what people had always said, ever since the Normans first crossed the sea. They had no interest in us or our lands north of the Humbre. Two years had come and gone since

207

the foreigners had first set foot on these shores. So far we had remained untouched by the wars that had afflicted the rest of England. No Frenchman dared set foot in these parts nor held a single scrap of land, because they'd heard that the Northumbrians were a fierce people, a proud people, and they didn't dare anger us. They had enough trouble in the south as it was; they didn't want to spread themselves too thinly across the kingdom and so make it easier for their foes to attack them. And besides, it was said, King Wilelm knew we would never suffer a foreign lord. Not like the folk of Wessex, whose necks were easily bowed. He feared us and respected us in equal measure, and was content to leave us be as long as we paid the dues that we owed him.

'I don't know,' Skalpi murmured. 'I don't know.'

And suddenly I saw those boasts for what they were. Lies we'd told ourselves, although for a long time they'd seemed true enough. The quiet times we'd enjoyed, which we should have known wouldn't last, were gone. For Eoferwic had fallen. Eoferwic, the great city, only a couple of days' ride from Heldeby.

At any moment they might arrive, I thought. If I ran down the stairs and out into the yard, already I might spy the dust cloud rising in the distance, kicked up by their horses' hooves as they pounded the road. They would come along the track, across the bridge, in their byrnies of mail and their helmets shining bright, bearing steel in one hand and a sealed writ from King Wilelm in the other. And they would bring with them a priest or a monk from the minster, one who spoke both tongues: an Englishman who would tell us, stuttering because he was nervous, that the king had granted our land to these foreigners and that they were now the rightful lords. That this manor, these barley fields and pastures, orchards, fish weirs and grain stores, this hall, the mill, the sheepfolds and the pigpens and the cowsheds – all of it now belonged to them.

And Skalpi would protest. He would spit and curse, and when none of that made any difference he would fly into a rage, and Orm and Ketil too, and perhaps blood would be spilt and there would be screaming, and there would be children wailing, and the cottars and geburs and slaves would cower in their houses because they wouldn't know what was happening, and there would be nothing anyone could do. And they would cast us out. If we were lucky they might give us until dusk to gather our belongings, one pack-full, maybe, and then we would be made to leave, and if still we refused then they would cut us down where we stood.

That was what I was thinking. I could see it so clearly. We'd all heard the stories coming out of the south, which had reached us on the tongues of exiles and pedlars and travelling priests. Always it was the same.

When eventually I could speak, I asked, 'What do we do?'

He didn't answer. But then what was I expecting him to say? What could he say? He knew just as well as I did how helpless we were if the Normans did come. There was nothing we could do. Only wait and hope.

Outside a nightingale trilled gently, but I didn't feel her joy. If only I had wings, I thought, then I would be able to fly away. That was the first time I'd ever felt truly afraid. You know what I mean: the sort of terror that clutches at your heart and steals the breath from your chest and seizes your limbs so that you can hardly move. The same that I feel now, sitting here with you, not knowing what's going to happen or if we're even going to survive this night. Knowing that they're out there somewhere, and that at any moment they could find us . . .

Anyway, I don't know whether it was because I was frightened and cold, or because, like Skalpi, I too was looking for companionship, or because I was desperate to do something, anything, to raise him from his sorrow. Probably it was all of those things. I don't remember any more, if I even knew at the time. I was confused, I know that much. It was like I had a hundred voices all shouting in my ear, trying to drown each other out, and nothing I could do would make them go away.

Maybe it was one of those voices that told me what I needed to do then, because I found myself shedding my shoes, my dress, my undergown, and sliding under the coarse blankets into the warm bed beside him.

'And?' Oslac asks with a smirk on his face that Tova doesn't like. 'What happened next?'

'I've just told you,' says Merewyn indignantly. 'If you can't work it out for yourself then you're more stupid than you look.'

'I thought we might hear the rest of it, that's all. It'll be something to cheer us and keep us warm through the night.'

She regards him with disgust. 'What do you take me for?'

'A good storyteller always gives his listeners what they want. That was one of the first lessons my father taught me.'

'Well, you've got as much as I'm going to give you. And you can stop looking at me that way.'

After that things remained uneasy for a long time. We learned later that hardly had Eoferwic fallen than the king had marched back south to quell some disturbance or other. He'd left behind him some men to hold the city and the surrounding lands, and appointed as shire reeve a Frenchman born to an English mother, whose authority he thought we might accept.

Despite my fears, peace of a kind prevailed, although it was an uneasy peace. From what little we heard, and it was only what we could gather second hand from such travellers who from time to time stayed as guests, the Normans seemed content to confine themselves to the city and the shores of the Humbre. I remember Orm saying that this only proved what men had been saying before: that the invaders feared the men of Northumbria. They were foolish words from someone who as far as I knew had never actually seen a fight in his life, as much as he loved his spear and shield practice, but he wasn't the only one saying such things.

Nevertheless I had the feeling that this wasn't the end of it, and that either later in the year or else in the spring the king and his army would be back. The sparrowhawk was hovering, watching and waiting for the right moment to stoop and strike. That's what I said to Skalpi, although he surely knew it already. His temper grew shorter and those grey moods of his ever darker as the harvest season passed, the slaughter month began, the trees shed their golden raiment and the first frosts came. He would ride with me and sit with me in the orchard and let me read or sing to him, but he also continued to spend much of his time alone, and in those moments when the gloom overtook him there was little I or anyone could do to stir him from it.

In the meantime life at Heldeby continued much as it had done. As it had to, if we wanted to place food upon the table and have fuel and warm clothes to last us through the winter. I often confided in Tova, and she in me. We shared our worries and exchanged tales, and over the months I suppose we gradually became friends. I'd grown up surrounded by boys, you see. All my life when I was young I'd wanted a sister I could play with and whom I could confide in when I was feeling sad. Eadmer and I were close, but that was different. While our brothers were alive he was more interested in being with them and joining in their adventures. Exploring the woods near the house, stretching hides over wicker frames to make boats that they could use to see what was downstream. Wrestling with them, even though they were much bigger and stronger and so always bested him.

I never had anyone I felt I could talk to. There'd been my mother, I suppose, but she hadn't had much time for me. So I never had a friend, a true friend, until I came to Heldeby and until I met Tova.

It helped, I think, that we had a lot in common, strange though that probably sounds. We both found ourselves in situations not of our choosing. We were both looking for companionship and both desperately needed an ally, in particular against Orm, whose father seemed to have given up trying to restrain him.

It was about that time, as winter approached, that we first began to hear rumours of the rebellion, of a great host gathering somewhere beyond the old wall to drive the Normans from the kingdom and back across the Narrow Sea. And we heard as well that the ætheling, Eadgar, who had been deprived of the throne by Wilelm and kept as a hostage at his court, had managed to escape his captors and had fled. To join the rising, some said; others said to lead it. But there were so many rumours coming from all quarters in the weeks before and after Yule that it was hard to be sure which held any sort of truth at all and which were just wishful thinking.

Orm, for his part, wanted to join the ætheling, to take up arms and fight. Skalpi, though, forbade it, insisting that the rebellion was nothing more than foolish hearsay, and in any case no army ever chose to march in winter, when the ground was hard and the weather foul and food scarce, when seasoned fighting men could drop dead of a chill while the enemy were safely ensconced behind the walls of their strongholds, keeping warm by their hearths, as all sensible folk did in the cold months. Orm sulked and lashed out, and managed to put out the eye of one of the neighbouring ceorls he often sparred with, and the longer it went on the worse he became, and Tova was worried, too, weren't you? You didn't know what he might do next and if he might threaten you again, or worse.

You came to me, I remember, seeking my help because you didn't know who else to go to, and I promised he wouldn't touch you and that I would make sure of it, although at first I wasn't sure how, but I'd given you my word, and so I went to Skalpi that afternoon – about a week before midwinter I think it was – and asked if he might grant you your freedom. I didn't give him the real reason why, but said that we had more than enough slaves to work in the kitchen and in the dairy and in the fields, whereas I needed a maidservant, someone to help in the house and hall who could keep me company in the afternoons while I was at my stitching and my weaving. All of those things were true, of course, and I knew that as long as you were with me and a part of the household, Orm would never dare come near you.

Of course he agreed, as I knew he would. More than anything he wanted to please me, and so he made the arrangements. Thorvald was heartened when he heard what Skalpi intended, because granting someone their freedom was the mark of a generous soul, and God would duly record such a worthy deed in his book and remember it when the end of days came. There was a ceremony of sorts, although it was only myself and Skalpi and his sons and Ælfric who witnessed it, together with maybe half a dozen men from nearby manors, with the priest there to preside.

We went out on foot to the crossroads where our lands abutted our neighbours', even though it was raining and the tracks were clogged with mud. There my husband and I in turn clasped Tova's hands while Thorvald spoke a prayer in Latin and Skalpi said the necessary words, and then when we returned to the hall he brought us forward one by one, to make our marks on the charter that Thorvald had prepared confirming Tova's freedom. I was first to be called, and out of the corner of my eye I saw Orm scowling. I tried to ignore him, to put him from my mind, but I couldn't help but smile at the victory I'd won over him, small though it might be.

Thorvald pointed to the place where I was to place my cross, forgetting that I knew how to read and so could see my name already spelt out below Skalpi's. Or close enough, anyway: the priest's spindly letters were bunched up so tightly together that I wasn't sure that they were all present, but they were recognisable, and I supposed that's all they needed to be. After that I swore myself to keep and defend Tova, and you swore that you would serve me faithfully always. We both shed some tears, didn't we? I even saw the old priest weeping a little too, and I hugged him and Skalpi and thanked them both.

'Forgive me,' says Guthred, 'but what does all this have to do with why you were running?'

'I'm coming to that. I'm only telling you this because I don't want you to think badly of me for what happened.'

'Why?' asks Beorn. 'What did you do?'

Tova meets her lady's gaze, and she sees the trepidation in her eyes. But it's too late for Merewyn to have any second thoughts, especially now that she has come so far in her story. What choice does she have now but to tell them how it ends?

Winter came and went. It wasn't as harsh as some, not as bitter as this one, but the winds came rushing down from the high moors, and rain battered the hall for days on end. There was a storm one night that screeched and roared and made the whole house creak, waking everyone. In the morning we found that it had torn the thatch from one of the barns, and Skalpi crossed himself and said the old gods, the gods of the Danes, the gods of his father's father, were stirring from their slumber, beating their war drums as they marched to give battle with the new religion, and that was the surest sign that bad times were to come.

Then, just as the days were beginning to grow bright again and the first shoots were bursting forth, there came another long spell of rain. The rivers rushed and frothed and swirled and swelled until eventually they overspilled their banks and all the meadows were under water. The timber bridge, which had apparently stood for forty years, was swept away, and the wath was too dangerous to cross for weeks afterwards, so we were cut off for much of that time, and that meant that tidings of goings-on elsewhere were hard to come by. We'd hear things sometimes if we needed to send to manors further up the valley to trade fleeces for flour or salted pork for rolls of linen, but it was only what they'd learned from others, who themselves had heard it in turn from Byrhtred, who'd been told it by Æthelwulf, who had first heard it from Maning, so it was difficult to know how much of what reached our ears was true, if anything.

Of course it turned out it was all true: the rumours of rebellion which Skalpi had dismissed as mere fancies, everything. Some time before Christmas the ætheling had fled King Wilelm's court and gone into St Cuthbert's land, where he'd made common cause with the lord of Bebbanburh and other noble families and had marched south. A great battle had followed at Dunholm, where the Normans had been slaughtered in their thousands, or

215

so it was said, until the streets were choked with their corpses and the river below the town had run red with their blood.

Not long after, the ætheling had retaken Eoferwic, and the Norman whom the king had made shire reeve was besieged inside his castle, and suddenly men began to think that young Eadgar might be the one to drive the Normans from this land back into the sea. But then, as you know, the king rode north with great haste, gathering his vassals, his foot warriors and his riding men as he went. He came upon the ætheling and his army before dawn one morning, forced his way inside the city and took them by surprise, routing them and causing them to flee back into the north.

So it was told to us. The great rising against the Normans, over before it had hardly begun.

When he heard the news, Orm was livid. I was in our chambers with Skalpi eating our midday meal when he burst in uninvited.

'You should have let me go,' he said without so much as a greeting. He didn't glance at me; I don't know that he even realised I was there, so consumed was he with rage. All his attention was on his father. 'Now the rebellion is over, and instead of marching under Eadgar's banner all I've done is waste my time here.'

'Do you think the rebels failed because they lacked your spear and your shield?' Skalpi asked him. 'Do you? Don't be foolish. If you'd gone, you'd most likely have got yourself killed.'

Orm stood across the table from his father. 'At least I have the courage to fight for my land and my people, something you would never do!'

Red-faced, Skalpi rose. 'Apologise,' he said.

'Why should I apologise?' Orm retorted. 'Why should I say sorry for speaking the truth?'

And Skalpi struck him.

I'd never seen my husband take his hand to anyone, not even a slave, and certainly not his own son. As long as I'd known him, he'd always been among the most mild-mannered of men. I'd heard that in his time he'd fought in wars and had killed men, run them through with spear and sword. That was not the Skalpi I knew, but in that moment there was such a wildness in his eyes. As if something inside him had broken, I thought, as if the Devil had somehow taken hold of him. His mouth was twisted into an expression I'd never seen before, an expression I'll never forget as long as I live. His teeth bared. Breathing hard. Like a hound gone mad. And I was afraid of him suddenly, as I'd never been afraid before.

He struck his son across the side of his head, hard enough to send him reeling, stumbling sideways so that he almost fell over a stool. How Orm managed to stay on his feet, I don't know, but he did. His ear was bleeding where I guessed Skalpi's ring had cut him, blood streaming down his face, dripping on to the rushes and the straw. He put a hand to his cheek, and his fingers and palm came away smeared red, and he just looked at them, bewildered, his mouth hanging dumbly open like he didn't understand what had happened, like he couldn't believe what his father had done.

'You dare disrespect me?' Skalpi roared. 'You don't know what I've given for this kingdom, for my people. I've marched until my feet were raw and bloody. I've stood in the shield wall with Earl Siward against the Scots, in fog and hail, wind and snow, my fingers so stiff with cold that afterwards I couldn't make them let go of my spear haft. I've killed more men than you've winters to your name. I've done things I hoped I'd never have to do, seen horrors you wouldn't believe if I told you. I've done more than you ever will, and I did it all to defend these lands, you ingrate. These lands, which our family has held by charter right since the days of my father and his father, so that you and your brother might in turn inherit them from me some day. Do you hear me?'

That's what he said, more or less, while Orm simply stared at him. For once he had nothing to say.

'Next time you think about accusing me of faint-heartedness, remember that,' said Skalpi, then went out, without finishing his meal, without as much as another word either to Orm or to me, as if in his anger he'd forgotten I was there as well.

Maybe part of the reason he was angry was that he believed Orm was right, even if he didn't want to admit it. He might have been nearing fifty and as far as I knew hadn't lifted a blade or donned byrnie or helmet in years. He certainly hadn't in the months I'd known him. In spite of that, I think he felt he should have been there, riding with Eadgar, fighting against the foreigners, doing what he could to defend the land he loved, the land in which he had grown up. The one thing that gave him hope was that the ætheling had escaped the battle and probably still lived. As long as he did, the remaining rebels, the ones who'd survived Eoferwic, had someone to rally around.

Those were strange times. All that anyone talked about, in the fields or the hall or the yard or the pigpens, was the war against the foreigners. Whenever more news came our way, Skalpi would summon Ælfric to consult with him as to what he should do. There was great excitement but at the same time great uncertainty, because no one knew what the Normans would do next. King Wilelm himself had gone back south to put down risings elsewhere, but he'd left behind even more men to occupy Eoferwic and the surrounding country. They were seizing manors close to the city in reprisal for the rebellion, and we heard of scouting parties riding north into St Cuthbert's land to try to root Eadgar out. We knew they hadn't succeeded, though, because just after midsummer a man arrived at Heldeby, sent by the ætheling himself.

He came alone, arriving one bright morning. He rode a white horse, and not some old nag but a stallion, well bred and spirited. Weeks of dust and dirt caked his shoes and his cloak and his trews, which were full of holes, some of them stitched back up and others not. By the state of him he looked poor, but his clothing was fine, or at least it had been at one time. I remember thinking that his tunic must once have been reddish in colour, although it had faded to a sort of mud-brown, and it was embroidered at the cuffs and the neck and hem and along the sleeves, but all the threads were coming loose. He was about the same age as you, Beorn, or maybe a bit older. It was hard to tell; his face was drawn and he had dark pouches under his eyes, as if he hadn't slept properly in several days.

The stranger drew to a halt in the yard, surrounded by a cloud of dust that his mount had kicked up, and demanded that the lord or steward or whoever held this manor come out to greet him, for he had been sent by Eadgar himself. As soon as he said that, there was a great commotion. Word was passed around, and everyone set down their tools and whatever it was they were supposed to be doing, and flocked to see this man and hear what he had come to say. Skalpi was out with Orm and Ælfric riding Heldeby's bounds, as they did every week, examining fences and hedges that might need repairing, drove roads and tracks that needed to be cleared of brambles and nettles, which were always encroaching and making passage difficult for travellers. I sent someone out to look for them and bring them back while I stepped forward and told him plainly that in the meantime the stranger should address himself to me, the Lady Merewyn, Skalpi's wife and head of his household.

He looked at me down his nose, from atop his white horse. I guessed he was unmarried since he was clearly not used to being spoken to in that way by a woman or to showing her any courtesy. But everyone was clamouring for him to speak, pressing close on every side, and so, puffed up with his own self-importance, he gave in. He called himself Ascytel and said that he was a staller in King Eadgar's service. Not ætheling but king. That was the first time I'd ever heard him called by that title, his real title, and it sounded strange, although it probably shouldn't have, given that many people say that it was his right by birth. Ascytel said that he had travelled across field and fell, brook and marsh and moor, that he had come from beyond the old wall in the far north, where a host was gathering. Gathering, he said, for another campaign. Another attempt to take back the kingdom from the invaders who sullied the earth with our blood. Many had died at Eoferwic, but many more still lived, he said, and they were determined that one defeat should not be the end of their ambitions. King Eadgar was sending word throughout the land, sending men like him, like Ascytel, into each shire, each wapentake, each manor, to rally support among the English. Sending the message that we were not defeated, that the rebels' fire was undimmed, and that despite all the hardships they had suffered, the struggle still went on.

We could yet wrest the crown from the usurper's brow, he said. We could yet strike him down and drive the Normans from these shores. To do that, though, Eadgar needed our help. He needed the help of every able-bodied man in England. Every man who already possessed a shield or helmet, his own shirt of leather or of mail, and even those who were lacking. If he knew how

220

to wield an axe or sword or seax, if he knew how to thrust and trap and cut, if he had fought before, then so much the better, but if he did not and had not, it didn't matter. As long as he had hands with which to hold spear or spade or hoe, and feet with which he was willing to march for victory and in the name of the kingdom, in the name of the English people, that proud and ancient race, that was what counted.

Even then I remember thinking it was madness. A man from every carucate of land – that was what was required by kings in times of war, according to both the law and ancient custom. Heldeby was ten carucates in size, and we could manage without that many men if they went away to fight. Not easily, because the others would have to take on their work, but it could be done. If we willingly gave up every able-bodied man, though, or half or even one third of them, what were we to do if they still had not returned by harvest-time? How did Ascytel expect us to keep up the manor? To feed ourselves? Surely he didn't expect us to starve for the rebellion's sake?

But when I asked him he only shrugged. 'This is what I've been told to tell you,' he said, and that was all he would say to me, insisting that the rest he must discuss with my husband and my husband alone.

Skalpi returned soon after that, and they went to his chamber, where they had long discussions which I was not invited to attend. These were matters of war, Skalpi said, and should be talked over between men. And they did talk. For over an hour they talked, before finally they emerged and Ascytel mounted his stallion and rode off to the next manor and the one beyond that and the one beyond that, with the same message for all of them.

'What did you say to him?' I asked Skalpi when our visitor was no more than a white dot disappearing over the brow of the hill.

'I said what I had to,' he said, tight-lipped. He clearly didn't want to speak any further, but he was mistaken if he thought I was going to leave it at that.

There was a stiffness to his bearing that I didn't like as he went back inside the hall.

'And what was that?' I asked.

'I promised ten men, because that's what I owe. The strongest and the fittest because they're the ones most likely to make it back.'

'No more than ten?'

'That's what I promised,' he said and then hesitated, but when I pressed him he went on: 'I'm not going to force any man to go who doesn't want to, but at the same time I won't deny anyone who's able and willing the chance to take up arms and join us. Ascytel was right about that much. We need every spear we can muster, if we're to have any chance of defeating the foreigners.'

I remember the feeling in my stomach at that moment. '"We"?' I echoed, my voice small.

He placed his hands upon my shoulders and looked straight at me. 'If we lose this war, we will lose everything else as well. I can't stand aside while others risk their lives on my behalf. I might be old but I can still ride and I can still lead men. I know what it means to fight in the shield wall. So you must see that if Eadgar is marching, then I must march too.'

But I didn't see. 'You can't.'

'I have to,' he replied and turned away. He'd made up his mind, he said, given his word to Ascytel to give on his behalf to Eadgar himself.

I clutched at his arm and tried to persuade him to send someone else in his place. He didn't have to go himself. I tried to hold back my tears. I didn't want him to dismiss my pleas as those

222

of a desperate and foolish woman. He listened patiently, as he always did. Although I didn't love him as he had hoped I would, I'd grown fond of him. And I was worried for him. He had the resolve and he was afraid of nothing. That he was strong enough in that sense, I had no doubt. And it was true that he didn't toil for breath or walk with a limp or talk about his creaking bones, as did many men his age. He wasn't in ill health, but he wasn't battle-fit, and surely he knew that.

I asked him when was the last time he'd drawn his sword from its scabbard, or even when he'd last lifted it from the kist beneath his bed.

He didn't answer. He had none to give.

I couldn't help thinking that if Eadgar's first rebellion had failed, why should it be different this time? How many more would die?

And I confess I was worried for myself as well, although I would never tell him so. Why not? Because it would sound as though I had no confidence in him, and also because I feared it would sound selfish. And it was selfish, I suppose. For I was asking myself, if he didn't survive, what would happen to me? As his wife I commanded some respect, modest though it was, and had protection in law. As his widow I'd have hardly any of that. I'd either have to take another husband, go back to my brother's house or else go into the cloister, and the thought of any of those things made me despair. For while life at Heldeby was not always easy, the truth was that I'd grown comfortable there. Like the sapling, I was at last beginning to flourish, and I didn't want things to change.

But I said none of this. He sat upon a stool on the dais while I paced around and around.

'I am a warrior,' Skalpi said eventually. He spoke quietly, but his words filled the hall. 'My father was a warrior, and his father too. Both of them strove hard to defend these lands of ours. And I must do the same.'

I didn't try to argue with him. Not when he said that. I'd done all I could and knew if I said anything more it was likely only to strengthen his determination. He was like that.

The next few days swept by in a haze. For so long things had been quiet; from where we were, in the hill country on the edge of the high moors, the wars against the Normans had seemed a world away. But suddenly everything had changed.

Preparations began that very evening. Skalpi called a muster at the ancient stone that stood in the meadow not far from the crossroads, to which he invited every man and boy over the age of eleven, which included Orm but not Ketil. As the sun grew low, two dozen came, of whom he sent away four because they were too young, another because he could only walk with the aid of a crutch and was nearly sixty besides, and lastly Wulfrun, the smith's wife, because she was a woman, though she protested she was as strong as any man, and proved it too by clouting around the ear one of the younger men who laughed.

That left eighteen, whom Skalpi watched over the coming days as Ælfric sparred with them in the training yard, using poles and wicker shields in place of the real things. He watched as they were formed into groups and made to practise the shield wall, and he watched as they were each handed a spear and, one by one, took it in turns to run at a scarecrow and impale it. He watched as they hurled javelins at targets in the fallow field beside the coppice, and gave advice to each man on how to hold the shaft and how to plant his feet, and where his head should be as he aimed and then loosed it. At all of this there were some who were better than others, and equally there were some who clearly had no skill and would not survive long. He dismissed these, saying the last thing anyone in battle wanted was someone on his flank he couldn't trust to hold his own, because when the lines clash each man relies on his friends to help keep him alive. If the shield wall breaks through ineptitude or cowardice, then everyone dies. He had seen it happen, time after time. So he would take only the best.

That's how he explained it to me, anyway.

The smith was busy too: the sound of steel on steel rang out from dawn till night as blades were sharpened and dents in helmets hammered out and new links added to Skalpi's mail shirt to repair holes and because he was a little wider around the stomach than he had been the last time he'd donned it. Provisions were set aside from the storehouses to last the men for a couple of weeks, since we had no idea how well supplied the army would be when they joined it. While all that was happening, Tova and I worked to repair Skalpi's faded banner, helped by some of the younger slave girls, whose fingers were nimble and whose sight was good enough. It was a task for more pairs of hands than we had, but the other women were all busy mending cloaks and tunics and caps and shoes and everything else their husbands and sons and brothers might need.

The banner had been stored in the same strongbox as his silver, beneath the floor of Skalpi's chamber. In brown and blue thread, it showed an owl in flight with wings outstretched, but over the years the damp had got to it and caused one corner to rot away, while colours that once had been bright were now muted.

'An owl,' Skalpi said when he came to see how we were doing, 'because it is ever watchful, because it chooses to hunt while other creatures sleep, and because it is wiser than all the other birds.'

By the time he was ready to leave, it looked more or less as it

225

was meant to. We had no brown thread and no time to buy more at market, so we used black instead, but Skalpi was pleased, and that was all that mattered.

That was a sad day. I couldn't bear even to watch as the band mustered in the yard. Instead I stayed at my stitching while outside Skalpi barked instructions to the men he was taking, fifteen in all. Horses whickered, men called to one another, and their wives and daughters were crying. I could hear Father Thorvald's dull voice as he said Mass in the open and prayed that the Lord kept his warriors safe from harm.

I didn't want to see them. Most of all I didn't want to face Skalpi. Eventually he came looking for me, as I knew he would. He held me tightly against his chest, and I wrapped my arms around him. Neither of us spoke, and the only sound was that of my sobs. He kissed me on the forehead and then on the cheek and lastly and longest on the lips. Then all too soon he broke off our embrace and I knew it was time. I thought about trying to sway him once more, but I didn't. I knew it wouldn't make any difference. All I could do was wish him well and pray that he returned safely.

I followed him out into the yard, where he told Ælfric to take care of me and of the manor in his absence, and then he mounted Hengest, his gelding. I saw men young and old, some of whom I knew had seen battle before because they had the scars to show it, although most hadn't. Almost all carried around their necks some rune charm or trinket given to them by their loved ones; each had a spear and a knife or seax, most had a shield and a handful had helmets. A couple had padded jerkins of cloth, a couple more had leather shirts. None possessed mail – save Skalpi, of course, and Orm, who was in as bad a temper as I'd ever seen him. His eyes were dark as if he hadn't slept, and he had a look about him of such fury. He snapped at everyone who approached him as if they'd personally slighted him, and kept his distance from his father. I didn't know if someone had said or done something to upset him. I had supposed he would be happy because he was finally getting his wish. He was riding to war, being given the chance to prove himself, but evidently even that wasn't enough to please him. A part of me was glad he was taking his anger elsewhere and putting it to good use, but that wasn't much consolation.

All of Heldeby had gathered to watch them go. I stood with Tova and a few of the alewives and the miller's daughter. Children stood beside their mothers, the younger ones clutching their legs, some of them wailing. They didn't understand what was happening, what everyone was doing in one place, why they were all hugging and crying, why their fathers and brothers were leaving or where they were going. And how could they? I didn't understand it, not entirely, and if it didn't make sense to me then how could it make sense to them?

We followed them to the crossroads. That was as far as Skalpi wanted us to come, so we halted there, at the edge of the manor. He told us to be strong and to pray for victory, and his gaze found me in the crowd. I can still remember the look in his eyes. Until then it had never occurred to me that he might be just as anxious as me. As I said, it had always seemed to me that there was nothing in the world that frightened him, but I understood then how wrong I was. Maybe no one else noticed it, but I did – a look in his eyes, as if he wasn't sure whether he would be coming back.

He must have realised what I saw, realised that he'd betrayed himself, because the blood rose to his cheeks. He tried to hide it by quickly turning away and raising a cry for King Eadgar, for Northumbria and for England. He rode to the head of the column, and then they were on their way. All the men waved as they went, calling out to their children and womenfolk, who waved in return, wishing them luck.

All the men, that was, except Skalpi. He didn't falter or glance over his shoulder. Not once. Not even for a moment. I suppose he thought that if he looked back others might see what I had seen. It wasn't that he was proud, or it wasn't just that. He knew that men were looking to him as their leader, relying on him to give them encouragement and strength. More than anything, he needed their respect and their confidence. And so he just rode on, his gaze fixed on the track ahead. I watched as they grew further and further away, until they were dots amid the haze: dots that became pinpricks and then were no more.

He was gone.

It was weeks before we had any news. When we did, it was never much. Often it didn't make sense, and we were never sure of the order in which things were supposed to have happened. A battle here, raiding and hall burnings there. The king of the Danes had supposedly sent a great fleet bearing thousands of warriors, which had entered the Humbre and sent messengers to Eadgar to seek an alliance with him. He'd accepted and together they had marched on Eoferwic and this time had burned it to the ground.

I know now that's what happened, but at the time it all sounded so far-fetched we didn't know what to make of it all. This was the first any of us knew about the Danes' arrival, and we didn't know whether it was a good thing or not. Besides, we had worries of our own: every week we heard stories of brigands and outlaws roaming the shire, taking advantage of the uncertainty to waylay travellers, to steal sheep and grain and whatever else they could lay their hands on, to extort silver with the threat of violence from stewards and village priests, who had no choice but to give them what they asked because their lords and protectors were away fighting. If they couldn't pay or they refused, they were beaten or killed, and their homes torched.

And so we lived in fear. Fear for our own safety, and in my case fear for my family as well. We used to exchange letters every few weeks, but I'd heard nothing from them in months. I didn't know if Eadmer had also gone to join the rebellion; he was still young and I didn't like to think of him standing in the shield wall facing the Normans. I was desperate for the war to be over, and I didn't care whether it was defeat or victory, as long as Skalpi came home safely, and soon. Where he was and what had happened to him, I didn't know. If he'd sent us any messages, as I kept hoping he would, they never reached our ears.

In the meantime I looked after Ketil and did my best to keep him busy by teaching him his letters, although he was becoming more difficult as he grew older. More like his brother. He was a sackless boy, refusing to sit still for long, and was easily frustrated, but I persisted because I knew it was what Skalpi would want. When I wasn't with him, I was helping Ælfric, doing my best to keep the manor running as it should, although the fact that so many of the younger men had gone away made the work more difficult, especially as the months passed and the harvest came round and we needed as many hands as possible to reap and sheaf and stook, to plant turnips and mow hay, to pull up leeks and onions and carrots from the vegetable garden behind Thorvald's house. I was out there in the fields with them, with my sleeves bunched to my elbows, and my dress rolled up, helping where I—

Why is that funny? Do you think I spend so long at my weaving

229

and my sewing that I don't know how to use a scythe or flail or winnowing basket? I might not have seen as much of the world as some of you, and maybe I don't have as many calluses and my face isn't as weather-worn as yours, Beorn, but I know what it means to work hard.

As I was saying, the months passed and the seasons turned. It wasn't until after the winter barley had been sown that we had the first news of the rebellion. The first proper news, I mean, because that's when our men started coming back.

'And was your husband among them?' asks Guthred.

Merewyn shakes her head.

Tova knows this part of the story. Seeing them again after so many months, the joy that turned so quickly to anguish, as she and everyone else abandoned the pails they were carrying, the firewood they were chopping, the shovels they were using to clean out the groops, and rushed out to greet them, only to see how few they were.

Even now it hurts her to think about it. How Merewyn can talk about these things without faltering or breaking into tears, Tova has no idea.

No, Skalpi wasn't with them. There were just four, and he wasn't one of them. When I asked where he was, they looked at each other blankly until one spoke up. Ceolred the miller's son, it was, although at first I didn't recognise him because his face was blotched yellow with so many bruises and his nose was out of shape. He couldn't have been much older than seventeen years, but he was hobbling like a greybeard, leaning on his spear haft for support.

Ceolred said they didn't know where their lord was or what

had happened to him. When the Danes abandoned them and the rebellion collapsed, he said, all fell into chaos. He told me that one afternoon the four of them had returned to camp having spent the day collecting armfuls of firewood to find everything in disarray, men running everywhere, saddling their horses if they had them, abandoning tents and cooking pots, making for the hills. Eadgar and his huscarls had fled back into the north, and word was that the Normans were only an hour away, that King Wilelm was riding at the head of a mounted army thousands strong.

They didn't even have time to strike camp, Ceolred said. They just snatched up what they could, and then, like everyone else, they ran. They thought if they could make their way back home they'd perhaps find Skalpi here.

Others returned over the next few days, alone or in pairs, all with tear-filled stories of the things they'd seen and friends who had died at Norman hands, and there was much grieving. The brothers Ubba and Uffa, both gaunt-faced, bruised and hungry. Hæsta the smith and Saba the goatherd.

Last of all to come was Orm. He arrived on foot and he arrived alone, his cheeks scratched and cut in a hundred places, his lip scarred, his eyes dark and hooded, clutching at his side where his tunic was matted with blood. He still had his sword, but his shield rim was cracked and the leather facing flapped where it had come loose. He didn't say what had happened to his horse, and he knew nothing about his father, except that they'd become separated when they ran into a Norman scouting party on the road home. He had searched for Skalpi but couldn't find him, and he had feared the worst. When Ælfric and I told him that his father hadn't returned, he stared at us for the longest time, his eyes hollow. None of us wanted to believe he was dead, but as the days and the weeks passed, the harder it became to deny. I kept waiting, waking every dawn hoping that would be the day when he came back.

But he never did. Each morning the frosts lay heavier across the land. That's when we first learned about the raiding armies that King Wilelm was sending into Lincolnescir and Heldernesse to root out the remaining rebels. Even then we never thought the enemy would have any reason to come to Heldeby, and indeed as the weeks went by we heard less and less about the Normans and so assumed they must have gone back to their strongholds for the winter, which was fast approaching.

The leaves had long since fallen and the days were growing ever shorter, which meant Ælfric and I were supposed to be discussing how many hogs we should slaughter and how many cattle we'd be able to keep fed and so how many we should sell at market, and what price we might expect to get for them. But I couldn't face it; my mind was filled with worry about my brother, and about whether or not my husband still lived, and so I spent more and more time alone in my bower. Tova would bring me food from time to time, and if she wasn't busy with other things she would come and sit with me for a while, and we would spin yarn together, sometimes talking and sometimes not.

After a few days Thorvald came to me. At first he seemed reluctant to speak and kept on fingering the cross that hung around his neck, as he often did when he was nervous. Once he saw I was growing impatient, though, he came out with it. He said he had been discussing matters with Ælfric, and they had agreed that if I wasn't well enough or willing to fulfil my duties as lady then perhaps it would be better for me to allow Orm to take on those burdens, as Skalpi's heir.

I replied indignantly that this was no time to be talking about heirs, since we didn't even know yet whether or not Skalpi was dead, and that until I saw his body I refused to believe anyone who claimed that he was. I'd convinced myself that he must have fallen into the hands of the enemy, which was why we'd heard nothing from him. All I could do was pray that they had spared him, although in truth I had no idea how likely that was.

Thorvald wrung his hands and tried to soothe me, but I would not be soothed. I shouted him down and ordered him to go away, which he did, meekly in the end. That evening, though, he came to see me again, and this time he brought with him Orm and Ælfric.

'Everyone is concerned for you,' the reeve said. 'As much as we all miss Skalpi, we can't go on hoping against hope for ever. Sooner or later we have to accept the truth. He won't be coming back.'

When I heard this, I broke down, sobbing, sitting on the edge of the bed with my hair in my face, while Ælfric explained solemnly that I would keep the portion of land that had been set aside on my marriage as my morning gift, but Orm would become lord of Heldeby, as was his right. I saw the priest nodding sagely, and through my tears I caught Orm smirking. It was the merest glimmer of a smile and swiftly concealed, vanishing almost as soon as it appeared, and I knew he hadn't meant me to see it. But see it I did, and it was all I needed.

I rose and hurled myself at him, fists flailing, screaming all the most hateful things I could think of, every insult, every curse. Words he probably thought I didn't know. Words I'd hardly ever spoken before. I seized his collar and shook him, or tried to, and for the first time said what I really thought of him and that he wasn't fit to be his father's heir. He tried to fend me off, but I was quicker and I slapped his face. At first he just looked stunned, but then he made as if to strike me back.

Ælfric seized my arm and held it firm, and though I struggled I couldn't break his grip. 'Enough,' he bellowed at Orm, whose hand was raised. 'She's your father's wife.'

He spat on the floor at my feet. 'His widow, you mean.'

'Maybe so,' Ælfric said, 'but she still deserves your respect.'

'Why? You see how she hates me. She doesn't respect me.'

'Because you're a vile creature,' I said, and suddenly all those thoughts I'd never dared voice all came tumbling out. He was an evil child who cared for nothing and no one but himself. Skalpi had been ashamed of him, ashamed of what he had grown into.

'Don't talk to me about him,' Orm warned me.

But the weir had burst. The reeve and priest tried to calm me, tried to shout me down, but they couldn't stop the torrent. And so I went on. How Skalpi used to confess to me his despair, because all Orm seemed to dream about was war and violence and killing and glory. Because he refused to understand that a good lord had responsibilities and couldn't simply do whatever he wanted, whenever he wanted. Because Skalpi thought he had failed him and failed as a father. How sometimes he doubted whether Orm was even his own son, or whether Ælfswith's falseness had led to him raising a cuckoo in his nest.

Orm's eyes grew narrower, his cheeks redder, and I thought he might again try to take his hand to me. Instead he just turned and went without saying anything, and I think that was the first time I ever saw him lost for words.

I took ever greater care to avoid him after that, although it wasn't easy. Whenever I saw him he greeted me with a stare that made my skin prickle. I thought about going back to my brother's house for a while, or perhaps for good. When a pedlar arrived a few days before Yule selling wax candles and herbs and spices, I asked him if he might take a letter to Eadmer. He agreed, but whether it ever got through, I don't know. From what he told us, in the wake of the rebellion's collapse all order had broken down, and the roads were growing ever more dangerous. Everyone lived in fear that the Normans would come and take possession of this land, but most agreed that wouldn't happen until the spring if it happened at all, and there was a good chance that it wouldn't, if King Wilelm was merciful.

You'll tell me now that we should have started making preparations to leave without delay, that it was reckless hope we were clinging to, that we should have known that eventually the Normans would come. But it was our land, our home. Many of those who lived there had hardly set foot outside the manor bounds; as far as they were concerned, that was their world, and so it would remain until the day someone came to take it from them. And so we waited and prayed, and tried not to lose faith but to convince ourselves and each other that no matter how dark things seemed at that moment, all would be well and God would deliver us from harm. It was all we could do.

That was the least joyful Christmas I can remember. No one was in the mood for feasting or celebrating, although there was a lot of drinking, most of it done by Orm, during the day as well as in the evening. He would lash out unexpectedly, usually for a petty reason: if his food reached the table cold or if the girl holding his cup happened to spill some because she was trembling so much. He would argue loudly and at length with Ælfric about matters to do with the running of the manor, thinking he knew better and saying he didn't know why his father had put up with him for so long. Maybe their broken friendship was the reason he was so angry. He refused both confession and communion, which upset Thorvald. And so he slighted the two men who might otherwise have been his most useful allies. I noticed

235

too that Ketil, who had always been his most loyal friend, spent less and less time with him. They had often enjoyed playing tæfl together, but now when he lost Orm would shove the board from the table and send the pieces flying across the chamber.

Maybe he felt abandoned, and that's why he began seeking solace and companionship elsewhere. The slave girls quickened their step whenever he was near, and fathers took care to keep their daughters within sight. I took to eating my meals in my bower so that I didn't have to suffer his gaze from across the dining table. Some days he would hardly touch his food. His hunger was of a different sort, I knew – one that was less easily sated.

At night I struggled to sleep unless I knew he'd already taken to his bed or had drunk himself insensible on the floor of the hall. I'd lie awake for hours at a time, listening until everything was still and I felt safe enough to close my eyes. He'd never dare come into my chamber, I tried telling myself, but I didn't really believe it, and so after a while I moved myself and all my possessions into my own house on the other side of the estate. It was more confined and simpler, built of daubed wattle rather than oak, but it was further from Orm, and that was all that mattered. Some nights I'd ask Tova to stay with me and either sleep in the room below or else on a mattress on the floor of my chamber, but that was as much for the sake of her company, so that I didn't have to be alone with my sorrow and my fears.

Skalpi was gone. The rebellion had failed and there was no telling what would happen now. Foreigners were overrunning the kingdom and everything was passing into shadow and ruin. I felt under siege, with enemies everywhere I turned, not just outside but now also within my own home, so that it no longer felt like a place of safety but somewhere I needed to escape, if only I knew how.

Desperation changes you. You stop seeing things clearly and instead do things you'd never otherwise imagine, because there is no other choice. Before, I'd heard it said that in times of hunger poor folk would sometimes gather together all their shoes, put them into a great cauldron and boil the leather into a broth because there was nothing else to eat and that was the best they could manage. As a child I'd squirmed when my father said things like that, which were supposed to teach me how lucky I was to be the daughter of a thegn and to have warm clothes, a timber hall to sleep in and as much meat and ale as I needed, but I'd never entirely believed such stories because I never understood.

I understand now.

'What I still don't understand is why *you* couldn't have gone away,' Oslac says. 'If things were as bad as you suggest.'

'I know,' Merewyn says. 'And I did think about it. Mainly it was pride. Heldeby was my home as well, and I didn't see why I should be forced to leave. But it was also hope. A part of me still thought that, any day, Skalpi would come back and all would be well again.'

'So what happened after that?'

Merewyn breathes deeply. 'Three nights ago he came to my house. Orm, I mean. It was late or early, I'm not sure. I was anxious and my head was so full of worry that I hadn't been able to settle. I'd struggled to sleep and kept on waking, each time in a fright. I heard footsteps in the room beneath my chamber—'

'Was there no lock on the door?' Beorn asks.

'There was. I was sure I'd locked it before going to bed, but maybe he had smashed it. Maybe that was what woke me, although I don't remember hearing a sound.'

'Or else maybe you forgot,' Oslac says.

'No,' says Merewyn firmly. 'I remembered, I'm sure of it. Especially because I didn't know if was just Orm I ought to be frightened of.'

'What do you mean?'

Earlier that evening, just as the light was fading, Ælfric had returned from riding the bounds looking pale, which was unnerving in itself because he usually wasn't one to let his fears show. He'd spied smoke, he said, rising some way beyond the woods to the south, in the direction of one of our neighbours' halls, and it wasn't the thin kind you might expect to see from a hearth fire or forge, but thick black coils that made a blotch upon the horizon. We wondered what could have happened, but there was an obvious explanation. Everyone was probably thinking the same thing, but no one wanted to say it plainly.

Thorvald suggested we leave immediately and seek refuge up on the moors, just in case. Ælfric agreed, and Ketil tried to persuade his brother that they spoke sense. Orm, though, said there could be any number of reasons for the smoke that had nothing to do with brigands or the enemy, and that since we didn't know for sure there was any danger, we shouldn't worry. Instead, he announced, he would lead a riding party at first light to find out what had happened.

But we did worry. That night Ælfric arranged sentries to sound the horn if anything happened, and agreed to take one of the watches himself, but said we should try to keep this news a secret from everyone else. He didn't want to cause panic. Orm ridiculed him for being frightened of a little smoke; the reeve answered that he would rather be fearful and live than die because he had been drunk and foolish. They argued loudly, and were still going at each other long after dark. I was in the chapel, praying alone by candlelight, across the yard from the hall, and even from there I could hear them hours after most people had gone to their beds. Eventually they came out from the hall, still shouting at one another.

'Lady Merewyn was right,' Ælfric said, and it was hearing my name that caught my attention. 'You don't care about anyone but yourself.'

Orm protested that wasn't true, but the reeve spoke over him: 'If your father could hear you now—'

Orm said, 'I don't care what Skalpi would think. And anyway he's dead.'

'The folk of Heldeby have put their faith in you,' Ælfric said. 'You're their lord. They're looking to you for protection. If you betray their trust and they die because of your recklessness, then may you perish in Hell.'

Orm shot back that he wasn't stupid, that he was no longer a child and that he didn't deserve to be spoken to in such a way, especially not by his own reeve. Besides, he said, he knew what he was doing.

'I doubt that very much,' Ælfric said.

After that things went quiet. I assumed the reeve had gone to take up his watch, and I thought maybe Orm had gone back to the hall to slump on a bench there, as he usually did.

I peered out of the chapel door. When I was sure he wasn't about I went back to my house and to bed. I was halfway between dreaming and waking when I heard movement below. At first I thought it must be dawn and that Tova had come to lay the fire, and then I was confused since usually I had to come down to let her in. But I heard footsteps on the stairs and suddenly none of that mattered. They were heavy footsteps, but slow. Not constant either, but unsteady. I knew then it wasn't Tova. It was him.

239

There were only two chambers on the up-floor: the first led to the second, and that was where I had my bower. I could hear him crossing the room from the stairs, barefoot by the sound of it, and could hear my own heart thumping as I fumbled for the knife under my pillow, the one my father had left me, with the hilt inlaid with silver crosses—

'A knife?' Guthred asks, glancing at the others. 'You kept a knife under your pillow?'

'For protection,' Merewyn says. 'I always told Tova she should do the same, just in case, although in my heart of hearts I never really thought he'd go that far. I just wanted to be ready for him, and to have some way of fending him off. I never planned—'

'But I thought you said Tova was there with you.'

'Not that night,' Tova says. 'I wasn't there every night.'

'That's why I had the knife,' Merewyn explains.

Oslac says, 'He knew you were alone, then.'

'Maybe. I don't know. He was drunk, worse than usual. He was so far gone in his cups that he didn't care. I didn't know what he might do, and I don't think he did either. I was frightened like never before, like I never knew I could be.'

'What did you do?' asks the priest, but from the look on his face Tova guesses he already has some idea.

What did I do? Well, as I was saying, I could hear the groans of the boards, the shuffling of his feet as he crossed the floor. I lay there, as still as anything, clutching the knife in my hand, hardly daring to breathe as I watched the door and listened. At one point he seemed to pause, and everything was so silent that I thought maybe he'd gone away, but then I heard the footsteps again, closer this time, and a fumbling at the latch.

I lay stiff as a board, my whole body gripped by fear. If I screamed, who would hear me? The door swung open, and he ducked beneath the lintel into the room. It was so dark I could barely make him out.

'Don't come any closer,' I told him before he could take another step.

'I didn't mean to wake you,' he mumbled. His words were slow and uneven. It looked like he had something in his hand. A flagon, probably.

'Get out,' I said.

He didn't seem to hear me, or if he did he chose to ignore me. I sat up, one hand drawing the blankets up around me because the night was cold. He came closer, and beneath the covers my fingers curled more tightly around the knife's hilt, but he stopped at the foot of the bed, sitting down with a sigh, facing away from me. I heard the splash of something that I took to be ale, or more likely mead; he favoured stronger drinks when he could lay his hands on them. There was a sourness on him that even from the other end of the bed I could smell, like he'd been sick over himself.

'They hate me,' he said quietly but with an edge to his voice. There was a twinge in my gut as I was reminded of Skalpi. He'd said much the same, if not those exact words, that time all those months ago.

I didn't know if he wanted me to answer and decided it was better to stay quiet and wait to see what he did next. If I just let him say what he wanted, I thought, then maybe he would leave.

'They hate me,' Orm repeated, in case I hadn't heard or because he'd forgotten having already said it. 'All of them. Even Ketil, worm that he is. He used to be my friend, but now they've poisoned him against me. He'll hardly speak a word to my face.

241

They think I don't know the things they say about me. They think they're so clever and that I'm stupid. They think I don't see what's really happening. But I do. You know that, don't you?'

'Of course,' I said, trying not to let my voice tremble. Better just to agree, even if I didn't entirely understand what it was I was supposed to be agreeing with.

'Whatever I do, it's never enough for them. They want me to be like Skalpi. Well, I'm not him, and I never will be. And he's not coming back.'

You don't know that, I wanted to say, and was going to tell him that if Skalpi had been captured there was a chance King Wilelm might sell him back to us. But I decided against contradicting him, and it was a good thing I did, because if I hadn't then I might never have heard him say what he did, and then we might not be here now.

'It's because of me that he's dead,' he said. 'It's all my fault.'

And then something else happened that I wasn't expecting: he started sobbing.

'No, it isn't,' I said, and even then I remember asking myself why I was trying to comfort him, but I was scared and didn't know what else to do. 'It's not your fault. How could it be?'

The tears kept coming. 'It was me,' he said. 'There was never any Norman scouting party.'

He broke off, and it was then that I realised what he was saying. I couldn't feel my limbs any more, could barely breathe. The room was swirling and the darkness was rising all around me.

'What did you do?' I asked, almost choking on the words, but I had to get them out. It couldn't be true, surely? But what else could he mean?

He killed him, I thought. His own father. My husband.

And now he was here, in my chamber, and I knew that I had

to get away from him. I wanted to get up and run, out the door and down the stairs and into the yard, and lose myself in the night, but fear held me. Even drunk he was probably still faster on his feet than me, and besides I had to pass him in order to reach the door.

'He never loved you,' he said as if he hadn't heard me. The tears were gone and his voice was hard. 'Not like I love you. He never cared for you as a man should.' His weight shifted on the end of the bed as he turned towards me. 'But I can.'

'You don't love me,' I said as my blood ran cold. 'You don't.'

Just hearing him say that made me feel I'd done something I shouldn't, something shameful.

'He never deserved you,' he said, and told me that I ought to have married him instead of Skalpi. That he knew how to treat a woman properly, and that if I were his wife, he would make sure to plough me every night, over and over and over, until we were both of us hurting and I was crying for him to stop.

He edged closer, and I tried to draw away. The flagon slipped from his fingers and thudded upon the floorboards, and he was grasping at the blankets covering me, trying to pull them away.

I scrambled out of the bed, so that I stood barefoot in just my undergown, with the blade still in my hand. He followed me, but the mead had made him slow, and I was able to duck out of the way of his hands.

'What did you do, Orm?' I asked again. 'Tell me!'

My path to the door was clear now, but I was no longer thinking about running. I wanted to hear him say it. I wanted him to confess what I knew he'd done. And so I stood my ground, the knife before me pointing in his direction. But still he kept coming. Maybe he didn't see the glint of steel, or maybe he didn't care. I swung wildly, but he caught my wrist and seized it in his hand.

Before I knew what was happening he'd thrust his other hand against my collarbone and I was pinned back against the wall. I tried to break free, but his grip was firm and all those months spent in the training yard had made him strong. His breath was like fire upon my face, and as well as the sour reek of vomit I could smell the mead on him, and I was panicking because I'd lost my one chance of escape and now there was nowhere to go.

'You killed him, didn't you?' I asked, almost in tears myself. I was thinking of Skalpi, who had always been kind, who had always been generous, who had done nothing to deserve his fate. 'Say it. Say you killed him.'

He squeezed my wrist hard; I cried out and dropped the knife, and then he threw me to the floor beside the bed. I fell awkwardly on something hard and round that knocked the breath from my chest. Orm's empty flagon, I realised. I fumbled for the handle as he stepped towards me and leaned down to grab at my hair. At that moment I swung the vessel towards his head. It struck him underneath the chin; he stumbled sideways and fell over his feet, landing in a heap by the kist where I kept my clothes. He was swearing and swearing and swearing, and clutching at his jaw, and I leaped to retrieve the blade lying on the floor.

I didn't stop to think whether what I was doing was right. I was burning inside, and there was only one thought running through my mind.

Orm saw me coming towards him and, still in a daze, tried to get to his feet. His teeth were clenched and there was blood running from his mouth and from cuts on his cheek. The whites of his eyes gleamed in the darkness as I flung myself at him, and I saw that he was frightened.

He thrust out an arm to try to fend me off. I was probably screaming, but if I was and what I was saying, I don't remember.

244

What I do remember is letting the hate and rage pour out – all those feelings that for so long I'd kept buried inside.

Something warm gushed over my hand, as all at once the fight went out of him. I drove the blade deeper and deeper and deeper, until it met something hard and would go no further. I ripped it free, and he let out a wordless gasp as he tumbled to the floor. Before he could so much as think about getting up again I was on him, plunging the steel into his thigh and his gut and his groin and his neck and his chest and his face, each wound a punishment for the hurt he had done to me, to Tova, to his father and to others.

Over and over and over I did it, again and again until he was no longer moving, and still I kept going until the hilt slipped from my fingers and the blade clattered away across the floorboards and I sank to my knees and sobbed into my sticky hands, into my undergown's soaked sleeve, with my hair in my face and blood in my hair. Blood everywhere, pooling underneath his body, running over my fingers, spattered all across my skirt. He lay in front of me, crumpled and empty-eyed.

It makes me sick even to think about it. About what I did.

He was just a boy. He was younger than me. And I snuffed out his life, stole it from him. I killed him. With my own hand I did it. And do you know what the worst part is? I enjoyed it. I enjoyed watching him die. I thought it was justice.

But now? Now I don't know. Every time I pause to think about it, the less sure I am. Was it the right thing? I tell myself I had no choice, but maybe there was some other way. Some way that I didn't have to . . .

I'm sorry. I'm all right, really I am.

What was I saying?

How long I knelt there, I don't know. Eventually I had no

245

more tears to give. Only the sound of my own breathing broke the stillness.

That's when I panicked. My gaze settled upon his still form. Lying there he looked so peaceful, nothing at all like he'd been in life. His mouth and eyes hung open, not so much in pain, I thought, as in surprise. That was when it struck me what I'd done. What I'd become.

I knew what I had to do. First I took off my undergown and went to the stone basin in the corner, which was filled with water drawn from the well. I splashed some in my face and almost choked because it was so cold. My breath came quick and short, forming clouds in front of my eyes, and I was shuddering, partly from the cold and partly from fright, but there was a voice inside me telling me I shouldn't waste any time, that the longer I spent here the greater chance I'd be discovered. As quickly as I was able, then, I rubbed down my hands and my arms, trying to cleanse the worst of the blood from my skin, then dried myself with the blankets on my bed, before throwing open the kist and searching for fresh clothes. There was another shift buried in there, I knew, threadbare in places and frayed at the hems, but it was the best I had apart from the one which lay in a sodden pile by Orm. I found it and tugged it on, followed by the thickest dress I had, then my winter cloak on top of that and lastly my shoes.

There was nothing I could do about Orm's body. He was too heavy for me to move, and if I did it would do no good; there was so much blood. And so I left him where he was. Sooner or later they would find him. I could only hope it would be later, by which time with any luck we would be long gone.

Maybe I should have stayed and told them what had happened. Maybe if I had, if I'd told them everything I've just told you, they'd have believed me. Maybe they would have forgiven me, but I didn't know that, and so I did the only thing that made sense at the time.

I fled.

I gathered everything I thought I might need, and then I ran like I'd never run before, from the house along the path and past the church to the kitchen, where the servants sometimes slept during the winter. That night was mild, but I knew Tova felt the cold more than most, so I hoped to find her there, and I was right. She was curled under the blankets next to Cene, who was one of our best running hounds and had always been Skalpi's favourite.

Cene stirred first and began yapping, so loudly that I knew he would wake the other servants in their quarters across the yard if he carried on much longer. I did my best to calm him at the same time as I woke her. Once he saw it was me he stopped, but I knew that any moment someone might find us. I told Tova to get dressed and pack whatever she needed. Cene went after her; I think he sensed she was nervous and was trying to protect her, but I found some meat in the storehouse and put it down for him, and hoped that would keep him quiet for as long as it took.

I saddled horses for both of us, and led them towards the bridge, where Tova was already waiting for me, and there was Cene again, at her feet, circling her, bounding with excitement. He thought this was all a game, and began to follow us as we rode away. I told him to stay, and God be thanked he didn't try to come after us, although it wasn't long before he started barking again, and whining, and barking some more. I was sure the noise would rouse everyone on the manor, and it wouldn't be long before they realised we were missing.

I didn't dare look back as we made for the hills, riding as fast as we could through the darkness, leaving Heldeby behind us.

That was the last time we saw home.

'After that we found Beorn, or rather he found us,' she says. 'He came just in time to save us from a band of Normans. He said he would take us to Hagustaldesham, to safety. And here we are, talking to you now.'

'Orm killed Skalpi?' Tova asks weakly. She can hardly speak. It can't be true, she thinks. Please, God, don't let it be true. Like everyone else, she'd long ago given up hope that he might ever come back. But to be betrayed by his own son . . . he didn't deserve that fate.

Merewyn's voice, when she speaks again, is small. Even now, days after it all happened, still her hands tremble, and not just her hands but her shoulders too.

'He did. He killed him. I know it. He wouldn't speak the words aloud, but there was no mistaking what he meant.'

'He was drunk,' Oslac says. 'Have you thought that maybe he didn't know what he was saying?'

'Mead often loosens a man's tongue,' Beorn points out. 'And he didn't deny it when you asked him directly.'

'That's not the same thing as admitting it, though, is it? What if he didn't do it? Then she killed a man for no good reason.'

Beorn says, 'She was defending herself. What do you think she should have done?'

Only the priest stays quiet. He's torn, Tova thinks. On the one hand he doesn't approve, but on the other he knows he's in no position to judge.

Tova asks her, 'Why didn't you tell me all this before?'

Isn't she supposed to be her lady's most trusted friend? Like sisters, she said they were. There aren't supposed to be any secrets between them. Not ones as big as this.

'I should have said, I know. I'm sorry. I didn't know what to say. I didn't think you'd understand.'

'Of course I'd understand. Whatever made you think I wouldn't?'

Merewyn shakes her head. 'An eye for an eye. It isn't lawful. It isn't just. What would Father Thorvald say? But when I heard Orm say those things about Skalpi, about how his father's death was his fault, I couldn't help myself. I was so full of rage that I couldn't suffer him to live any longer. All I wanted was revenge.'

She turns to Guthred. 'God will understand, won't he, Father? He'll forgive me. There must be some penance I can undertake. Whatever it is, I'll do it.'

Absolution. That's what she wants. All he has to do is say the words.

But the priest doesn't seem to hear. He sits, staring at the ground, unblinking.

'Father?'

Guthred looks up. 'I wish I could tell you what you want to hear. But I fear that gift is not mine to grant. Not any longer. I can pray with you, if you wish. I can help you find the words. But I can't promise you any more than that. I'm sorry.'

She nods, sniffing. 'I am too.'

'That's not how it happened, is it?' Tova asks later, when they are alone.

The others are back at the camp; the two of them have gone together to gather more wood for the fire. The pile is getting low, and they're going to need plenty if it's to keep burning through the night. The rain has stopped and the skies are beginning to clear. There'll be a thick frost come the morning.

Merewyn picks up another branch and tucks it under her arm. 'What are you talking about?'

'I know it isn't true – what you said. About Orm. About what happened that night. If it were, you'd have told me already. You wouldn't have kept it from me until now.'

'Tova,' Merewyn says in that warning voice that she has grown to know.

But Tova will not be deterred. She will not be put in her place. Not this time. Even as her lady was telling her story, she thought that there were some things that didn't quite make sense. Now that she's worked it out, she's not going to stop until she has answers.

'He didn't try to attack you, did he? All that about the lock on the door—'

'You have no right to speak to me like this. To accuse me.'

'Of what? That's why you didn't want me there that night, isn't it? Because you had it all planned. He didn't come to your chamber on some whim; he came for a reason. He came because you'd invited him there, hadn't you?'

Saying afterwards that she never meant to do it. Of course she did. She knew exactly what she was doing. Tempting him to his death.

'Don't lie to me any more, please,' Tova says. 'Just tell me. You trust me, don't you?'

Merewyn hesitates and then says quietly, 'I left him a message on a scrap of parchment. I wrote that he should come to my chamber that night after everyone else was asleep.'

'You deceived him. You lured him with false promises so that you could kill him.'

'No!' Merewyn protests. 'I mean, it wasn't as simple as that.'

'What do you mean?'

250

'I did it so that I could find out the truth. About what happened to Skalpi. A part of me had long suspected, I suppose, ever since Orm returned. It was a feeling I had, nothing more than that. Not until that day when they took Heldeby from me and gave it to him, and I saw that hateful smirk on his face. Then I started putting things together. Why, when I said how Skalpi wasn't sure if Orm was his own son, he acted as he did. Because he'd guessed it himself, long ago. He knew that if Skalpi ever disowned him, by claiming he wasn't of his blood, then he'd lose all right to Heldeby. And that's why he did it. Not just because he hated Skalpi, but to make sure he didn't come back. To make sure that no one ever found out.'

'It was true, then?' Tova asks.

'Maybe it was. Who knows? Skalpi had wondered ever since he cast Ælfswith out. The longer their quarrels went on, the greater his doubts grew.'

'That doesn't mean Orm killed him, though.'

'That's why, before I did anything, I had to be sure. I knew he'd never admit the truth normally, but I thought that if I gave in to him, if I could gain his confidence, then he would tell me.'

And Tova understands. 'No,' she says under her breath. 'You didn't. You can't have.'

She can't say it. She doesn't even want to think it.

Merewyn's back is turned. 'I did. Yes, I did. It makes me sick to think about it. But it was all I could do. I needed the truth.'

Tova wants to retch. The thought that Merewyn might willingly have offered herself, allowed him to . . .

'And did he really say those things?'

Merewyn nods.

'You could have told me. You could always have told me, even if you didn't want the others to know.'

251

'I was frightened of what you might think. I wanted you to see that I didn't have any choice.'

'You were frightened of what I might think?'

'I didn't want you to think badly of me. That's why I lied. It was wrong, I know. I ought to have told you everything from the start, but I was ashamed. Can you forgive me?'

For what? For trying to hide the truth from her? Or for the things that she did?

'It's all right,' Tova says, to reassure herself as much as Merewyn. The words sound as if someone else is speaking them. 'I forgive you.'

But it isn't all right.

Hours later the thought of it continues to eat away at her. She can't settle. She can't sleep. She turns over and over, coiled tightly inside her blankets, trying to rid her mind of the pictures that keep forming, unbidden.

It isn't that she feels sorry for Orm. She had as much reason to hate him as Merewyn. It might have been the right thing to do. It might have been only what he deserved. God will judge, she supposes, when the end comes.

Why, then, does she feel so uneasy? Because she never thought her lady capable of such trickery? Or because she isn't, after all, the person that Tova thought she was?

She can imagine how it would have happened. It would have happened something like this.

He enters, flagon in hand, just like her lady described, except that Merewyn is expecting him, waiting by the top of the stairs, listening for the sound of the door and for the creak of the floorboards under his feet. The smell of drink on his breath as she greets and kisses him. Shyly she leads him in the darkness across her chamber towards her bed. The smile of surprise and puzzlement and triumph as he follows, his mind so dulled by ale that he doesn't question why as they shed their clothes. She tells him she didn't mean the things she said about him before, that she has been foolish, that she wants to show him how sorry she is. He knows that, doesn't he?

He says that he does. But he will say anything.

Afterwards, she tells him that she'd wanted him for such a long time, but that as long as Skalpi was alive, as long as there was a chance that he might yet come back, she couldn't afford to let her real feelings show.

He never loved you, he murmurs, his words slurred. He lies beside her upon the bed, face buried in the sheets, the sweat on his skin glistening in the candlelight. He never loved you like I love you, he goes on. He never deserved you. He never cared for you as a man should.

She tells him she knows. She says that she understands now. She asks him baldly, Skalpi isn't coming back, is he?

No, he says. No, he isn't.

That's what she's been waiting to hear. Her trembling hand reaches up past her head. Slowly, quietly, so that she doesn't disturb him. Sliding underneath the pillow until she can feel the hilt. Her fingers curl around it.

Trying to keep her voice as even and as gentle as possible, she asks, What do you mean? How do you know?

But she already knows. She made up her mind long ago. And she's ready. She draws the blade out and sits up.

It was me, he says. There was never any scouting party. It was me. It's my fault that he's dead.

She waits until he's asleep, insensible with drink, snoring softly. And she takes the knife in both hands. And she kneels

253

over him. And she summons all her strength, all her anger. And she plunges it down into his back, through the back of his ribs. And again. And again. Driving it home until it is buried all the way up to the hilt.

And he lies as still as stone.

To take a man's life in desperation, out of fear for one's own safety, that's one thing. To take that same life coldly, out of hatred, that is something else entirely.

Merewyn was always so good, so pure. Someone to be looked up to. Virtuous and honest. Strong in her own quiet way. Incapable of malice or of harm.

So she used to think, anyway.

Now she isn't so sure.

FOURTH DAY

They rise early, in the chill grey half-light that comes before dawn. There's a ford a mile upriver from their camp, says Beorn, who's been up for some hours already, riding on and back to check whether the way ahead is safe. No sign of the enemy. As long as they keep moving, they'll be all right.

A glimmer of light as they lead the horses down the muddy, crumbling path towards the river. The very sky aflame. The clouds lit from below in searing orange, on top as black as charcoal. A sea of marsh mist. Hills rise as islands out of the thick murk. Lost amid those swirling wispy veils is the sun's feeble disc, too craven and timid to show itself fully.

Tova slips off her shoes and puts them inside her pack and tucks her skirts into her belt, where they'll be out of her way. The last thing she needs is to get them wet. She curses as she tests the water with her toes, but there is nothing for it. Beorn and Oslac are beckoning her on, and behind her Merewyn and Guthred are waiting. The river is high and swift-coursing, rising more than halfway to Tova's knees. She tugs on Winter's reins, urging her on. The riverbed is thick with mud which sucks at her soles, forcing her to tread carefully. She grits her teeth against the biting cold. One step, then another, then another. By the time she reaches the other side she can hardly feel her legs, they're so numb; it's a wonder her toes haven't dropped off. She's seen it happen: a decrepit pedlar that Ælfric found out by the crossroads after a blizzard. Barely alive when they brought him into the hall, his lips were blue and his fingers and toes purple, turning soon to black as they withered away. He lived, but he was lucky.

They pause on the north bank to dry themselves off and let the feeling return to their limbs, but they don't dare tarry for long. By the time they're on their way the sun has disappeared again into the grey. Tova wonders how many more dawns she'll get the chance to see.

Three more days, maybe four. That's how long Beorn reckons it will take them to reach Hagustaldesham. If they move quickly. And they're going to have to.

'The wind's changing,' he says as he pauses to look up at the sky. 'Colder weather to come. There could be snow on the way.'

'How soon?' Guthred asks.

'Your guess is as good as mine. Tomorrow, maybe, or the day after. It's a feeling I have, that's all. Just as in summer you can sense a storm in the air. You can feel it on your skin long before it arrives. It's like that. If you spend any time at sea, as I've done, you learn to recognise the signs.'

'You didn't tell us you'd been to sea,' Tova says.

'I've been to lots of places.'

She has only seen the sea once in her life, although of course she has heard many songs and stories about ships and the beasts of the deep, and the lands that lie across the water, and the strange and wonderful creatures that live there. What it must be like to be out there on the vast, open whale road, she can't begin to imagine.

'Have you been to Miklagard?'

'Not Miklagard, no. Never that far.'

'Where, then?'

She wants to know more about these faraway places she's heard of, but this time from someone who has actually seen them with his own eyes.

'Yrland and Ysland. Orkaneya. The kingdom of the Danes. Sometimes to the lands of the Moors.'

'They say that the Moors have skin that's as black as coal,' she says. 'Is that true?'

'Not quite. Not the ones I've seen, anyway. But dark. Much darker than you or I or anyone living in England.'

'What about the Yslanders? I've heard they live without a king, and instead they rule themselves through councils, and that the earth itself spits fire, and there are giants living in the mountains.'

'That's right. Everything except for the giants, anyway.'

Oslac looks doubtfully at him. 'The earth spits fire?'

'Spits it high into the sky, and spews it over the land, too. Rivers of flame, flowing like water from crevices in the hills. Towering black clouds, higher than you can imagine. Ash raining from the sky. Sometimes at night, high above the clouds, strange lights. Curtains of green and orange, brighter than the moon. Dancing and swirling like dragons' breath. Like the heavens themselves are on fire.'

'Really?' Tova asks.

Beorn nods. 'I've seen it.'

There's so much of the world she doesn't know about. So many things she never knew existed. So much strangeness, so many wonders. So many places she would go, if she could.

'What else have you seen?' she says excitedly. 'Is it true there are whole islands made of ice, just floating adrift on the waves? And there are snow bears living on them?'

'I never saw a snow bear myself, but I know men whose word I trust who say that they have. Where did you learn about such things, anyway?'

'In stories. I didn't know they were real.'

'I don't doubt that they are.'

'And the ice islands?'

'Those I know about. In the northern seas you have to be always on the lookout for them. They drift with the currents across your course, rising like white cliffs out of the dark water. At night they can be hard to spot, especially if the moon is new. You need a good crew and a good steersman. Folk you can trust with your life.'

Merewyn asks, 'What were you doing in Ysland?'

'Trading.'

'Trading what?'

'Wool cloth for furs. Quernstones for walrus ivory. Things like that.'

'Slaves?' Tova asks.

She didn't mean to say it. The question had already slipped from her lips before she knew it. But it's too late to take it back.

He stiffens in the saddle, ever so slightly. His gaze fixed on the way ahead. His jaw set firm.

'Beorn?'

It's the first time she's seen him wrong-footed. Until now he's always had an answer for everything.

'Yes,' he mutters without looking at her. 'Once or twice, when my lord thought we could fetch a good price for them.'

'You did?'

'Only because if we didn't, our families would starve that winter because we had no silver to buy food and clothing. Did we like it? No. But we had no choice. Understand?'

Tova clenches her teeth to stop the anger spilling over. She can't look at him. She tries not to think about those helpless wide-eyed folk, in frayed clothes either too large or small for them, being led in chains to places at the edge of the world.

Like Ase, maybe. Like Gunnhild.

Just as she thought she was beginning to understand him. What else is there, she wonders, that he isn't telling them?

Right now she isn't sure that she wants to know.

They come to the old road around midday. Straight as a pole, it runs north as far as the eye can see, across the hills. Like a knife cut across the land. No sign of the Normans in either direction, but there's no doubt they've been this way.

Hoofprints everywhere, too many to count. The way has been churned into a mire. Long stretches ankle-deep with dirty rain-water. In the ditch by the roadside an iron cloak pin, bent out of shape, tossed away. A shoe with a hole in the toe. An ale flask. A battered drinking horn, chipped at the rim. A helmet with a dent that nobody could be bothered to hammer out.

'There must have been hundreds of them,' says Oslac. 'A whole army, by the look of it. And not that long ago, either.'

He looks at Beorn, who nods. It might be the first time the two of them have found themselves of the same mind on anything.

'All the more reason to keep moving, then,' says the priest.

Tova couldn't agree more.

They find the man by a stream, curled up in a ball like a child, whimpering softly to himself. Not dead, but hardly moving. His cloak and his brown robe are plastered in dirt and sticks and leaves; he has no shoes.

No one else around. No other sound save for the birds.

261

'Who's that?' he says in a shaky voice as they approach him. 'Is there somebody there?'

He stirs, raising his head a little: not so they can see his face, but enough for Tova to catch a glimpse of his bald pate with its crown of trimmed brown hair.

A monk.

'Someone you might know?' Oslac murmurs to Guthred, who sits in his saddle as still as stone.

Whoever he is, he's hurt, and badly. While the others just stand there, Tova hurries over, splashing through the stream, and kneels down on the damp ground beside him. She rests her hand upon his shoulder. He flinches at her touch, gentle though it is.

'It's all right,' she says softly.

He lies on his side, his head turned away from her, hidden underneath his cloak. A bloodstained hand clutches glass, amber and jet prayer beads on a scarlet thread with a cross hanging from the loop, and a tiny glass phial filled with a golden liquid about half the length of her little finger.

Holy oil. She knows what it is because old Thorvald had one much the same, which he wore on a chain around his neck. She remembers him telling her how, many years earlier, he'd made the long pilgrimage to Cantwaraburg to fill it from the gilded reliquary that held the saint's remains.

'P-please,' he says. 'Have mercy.'

His voice sounds young, if strangely muffled. And he seems young, from what she can tell.

'There's no need to be afraid.'

She reaches a hand up and peels back his cloak slowly so as not to distress him—

And recoils, shrieking. She stands up too quickly. Her feet don't feel like they belong to her.

Blood everywhere, streaked across both his cheeks. An angry, crusted gash along his jawline. Where his nose ought to be there's only a sticky mess. In place of his eyes, dark, hollow sockets.

'Have m-mercy on me,' the man says again as he turns to face her. 'I beg of you, please.'

She thought she'd seen everything these last few days. She didn't think there was anything the enemy could do that could be worse than what she's already witnessed.

His eyes. They put out his eyes.

'Oh, dear God,' says Guthred as he raises his hands to his mouth and looks away quickly. 'Sweet Christ.'

'Who did this to you?' Beorn asks. 'Who? Was it the Normans?'

But the man isn't listening. He has started whimpering again. She can't begin to imagine the agony he must be in.

'Ale,' says Tova, when she finds her voice again. 'We need to give him some ale, or some water. Something. Anything.'

Merewyn is already there with a leather bottle in her hand, kneeling beside him. 'We need to sit him up.' She gestures to Oslac, who is closest. 'Help me.'

Together they manage to drag him over to a tree and rest his back against it. That's when Tova sees just how badly he's injured. For it isn't just his face. His other hand, his right hand, is missing, severed below the wrist, while the front of his robe is dark and moist where his flesh has been pierced. Whoever did this to him must have hearts of stone.

'A knife or a seax,' Beorn says after he's had a chance to look carefully at the wound. 'Too narrow to be a sword. But deep. Gut-deep. Recent too.'

'How recent?' Oslac asks.

'A few hours. He's lucky not to be dead already.'

'We can help him, though, can't we?' says Tova.

Beorn doesn't answer.

'He'll live, won't he?'

He gives her a look that suggests she shouldn't be asking such a foolish question. But it doesn't seem foolish to her.

'Won't he?'

'If we could find him a leech doctor or a wise woman,' he says in a low voice, 'they could give him something for the pain, maybe, but nothing more than that.'

'Could we?'

'Could we what?'

'Give him something for the pain. Something besides ale.'

'I don't know what, girl. Do you?'

The man groans. Beads of sweat roll off his forehead. His lips quiver, but there's barely any sound behind them.

'I think he's trying to speak,' Merewyn says.

Beorn crouches in front of him and gazes into the monk's unseeing eye sockets. 'What's your name?'

He swallows. 'Godstan.'

'Did the Normans do this to you, Godstan?'

The young man makes a mewling sound in his throat as, almost imperceptibly, he shakes his head.

'Who, then?'

'Four. There were f-four of them.'

His words are so faint Tova can barely hear him. She watches his trembling lips.

'English folk?' she asks.

Godstan nods. 'English. Three men and a w-woman. They took everything. My knapsack. My horse. They spat on me. C-called me pious filth. Then . . . then they . . .'

But he doesn't finish. He is crying now, or would be if he had eyes to cry with. He wheezes as he breathes, and clutches at his

264

stomach with his one remaining hand. Why would anyone attack a monk? Why would anyone ever do such things to another man?

'What else do you remember?' Beorn asks.

The monk shakes his head. His teeth are gritted against the pain. The last thing he needs, Tova thinks, is to be besieged with all these questions.

'Wulfnoth,' he says.

Tova stares at him for a few moments, unsure whether she's heard him properly. She turns to the priest, who has gone suddenly pale.

'What did you say?' Beorn asks Godstan.

'That's what they called him. Their leader. W-Wulfnoth.'

It can't be the same one, surely. There must be scores of men in the world by that name.

But how many make it their business to prey upon men of the Church? To attack and steal and maim? To leave a man for dead?

His eyes. They put out his eyes.

'He's coming after you, isn't he?' she says to Guthred. 'He's coming after the book.'

Guthred's eyes are glazed, unseeing, his mouth half-open. Stiff with fright.

'It has to be a coincidence,' says Merewyn. 'Surely it can't be him. It has to be another Wulfnoth. It must be.'

'What's h-h-happening?' says Godstan weakly. He turns his head at the sound of each voice. She imagines that his eyes, if he still had them, would be wide, desperate. He must realise that his time is short. 'P-please, tell me.'

'We can't stay here,' Beorn says, ignoring him. 'They could still be close by. We need to keep moving.'

'Which way?' Merewyn asks. 'Back towards the old road?'

'We could ask him which way he thinks they went,' Oslac says.

'Of course, because he'll have seen them leave, won't he?' Beorn retorts. 'Do you even think about some of the things that come out of your mouth?'

'I was only making a suggestion.'

The monk's lips are moving. He's trying to say something, but Tova can't hear what it is for all their arguing.

'Quiet,' she says as she kneels back down beside him. 'We're listening.'

'Don't l-leave me,' Godstan says. 'Don't let me die alone.'

Tova glances desperately at Beorn. 'We have to do something. We have to help him.'

'We can't take him with us, if that's what you're thinking. You know we can't. He'll only slow us down.'

Merewyn places a hand on her shoulder. 'I don't think there's anything we can do.'

Very gently Tova slides her fingers into the young man's palm, trying to reassure him. She wishes now that she hadn't jumped when she first saw his face. More, she wishes she hadn't shrieked.

'There must be something,' she says.

They could concoct some sort of infusion, couldn't they? She's heard that willow bark is good for headaches and other pains; if they could find some, maybe they could boil it in water for him to drink. At the very least they could bind his wounds.

It won't stop him from dying, of course. She understands it's too late for that.

'There is one thing we could do,' says Beorn.

She turns. They all turn.

'What?' asks Merewyn.

He hesitates. Whatever it is, he clearly doesn't want to say, at least not out loud. He reaches up to the back of his head; for a moment she thinks he's scratching it, until she realises the motion he's making. How he's holding his hand. Flat, like a blade. The edge striking the back of his skull.

'No,' says Tova under her breath. 'No, we can't.'

He's thinking it's the kindest thing they can do for him. The merciful thing. They can put an end to his pain here and now. Let him be with God, where he belongs.

That doesn't make it right, though, does it? Taking someone's life, when for days all around them they've seen only death. What would that make them? He's not some old nag that's gone lame.

Why didn't the ones who did this finish him off when they had the chance? Why did they have to leave him like this?

But she already knows the answer. To make him suffer for as long as possible. They didn't want his end to be easy. No, of course not. That's why they did it.

But if the five of them were to leave him now, they would only be condemning him to a slow, lonely death. That's exactly what Wulfnoth and the others did. They would be no different.

'I agree with Beorn,' says Oslac.

'It's the right thing to do,' Merewyn says. 'We might not like it, but it is.'

Tova doesn't like it. But she knows in her heart of hearts that they're right.

'What do you say, Father?' Merewyn asks.

Guthred blinks and stares at her. There is a look of terror in his eyes, as if he has been shaken from sleep and has forgotten where he is. He looks surprised that someone should be addressing him or interested in what he has to say.

The monk coughs, and Tova reaches for the ale flask. Cradling his head, she raises it to his lips, letting a few drops at a time into his mouth. With every swallow he groans.

'Is there a p-priest with you?' he asks when he has finished. 'I

267

would very much like to speak with him, if I may. T-to pray with him, before it's too late.'

Tova squeezes the young man's hands one last time, then stands and lets Guthred take her place by his side. He does so slowly, gingerly, as if not quite sure what he's meant to do. The frightened look hasn't vanished but seems to have become frozen on his face.

'I'm here,' he says as he takes the monk's hand, which still clutches the rosary, and cups his own around it.

Beorn alone remains behind with them; Tova and Merewyn and Oslac carry on a short way down the track. For a while she's able to make out Guthred's soft murmur, but then they're too far away.

They halt and pace about while the horses graze.

'It's the right thing,' Merewyn says again, as if she needs to convince herself.

Tova doesn't hear the axe fall. There is no cry. No sound at all. Nothing but the wind buffeting her cheeks and blowing her hair in her face. But somehow she can sense the moment when it happens. A fleeting stillness. A chill. She closes her eyes and says her own silent prayer for the young monk's soul. For all their souls.

When she opens them again, she sees Guthred, his head bowed, leading his horse up the path after them. A short way behind him is Beorn, his axe slung over his back as usual, his expression as flat as always, as if nothing has changed.

It's done.

'You shouldn't have told Wulfnoth you were going to Lindisfarena,' Oslac tells the priest. It's been at least an hour since they left Godstan. An hour since any of them has spoken.

'I wasn't thinking,' Guthred says in a quiet voice.

'You realise, don't you,' the poet goes on, 'that if you hadn't told him, he wouldn't now be looking for you, and we wouldn't all be in danger? This isn't just about you and your precious book; this is about all of us.'

Beorn looks over his shoulder at him. 'You didn't think we were in danger before now?'

'I didn't say that. I just meant—'

'What? That the thought of being put to the sword by the foreigners doesn't scare you? Is that what you meant? Because if it is, then you're a braver man than I.'

'There's no need to be like that,' Merewyn scolds. 'He misspoke, that's all.'

'I hope so. Because you ought to be afraid. All of you. If you think the Normans will show any more mercy than the priest's friends, you're wrong.' He pauses to let his words sink in, then goes on: 'Besides, it's only Guthred here who has anything to fear. They don't care about the rest of us; they don't even know we exist. All they want is to get their treasure back.'

'It's not their treasure,' Guthred says. 'I told you. It belongs to the Church.'

Tova turns to Beorn. 'What are you saying, then? Are you suggesting that if they find us, we should just hand it over to them?'

'I'm hoping that they don't find us at all,' he replies. 'And they won't, as long as we stay far enough ahead of them. Or far enough behind.'

'But what if they do?'

'There are four of them. There's only one of me. I can only do so much.'

'You fought off five Normans before—'

'And nearly died doing so.'

'But—'

'Girl, you expect too much of me.'

'So tell us, then,' Merewyn says. 'What would you do?'

'Hand over the book and hope they're satisfied with that, without any bloodshed.'

'No,' says Guthred. 'If they want it, they'll have to kill me first.'

Beorn sighs in despair. 'Don't be a fool. If it's a choice between living and dying—'

'It's more than that. It's a choice between eternal life and eternal death. I've tried my hardest to explain. I don't expect you to understand.'

'I understand one thing, priest: I'm not about to risk my life for the sake of a few parchments, no matter how ancient or how precious or how holy they are.'

'You might as well give me up at the same time as the book, then. Because I won't be parted from it.'

If they did those things to the monk, though – a man they didn't even know – imagine what they might do to Guthred, who has already crossed them.

'They wouldn't kill you, would they?' Merewyn asks. 'You said that wasn't their way.'

Guthred shakes his head. 'I don't know anything any more.'

They manage to find a hall to spend the night in, one that's still standing, which the Normans haven't taken the torch to. But someone has clearly been there already; the place has been ransacked. The great doors are open; inside, the benches along each wall have been overturned, floorboards ripped up to reveal hiding places below. Wall hangings lie torn and trampled in heaps upon the floor, which is littered with old rushes. There is a musty smell everywhere – of damp and rot and mouse piss.

Something small scurries away into the darkness as they enter. Above, the thatch rustles.

'Something happened here,' says Merewyn. 'There must have been some kind of struggle.'

Oslac says, 'I don't see any bodies.'

No bodies, or pools of blood where bodies might have lain. No other signs of fighting, either. No scorch marks where flames might have licked at timbers. But whoever was here clearly got what they came for. Sturdy iron-bound chests lie open. Empty. Kists with their locks and their lids smashed in. A single tiny silver penny all that's left of whatever treasure they once held. On one side of the coin a bearded face with a crown and sceptre. On the other some writing that Tova doesn't understand: three letter shapes, one of them like a cross that's been turned slantwise.

'It's a coin of King Harold,' says the priest, when she gives it to him to look at. He squints at it, turning it over in grubby fingers. 'The one who was killed by the foreigners in the battle at Hæstinges.'

'What does the writing say?'

'*Pax*. It's Latin.'

'What does it mean?'

He looks at her with such defeat in his eyes, such gloom and despondency, that he seems suddenly twenty years older.

'What?' she asks.

His voice, when he speaks, is bitter. He says, 'It means "peace".'

They hack pieces from one of the benches to use as firewood, and from it build a good fire in the hearth. It's a relief not to have to sleep under thin hides or on the hard ground, and with a roof that doesn't leak over their heads. The rushes might be old but they're soft. Tonight, at least, they will be warm and comfortable.

Enjoy it while you can, Tova tells herself. You might not get the chance again for a while.

'How many men have you killed?' Tova asks Beorn some time later that evening, as they're sitting around the hearth.

Beorn stops running a whetstone up his knife edge, and stares at her. 'What?'

At once Oslac stops plucking his harp. Guthred looks up from the book; he's taken it out so that he might draw comfort from its words. Merewyn stops chewing mid-mouthful.

Everyone's looking at Tova.

She could apologise, say it isn't important, that it isn't any of her business and she doesn't mean to pry.

But it is important.

'How many?' she asks again.

'More than I'd care to admit.'

'Twenty? Thirty?'

He looks away in what she takes either for embarrassment or shame.

'More than that?'

'You ask too many questions,' he mutters as he begins sharpening his blade once more. The steel sings softly with every stroke.

She tries another approach. 'You said you fought in the rebellion.'

'That's right.'

'Tell us about it. All we heard were rumours, little bits from the ones who came back, but those who did speak about it didn't want to say much.'

'I don't blame them.'

It's like trying to draw water from a stone. He won't give them anything.

'Who are you, really?' she asks.

He says nothing but simply carries on running the whetstone up the knife, over and over and over.

'Beorn?'

He sets down his knife beside him. 'What makes you so interested suddenly?'

'You don't think we deserve to know? You expect us to follow you, to do exactly as you say, but we hardly know anything about you. How do you expect us to trust you?'

'I've kept us all alive this far, haven't I? Isn't that enough? You'd never manage on your own. Not against what's out there.'

'Why do you even care? Why are you helping us?'

'Why shouldn't I?'

'You're keeping things from us. I know you are.'

'So what if I am?'

He stares at her, daring her to challenge him. She meets his stare. She's not afraid of him any more. She won't be intimidated. She won't be cowed into silence.

And she's beginning to understand, or thinks she is, anyway. For despite his talk, his blunt manner, his harsh words, he feels as scared and as helpless as they do. He won't admit it, of course. He can't. That's not who he is.

Inside, she thinks, he's as uncertain and as lost as the rest of us.

'How many?'

'Girl, I'm warning you.'

She's trying his patience, she knows. But that's what she wants. Sooner or later he must break. And she will get the answers she's after. The answers they're all after.

'How many?'

'That's enough!'

His words ring in her ears. He rises. The hearth is behind him and his face is in darkness. His teeth bared, he looms over her. A shadow against the light.

'You really want to know my story? Do you?'

Tova tries to speak but can't find the words. They've become lost somewhere between her mind and her tongue. Her heart is thumping so hard she fears it might burst out of her chest.

The others are all on their feet, although no one wants to be the first to approach him.

Oslac says, 'Beorn—'

'Sit down,' the warrior barks at him. 'Sit. All of you.'

One by one they do so: Guthred at once, timidly; Merewyn more hesitantly. The poet is the last of all. The distrust in his eyes is plain to see.

'Since we're all unburdening ourselves of our secrets, purging our guilty consciences, confessing our sins, I might as well do the same, mightn't I? Fine. You want to know about the war? You want to know about the things I've seen, the things I've done? I'll tell you, although I promise you this: you won't like it.'

'It doesn't matter if we don't like it,' Merewyn says, and Tova is glad of her support, belated though it is. 'We have a right to know.'

'Very well,' Beorn says. 'I don't know how much you've already been told about the rebellion, or what you think you know. No doubt some of those who returned from the war told you stories about what happened and what they did. Whatever they said, though, you can guarantee that half of it will have been lies.'

'Lies?' Merewyn asks, frowning. 'Why?'

'Because often the truth is too much to admit. Think. Did you notice how those who went away so full of cheer and boasts came back quiet and withdrawn, shadows of themselves? Were there times when you asked them about the things they'd seen when they refused to answer no matter how much you pressed them? Did their tempers darken in an instant, like that? Did they strike out at their wives and their children?'

274

Tova remembers. She remembers how Ceolred was never the same after his injuries, but grew irritable and kept largely to himself. And she remembers seeing the bruises on the arm of Lufu, the goatherd's wife, when they were both fetching water one morning, though she quickly covered them and pleaded with Tova never to speak of them to anyone.

'I thought as much,' Beorn says. 'Take it from someone who has stood more often than he has cared to count in the front rank of the shield wall, waiting for death to claim him. When it comes to war, there are things of which you'll never get a man to speak, even if you count yourself among his closest friends. Silence is the only shield he has. His only way of protecting you. His only way of protecting himself.'

At last he sits with them. 'War is not glorious. It doesn't matter what the poets say. There is nothing noble in killing. There is no honour. We tell ourselves there is to make it easier to bear, but there isn't.'

He glares at Oslac, who holds his tongue, which Tova thinks is probably wise.

'We fool ourselves, over and over and over,' Beorn goes on. 'We're all guilty of it, everyone who lifts a sword in anger. And I'm as guilty as the rest. The rebellion probably seemed to you some foolish dream we were all chasing. But it never felt that way. I thought it was the campaign that would drive the foreigners from this kingdom once and for all. I believed that in my heart. I believed it was fate, I truly did, and that eventually we would prevail – that all we needed was time.'

He shakes his head as he picks at a splinter on one of the floorboards. 'For a while I did, anyway. I was wrong.'

beorn

BEORN

This is how it happened. The great rising against the Normans. I saw it all. I was there right from the very beginning. I was there when we slaughtered the foreigners in their hundreds in the streets of Dunholm that winter's night, a year ago now. I was there when, not a month later, we stormed Eoferwic's gates, and when not long afterwards we were driven from the city by King Wilelm, and forced to retreat back into the hills, with our hopes, like our banners, in tatters.

Just like your husband's son when he heard the news, we all thought that was our last chance. We had failed to grasp it, and now it was gone. The ætheling himself thought it; for days afterwards he wouldn't talk to anyone but would lie in bed for hours on end in the hall where he was staying. It was Earl Gospatric who rallied everyone, who settled the feuds and made men see that the struggle wasn't over, but that if we were patient the country would rise with us.

We fought for Eadgar, but Gospatric was the one behind it all, helped by others from the great Northumbrian families. You have to understand that the ætheling was – still is – not much more than a boy. Only a couple of years older than you, girl. Like all young high-born men he was eager and impatient and could be ill tempered, especially when he didn't get his way, which was often. That said, he was no fool; we would hardly have followed him if he was. He could hold a sword too, although you wouldn't call him a warrior. The closest he'd ever come to battle were sparring matches in the training yard. We needed him, for kingly blood flowed in his veins, but likewise he needed men who'd give him wise counsel and who could lead in his name.

Gospatric was one of those. The fiercest of them. The best of them. The most determined. Strong-willed yet patient. He must be nearly fifty now, a little older than your husband, I'd say. Not as old as you, priest. Already bald except for a crown of long white hair, he had a gut like he had a whole pig stuffed under his tunic. His fighting days ended long ago, but he knew how to inspire respect. He knew how to wage a war. And he never stopped believing. Even as we licked our wounds in the weeks after our defeat, he was sending out messengers across the kingdom, into every shire: men like the staller Ascytel who you say came to Heldeby. He wanted to get word to Englishmen everywhere: to everyone who was suffering under the foreigners, to all the scattered bands hiding in the woods and the marshes, to all those living in exile in the lands of the Scots and the Welsh and the Irish. He urged them to come together and make a common stand.

We didn't know who would come, if anyone. We all knew there was little chance of rousing the thegns in the south – those who had already given their oath to Wilelm so they might keep their lands. Too faint-hearted to fight, they were more worried about themselves and about what they would lose if they took up arms against their new lord and king. As for the rest, there was no telling whether they had the stomach for a long war, rather than the raids and ambushes and hall burnings they'd grown accustomed to. And how many common folk would leave their homes and their women and children and elders to join us? For we needed experienced warriors, but we also needed spears by the thousands if we were to stand a chance against the foreigners.

We had no idea, and as the weeks passed our hopes waned. A few heeded the call and sought us out, but not many. Not enough.

'But they did come, in the end, didn't they?' Merewyn asks. 'Men like Skalpi.'

Beorn nods. 'Men like Skalpi. Yes, they did. Over the summer months a strange thing happened. Maybe news of our victories at Dunholm and Eoferwic, short-lived though they were, inspired a willingness to fight that hadn't been there before. Maybe, like your husband, folk realised that if ever they could make a difference, it was now. Whatever the reason, just as men were whispering in Eadgar's ear that the cause was lost and he should start thinking about exile or else seeking a reconciliation with the king, suddenly that was when they started arriving. Just a slow trickle, it was at first – a handful here and there. But soon the trickle became a stream, and the stream in turn became a flood.'

From across the north came thegns and ceorls, hearth troops and fyrdmen, with their spears and swords, axes and shields. With them came swineherds, field labourers, millers and stable hands, bearing hay forks and hoes and whatever other weapons they could lay their hands on. Fresh-faced striplings with barely a wisp of hair upon their chins and time-worn warriors like your husband.

In all my years I've never seen anything like it. It was something to behold. That was when we – when I – really began to believe again. And the more that came to join us, the stronger that belief grew.

How many? Hundreds, thousands. Too many to count. More than I'd ever seen gathered together in a single place, all under the ancient purple and yellow banner of Northumbria, the adopted standard of our last great hope, the last in a line that stretched back half a thousand years. To most of us, Eadgar was the rightful king, deprived of his crown first by silver-tongued Harold and then by the outlander, bastard-born Wilelm. Eadgar was the man we would set upon the throne to rule justly over us and bring an end to the years of tyranny.

'But it didn't happen,' Oslac puts in, stifling a yawn. 'We know that.'

'Oh, am I boring you?'

'I'd just rather you got on with it.'

'And I will, if you'll stop interrupting me. You wanted to hear my tale, didn't you? Well, this is it, and I'll tell it how I choose. No doubt you'd tell it a different way if you'd been there, but you weren't. You know nothing.'

'Enough,' says Merewyn in that sharp tone of hers. 'Both of you. Oslac, let him say what he has to.'

'Yes, and listen well,' Beorn adds. 'Who knows? You might just learn something. Something you can use in one of your poems sometime. If we survive this.'

What is there to say, really?

Not long after we started south, we had word that the Danes had reached these shores and were raiding along the coast. As soon as we knew where they'd landed, Eadgar sent them envoys, hoping that some sort of settlement could be reached so that we and the Danes could direct our attacks against the enemy rather than each other. Those were nervous times. As it turned out, though, we needn't have worried. The Danes were only too eager to accept the offer of an alliance, and it wasn't long before we were welcoming them as brothers. Their leader, Jarl Osbjorn, met the ætheling, and there was much feasting and celebration and sharing of ale. We all sensed that this was the beginning of something great.

Not long afterwards we took Eoferwic, cutting down the enemy until the streets were slick with their blood and you could hardly move without tripping over the bodies of the fallen. Some survived and retreated inside their stronghold, where we couldn't get at them, but they were few. For those of us who had been there during that first rising, it felt like redemption after all our struggles. It would be different this time, we promised ourselves. We wouldn't be overcome so easily. We had numbers on our side now: more than ten thousand men, someone said, now that the Danes had joined us. We would take the fight to the enemy and, this time, we would win.

What we didn't know was that fate was against us. There would be no great battle, no clash of shield walls, no sword song, none of that.

The enemy didn't defeat us. They didn't need to.

We defeated ourselves.

Whether they or we burned the city, I don't think anyone really knows. Some say it was the Normans, trapped inside their castle, who hurled flaming brands on to the roofs of nearby houses, and shot arrows wrapped in cloth soaked in pitch that they set alight. Why they would have done that, I can't think. Others say it was an accident, that some drunken fools had built a great pyre on which they planned to burn an effigy of King Wilelm, but the flames grew beyond their control. It doesn't really matter. Before long half the city was ablaze. Houses, workshops, churches going up like so much tinder. The minster a writhing tower of flame. As soon as we realised what was happening, we gathered what we could and fled. The Normans did the same, abandoning their stronghold, choking as they ran through the streets and out the gates. We were waiting for them. They hardly put up a fight. Some of them had been in such a hurry to get out they had no weapons, no shields. They fell to their knees, pleading for mercy. We killed them anyway.

It was a victory of sorts, I suppose, but it didn't feel like one. The fire raged all day. When the flames died we realised the damage they'd done. Where the great minster church had stood, there was nothing but ash. The enemy's stronghold was a smouldering wreck; of the city's walls there was barely a stretch left standing that we could defend. As we picked our way through the ruins, it became clear that we weren't going to be able to hold the city, and that there was nothing left worth defending in any case. We'd heard by then that King Wilelm was on his way from the south at the head of a great army of barons and oath men, and we knew we had little time before he was upon us.

We retrieved what little we could from the smoking town; the Danes under Jarl Osbjorn carried their share to their ships. And then, by boat and by land, we retreated as swiftly as we could downriver to that marshy nook of land called Heldernesse, which lies between the wolds and the German Sea. And there we waited while our leaders tried to decide what to do next and how best to take the war to the foreigners.

Gospatric wanted to march forth and meet King Wilelm in battle in one last throw of the dice, but Osbjorn was more cautious. Having already braved a long sea voyage, his warriors weren't about to risk everything unless it was on ground of their choosing and on terms that suited them. Some had come hoping to win land, but more had come in the hope of plunder that they could take back with them to their homes across the sea.

No amount of silver and gold would be worth anything if they were dead.

'What did you do, then?' Guthred asks.

'Nothing,' says Beorn. 'We did nothing.'

For weeks we waited.

Eadgar and Gospatric and Osbjorn each sent out their scouts, men like myself, to keep an eye on the enemy's movements. We rode out and saw the king's army; we came back and reported what we'd seen, which was that the Normans showed no sign of seeking battle, but were content to wait while our provisions and spirits ran low.

And running low they were. We heard that the enemy had sent out raiding parties both sides of the Humbre. Groups of twenty, thirty, forty horsemen, who stripped granaries and storehouses everywhere so that the supplies we so desperately needed didn't fall into our hands. Not just food and ale but also firewood and lantern oil, things like that: all the things an army needed to keep warm and fed as the days grew shorter and the nights colder. And the less we were able to forage, the more had to be rationed, the hungrier grew our stomachs, and the more tempers flared. Men grew irritable; squabbles erupted over half-heard insults. Old wounds were reopened; long-standing feuds between families broke out afresh. There was fighting. Some were injured. Some died. Others swore vengeance. And so it went on.

And still we did nothing. The leaves began to fall and the first frosts arrived, earlier than expected; the land was becoming bare, and we all knew we'd struggle to support ourselves through the winter to come. Sickness was spreading through our camp, not helped by the foul marsh air. Every second man was suffering from flux, it seemed. Some of the Danes talked about making for home before the weather worsened and the seas grew too difficult for sailing, so that they could be back for Yule. They said it laughingly, or so we thought. Meanwhile Eadgar and Osbjorn quarrelled about the best course of action, and quarrelled some more, until they refused to speak to one another. Gospatric and some others tried to forge some sort of agreement, but it was no use.

We should have seen the inevitable coming. Instead we kept going, kept telling ourselves that we would march again soon. But we knew that the king was mustering more men by the week from other parts of the kingdom. His ranks were swelling while ours were dwindling.

It started with the Danes. One day they were there; the next they weren't. They left without a word, simply abandoned their camp overnight, took to their ships in the murky light of dawn and were gone, as if they had never been. We later learned that King Wilelm had been sending them secret messengers, promising them shiploads of silver and gold, as much as they could carry back with them and more besides, if they broke their compact with Eadgar. Like the grasping craven that he was, Osbjorn accepted.

After that, things only got worse. Shorn of allies and with no real expectation of victory, many in our own army began to question why we were continuing the fight, what we could hope to gain. Whether it was better to desert and beg the king's mercy. And so, riven by grievances, confined to the marsh country, without anything to strive for, with our leadership in disarray, spirits failing and hopes ground to dust, the rebellion crumbled.

'And what about you?' asks Merewyn. 'You haven't said what you were doing while all this was happening.'

'Yes, I thought this was supposed to be your story,' Oslac mutters.

'I was serving in the household guard of my lord, Cynehelm,' Beorn says. 'He was no one of any particular standing or wealth, just a merchant who'd prospered through many years' trading, until he'd earned the rights and rank of a thegn. He had a manor a short way downriver of Snotingeham, where we spent our winters between sea voyages, at least until it was burned by the Normans and his lands stolen from him while we were overseas. When we returned from our travels we found our home gone and our wives and children too. Some slain, we were told; the rest taken away to be sold at far-off markets. After that he vowed to take up arms until not a single Frenchman remained this side of the Narrow Sea, and the rest of us joined him.'

'You had a wife?' Merewyn asks.

'I did. Ingeborg, her name was. More beautiful than any creature I've ever seen, before or since. Kind in spirit, although stern when she had a mind to be.'

'Was she killed by the Normans?'

'No, she wasn't killed, although many were. She left this world three years ago. She was charged by a bull that had escaped his field while she was out milking. Her ribs were crushed and both her legs broken. She died soon after.'

He speaks the words, Tova thinks, offhandedly, without any feeling behind them, like he has said the same thing many times before and has grown tired of repeating it. If she was being unkind, she might say he'd rehearsed it.

'I'm sorry,' Merewyn says.

Beorn begins again: 'As I was saying—'

'Wait,' says Oslac before he can go on. 'You said some folk had been taken away to be sold. The Normans don't keep or sell slaves.'

'And what would you know of it?'

Oslac shrugs. 'It's what I've been told. Their bishops forbid it.'

'He's right,' Guthred says. 'I remember hearing that the dean once entertained a monk from France who happened to stop at Rypum overnight on his way to Lindisfarena. He denounced the dean for keeping so many unfree labourers to work the canonry's lands, especially when he and his fellow priests lived in such luxury. The monk grew quite angry, I heard, and said that they weren't fit to call themselves men of God.'

'Well, you weren't there,' Beorn says. 'I was. That's what I saw, and what I heard.'

'Maybe you were misinformed,' Oslac suggests, 'because if what you say is true it couldn't have been the Normans who burned your lord's manor.'

'Or maybe you're the one who was misinformed. Have you thought about that? Because that's what happened. Now, are you going to let me carry on with my story?'

The younger man scowls but says nothing, and that's probably just as well.

When the rebellion crumbled, it crumbled quickly. After the Danes, the next to abandon the cause were the swords-for-hire who had flocked from across these isles to the ætheling's banner. Once they realised the campaign was stalling and there would be no easy plunder, they took to their ships and sailed back to Orkaneya, the Suthreyjar, Mann and Yrland and wherever else they'd come from. Not long after that a number of the leading thegns began to slip away, some to renew their submission to the king and plead his forgiveness, others to skulk back to their manors, seeking the comforts of the hearth fire and the mead cup.

No one worried too much about them. Most of us were glad to see the back of weak-willed men who had no stomach for a winter campaign, men who didn't deserve to call themselves warriors. But the rot had taken hold, and now it spread to the heartwood.

Maybe Eadgar had already sensed the inevitable. Maybe he was thinking that the longer he held out and the more of his spearmen and fyrdmen deserted him, the closer the Normans grew to overcoming us entirely. Maybe he feared what might happen if he fell into their hands.

I don't know. None of us knew. The princeling kept his own counsel. He didn't let anyone into his chamber who wasn't one of his trusted retainers or advisers. Even men like Earl Gospatric, without whom he'd never have got as far as he had, were no longer welcome.

In the end the rebellion was finished by a rumour. The days were growing short and winter was almost upon us when one afternoon a story spread through the camp that the enemy were on their way. Their entire army. Thousands of Normans. They knew we were weakened, and now they were coming in force, only a few hours away from destroying us utterly.

Where the rumour came from, if it was true at all, or if the whole thing was just an enemy ruse, I have no idea. It hardly matters now. The end was near. It would have happened sooner or later.

It didn't matter then, either. No one wanted to wait to find out whether or not it was true, least of all Eadgar. I saw him and his huscarls, mailed and helmeted, with banners flying, mounting their horses and marshalling their men to ride out. I watched his servants emerge from his great tent carrying arm-fuls of clothes, cooking pots, weapons and helmets, with cloaks over their shoulders and ale flasks hanging from their belts and leather scrips slung across their chests. Four of them dragged out an immense chest that they must have found in the ruins of the enemy castle at Eoferwic, since I didn't know where else it could have come from, and stuffed silver chains and pouches of coins into their lord's packs and saddlebags.

Within the hour the ætheling was gone, despite the protests of Gospatric and everyone else who'd placed their faith in him, who'd pledged their swords and their spears and their shields in his support and were willing to fight to the last. He fled back into the north with his retainers, his clerks and his servants, his shield bearers and his stable hands. Into exile.

And that was that. After he left all was chaos. You heard how it was from those who returned. Men gathered their things and made ready to flee. We were so few by then; what had once been an army ten thousand strong was reduced to mere fragments. Those thegns who'd remained, who had stayed loyal to the cause through everything, rode back to the halls and the strongholds that they called home. I don't blame them. There was nothing more they could have done. Not by then.

And so our proud host broke apart, its various parts each going their separate ways, like a spear shaft shearing into so many splinters.

For us, though, that was just the start.

'Why?' Tova asks. 'What did you do then?'

Most, as I said, fled back to their halls and their homes. But we, Cynehelm and his men, had no home to go back to. There were others like us too: men who had stood in the shield walls at Fuleford and Stanford Brycg, who had given everything for this land,

and who weren't ready to suffer under the rule of foreigners. We all knew that submitting to the king would be futile. There would be no mercy. Not after we'd twice risen against him. And so we bound ourselves by oaths, pledged our blades to each other's service, and swore to continue the fight by whatever means we could. By whatever means we had to.

In all there were perhaps two dozen of us, never more than that. We were men of all ages, some barely out of boyhood while others were in their fortieth winter, and we hailed from all quarters of Britain. Honest men, noble men, fierce men, scoundrels. The one thing we had in common was that, for whatever reason, we could not or did not want to go home.

And Cynehelm was the one who led us. He didn't think himself much of a warrior, not really, although by anyone else's estimation he was more than competent. But then that was true of everyone who chose to ply their trade, as he did, upon the dangerous waters of the German Sea, where the sea wolves roam in search of vessels that ride heavy across the waves, laden with goods for distant markets.

He wasn't the easiest of men to like. He could be cold and sour-tempered at times. Cynehelm Caldheort, he was sometimes called, although never to his face and only by those who didn't know him. Cynehelm the Unfeeling. Those who were as close to him as I was, though, knew that he was a fair and generous lord, who always tried to do right by those who depended on him.

He wasn't much to look at either. He took little pride in his appearance. He didn't care for glittering arm rings or jewelled weapon hilts, fine-spun cloaks and ornamented sword belts, as some men did. He'd risen to his rank in life not through birthright but through his own hard toil, and he never felt the need for the trappings of wealth that others so adored. He preferred to let his deeds speak for him. Maybe that's why men sometimes underestimated him. He was patient, or tried to be, anyway. Only fools ever mocked him, and they never did so twice. To his followers, he was someone who knew how to command respect and how to win confidence.

He was a good lord, in spite of everything.

'Was?' asks Merewyn.

'He isn't any more.'

'Why? What happened?'

'He's dead. But I'm coming to that.'

When you're out on the open sea and a storm blows up around you, you don't try to fight the waves. Not if you want to live. No, you ride them, even if that means they end up taking you far from where you were intending to go. As the wind changes, you have to change with it. And that's what we did.

For everyone else the war was over. For us it was only beginning.

Even as the rest of the army was fleeing into the north, we ventured south, into the midland shires and what used to be known as the territory of the Five Boroughs, which the Normans had already brought under their heel. We abandoned our horses, going on foot so as to be less easily noticed, keeping off the main roads and tracks. We took to travelling by night, stealing our way through the shadows. By day we slept in ditches and in copses, though always with one eye open and with weapons close to hand.

Over the next month we lived off the land, surviving by our wits and our swords, laying ambushes for the enemy on woodland paths, slaying any French-speakers we came across, attacking supply trains that were poorly guarded, killing those we could and then emptying the contents of their carts into the nearest river. Barrels of salted pork and pickled herring, casks of ale or wine or butter – all of it. We took just enough to slake our hunger and thirst, and then in it went, the bodies as well.

But that wasn't enough. Not for Cynehelm. His home, our home, had been destroyed by the foreigners. He wanted vengeance. From waylaying convoys and scouting parties, we soon turned to more ambitious undertakings. We set the torch to mills and barns, stables and churches and even halls, barring the doors from the outside so that no one could escape, then watching from afar as the thatch smouldered and sparked into light and the flames swept across the roof until the whole thing was seething with flame. Then would come the screaming, as those inside realised what was happening, screaming that only grew louder when they tried the doors only to discover they were trapped. After that, the coughing and the choking, quickly drowned out by the roar as the beams and the wall timbers caught, and the building became one bright-blazing, twisting column: a beacon and a warning.

'But that's horrible,' says Tova.

'That's war. If you think it's anything like the tales that the poets and skalds sing, you're wrong.' He glares at Oslac. 'They know nothing. It isn't about heroes and kings. It's not about mighty shield walls clashing, the clatter of steel upon lime wood, the sword song ringing out or the glory of the kill. The man who claims it is hasn't seen battle. He has never been in a real fight, nor probably ever hefted a blade longer than a carving knife. Certainly he has never plunged it into a man's belly, driving deeper, twisting until the blood gushes thick and fast all over his arm, then stood bellowing in triumph, watching for the moment when the light goes out from his enemy's eyes and he voids himself all over the ground at his feet. They don't sing long into the winter nights about the joy of wading ankle-deep in pools of vomit and shit and piss and mud, do they?'

'No,' Tova says quietly.

'Well, that's what war is like, girl. It's about ambushes and raids. Looting. Seizing goods, cattle and sheep. Taking your enemy by surprise; striking when he least expects it. Letting him know that, as long as you live, you won't let him sleep quietly in his bed. And it wasn't just the foreigners. Many thegns, in the midland shires especially, had given their oaths to King Wilelm and marched under his banner. Marched with the foreigners. It makes me angry to think about it even now. Englishmen who'd turned against their people, who had even killed their own kins-folk. Who had begun drinking wine and were learning to speak the French tongue, who had set aside their wives so that they could take Norman brides, all to win favour.'

Tova swallows. 'What happened to them?'

'We did to them what we did to all our enemies. We knew who they were. We knew where they lived. And we showed them no mercy because we knew they would show us none.'

'You killed them?'

'What else were we supposed to do? They'd betrayed us. They didn't deserve to live. Listen to me, girl, before you say anything. What we were doing in those weeks, that's war. We didn't enjoy it. Of course we didn't, so don't for a moment imagine otherwise. No one enjoys it. Not unless their hearts are made of stone or they have given up on all that is good in the world. There is no glory in it, no honour, and it sickens you to the gut when you recall later what you've done. Every night I lie awake, thinking about the things I've seen, thinking about the blood that stains my soul, not wanting to close my eyes because I know that if I do, I'll see

291

the faces of all the men I've sent to their graves. Everyone whose bellies I've run through with spear and sword, whose throats I've slit, whose limbs I've broken and whose skulls I've beaten in. That's when you start to wonder if it's all worth it, whether it was the right thing to do. But you don't question it at the time. You do it because you have to and because you know that if you don't, they'll do the same to the people you care about.'

His eyes glisten in the firelight, but if he's expecting sympathy, he's going to be disappointed. She can't do it. She can't bring herself to feel sorry for him.

Does it matter whether or not his intentions were noble? Does it matter that he took no joy in it? He killed his fellow Englishmen. How is he any different from the Normans?

He says, 'As much as I despised every one of the men I killed, I hate myself more. For who I am. For everything I've done. Those marks cannot be rubbed out.'

'But they can, if you only give yourself to God,' Guthred puts in. 'Confess and do penance before it's too late, and there'll be a place for you in his kingdom.'

'Your god cares nothing for me. He cares nothing for any of us.'

Tova's breath catches in her chest. To hear him say such words openly, and to the priest's face . . .

Guthred's cheeks flush red. 'I understand your pain. I know you speak from anger. Without God's light and grace, there can be no resurrection on the Day of Judgement. You must know this. He's willing to accept you, if you'll only accept him. Otherwise there's only death.'

'Day after day, I see nothing but death everywhere around me. I've lived with it for so long now, I feel its stench clinging to my skin.'

'That's not what I mean.'

'I know what you mean. I've heard it all before, many times. And I'm telling you I'd rather spend an eternity in your god's hell than a moment in his heaven.'

The priest does well to remain patient, Tova thinks. Then again he probably heard similar things from the mouths of Wulfnoth and the other reavers.

'Why do you say that?'

'The foreigners worship the same god as you, don't they? So does he forgive their sins as well and allow them into his kingdom?'

'If they're true of heart and faithful to the Cross,' he says. 'If they repent before the Lord and atone for their wrongdoings, then yes, they'll find their place alongside him.'

'There's your answer then. I want no part of any heaven where I have to live among their kind.'

'I wish I had the answers you're hoping for. I wish I could tell you what you want to hear. But I don't. I can't. But you must find your faith, as I did. We toil and suffer and die upon this earth, and none of us can pretend to understand his purpose—'

'Because there isn't any. There is no life beyond this one, no promised kingdom, no heavenly design. There's only what we make for ourselves. After that, nothing.'

'You can't believe that.'

'Why not? You renounced your faith too, for a time. You told us so.'

'Yes, and then I saw the error of my ways.'

Beorn gives a snort. Desperately Guthred glances around the circle, perhaps hoping that one of them will say something that will help convince the warrior, will help him see more clearly and guide him towards the light.

Tova looks away before the priest's eyes can meet hers, feeling not a little guilty. She has had her own doubts, it's true, and there have been times in the past couple of days when she's wondered if Guthred is right about this being the end of days, and if the coming of the Normans truly is God's punishment for their sins. But at the same time she's determined not to end up like Beorn. If she surrenders her faith then what does she have left? At the moment it's the only thing keeping her going.

'Maybe you should carry on with your story,' Merewyn suggests.

For a long while Beorn doesn't speak, or do anything except sit there, his gaze turned towards the ground.

Sheer will is all that's kept him going, Tova realises. The fire hasn't gone out of him, not yet, but it has been dampened. He doesn't want to spend for ever fighting. For all that he talks about reaching Hagustaldesham and continuing the war against the foreigners, she senses there's a small part of him that would be happy enough to die. At least then it would be all be over.

So. I've told you about the rebellion. I've told you about our raids upon the enemy, how we ravaged their lands as we tried to take the war to their gates. But we knew we were fighting a losing battle. For all the damage we inflicted and all the Frenchmen we slew, it was never enough. We could never stay for long in any one place; we had to keep moving to avoid capture. All the while they were growing stronger as the other risings around the country were gradually put down, as they threw up great mounds of earth upon which they set the strongholds they call castles, and surrounded them with ramparts and ditches and timber palisades to defend against people like us.

The days grew darker, the nights colder. Our spirits were failing. Each evening we would pitch our tents and bed down on cold earth, and each dawn we would wake up, our limbs and joints as stiff as the frost that covered the land. After those early weeks, when we lived off what we could plunder, the Normans guarded their convoys more closely. We came to rely on provisions brought to us in our woodland hiding places by folk in the surrounding countryside who were friendly to us. They took huge risks on our behalf, slipping away from their manors in the dead of night to bring what they could from their own winter stores, even when they didn't have enough to feed themselves and their families.

Such kindness, though, could never keep so many hungry men fed for long. And that wasn't the only reason we were despondent. Our tunics and cloaks were ragged and dirty and full of holes, and we were each nursing some injury – bruised ribs, a broken nose, a missing finger or something more serious. We had all lost friends, good men who had given their lives for us. For all the care we took in planning our raids, we could never be sure when we set out which of us would be coming back.

The one thing that kept us determined, kept us fighting through those difficult weeks, was what the Normans were doing to the people under their rule. How in places they were treating the English folk who worked their land as little more than slaves. How they were seizing their treasured possessions, their hard-won harvests, as if it all belonged to them by right. How they didn't care whether that meant that those who had toiled so hard all year would starve. Any who dared challenge them, they hanged as examples.

From all across the kingdom we heard such tales. But there was one baron in particular whose name we kept on hearing and whose appetite for blood never seemed to lessen. Malger fitz Odo, he was called. Malger of Stedehamm—

'Did you say Stedehamm?' Guthred asks, interrupting.

'That's right. What about it?'

'Nothing really. It was just one of the places we used to visit when Master Æthelbald took us out with him into the shire, that's all. It was only a couple of days' ride from Licedfeld, as I remember. It wasn't much then. A few cottages. Not even a church. He had to say Mass in the open, on top of the moot hill, in the rain—'

'Do you want to tell the story, priest, or are you going to let me?'

This Malger was the cruellest of them all. Whenever a Frenchman was found dead on the roads that ran through his lands, he would round up all the men who lived nearby and demand that they produce the murderer within a week. If they failed, he would pick five of them and take their thumbs, or their ears, or some-times their noses as punishment. He would seize the womenfolk who lived on his manors and take them to his bed, even though he had a wife of his own back across the sea. If they tried to resist he would threaten them and their brothers and husbands and fathers with violence.

Even his countrymen thought he went too far, we heard.

Geburs and ceorls alike had been put to work building a new great hall, twice the size of the old one, sawing and jointing timbers, digging ditches and post holes, throwing up earthworks and hauling flagstones to set around the hearth and at the door. Anyone he and his steward decided wasn't working hard enough was stripped to the waist and flogged in the yard in full view of the rest, until his back was raw and streaked with scarlet, his flesh torn to ribbons.

When I heard all this, there was no question in my mind what we had to do. Nor in Cynehelm's. Nor in most of the others' too. We thought that if we could rid England of such a man, then we would have achieved something worthwhile, however small. A couple, though, said it was folly to pit ourselves against him. We were only fourteen in number by then. Several had left; others had died, including three of Cynehelm's own hearth warriors, men I'd known for many seasons, alongside whom I'd bent my back to the waves on many a voyage across the whale road. Their deaths came especially hard. Yes, others had joined us since, but they were mostly pups newly weaned from their mothers' teats, who for all their keenness barely knew one end of a spear from the other.

All the reasons the doubters gave were good ones. I wasn't so blinded by hatred that I couldn't see that. But for me they changed nothing, and I told them so plainly.

In the end the fairest thing, Cynehelm decided, was to put it to a vote. Even on our voyages he had always sought his crew's opinion when he could. When you're out at sea, far from shore, at the mercy of the winds, being battered by rain and hail, there's nothing worse than knowing your oarsmen are cursing you behind your back.

Anyway, we voted. Of the fourteen, twelve wanted to go after Malger, either out of anger or because they wanted revenge or simply because they didn't know any better. And so it was settled. For the two who had voted against, that was it. Cynehelm insisted that they should be allowed to depart with honour and without reproach, since they'd been staunch friends who had served well. Even so, it was hard to see them go, not just because they'd been there since the beginning, but also because they were two of our best warriors.

Æscmund I loved like a brother and trusted more than any other man in the world. He had served Cynehelm for nearly ten years. And there was his cousin Uhtferth, whose hide I'd saved more than once and who had saved mine in turn, whose good humour we could always rely on to lift our spirits in our darkest moments. Everything we'd seen and everything we'd done, though, had doused his fire. There was no laughter left in him, nor hunger to keep on fighting. They were good men, but they were spent, and so we had no choice but to say farewell. They begged me to join them, said it was pointless to keep fighting and that I should come with them.

'They asked you to abandon your lord?' Merewyn asks.

'They tried to sway him as well. They said we'd done everything we could but that it was time to give up the struggle. That this was a fight we could never win.'

'And what did he say to that?'

'His mind was set. So was mine. When they saw this, they shook their heads and turned away so that we wouldn't see their tears, but they didn't change their minds, and I didn't expect them to. They wished us well, and then with heavy hearts we parted ways. Where they went and what became of them, I don't know. It was only once they'd gone that I began to feel nervous. We were only twelve men then, a sorry knot of bedraggled warriors with little in common except the wish to bloody our blades. Maybe I should have stopped then to think about whether what we were doing was wise.'

'Would your lord have listened, if he was as single-minded as you say he was?'

'Yes,' Beorn says abruptly. 'Yes, he would have listened. To me, he would have, if to no one else. I'd always been closest to him. He trusted me like no other. He respected my judgement. And besides, I was the only one left.'

Tova asks, 'What do you mean, the only one?'

He gives her a strange look as he hesitates. 'Of Cynehelm's men. We were five to begin with and now there was just me, keeping company with men and boys who until a few weeks ago had been complete strangers.'

'So why didn't you say anything?' asks Oslac. 'If your lord trusted you and respected your counsel, why did you hold your tongue?'

'Because even then I still wanted what everyone else wanted. I suppose pride was part of it as well. If I'd changed my mind I would have looked a fool. And what else was I going to do? Where else was I going to go? So you see I didn't have much choice. Anyway, it was only a moment's misgiving, nothing more than that. As a warrior you always have doubts, but if you let them grow too powerful they turn into fears, and those fears cripple you, so you quickly learn how to push them away. You learn or you die.'

He pauses to swallow, as if the words are sticking in his throat and he is having trouble getting them out. There is silence. No one, Tova supposes, wants to be the one to ask what happened next. She isn't sure she really wants to know, but she has the feeling they're about to find out.

For three days we watched the great hall that Malger had ordered built. It stood on a mound within a loop of the river, surrounded by ditches and ramparts and a timber palisade. It was nearing midwinter; the frost lay heavily across the land and the ground was hard. Many of the streams were frozen, and there was a biting wind that stung our cheeks. We rubbed our hands and huddled deeper inside our cloaks, and all the while we kept imagining ourselves inside by a blazing hearth, feasting, swilling ale, playing games, telling riddles and sharing tales of things we had done and seen and others that we had heard, with our loved ones gathered around us, with beautiful women perched on our knees and children's shouts filling the air as they scurried around our feet.

Our loved ones, our children, who were all dead because of what Malger and others like him had done. The days grew colder and so did our hearts.

By day and by night we scouted around Stedehamm. Cynehelm divided us into pairs so we could take turns keeping watch and so there was always someone observing the comings and goings at the hall. Meanwhile the rest guarded our camp deep in the woods or else went out foraging for supplies or seeking information from the folk in neighbouring villages. I was paired with a man called Wihtred. I say he was a man, and he claimed to have sixteen summers behind him, but I think he was lying. Tall, he was, though, and as strong as a boar, with a boar's temper too, always eager for a fight. I suppose Cynehelm was thinking he might learn a thing or two from me. Not that you can teach much to those who don't want to listen.

Wihtred and I counted the guards on the gates, and we saw how often and at what times they changed watch. From that we reckoned he could have no more than ten hearth troops living on this particular manor, fewer than we'd expected, although still more than we wanted to face in a fight, especially given how inexperienced many of our own band were.

All the while we hoped for a glimpse of Malger himself so that we might know for ourselves the face of the man we'd sworn to kill. Wihtred and I thought we spied him that first morning, overseeing the repair of one of the fish weirs that the recent floodwaters had damaged. We were far away, though, so we couldn't be sure if it was him or his steward. It wasn't until the second afternoon that someone was able to say for sure that they had seen him, when he and his men grabbed one of the stable boys and dragged him outside the gates, where they beat and kicked him, for what offence no one could work out.

When they heard the boy's cries, the village folk stopped what they were doing, abandoned their tools and rushed to see what was happening. They were too afraid to do anything, though, and when Malger had finished and he saw them all looking on, he shouted and waved his arms at them until they went back to work, warning them against trying to help the boy, who was left lying in the dirt. Then a man and a woman who might have been his father and mother came with a flask of something for him to drink and a blanket to wrap around his shoulders and helped him to his feet.

That was what Leofstan and Thurgils said, anyway; they were the ones who saw what had happened. When we heard this, we decided we wouldn't wait for the right opportunity to come; we had to make something happen.

That same night Cynehelm sent two of the youngsters, Sebbe and Gamal, to get as close as they could to the hall and see if they could find any weaknesses in its defences. It was raining, a steady drizzle that would mask the sound of their footsteps and also with any luck dull their scent so the guard hounds wouldn't wake and give them away. They wore dark cloaks and smeared their faces with dirt so they could slip unnoticed through the shadows. They got so close to the gates that they could hear the sentries murmuring to one another, they told us later. They crept all the way around the ramparts, returning to camp shivering and soaked to the skin, with their hair dripping and plastered to their skulls, with little to show for their trouble, and yet despite that they were grinning from ear to ear at the adventure of it all, having been under the very noses of the enemy.

The one thing we learned from their expedition was that we had no chance of storming the defences, even if we had the numbers. The ramparts and palisades looked in good repair. No rotten timbers that might collapse if given a solid kick. Nowhere we could place a ladder and scale the walls. And so we had to find some other way.

It wasn't long before an idea came along. The next day Wihtred and I were out gathering kindling when we heard voices floating through the trees. At once we dropped what we were carrying and crouched behind a fallen trunk that the passing of the seasons had hollowed out. It sounded like they were speaking in English, but we couldn't be sure, and even if they turned out to be friendly we didn't want to be spotted. So far we'd been careful not to give ourselves away to the folk of Stedehamm itself. The last thing we wanted was for the enemy to get wind of our presence. This wasn't like before, when we were constantly moving from place to place. Then it didn't matter if the enemy learned of our whereabouts, since we were always long gone before they could catch up with us. Now things were different.

We kept low, Wihtred and I, not speaking, hardly moving as we strained our ears. The voices grew nearer. Two of them, both belonging to women. Young-sounding, I thought, although they were speaking too softly for me to make out what they were saying. Taking care not to make any sudden move that might give us away, I peered over the hollow log, trying to catch a glimpse of them.

And there they were. Two, just as I'd thought. Neither much older than you, girl. Sisters, although I didn't know that until later and you wouldn't have thought it to look at them. One was fair and short and the other dark and tall, and I supposed she was the elder of the two, although from where we were it was difficult to tell. What they were talking about, I don't know, but they were laughing. The tall one had a knife sheath belted around her waist; they both wore gloves, and under their arms they were carrying holly boughs. Until I glimpsed those winter-green leaves I'd entirely forgotten that it was nearly Yule, as I think had everyone else in Cynehelm's band.

A small part of me envied them. Even in those dark days, with everything that had happened and was still happening, they could still find cause for cheer. Still they went to gather holly to

302

decorate their homes, just as they'd done every winter in good years and in bad. Still they were able to laugh.

'Can you see them?' Wihtred asked, too loudly for my liking, although anything that came out of his mouth was always too loud, in my opinion. I waved him quiet.

They were coming closer, picking their way around fallen boughs, under bare branches, trampling the dead bracken as they went, taking care over the thick layer of leaves that littered the ground, which the recent rain had made slippery. That was when I saw that they had a dog with them: not as large as one of Malger's two great watch hounds, but a mangy grey-white thing that stood as high as the taller girl's knee, with a shaggy coat and an ear that had been half bitten off. Hardly had I spotted it than it must have caught scent of us; its ears pricked up and it bounded towards us, barking, barking, barking.

I threw myself to the ground behind the trunk, and just in time too, as I heard one of the girls call out.

I cursed silently. Cursed the noisy beast and wished I could wring its miserable neck.

'Did they see you?' Wihtred asked, and all I could think was: shut up, shut up, shut up.

I told him to keep down and stay still. My heart was pounding as I lay there in the dirt. If we tried to move, the wretched thing was bound to hear us, but if we stayed where we were and didn't make a noise then maybe, just maybe, the women would think it had smelt nothing more than some rodent or bird that it wanted to chase.

The animal was growling, and barking, and growling again, and Wihtred was whispering, asking what to do.

Nothing, I told him. We wait.

A rustling in the undergrowth. Footsteps, light upon the soft earth. Close, maybe ten paces away, I remember thinking. And then I could hear them talking. One was asking the dog what was the matter, and what had it found, while the other, the elder one, I think, was warning her to stay close in case there was danger, and that they should leave well alone, and, besides, everyone would be expecting them back soon. And then the first was asking, what sort of danger?

'Rebels,' the elder one said. 'Wild men. I overheard the smith talking about some near Ascebi who were hiding out in the forest. Half-men without souls, who live up trees and eat the flesh of the people they kill.'

I know it sounds silly, but that's what she said. We'd heard similar things before, for already those were the kinds of tales that people were telling about us, and about others like us. We reckoned the Normans were responsible for starting such rumours, to discourage folk from joining or helping us.

The younger one asked, 'Where's Ascebi?'

'Not far away. Herestan said there had been a hall burning near Lucteburne, too.'

That was us, I remember thinking. We had been to Ascebi, and before coming to Stedehamm we had raided around Lucteburne, although they were all becoming one in my memory. Had those raids been last week or last month? I didn't know any more.

'The wild men wouldn't hurt us, though, would they?' the younger one asked. 'I thought they only attacked the invaders—'

I was only half-listening, because at the same time I could hear sniffing, growling and the padding of paws upon wet leaves on the other side of the trunk from where we lay. Wihtred glanced at me but I had no more ideas. Another bark; this one rang in my ears and made my blood freeze. I've never liked dogs, ever since I was nearly killed as a child by the steward's deerhound.

It was a fearsome beast, the kind that would tear other dogs apart if given the chance, and word was going around that it had gone mad and that somehow it had got loose in the sheepfold. I didn't know what was happening, except that there was bleating and there was snarling, and the sheep, those that still lived, were running in every direction, their fleeces spattered with red, and the dead ones' necks had been savaged and their legs broken. All us youngsters rushed to watch while the men ran in with sticks and knives to try to kill it, but it was too quick for them, and too strong, and the next thing I remember was my father shouting at me from afar to run. I just stood there as it rushed at me, baring its teeth, which had strings of flesh and wool hanging from them, its muzzle slick and red-glistening. That was the first time I was ever truly afraid for my life. And the last.

I know, I know. I'm getting there, if you'll let me.

I could hear the girls' footsteps, so close now. The younger one was talking again to the dog, asking what had got him so excited. They were going to find us sooner or later, I realised, and it might as well be sooner.

I stood up. Wihtred hissed at me, asking what I was doing. But it was too late to have second thoughts.

The fair-haired girl was the first to see me. 'Ymme!' she shouted. 'Look out!'

I wonder what I must have looked like to them. I hadn't bathed in weeks; all my clothes had holes in them just as you can see now, and my face and arms were a mess of scratches and bruises.

Ymme didn't scream. Neither of them did. She opened her mouth as if she was about to, but then froze, not knowing whether or not to run, or what she should do.

I said, It's all right. We're not going to hurt you.

305

They could tell that I wasn't one of the foreigners, but at the same time they must have realised from my manner of speech that I wasn't from those parts, and so she was suspicious.

'Who's "we"?' Ymme asked, although I could hardly hear her above all the barking.

I glanced down at Wihtred, still crouching behind the log, looking at me as if I had lost my mind. Show yourself, I told him, or else I'll drag you to your feet myself, and he did so grudgingly, as sullen as ever.

'Two of you?' she asked. 'Or are there any more of you hiding there?'

Just two, I said. And you can call off your dog. We're not going to hurt you.

The animal was running back and forth, circling me like a wolf might approach its prey, growling and snarling, but not in a crazed way like the hound that almost killed me when I was young; rather it was anxious and excited, eager to please. At the sound of her voice it stopped and lay down quietly on the ground, but it didn't take its eyes off me. It wasn't until she called a second time that it padded reluctantly back to her side. She crouched down, placing a hand on it to keep it still, while the younger one huddled close to her.

'Who are you?' Ymme asked us. 'What are you doing here?'

And I told them. I started with our names and said that there were others elsewhere, a good twelve of us in all, and that we were warriors who had been with the ætheling's army in the north and had been fleeing the king's men ever since. I told her just what I've told you, about how we were carrying on the fight against the foreigners, how we had spent the past month in raids and ambushes, travelling from place to place, and that was how we came to be hiding in the woods.

'Wild men,' said the younger one under her breath, her eyes filled at the same time with apprehension and delight.

Ymme, though, had gone pale. 'You have to go,' she said. 'All of you. You can't stay here. Whatever it is you're planning, you're putting us all in danger just by being here.'

I assured her that we weren't going anywhere.

'Why here? Of all the places you could have chosen, why Stede-hamm?'

'Because of Malger,' Wihtred blurted before I could stop him. 'We've come to kill him.'

'To kill him?' asked the younger one. 'You mean it?'

'No,' her sister said quickly. 'No, you can't. You mustn't.'

Wihtred was frowning. 'Why not?'

'Because you can't!'

Listen, I said, while silently cursing Wihtred. You mustn't tell anyone we're here. You have to promise us that. If word gets out—'

'Do you know what will happen if you kill him?' she asked. 'None of us will be safe, and things will only get worse afterwards.'

I said, Worse than they are already? We've seen what he's doing. He treats your folk like they're his slaves. He deserves only death.

'But don't you see? Killing him won't change anything. After him there'll be another one just like him, except the next lord will be crueller than the last and will punish us all the more harshly, and so it will go on.'

I said, I can't just stand by and let these wrongs go unpunished. Not after everything I've seen. After everything we've fought for.

They began backing away, with the dog following. 'Then take your fight somewhere else. Somewhere far away. We've seen enough troubles here already. I beg you, don't bring any more upon us.'

Help us, I said.

It was a desperate plea, I knew it was, and there was something inevitable in the way Ymme shook her head.

'No. Don't ask us to help. Just go, please.'

At least promise you won't tell anyone you saw us, I said.

'Only if you swear that you and your friends will leave.'

Out of the corner of my eye I saw Wihtred shoot me a questioning glance, but he knew better than to say anything.

And I swore. I gave my oath to her. An oath that, even then, I wasn't sure if I could keep.

'Then you have our promise too,' Ymme replied. She turned to go, beckoning to her sister, who was staring us up and down, partly in wonder at being in our presence, I think, but also partly in dismay because of what I'd just sworn. I remember exactly what her face looked like then, the way her cheeks shone pink with the cold of the day, her fair hair all a-tangle, and I remember as our gazes met seeing in her eyes something else. Something that I hadn't seen in a long time, and haven't seen since.

Hope.

And right then, seeing the young one's face, I saw how much she was depending on us. How much she wanted to believe that we would do what we had intended. We were the only ones who could help her and her folk. There was no one else. And, in the end, that was what swayed me.

It's strange, I suppose, what makes us choose certain courses over others. But as I watched those girls and their hound disappear into the woods, I was more sure than ever that what we were doing was right.

Malger had to die.

'So you didn't mean what you said?' Mereywn asks. 'When you swore you'd leave.'

'I thought I did,' says Beorn. 'I was wrong.'

The fire has begun to dwindle; small flames dance and flicker amid the embers, and their light plays across Beorn's face, making strange shadows of the pits of his eyes and causing his yellow teeth to gleam.

Oslac yawns noisily, deliberately. 'When will you get to the point?'

'Am I boring you?' he asks. 'I thought you were the one who wanted to hear it in the first place.'

'I know, and I'm thinking now that I made a mistake.'

'The sooner you shut up, the quicker it'll be over.'

Oslac scowls again but says nothing.

Late that night, after Gamal and Sebbe had come back from their scouting, we held a council of war. It had been a few hours since we'd returned from our meeting in the woods and Cynehelm's mood had been steadily darkening. Doubts were creeping into his mind, and the longer we spent discussing what we should do the angrier he grew. He wasn't usually one to let his frustrations show, but he was angry then, and everyone knew it as they sat waiting for him to speak.

This threatened to ruin everything, he said. If the girl spoke—

She won't, I told him.

And why not?

Because she gave her oath that she wouldn't, and I believe her.

Her oath is worth nothing to me. Not when our lives are at stake. How could you be so careless as to let them find you in the first place?

It was fate.

It wasn't fate, he snapped, and he told me not to be foolish. For all we know, he said, word has already reached Malger, and his men are searching for us as we speak.

No, I answered. They're hardly going to venture into the woods after dark, when they could easily be ambushed.

We have to leave, he said. Before first light, before they come looking for us.

There were footsteps then, a rustling in the bracken, and we all looked up at once, drawing our weapons as we turned to face whoever it was, expecting the worst.

But it was only long-faced Pybba, one of those keeping watch that night. With him, though, was another figure, shorter and clad in thick wool. It was the girl from earlier. Not Ymme. The other one, the younger of the two. Pybba said he'd found her, or rather she'd managed to find him, which we all thought strange until it emerged she'd heard him pissing against a tree. She'd said she was looking for the outlaws, and since he didn't know what else to do with her, he decided it was best to bring her straight to us.

She looked terrified, and no wonder, seeing all of us turned towards her with bared steel in hand. I suppose she must have had some idea of what to expect after meeting Wihtred and myself, but even so we must have looked to her a rough lot, dirt-stained, bruised and travel-worn, dark under the eyes from so many sleepless nights. At last her gaze settled upon me. Seeing a face that she recognised seemed to calm her a little.

Leofstan asked me if this was the girl we had met that afternoon, and I said yes, one of them, anyway.

Cynehelm asked what her name was, and after a moment's hesitation she said in a small voice, no more than a squeak, 'Eawen.'

She'd brought with her a knapsack, which she presented to Cynehelm. Inside were cheese and sausage wrapped in cloth, a brace of carrots and a few handfuls of nuts.

'I'm sorry there isn't more,' she said. 'This was as much as I could safely take without anything being missed.'

She broke into tears as she said this, and none of us was sure whether they were tears of sadness or gladness. Small though her gift was, it was welcome, and we put the carrots to use straight away, tossing them into the broth that was cooking. I gave her my own bowl, ladling some out for her. She took it, cupping it in her hands as if grateful for the warmth, but she didn't eat. Maybe she was too scared to be hungry. She was probably eleven or twelve years of age, but huddled under all those layers of wool and linen, I remember thinking how small she looked, and how thin. Skin and bone and precious little else.

I asked, Where's your sister?

'At home,' she said, 'asleep like everyone else. Don't be angry with her, please. She's only thinking of what's best for everyone. She thinks she's doing the right thing.'

I said, Has she told anyone about us?

She shook her head.

I asked, Are you sure?

'She won't tell. She isn't like that. She isn't as heartless as you think. She's just frightened, that's all. We all are.'

I said, Does she know you're here?

She shook her head. 'No one does. I was worried that if I didn't try to find you tonight then you'd all be gone come the dawn.'

You risked a lot just to bring us a few provisions, said Cynehelm. If someone notices you're gone, there'll be questions.

'That wasn't why I came. I came because I want to help.'

Wihtred snorted. 'You want to help?'

'In five days Malger will be celebrating Christmas in his new hall,' she said, undeterred, and explained that was why she and Ymme had been sent to collect the holly. Malger had invited some of his Norman friends from nearby to join him for the feast, and after that he was going to rejoin the king's army. She said to me, 'If you're going to do anything, you have to do it soon.'

We would if we could, I said. We've watched him. He rarely steps beyond his gates, and when he does he's always well guarded.

That was when she told us that the very next day Malger was planning to ride to market to choose a hog for the feast, after complaining that the ones at Stedehamm weren't fat enough and saying he'd get a better meal if he slaughtered Herestan the swineherd instead.

Enough about the swineherd, Cynehelm said sourly. You said Malger will be going to market. Where?

'Ledecestre,' she said. 'He'll be taking six men with him for protection.'

I said, Just six?

'It could be more,' she said, 'but he usually leaves half his men behind to guard the hall. They'll be going at first light, so as to get there and back before the day is out. They'll be taking the winter road.'

We'd all seen enough of Stedehamm and its surroundings by then to know what she meant by the winter road. It was the one that made the steep climb up the ridge rather than the track that lay in its shadow, which the last few weeks' rain had turned into a thick bog that neither man nor horse could cross.

The old fort, Cynehelm murmured.

We all nodded, knowing what was in his mind, for we were all thinking the same thing. At the top of the ridge, a mile or maybe two from the village, the track passed a series of banks and ditches, which at some time in the distant past must have served as some sort of stronghold. An ideal place for an ambush.

Pybba said it was too risky to trust the word of a girl. His arms were folded, and he was frowning. Maybe he was still sour that he'd been shown up by her.

I pointed out that we wouldn't get a better chance than this, and that if we didn't take it we might as well give up. We put it to another vote. This time eleven were in favour, with only Pybba against, but he soon relented. And so it was decided.

It was foolish, I see now, allowing hope to get in the way of my better judgement, but at the time I really thought we could do it. Fate had delivered this girl to us. And fate would deliver us victory. Of that I was more sure than ever.

Eawen left us not long after that so that she could get back before anyone realised she was missing, although we insisted that she eat something before she went. She'd taken an enormous risk on our behalf, and we were all grateful to her.

As soon as she'd left, we gathered our helmets and our shields, our swords and knives and seaxes and bows and axes and spears. We fastened our sword belts and baldrics and buckled up our shirts of leather. Our tents and all our other belongings – our packs and our cooking pots and everything else – we left behind, thinking we could come back for them once it was done. We threw water on the fire and stamped upon the cinders and ground them with the toes of our shoes into the earth, and then, under the cover of darkness, under a starless sky, we set off. We had some miles to cover, across fields and streams, tramping through flooded water-meadows, scrambling up hillsides with uneven tussocks and muddy paths that kept giving way beneath our soles. The fog was closing in and at times we could barely see our own feet, let alone who was in front of us, but somehow we kept going.

It was still dark by the time we found the winter road and arrived at the old fort, or what remained of it. There was a short stretch where the rutted track ran within perhaps ten paces of part of the encircling ditch, and we chose that as our hiding place. Ten of us huddled down on the wet slopes, surrounded by thorns and bramble bushes, with the ramparts at our back, while Cynehelm sent Sebbe and Gamal to keep watch across the valley. They were to hurry back as soon as they saw anyone approaching from the direction of Stedehamm.

We didn't sleep. We couldn't. We spoke in low voices, shared a little bread and ale and did our best to keep warm. It wasn't that we were nervous. I wasn't. It was more the anticipation, knowing that finally our chance had come not just to carry out the promise we'd made to ourselves at the start, but also to fulfil the duty we owed Eawen and these people. None of us wanted to let this chance slip. The fate of kingdoms might not have rested upon our shoulders, but we knew how important this was. We would send a message to the foreigners. The English people were not defeated. They would not simply bow their heads to the yoke. We would fight on, and so long as we did, no Norman was safe.

Morning came. The fog still hung close. The skies grew lighter, and still we waited. Eawen had told us they'd be riding out at dawn, but an hour must have passed since then and there was no sign of them. No word either from the two youngsters keeping watch. Someone murmured that she'd lied to us. Wihtred, I think it was, but I'm not sure.

Someone else, more charitably, said she must have misheard. Whatever she thought she'd heard about Malger riding to Lede-cestre, she was mistaken.

Cynehelm said nothing, but I could tell he was thinking the same thing as me: we were wasting our time.

Pybba was asking how much longer we were going to wait when through the fog from the direction of the manor came the clinking of harnesses, the dull thudding of hooves upon turf.

It's them, said Cynehelm. He told the others to stay low to the ground and to wait for his signal, then he and I scrambled, as quietly as we could, further up the side of the ditch so that we might have a better view of whoever these people were.

I asked, Where are Sebbe and Gamal? They were supposed to come and tell us if they saw anyone.

They must have fallen asleep, Cynehelm said and swore under his breath, saying that he should have sent someone older rather than entrust such an important task to them.

Malger was late, and we hadn't heard from the two boys. Alone, each fact meant nothing, but taken together I couldn't help but see them as signs. There was a tightness in the pit of my stomach, a tightness that only grew worse with every passing moment. Why hadn't Sebbe and Gamal returned?

I said, This isn't right.

He replied, You're just anxious.

The horsemen were growing closer. We pressed our bellies against the dirt, breathing as lightly as we could. I could hear my heartbeat sounding through my entire body as we lay there, peering out from behind a thorn bush, trying to catch a glimpse of our enemy.

And there they were. Four shadows in the gloom.

This should be easy, said Cynehelm.

He was thinking that we had three men to every one of theirs, but I was thinking that they were missing at least two of their number. Hadn't Eawen told us there would be six?

No, I said to him. Something's wrong.

Enough, he told me, stopping me before I could go on, and in a way he was right to, because by then it was too late to change our plan. They were getting close now, riding at a gentle trot. Clad all in mail from neck to knee, with long spears in their hands and strips of coloured cloth flying from the shafts of those spears. I forget what colours they were.

But not one of them looked like Malger.

It was hard to tell, because of the fog and because they all wore helmets like the one Cynehelm had, with a piece to protect the nose, and so it was hard to make out their features. I knew, though, that Malger was short and broad of shoulder, with a round face, nothing like the riders approaching, and the closer they came the surer I was.

He wasn't among them.

And I knew. Somehow, suddenly I knew. I could feel it right here, in my gut. Even as, out of the corner of my eye, I saw the others sliding their blades from their scabbards, I could feel a wrenching, a twisting, a churning.

That was when I heard my name. It came from somewhere beyond the rampart behind us, and it sounded like the girl's voice. Eawen's, I mean, but it couldn't be, I thought, not all the way out here. I must be imagining things, I told myself.

A cry went up and I turned, and suddenly there they were, Malger and his men, half-running, half-sliding down the grassy bank with swords in hand, while others stood on top of the rampart with bows, loosing arrow after arrow into our small band. Wihtred fell and Thurgils too, and there was blood everywhere, over their tunics and their faces, blood on the frosted ground, and everyone was shouting all at once, and no one knew what to do. We were caught like eels in a trap, and there was no way out.

At once Cynehelm threw himself into the fray, yelling at us to kill them, to kill the foreigners. They had reached the bottom of the ditch, where battle was joined. One of our younger men went down to a blow across the shoulder and neck and did not get up; I saw Malger plunging his sword into Pybba's gut and ripping it free. He was whooping with joy, and I wanted to strike that grin from his face, to bury my axe in his skull, but there were too many men between us.

Then, above the shouts and the cries of pain, I heard the shrieks. A girl's shrieks. On top of the ramparts on the other side of the ditch was Eawen, and I knew then that I hadn't imagined her voice. She was trying to break free from the grasp of one of Malger's men.

'I don't understand,' Tova says. 'What was she doing there?'

'I didn't understand either. Not at the time, with all that was going on. It was only later, when I was far away from there, that I was able to make sense of it all, that I was able to work out what must have happened.'

'And what was that?' asks Merewyn.

'My guess is that while Eawen was with us the night before, someone noticed she was missing. Her sister, maybe. When eventually she came back, they made her say where she'd been. As soon as they discovered she'd been with outlaws, they must have gone to Malger.'

'But why?'

'For much the same reasons as her sister gave, I suppose. They were scared they would be accused of conspiring against him. They were scared of the consequences.'

'So it was Ymme who betrayed you, then?'

'Maybe it was. Maybe she was right to.'

'That doesn't explain why the Normans took the younger one with them that morning,' says Guthred. 'All she'd done was bring you food. She had no hand in what you were doing.'

'No, but she'd spent long enough with us to see not just how many we numbered, but also how well armed we all were. Also where we had made our camp and where we were planning our ambush. I suppose they took her so that she could show them the way. Maybe they were also thinking she might make a useful hostage as well, if it came to it.'

At the time, though, as I said, I didn't know how or why Eawen was there, but it hardly mattered. There she was, shrieking, limbs flailing as she struggled against her captor. His arms were around her middle, and there I was, with the ditch and more than a dozen of the foreigners between me and her, and there was nothing I could do.

Run, Cynehelm was shouting, but there was nowhere we could go. The foreigners had us hemmed in on both sides: from the ramparts and from the track, where the horsemen were riding down any who scrambled out from the ditch. They were killing us, tearing us apart.

One of the Normans came at me, his sword raised, but his mail and his shield made him slow, and I was able to duck under his swing and clatter my axe into his neck. His head jerked back and he fell, and I hurled myself at the next. I was howling with rage, seeking vengeance for all my friends they'd killed. Before he knew what was happening I'd brought my blade round and smashed it into his face, carving a gash from temple to jaw. His cheek was gushing crimson, thick and dark, and he was yelling something in his own tongue that I didn't understand, and I was turning, stumbling over the corpses underfoot, the corpses that lay sprawled over one another, arms outstretched, legs crooked.

The soles of my shoes were slick with mud and blood, and the ground was still hard with frost, and when I glanced down the faces of Leofstan and Eadbald stared up at me, their eyes empty and their mouths hanging open. Their bodies broken. Wihtred too, lying on his belly, his face buried in the grass, a feathered shaft lodged in his back, his tunic soaked and matted against his torso.

Another scream from the rampart. I looked up at the Frenchman holding Eawen. Drawing his knife. Raising it to her face. Her eyes were wide, and she was shaking her head from side to side, twisting and kicking and twisting again, doing everything she could to get away from that blade, and she was shouting my name, screaming for help. Over and over and over she called out, and even now I hear her cries every night in my dreams.

He breaks off, trying to hide his face behind his hand. The tears are streaming down his face and the fire is reflected in his cheeks.

'What?' Tova asks. 'What happened to her?'

But she can already guess.

I don't know if she'd seen me. Maybe she hadn't and just supposed I was there, but anyway she kept on calling my name, and it was like a great spear was being driven through my heart and twisted, twisted. At once all the strength left my limbs, and I felt helpless like I've never done before or since. Another of the Normans was coming at me, and behind him was another, and behind him two more, but I knew somehow I had to get to her.

She was still shouting my name, and maybe there was more but that's all I was able to make out.

Eawen, I yelled as I ducked beneath the first Norman's strike and hooked my axe around his ankle, bringing him down.

Eawen, I yelled again, and I hoped that over the shouting and the dying and the ringing of steel upon steel she could hear me and know that I was there and I was coming.

She didn't answer. I risked another glance up towards her.

A bright line blossomed straight across her throat where the

Frenchman's knife had slit it. He was holding her up by the hair as she raised a powerless hand to her neck, and I was roaring, refusing to accept what I was seeing, but there was no denying it.

Eawen, I shouted and shouted again. Eawen!

He let go, and her limp body sank to the ground, the weight of her head carrying her forward, down the slope, rolling and tumbling, her arms and legs everywhere. Her brow struck a stone on the way down, her neck jerked back, and when she reached the bottom she was still.

After that I don't remember much. Things happened so quickly. I remember Cynehelm yelling above the clash of steel. I remember the clatter of lime wood and the shouts of pain and the Normans' war cries and the pleas for mercy. I remember the hatred pounding inside my skull. Cynehelm's helmet had come off, and his cheek was grazed and his nose was streaming and his lip was cut and his tunic was torn where his shoulder had been gashed. It was just him and another man, Tatel with the red hair, I think it was, against four of the foreigners, but he wasn't giving in. He was swearing death upon them, striking out on all sides, fighting like I'd never seen him fight before, but there were too many of them, and I think he knew that his death was near.

Run, Cynehelm was saying, over and over and over. While you still can, run!

But I wasn't going to give up the fight, not like that. I heaved my axe into the mailed back of one of his attackers, sending him sprawling to the ground, but just as I did so, another of them plunged his sword into Tatel's gut, driving it deep, so deep that it went all the way through, and I was yelling through my tears. A little way off, where the thorns grew dense and tall, there was more fighting, but there could only have been one or two of our

320

band left by then. They were surrounded, and I realised there was nothing I could do for them.

Then I couldn't hear Cynehelm shouting any more, and when I glanced around he was nowhere. And I knew. I didn't need to see his bloodied corpse to be sure. He was gone. Cynehelm was dead.

And so I ran. I didn't wait for Tatel's killers to turn on me; I just fled. I remember scrambling on my palms and knees up the side of the ditch, through the grass and the thistles, in the direction of the road. I remember hearing a voice and thinking it was Malger's although I'm not sure why, and he was bellowing something. The air was whistling as arrows spat down around me, out of the fog to my right and to my left, burying themselves in the turf. One came right over my head, and I thought I felt it graze my scalp, but I kept going, and then one struck my shoulder, and it was like I'd been slapped hard on the back. I'd reached the top by then and I almost fell, but somehow I stayed on my feet and kept hold of my axe, and it was just as well, because that's where the horsemen were, waiting to cut off our escape.

They saw me and wheeled about, then charged at me with their long spears. I ducked under the blade of the first, threw myself out of the way of the second, rolling across the hard earth, and then as the third came past I raised my axe, hooking the under-edge of my blade around his leg and wrenching hard so that he fell from the saddle. His steed ran on a little way up the track, and I chased after it, not stopping to finish the Frenchman off. My chest was burning and I was running like I've never run before, willing it to slow, to come to a halt.

Eventually it pulled up. I caught up with it and swung myself into the saddle, and then I was galloping down the track. I kept my head down as another one, two, three arrows whistled past.

I've never been the fastest of riders, but I rode then like I was fleeing the world's end. They came after me, of course; I could hear them behind me, and how they didn't catch me I'll never know, but I knew that if they did it would be the end, and so I didn't look back but just kept going through the swirling fog, following the track along the high ridge, away from the foreigners, hoping that eventually I'd lose them. Away from Stedehamm, away from all that death and all that pain.

At what point I realised they were no longer behind me, that they'd given up the chase, I don't know. It didn't matter. For hour after hour I rode, hardly slowing, not once pausing to rest. The further I could get away, the better.

The fog passed and the wind rose and the rain came, and I welcomed the hard, bitter drops as they stung my cheeks. They rinsed the blood, the grime and the sweat from my face and my clothes, but they did not rinse away the memories. I drove the animal on, through the rain and the mud, on ill-trodden paths far from anywhere, until eventually his foot lodged in a rut or struck a stone or a root. I don't know what it was, but he stumbled and fell. I was pitched over his neck and thrown into a hollow by the side of the track, and that was where I lay, bruised and bleeding and hurting, in the cold dirt and with the rainwater pooling around me, for hour after hour, weeping and weeping and weeping. How long I lay there I don't know. By the time I finally found the strength to get up, it was nearly night. My horse lay still and silent; I suppose it was exhaustion that did for him.

I could have given up in the same way. I could have lain there and waited for the night to come, for hunger and cold and sorrow to sap what was left of my strength. For death to take me. But that would have been the coward's way. And so I wandered. I had no home to go back to, and so I walked from place to place, sleeping in ditches and in hedges, just like before, only this time I did so alone. At first I tried to make snares to catch small animals to eat, but I didn't really know what I was doing and so turned to stealing what I needed from the villages I came to. A chicken here, some cheese or ale there, a winter blanket or two to keep myself warm at night. Stealing, because I was too ashamed to beg.

Whenever I spied any Frenchmen travelling on the road, alone or in small groups that I thought I could overcome, which wasn't often, I'd lie in wait to surprise them and then slaughter them. Whether they were warriors or not, it didn't matter. I killed them anyway, and after I killed them I'd take their provisions, and whatever else they had that was useful. A whetstone, a cloak. Shoes to replace mine, which had worn through. Arrows, a pack, a tent, a new horse: all these things I took. I would smash in their faces with my axe and slice open their bellies so that their guts spilled out, and I would leave them in the middle of the path where they would be easily seen, so that they might serve as a warning.

I didn't enjoy doing it, but it was justice.

It was from one of the Normans, a young man, a messenger on his way to Lundene, that I heard about the army that the king was gathering to lay waste the north. It was from him that I learned about the rumours of the rebels coming together at Hagustaldesham. As soon as I heard this I knew that was where I needed to be. I thanked him for his help and then buried my blade in his neck. After taking his precious parchments and tossing them to the winds, I left his body to the carrion birds.

And set out on the road north.

'And that was that.' He sits hunched over like a man twice his age, his voice small and weak. The tears, which were streaming down his face not long ago, have ceased. 'A few days afterwards, I happened to find you. The rest you know.'

Tova feels numb. All she can think about is that girl, that poor girl.

'It wasn't your fault,' Merewyn says, resting a hand on his arm. 'None of it was.'

'Yes, it was. If we hadn't got it into our heads to carry out that foolish plan, they'd all be alive now. And if I hadn't opened my mouth, if I hadn't told the girls who we were and what we intended, Eawen would never have come to us that night. She wouldn't have become involved. She needn't have died.'

'You didn't know,' Guthred says. 'How could you have done?'

'She was just a child,' Tova thinks, and is surprised to find herself murmuring the thought out loud.

Beorn nods. 'No older than you, certainly. But she had been consorting with us. That was enough to seal her fate.'

Merewyn asks, 'What about her sister?'

'Ymme? Probably they killed her too, when they returned to the manor later that morning.'

'Killed her as well?' Tova doesn't believe it, or maybe she just doesn't want to believe it, which she realises is a different thing.

'Why, though?' the priest asks. 'If she gave her sister up to them. If she was the one who betrayed you.'

'I can't say for sure that's what happened, because I don't know. But it wouldn't surprise me. Obviously she didn't know quite as much as Eawen. She knew we were there, though, hiding on Malger's lands, and she knew what we'd come to do. She'd deliberately hidden that knowledge from them. She'd pledged us her silence. Once they found that out—'

'She might yet live,' Guthred says.

'In the days afterwards I heard many stories from Stede-hamm. How many were true and how many were exaggerated, I don't know. But they were all bad. Men killed in reprisal, their daughters and wives given to Malger's guests for their pleasure when they arrived for the Christmas feast. We brought that upon those folk. We did that.'

'You can't blame yourself for the crimes of others,' says Merewyn.

Beorn doesn't seem to be listening. 'She didn't even know what she was doing. She didn't know any better. She trusted us, and we took advantage of her trust. Of her innocence. They didn't betray us. We betrayed them.'

Tova's beginning to understand, or thinks she is, anyway. 'Is that why you saved us? Because of them?'

'I'd been riding north for I don't know how long. Five days, maybe six, maybe longer. All I know is that it was slow going. I travelled by night and hid during the day so that I could rest, except when I knew the Normans were near, in which case I kept moving. I had a reason to live again, you see. Then late one afternoon I caught sight of the two of you riding down from the high moors, and I wondered what you were doing all by yourselves, and so I watched you, to see where you were heading. I didn't show myself because I didn't want you to be afraid, and because I remembered what happened the last time I'd tried to do a good thing. When I heard those Normans coming, I hid and hoped you'd do the same. As soon as they found you, though, I knew I had to do something.'

He looks straight at Tova. 'I heard Eawen's voice calling to me, and I knew I couldn't let the same thing happen again. I couldn't.'

She doesn't know what to think. On the one hand she knows she should be grateful, and she is, because he risked his life to save theirs. But on the other she resents the idea that the only reason they're here now is because others before them had died. Because he needed a way to assuage his wounded soul.

325

And wounded it is. His scars run deeper than the skin. His world is gone. What dreams he had are all but shattered; his hopes stamped out.

The desire to keep fighting is the only thing still keeping him going. It's all he has left. Without it he is nothing.

The hearth fire has died. The hall grows cooler as the shadows deepen. Guthred is snoring. Merewyn is also asleep, close beside her. Tova is on the verge of sleep herself when she hears Beorn and Oslac murmuring to one another. She lies as still as she can, her eyes open. She can't see them, but they're near.

'Let me understand this,' the poet says. 'The only reason you have it in your mind to go to Hagustaldesham is because of a rumour you heard.'

'What of it?'

'So you don't really know that's where the rebels are gathering, if they're gathering at all.'

'I heard it from one of the king's men, and he must have heard it from somewhere. From their scouts and their spies, probably.'

'How can you be sure he was telling the truth?'

Beorn says, 'I had my foot on his chest, my axe in one hand and my knife in the other. He knew if he didn't speak I was going to kill him.'

'You were going to kill him anyway. He could have told you anything and it wouldn't have made the slightest difference.'

'I saw the fear in his eyes. He wasn't lying. I'd have known if he was. Believe me, I can always tell.'

'The rebellion is finished. The war is lost.'

'Not yet,' says Beorn. 'Not yet.'

FIFTH DAY

Tova wakes in the early light with a dull ache at the front of her head. Cold air upon her face, swirling, teasing, tearing her from her dreams, bringing her back to the world. To the hall and the damp rushes and the smell of mouse droppings. To the sound of rain pattering upon the ground outside.

She rolls over, blinking to try to clear the bleariness from her eyes, wondering what woke her and why it's so cold.

The doors are open. Not by much, but enough to let in the grey morning. In the dip at the threshold a muddy puddle has formed that glitters as ripples race across it.

They closed the doors last night to keep the heat in, and barred them from the inside so that the wind, which was getting up at the time, wouldn't blow them open. Still befuddled by sleep, Tova thinks for a moment that's what must have happened, somehow. But then she notices the bar resting up against the wall.

She gets to her feet and looks around. Merewyn is still sleeping and so are Beorn and Guthred. But where Oslac was lying, on the bench by the wall, he is no longer. His blankets are gone, his pack too.

She hurries to the door, stopping only to put her hood up before she steps outside. The yard outside the hall has turned overnight into one great lake. She picks her way around it as she searches in all directions.

Of course he could be long gone. If he left in the middle of the night chances are he's already many miles away.

She looks back the way they came, towards the woods, then the other way, down to the burn and the mill below, but she can't see anything. A few sheep grazing that must have been left behind. A deer down by the water's edge. She glances towards the west and the tiny timber church where Guthred went to pray last night before they all settled to eat and warm themselves by the hearth, then eastwards, along the track that runs between the hedges, that leads past the well and the cattle byre.

And she sees him. Or a figure that could be him. She thinks about shouting but reckons he's too far away to hear. What's he doing?

She runs after him, as fast as she can manage down the muddy track. The rain is hard, almost like hail; it stings her face and her hands. The cold air pains her throat and her lungs.

'Oslac,' she calls when she is nearer. 'Oslac!'

He too has his hood up against the rain, but he must be able to hear her, surely.

She carries on after him, calling his name again. Does he quicken his pace? She isn't sure.

She's almost reached him when at last he does turn. His eyes have a dark, sunken look, as though he hasn't slept.

'Why are you following me?' he asks angrily.

'Why am I . . . ?' she says, taken aback. 'What about you? Where are you going?'

'I'm leaving.'

'Leaving?'

'I can't do it any longer. I don't trust him. I never have, from the moment we met. After what he's told us, I trust him even less.'

'Who?'

'Who do you think?'

'Beorn?'

'He's hiding things from us still, I know it.'

'So you're running away?'

'As should you, if you have any sense. I can't follow him blindly to my death. I won't. Because that's what's going to happen if we let him lead us to Hagustaldesham. This war that he believes he's still waging, it's nothing more than an empty dream. It's a lie. The rebels are destroyed. They were destroyed long ago. England is lost. You only have to look around you to see. Look at this empty land. There's no sense fighting any more. The time for that has passed. It's over. The Normans have won.'

'What are you going to do, then?'

'Survive,' he says. 'That's all any of us can do now. Survive, however we can. And I know I stand a better chance of doing that if I go my own way. I've always travelled alone before now; I'll do it again.'

'What about the rest of us?'

'You have to make your own choice. I can't do that for you. But if you're sensible, you'll take my advice. Do what I'm doing. Run. You and your lady, and the priest as well. All of you. Get as far from him as you can, as soon as you can. He's dangerous. His wits have gone. He doesn't know what he's doing any more. He only knows one thing, and that's how to fight.'

Does he think she doesn't know that? She was there. She saw. She knows what he can do far better than Oslac does.

'As long as you stay with him, you aren't safe,' the poet continues. 'He's a broken man.'

'He's all we've got. He's all that stands between us and those who would kill us if they had the chance.'

'I'm not going to stand here arguing with you. I have to go. Call me a coward, if you like. Call me anything you want. I don't care. I'm not asking any of you to come with me. Tell the others I'm sorry. But think about what I've said. For your own sakes. Before it's too late. Will you do that?'

She doesn't answer. She can't believe he would abandon them.

'Forgive me,' he says.

He turns. She watches him go. He must see how selfish he's being. Any moment now he'll realise what he's doing and change his mind.

But he doesn't. Not so much as a glance over his shoulder as, his pack slung over his shoulder, he trudges down the slope, through the rain, which is growing heavier, until the path turns and he disappears behind the hedge and she can no longer see him.

'Did he say where he was going?' Beorn asks.

'No. He didn't tell me anything.'

'He was going east?'

She nods.

'Back towards the old road,' he mutters. 'He should have gone west instead, made for the high hills. The Normans will find him. He'll get himself killed.'

'There's no chance, I suppose, of catching up with him?' Guthred asks.

'If he has almost an hour's start on us, he could be anywhere by now,' Merewyn points out.

Beorn says, 'You should have woken us straight away, girl. You should have woken me.'

'So that you could have done what?' she asks. 'Dragged him back here? His mind was made up.'

'Did he even say why?' the priest asks her.

She shakes her head. She can't bring herself to repeat what Oslac said, certainly not in front of Beorn.

The warrior says, 'We're better off without him. I never trusted him anyway.'

And so they are four.

They saddle up and ride on, through the mist that hangs in the dales and the cloud that clings to the hilltops. Somewhere far off a cow lows forlornly. Flocks of sheep are untended in their garths. A shepherd's hut but no shepherd. The ash in his fireplace is as cold as the earth; he must have left some time ago. They take what they can, which isn't much: a small bundle of kindling and three loaves, each the size of Tova's fist and rock-hard. Going mouldy, but they can cut those parts off. The rest they leave: the tally stick, the whittling blade, the necklace of jet beads, the water pail standing outside the door.

They travel cautiously. Beorn no longer rides on ahead to scout out the way. Instead he stays close, and Tova is glad that he does. Up here on the hills, under the wide, white sky, Tova feels more exposed than ever. She can see for miles whichever way she turns, which means that they too can be seen by anyone with keen enough eyes who cares to look.

More than once that afternoon they spy horsemen in the distance, or think they do; in the darkling day the slightest flicker of movement or glint of light could be a person or people. Maybe they're friendly, but they have no way of knowing and Tova would rather not wait to find out. They seek cover in woods and in ditches by the roadside, leading their horses quickly into the trees where they won't be seen, before crouching low amid the thorn bushes. There they wait, watching, hardly daring even to breathe, until they can be sure that whoever it is has moved on, before finally they emerge with twigs in their hair, with scratches on their faces and their hands, with holes in their sleeves where the brambles have taken hold.

More hoofprints, these ones not so recent. The edges are blurred, washed away by the rain. Half a mile further on, the remains of a campfire, set a short way back from the path. Wooden plates and cups. A knife. Half-eaten bread amid the leaves. Blankets soaked by the rain strewn on the ground. A carved wooden horse – a child's toy, perhaps – lying forlornly on the ground.

And that's not all. Hardly fifty paces beyond that, at a fork in the path, four figures strung up from the thick branches of an oak, hanging by their necks. Ashen-faced. Stiff. Eyes closed, mouths open: even in death they still gasp for air. Barefooted, their shoes missing. A woman, two girls and a man. A whole family, Tova thinks. The girls even younger than her. Their clothes are rough, travelling garb, frayed at the hems.

'They must have been important,' Merewyn says.

Guthred asks, 'What makes you say that?'

'They could have just killed them; instead they chose to make an example of them.'

'Why would they do that? Who's going to see them?'

'Well, we did.'

'But how many others are going to be travelling this way?'

'They didn't kill them as a warning,' Beorn says as he examines the bodies. 'They killed them one by one. Hanged the first to put fear into the others' hearts. Then the second, then the third. Him last of all.'

'How do you know?' Tova asks.

'I've seen it done before.'

He doesn't look at her as he speaks. She would ask when and where, and what does he mean when he says he's seen it before, but she isn't sure she wants to know the answers.

'Maybe they knew something,' he goes on. 'Or the Normans thought they did, and wanted to get it out of them.'

Guthred makes the sign of the cross. 'I think we should go.'

'Are you sure this is the way?' Tova asks when Beorn leads them down a trail so brant and rough that she thinks it must have been trodden by goats, not people.

'I'm sure,' he replies.

When at last they come to the bottom of the slope and find the river too deep and fast-flowing to ford, with no sign of the bridge he said they'd find, however, his mood changes. A cloud comes across his face as he looks first upstream and then down.

He doesn't shout. He doesn't curse.

Instead he squats down on his haunches and presses his clenched fists to his brow. His eyes are closed tight. He looks in pain.

'Are you all right?' Merewyn asks.

He says, 'I'm trying to think.'

'We could go back the way we came,' Guthred suggests. 'We probably took the wrong path, that's all.'

'No, we didn't. We took the right path. I remember the bridge. It was here.'

Even if it was, it isn't any more. Maybe it fell down and washed away. Maybe it was destroyed by the Normans. Or maybe . . .

She doesn't want to say what she's thinking, but she has to. 'We're lost, aren't we?'

He rises, gazing down the valley towards the east. 'Follow me,' he says.

They've been this way before.

For the last hour she's thought that each hill, each ridge, each clump of trees and outcrop of rock had a familiar look about it. Now she's sure of it. They've doubled back on themselves. They might as well have followed Guthred's suggestion.

How many hours have they wasted? It's long past noon already; they can't have much of the day left.

At every fork in the track Beorn halts. He gazes up at the sky, but the sun remains hidden. He looks to see which way the trees are bent, and on which side of their trunks the lichen is growing. He seems so hesitant suddenly, for no reason that she can work out. So uncertain of himself.

Was Oslac right to go his own way? Tova can't help but wonder. She hopes he's all right, wherever he is.

'If we can find the old road again, then we'll know where we are, won't we?' Merewyn asks the next time they stop. 'I don't see why we can't just follow that north.'

'I've told you why,' Beorn says. 'King Wilelm and his army are using that road.'

'Then what do we do? We can't keep going round in circles.'

'Do you think I don't know that?'

He whirls about and advances upon her. Anger flashes across his face. His eyes are wide and bloodshot. Merewyn takes a step back, then another. Tova clasps her lady's hand. Her skin is cold. Tova holds her breath as he comes towards them, teeth bared.

He stops. He realises what he's doing and stops mid-movement. He blinks once, twice. At once all the fury appears to drain out of him. He breathes deeply. His eyes are moist and red around the rims. Has he always looked so exhausted, and she has just never noticed before?

'I'm sorry,' he says quietly as he turns away.

How much sleep has he had? Not enough, obviously. But it isn't just that. His weariness, she senses, runs deeper than that.

She glances at Merewyn. Her lady's face is pale, and she's still shaking.

It's getting colder. Tova can feel it in her fingers, even inside her gloves. The rain is turning to sleet. Softly but steadily it falls, with no sign of relenting. The skies are dark and growing darker.

Beorn keeps saying there'll be worse to come. In that, at least, she believes him.

She's catching something, she's sure of it. There's a roughness at the back of her throat, which she would scratch if only she knew how to reach it. Instead all she can do is swallow, much good that does. For a few moments she has some relief, but then she feels it again, still there, still dry, still tickling.

Stay strong, she tells herself. It can't be much further. Five days they've been travelling now. Five days since they left Heldeby. They must be close, surely.

The cart lies on its side in the middle of the droveway, between high earthen banks. The grey skies are barely visible through the criss-cross of overhanging tree limbs. On the ground in front of it the unmoving forms of two oxen, still yoked, their tongues lolling out of their mouths.

Beorn tells them to wait while he approaches, axe in hand. He looks all around. If someone wanted to ambush them, this would be the place to do it. He lifts the oilskin sheet that lies in

337

a heap on the ground to see if there's anything underneath it, then rounds the cart slowly, making two full circuits.

He beckons them forward. 'There's nothing. It's empty.'

There's no sign of its owners either. Not until they venture another hundred paces along the rutted track and they see the body lying in the dirt. His face is buried in the mud; his white-grey hair is a bloody, tangled mess where a blade of some sort has felled him.

She ought to be sickened, she knows. But she isn't. In the last few days she must have seen almost every way there is of killing a man. Now there's nothing more that can shock her. She crouches down beside the old man. Tentatively she reaches for his hand, which is dry and wrinkled. Stiff. He's older than Guthred, she reckons. Maybe even as old as Thorvald.

'Cold,' she says under her breath. She lets the man's fingers fall from her grasp with a shudder.

Beorn glances about again, quickly. Is it just her imagination or has everything suddenly gone still?

'No,' says Guthred from a short way further up the track. 'Oh no. Oh Lord.'

He's kneeling down by the side of what looks like another body. He's sobbing as he throws his arms around its neck and presses his cheek against the figure's chest.

'No, no, no, no,' he says through his tears.

They gather around him but he doesn't look up. His face is buried in the boy's bloodstained cloak and tunic. A boy, not a man. Twelve years old perhaps, no more than that. His face and neck are covered in red blotches and tiny yellow pustules. He lies on his back, eyes open but unseeing.

'I'm so sorry, Hedda,' says Guthred. 'For everything. I failed you. Please, God, forgive me.'

338

That name. Hedda. Wasn't one of his students called Hedda? It can't be, surely. What is he doing here, this far from Rypum?

'Look,' says Beorn. 'There are more of them.'

He's found the others: Hedda's fellow students. She recognises them at once, for they're just as Guthred described them. They managed to get a little further before they too were struck down. As soon as they can prise the distraught priest away from Hedda's limp body, they lead him first to the chubby-faced and fat-fingered Wiglaf, and then to Plegmund: taller, dark-haired, with thick eyebrows that meet in the middle.

On seeing them the priest's legs give way. Fresh floods of tears break forth, until eventually he has no more to give. He can barely stand, barely even raise his head.

In all there are eight bodies: the three students, the old man, whom Guthred says was Father Osbert, and four others – Dean Deorwald and three more of the Rypum canons. Guthred says there used to be ten of them, or there were when he last lived there. Something must have happened to the others. God only knows what.

'They were trying to get north, like us,' the priest says, sniffing. His eyes are puffy and he looks ready to collapse at any moment. He takes deep breaths. 'That's all they were doing. Trying to escape the Normans, to take the minster's treasures somewhere they'd be safe. For that he killed them. He killed all of them.'

She is afraid. Truly afraid, like never before.

She has spent these last few days glancing over her shoulder, jumping at the slightest noise, tensing whenever birds flock up from a distant thicket, worrying whether that glint of light could be a spear point. But that was a different sort of fear, a constant, simmering, back-of-her-mind fear. In all that time she never felt as she feels now: that death could come at any moment, without warning.

Their enemies are close. She knows it. Beorn knows it. They all know it. No one says it, but they do.

How much more of this she can endure, she isn't sure. They can't keep running for ever. They can't live like this, on whatever scraps of food they can scavenge, in clothes that aren't even their own, sleeping on the hard ground, in tents or amid the hay in half-ruined laithes. They've been lucky so far, but for how much longer?

'I can't do this,' she says to Merewyn the next time they're alone. 'I can't.'

'We have to.'

'What's the point? We're going to die, aren't we? Maybe it won't be today or tomorrow, but it's going to happen.'

'We're not going to die. Everything will be all right.'

Tova feels like she could burst. 'You keep saying that! You keep saying it like you know it, but you don't. You don't know it at all.'

'But we're so close now. Another day or two and we'll be there, you'll see.'

Hagustaldesham, she thinks bitterly. It seems as far away now as it ever did. And even if we do manage to get there, what will we find? There'll be no friends and kin to give us comfort. No hall and hearth fire and music and revels. Only sorrow.

'What about afterwards?' she asks her lady. 'When the Normans have finally gone, what will we do then?'

'We'll work that out when the time comes. But we can't abandon hope yet, not—'

'What hope? What's left for us? There isn't going to be a home for us to go back to, because they'll have destroyed everything. Everyone's dead. Everyone.'

It all comes spilling out, everything she's been keeping inside these past three days. The anger, the pain, the hunger, the tiredness, the fear. The torture and the guilt, her constant companions. Guilt, for daring to live when so many do not.

She doesn't remember when she last spoke so bluntly, so boldly, in her lady's presence. Maybe never. At home Merewyn wouldn't have stood for such an outburst. But they aren't at home. They aren't mistress and servant any more. None of who they used to be matters any more. All that ended when the Normans came.

'Let them find us,' Tova says. 'Let them do what they will. At least then we won't have to run any more. We won't have to live like outcasts in our own land.'

'Don't say such things. It'll be all right. I know it will.'

Stop it, she thinks. Just stop it. I can't bear to hear those words any more.

One foot after another, somehow she forces herself to keep moving. It's all she can do as she tries to ignore the voice in the back of her mind. The voice of reason. The voice of doubt.

Run, walk or crawl, she tells herself. It doesn't matter how. Just keep going. She keeps on murmuring it to herself, quietly so that no one but her can hear, trying to keep that other voice at bay.

That other voice, which whispers to her, soothingly, even sweetly, repeating the same few words again and again and again.

Let it be over.

The wind is rising, howling down the dale. They struggle against it for a while but make little headway. Days of rain have made the slopes treacherous; sooner or later, one of them will slip and hurt themselves. And there is snow in the air too – a few flakes, nothing more, but enough to worry Tova.

Beorn wants to press on, to cross this ridge before dark; Merewyn is desperate to turn back. Eventually he hears her pleas and they descend through thickly wooded slopes into the lee of the hill. Close to the old road, which is what they wanted to avoid, but they have no choice.

'There's a ford an hour upstream from where the road crosses the river, if I remember rightly,' Beorn says. 'We'll make for that. If we're lucky we can cross before nightfall.'

'You're sure this time, are you?' Merewyn asks.

He doesn't answer.

The snowflakes continue to dance and swirl. Few enough that Tova can count them one by one as they fall, but with every hour that passes, the clouds grow blacker, lower, heavy with the promise of more to come.

Upon the horizon to the east, a fire blazes. It licks the sky, sending up great plumes of grey-white smoke. A warning beacon, perhaps, or more likely another hall burning. Three, four miles away. From somewhere unseen in the distance comes the tolling of a church bell. On and on it rings, by turns clear and then muffled, faint and then strident, as the wind gusts and dies away.

They hurry, pick their way down into a steep griff, down tracks that are slippery with leaves and often seem at first to lead nowhere. It's quiet. They could be the only four people in the world. The only four living creatures anywhere.

It's almost dark when Tova hears water trickling, tumbling, rushing. They're close.

A little after that, between the trees, she spies the shadowy remains of an old mill. It must have been abandoned years ago.

The roof has rotted away and so too have parts of the walls, although the timber posts are still standing. The leats and mill-pond have filled up, clogged with leaves and reeds. Brambles and ferns grow thickly all about.

The path leads down towards the river. And there, in front of them, is the ford.

'I told you we'd find it,' Beorn says.

Not a moment too soon, either. Night is closing around them. White specks dance and twirl around her. They settle on the ground and disappear in an eyeblink.

Don't let it snow yet, Tova thinks. Not until we're somewhere warm and sheltered. Somewhere with a roof. Then it can snow all it likes.

This river isn't nearly as wide as the one they crossed yesterday morning. It doesn't look as deep either. But the waters, thick and murky with mud, look every bit as cold. This time she decides not to take off her shoes; some of the stones look sharp.

Guthred goes first this time. Merewyn is behind him and Tova next. Beorn last of all. She picks her way carefully down the crumbling bank towards the water's edge, tugging sharply at Winter's reins, making encouraging noises as she coaxes her on. The mare doesn't want to enter the river, and Tova doesn't blame her. She's tired, like the rest of them. But they can't rest yet. Just a little further.

A rustling in the reeds on the other side; a bird chirps indignantly. Something long and sleek slides into the water and vanishes beneath the surface. An otter, maybe.

The current swirls around her ankles. She splashes through the river with Winter in tow, doing her best to ignore the icy water as it floods inside her shoes and seizes her toes. Instead she imagines the fire that they'll soon have burning, and how good it will be to warm her feet beside it. And her hands, and her face. If she thinks hard enough she can almost feel the heat upon her cheeks. Small comforts.

She's so lost in her thoughts that she almost collides with Merewyn, who's stopped in front of her, in the middle of the river. Her lady cries out. Behind her, Beorn is shouting something she can't make out.

'What's going on?' she asks, just as she looks up and sees the figures standing in the middle of the path on the opposite bank. Two of them, blades glinting coldly in the twilight.

'Quickly,' Beorn is yelling. 'Back the way we came! Now!'

Tova doesn't question him, but does exactly as he says. She whirls to follow him, ready to scramble back up the bank, only to see their path blocked by another two figures, both with weapons drawn.

Their enemies have found them.

'Well, well,' comes a voice from the near bank. A man's voice. Older. Thick with scorn and with spite. 'What a happy turn of events this is. Look, it's our old friend Guthred.'

And she knows. She doesn't have to see his gap-toothed smile, his scarred face, his thick eyebrows, those large ears. Like serving dishes, the priest said.

It's him. The murderer, the priest slayer, the killer of children, who has raided and thieved and cheated and preyed upon the weak, who has tortured monks without compunction.

'Wulfnoth?' Guthred says.

'Did you think you could run from us? Did you think you could steal from us and we would just let you get away?'

'You can't have it,' Guthred shouts back. 'I won't let you.'

Laughter. Not just from Wulfnoth but from the others too, on both sides of the river. Among them a woman's voice. Gytha, she thinks. Who else did Guthred say was left by the end? She tries to remember but can't gather her thoughts properly. One of the two brothers, she thinks, and the deaf one as well. Halfdan. Was that his name? Or was that Sihtric? She isn't sure.

Beorn asks, 'How did you find us?'

'Providence,' Wulfnoth says. He sounds pleased with himself. Tova can't see, but she can imagine the grin on his face. 'Or fate, or destiny; whatever you want to call it. God willed it, and so it happened. He delivered you to us.'

'He'd never help you,' the priest shouts. 'You're Hell fiends, all of you.'

'Oh Guthred, you pious fool. You never were one for jokes, were you? No, of course it wasn't God's doing. We've been watching you. Watching and following, waiting to see what you and your new friends would do. And now here we are. And here you are. What happened to the other one who was with you?'

'You can have the gold and silver,' says Beorn flatly, ignoring his question. 'The book too. Everything. We don't need it. It's yours.'

'No, it isn't,' Guthred blurts. 'It doesn't belong—'

'Shut up.' Beorn turns to Wulfnoth. 'You can have it, if you'll leave us in peace to go on our way. No one needs to get hurt.'

He extends his hand towards the priest, gesturing for him to give the treasure over, but Guthred shakes his head. 'You'll have to pry it from my dead fingers,' he calls to Wulfnoth.

'Priest,' Beorn says warningly. 'Do you really want to get yourself killed for the sake of a book?'

'Listen to him, Father,' Merewyn says. 'Think about it. If you die then you won't be able to atone, will you?'

'Atone?' Wulfnoth asks, laughing. 'Do you really think the Lord will forgive you after everything you've done?'

345

Just do it, Tova implores silently. Please, for our sakes, just let him have what he wants. God will understand, won't he?

Beorn gestures towards Guthred. The priest hesitates before reluctantly passing the strap of the scrip over his head and handing it to him. Beorn tosses it across to the bank where Wulfnoth and his friend are standing. It lands with a dull thud and a clatter of metal.

'There,' he says. 'You have what you came for.'

Wulfnoth picks it up and loosens the drawstring. He casts a brief look inside before letting it fall at his feet. 'Not yet.'

'What?' Beorn glances at Guthred. 'It's all there, isn't it?'

Wulfnoth gives a snort. 'Do you think we've ridden all this way just to take back a few shiny trinkets and a worthless bundle of parchment? We want Guthred. Hand him over to us and then you can go.'

'Guthred?' Tova asks. 'Why?'

'He knows why,' shouts the woman, Gytha, from the other bank. She stands under the trees, in shadow, all but hidden. 'He betrayed us. We trusted him and he betrayed that trust. He stole from us.'

'You crossed me, Guthred,' Wulfnoth says. 'You crossed me twice. You made my life a misery. You took everything from me. But you can't run any longer.'

He takes a step forward, then another. He walks with a limp, but at the same time with an air of confidence, as if he has mastery of the world and everything in it, and there is nothing that frightens him.

Silvery hair, thinning on top. Ears protruding from the side of his head. Those ridiculous ears, Guthred said. They don't look so ridiculous now.

Behind Wulfnoth is possibly the tallest man Tova has ever

seen. Taller even than the Norman giant Beorn slew that night when they met him. This one, though, is beanpole-thin. In his hand is a sword, the blade of which is long and narrow to match his build. She tries to remember what the priest said was his name. Cuffa? Was that it?

They step down towards the water's edge. At once Beorn's axe is in his hand. He drops his pack, lets it slide from his shoulders. It falls into the river.

'Don't come any closer,' he says. 'You have the book, the silver. Everything. You don't need him as well.'

'You're defending him? That worthless turd, that stinking piece of goat filth? Hasn't he told you who he is? Hasn't he told you what he's done?'

Merewyn shouts, 'He's told us enough. He's told us about all of you.'

'And you believed him?' asks Gytha. Now out of the shadows, she spits noisily on the ground at her feet. Dressed in tunic and trews, and with her hair cut so short she might easily be mistaken for a man, were it not for the shape of her face and the pitch of her voice.

Tova stares at her, half in wonderment and half in shock. When Guthred first mentioned Gytha, she couldn't help but be intrigued. Now that she sees her with her own eyes, the feeling she has is closer to revulsion.

'Whatever he told you, he was lying,' Gytha goes on. She spits the words rather than speaks them. 'His head is so full of shit he doesn't even know what he's saying. You can't believe anything that comes out of his mouth. He'll tell you one thing and then deny it a moment later. He's nothing but a worm. A mawk, that's what he is, a spineless, slimy, dirty, squirming—'

'That's enough, Gytha,' Wulfnoth says. 'And you can put your axe away, you there. The big fellow. Our business is with Guthred, not with you. If he gives himself up, then we'll leave you alone. On that you have my word.'

'Your word?' Merewyn echoes. She sounds like she is about to laugh or cry, or maybe both at the same time.

Tova sees Gytha make a signal to the mute one with rapid flicks of her hands, tapping first the side of her head and then her chest. He nods, following her as she advances, still keeping to the riverbank but nearly at the water's edge now. He isn't as tall as the other men, but he has a blacksmith's arms and a neck like a tree trunk.

Both Guthred and Merewyn edge away from them towards the middle of the stream. Winter shifts restlessly; Tova holds tightly to the reins. The animal knows that something isn't right and she's impatient to get going again.

Please, Tova prays. Don't let there be bloodshed. There has to be some other way to settle things. A way that doesn't need weapons.

'What's it going to be, Guthred?' Wulfnoth calls. 'Are you going to come willingly to your fate and save these good people, these new friends of yours, from any trouble? Or are we going to have to drag you?'

The priest stares back at him with empty eyes, his mouth agape.

'If you want him,' Beorn says, 'then come and take him. But you'll have to kill me first.'

No, no, no, no, thinks Tova. This isn't the way. It can't be. Don't you see? Wulfnoth and his band will stop at nothing. They don't care what they have to do to get what they want. That's the kind of people they are.

That's what she wants to say, but the breath catches in her chest and her tongue, like the rest of her, is frozen.

348

Wulfnoth exchanges a glance with the tall man next to him, then says loudly, 'Put down your weapon and hand Guthred over to us. I won't ask again.'

This time the edge in his voice is unmistakable.

This is it, Tova thinks. This is how it ends. This is how we die. At the hands not of the Normans but of wretched oath breakers and desperate outcasts. The dregs of mankind, the basest of all God's creatures.

'Beorn,' says Guthred in a small voice. 'Don't do this. It's all right. I know what I have to do.'

'Stay exactly where you are,' the warrior says. 'Don't move.'

Tova isn't sure whether he's talking to the priest, to her and Merewyn or to Wulfnoth, but she does as he says anyway, staying as close as she can to her lady. Here in the midstream the current runs quickly. Her dress is soaked to the knee; it clings to her ankles and her shins. She can't feel her feet any more. Winter is growing ever more agitated; she struggles against the reins and tosses her head.

Wulfnoth takes another step forward, and Cuffa too. Into the shallows, where the water laps against the bank.

'I'm warning you,' Beorn says. 'Any closer and—'

But Wulfnoth's patience has run out. He breaks into a charge, splashing through the water, yelling as he comes, with Cuffa behind him.

A rush of feet, a flash of steel, a roar of anger, a cry of pain. Winter rears up, spooked. The reins slip through Tova's fingers as her faithful mare tears herself away and crashes through the river, kicking up mud and gravel. Some place in the darkness where Tova can't see, Guthred is yelling. Merewyn screams as the deaf one seizes her dress, and she's struggling, waving her arms, twisting and falling all at the same time, trying to get away. More

349

splashing; the horses in confusion go first one way and then the other, getting in each other's way, narrowly missing Tova, casting up great slews of water.

Between the horses and the enemy there's nowhere to go. Out of the corner of her eye Tova spots a shadow rushing towards her. She turns, sees Gytha bearing down on her. She steps back. One pace, two. But she's too slow. The she-wolf seizes the collar of her cloak.

'Let me go!' Tova yells, but the woman's grip is strong. Strong like a man's. She flails, trying to tear herself free.

Ripping cloth. A hand across her cheek. Hard, sharp, stinging.

Tova yells out, in surprise more than pain, and stumbles back, almost losing her footing on the loose stones of the riverbed. The current tugs at her skirts, trying to drag her down, but somehow she manages to stay on her feet.

Merewyn shrieks as the deaf one stands over her. She scrabbles, spluttering, in the stream, trying to stand up. Her hair and face are wet, her clothes drenched and clinging to her. Too far away for Tova to help her. Gytha comes for Tova again but this time she's ready. She ducks to one side, out of the woman's reach.

'Beorn!' she shouts as she fumbles at her belt for the hilt of her knife.

Axe whirling, Beorn strikes the tall one high on the arm. An anguished howl as the blade rips through flesh, and Cuffa reels. His seax falls through his fingers and disappears into the black of the river, and Beorn is turning as Wulfnoth rushes towards him, steel flashing silver—

Gytha shouts. Tova turns, gripping her knife, back to face her, at the same time as a cry goes up. Not one voice, but many, all at once, coming from amid the trees on the south bank of the river.

And suddenly she sees what Gytha sees. Helmets, swords,

shield bosses, mail byrnies. Too many to count, gleaming in the moonlight as they hurry down the narrow path. Steel clinking, feet thundering. Calling to one another in words she doesn't understand. Foreign words.

Normans.

Three, four, five, six, seven of them, scrambling one at a time down the narrow, muddy path towards the riverbank.

It can't be, she thinks. Not now. Not after we've come so far.

But it is. They're here.

'What are you waiting for?' Beorn roars as he ducks under a wild swing of Wulfnoth's seax. 'Run! Now!'

Gytha is shouting Wulfnoth's name, desperately trying to get his attention, to warn him of the danger. The deaf one doesn't seem to have noticed that anything is amiss. Guthred is on his knees in front of him, his hands together and pointing to the sky, pleading for mercy. Halfdan kicks him hard in the stomach.

Tova glances at Merewyn, then back at Guthred, before rushing to her lady's side. She still hasn't got up; her eyes are wide and her breath comes in quick, short bursts. Is she hurt or just frightened?

'We have to go,' Tova says desperately as she reaches out a hand and drags Merewyn to her feet, struggling against the weight of her drenched clothes. 'Now!'

She glances up, sees the Normans nearly at the water's edge, their swords drawn.

'Now!' she says again, wrenching at her lady's sleeve. But Merewyn doesn't budge; instead she stares, panic-stricken, at the oncoming Normans.

And then, above the din, a voice from somewhere unseen, shouting urgently and for some reason in the English tongue: 'There he is! That's him, over there!'

The voice sounds somehow familiar, but she isn't sure why, and she isn't about to wait to find out. She pulls harder at Merewyn's sleeve, and this time her lady does move. They splash through the swirling, frothing, icy water towards Guthred, who is on his knees, doubled over, coughing.

'The book,' he splutters, his eyes wide, as together they haul him to his feet. He winces as he clutches his side. 'We have to go back for it. Where is it?'

'There's no time,' Tova says. 'It's theirs now.'

She looks about for their horses, but she can only see Beorn's, charging off downstream, crashing through the bare branches that overhang the stream.

Gytha is running now; Halfdan too has seen the danger. They splash away downriver in the direction of the mill, chased by three of the Normans. Cuffa's seax is in his hand once more; he rises to face the men bearing down on him.

Wulfnoth continues to hurl himself at Beorn. Either he hasn't realised what's happening, or he doesn't care.

'Go!' Beorn roars again. 'Do you hear me? Go! Go!'

He brings his axe about; it strikes Wulfnoth on the thigh. The outlaw's leg buckles beneath him and he falls back with a yelp.

And then the Normans are upon Beorn. In their mail and their helmets, with their swords drawn, they encircle him, and he is hurling himself and his axe at their shields: battering, twisting, striking low and high, trying to break through.

'This way,' Merewyn shouts as she makes for the other side of the ford. 'Tova!'

Tova's about to follow, but when she looks about to see where the priest is, he's no longer there. Instead he's running back towards the Normans surrounding Beorn.

'Guthred!' Tova cries, but it's too late.

The priest throws himself at the flank of the nearest foreigner, grabbing at his sword arm, tearing him off balance, bringing him down with a crash of mail and water and gravel. The priest throws himself down on the man, pressing his head under the surface, and the foreigner is struggling, choking, kicking, trying to shake him off.

'Tova,' Merewyn calls. 'Quickly, this way!'

She knows she should go. She knows it's the only sensible thing to do. But she's had enough of running. All this time on the road, exiles in their own land, and what good has it done them? However fast they flee, however many miles they travel, it isn't enough.

Wherever they go, their enemies will always be there, hard on their heels. They will never escape. They can never go home. Nowhere is safe. And she realises she can't do it any more. She won't. If her fate is to die, then she'll go to it with her head held high. Proud. Defiant. Not like a coward; like the heroes in the songs that she used to love. Fighting to the end, knowing she did everything she could.

Knife in hand, she tears across the ford, through the tumbling waters, crying out in anger. For all the blood they've spilled. For everyone at Heldeby. Everyone she ever knew.

She sees Cuffa crash his blade into the back of one of the Normans' helmets. She sees Wulfnoth rise, his damp hair flailing, and lunge at the midriff of another. She sees Beorn swing his axe against one of the enemy's heads. It clatters off his helmet, steel upon steel, and the Norman goes down, and Beorn is shouting something, but she can't hear what.

She sees his face, dark with spatters of mud, or maybe blood. His eyes white with hate. She sees one of the foreigners shove his shield boss into Beorn's jaw. She sees him reel back, barely out of reach of his foe's sword point.

She sees it all happen slowly, as if time itself is drawing to a standstill. Every beat of her heart seems like an eternity as she prepares to fling herself at Beorn's attackers. They haven't seen her yet. She can hear Merewyn screaming her name, but only distantly.

And through the confusion and the flashing steel and the spray and the darkness, scurrying down the bank after them, she sees—

Oslac?

She stops. Is it him?

It *is* him. She recognises his cloth cap with the ear flaps, the curly hair trailing from underneath. What is he doing here?

He reaches the water's edge and bends down. When he stands up again there's something slung across his shoulder.

The scrip. Guthred's scrip, with the book inside.

He glances up, and their eyes meet. And he yells something at her. She doesn't hear what, but she can tell from the way he moves his lips.

Go, he's saying. Go!

Where did he come from? Have the Normans seen him? Has Beorn? Has Guthred? She wants to shout and tell them, but she knows they won't hear her.

Joy blossoms inside her. He didn't leave, after all. Or he did, but he came back, and that's what matters. He came back.

'Don't just stand there!' Oslac yells. 'While you still can, go!'

Here he comes, across the river, half-running and half-wading where it's deeper, weighed down by the scrip, nearly falling a couple of times. The Normans still haven't spotted him. Beorn lands a kick upon his foe's chest, sending him sprawling, and he is twisting away, aiming a swing over the shield rim of the next man, smashing the edge into the enemy's face—

And Guthred? Where is he?

A hand on her shoulder. She spins round, stepping back, thrusting her knife out in warning, but it's only Merewyn. Clothes soaked and clinging to her skin, hair plastered against her face.

'Come on,' her lady is saying. Her eyes are wide and she is trembling from head to foot. 'What are you doing?'

Seeing Merewyn's face, Tova remembers where she is. All the courage she'd built up, all the hatred that was coursing through her only moments ago, drains away faster than she can blink.

She takes her lady's hand, and they are running together through the shallows, away from the tumult, away from the noise, away from the screams, away from the killing. Scrambling on hands and knees up the bank, through the mud and the leaves and the darkness, into the trees. Fighting the undergrowth, the brambles and the ferns, the low-hanging branches. Stumbling, falling, rising, stumbling again. On, on, on. Her face and hands are scratched and her dress is full of holes where it has caught, and her cloak is torn, but none of that matters.

'Keep going,' Merewyn says, over and over. 'Just keep running.'

Guthred and Beorn, Tova thinks. Oslac as well. We've left them all behind.

They plunge onward, the two of them, over fallen trunks, through muddy hollows, down into ditches and up the other sides, deeper and deeper and deeper into the woods, further and further from the river.

Eventually they collapse, breathless, the two of them huddled together, alone, behind the trunk of a broad-bellied oak. How long have they been running? Tova gasps for air. Her chest is aching. Her arms and legs are bruised. She's sweating all over. Shivering.

If she holds her breath and keeps still she can make out

shouting somewhere behind them. The sound of steel on steel rings out faintly, and she's reminded, for no good reason she can work out, of the sound of the handbell with which Skalpi, when he was alive, used to summon everyone at Heldeby into the hall for the Christmas feast.

They say nothing at all, but sit in silence, backs pressed against the knotted bark, keeping as close as they can, trying not to move for fear that any sound might give them away. Tova can feel Merewyn shuddering; carefully she prises her lady's sodden cloak from her shoulders, before taking off her own to wrap around her. Merewyn's cheek is stone cold. Her hands too. Tova holds her close, trying to keep her warm. Sooner or later they're going to have to move and find some place where she can dry off, before she catches a chill.

For now, though, they have to wait. She shuts her eyes tight and listens to the sound of her heart. Still racing. Thump, thump, thump, thump. Like the hammer at the smith's anvil. There's more shouting, but it's far away now. The breeze stirs the undergrowth. When it dies down again there's no sound of anyone.

'I think they've gone,' Tova whispers after a while longer.

Merewyn doesn't say anything, just nods.

All the same they don't move. Not yet. Not until they can be sure. What if the Normans come this way, or Wulfnoth?

No sooner has the thought crossed her mind than she hears a rustling in the undergrowth, close by, in the direction of the river. She tenses, holding her breath. She glances at her lady and they shrink back behind the tree. Is that them?

Stay still, she thinks. As long as they don't make a sound, there's no reason whoever it is should find them.

A voice calls out: 'Tova! Merewyn! Guthred!'

It's Oslac.

Should they shout back? What if the enemy are out there as well? What if they hear?

He calls again. There is a muffled sound like something suddenly hitting the ground. He curses loudly, then moments later calls again, only his voice is fainter this time. He's moving away, Tova thinks.

'We're here,' she calls as she gets to her feet, rubbing her arms against the chill of the night. 'Oslac!'

'Tova?'

'Over here!'

'Where?'

At last he finds them, emerging from the trees, covered in thorns and bits of leaves, with twigs sticking out of his hair.

'Oh, thank God,' he says when he sees them. 'You're all right. You're all right.'

Tova throws her arms around him, surprising him, and herself. This was the man who, after all, deserted them only a few hours ago. She breaks away, feeling suddenly awkward. But he's back with them now, and he still has the priest's scrip.

'Is Guthred with you?' Merewyn asks.

'I thought he was with you. He's not here?'

'No. We don't know what happened to him.'

Oh, no, Tova thinks. She has a terrible feeling in her gut. 'Do you think . . . ?'

'I don't know,' Oslac says.

'What about Beorn?'

'The last I saw, he was still fighting, but they had him surrounded. Then they started after me, three of them. I had no choice but to run. I didn't see any more than that. I think the Normans went back the other way; I didn't hear them after that.'

Not Beorn as well. He can't be dead. He can't be.

357

'He'll be all right,' Merewyn says, still shivering. She looks a sorry sight. 'He'll have managed, somehow. Won't he? He'll have got away. He must have.'

Oslac nods. 'I hope so.'

Tova asks, 'What happened to you? Where did you come from?'

He stands, catching his breath for a moment. 'I don't know where to start. This whole day . . . After I left you, I walked for a couple of hours and then ran into a Norman raiding band. They took me captive. I thought they'd kill me there and then, but they didn't. They were searching for some rebels on their way to Hagustaldesham. One of the Frenchmen spoke our tongue; he asked me if I knew anything about them. I said I didn't, but I think he could tell I was hiding something. He said that unless I told them, they'd kill me, and they'd do it slowly so that before long I would be begging them to let me die. They made me tell. I didn't want to, but I had no choice. Please, understand. I was frightened for my life. I said there was a band of four – two men and two women – heading in that direction across the hills. I thought they would let me go after that, but they took me with them so that I could lead them to you. This one who spoke English, he said that if it turned out I was trying to trick them they would kill me anyway. They'd slice open my belly and leave me as food for the—'

'Lies.'

Tova looks up. She knows that voice. She would know it anywhere.

'Beorn!'

He doesn't look at her. Instead he makes straight for Oslac, who retreats, but not quickly enough.

Beorn hurls his fist towards the poet's face, striking him

358

on the jaw. Oslac reels back, shouting out in protest and in pain.

'What are you doing?' Merewyn shrieks.

But Beorn's eyes are fixed on Oslac. 'You led them to us.'

The poet turns to run, but he's barely taken two steps when he slips. He flounders and falls, landing on his back.

'They made him,' Tova says, grabbing at the warrior's arm. 'Didn't you just hear what he said? He didn't have a choice.'

Beorn shakes her off as he advances and spits at Oslac. The poet turns his head, and it lands upon his cheek.

'They didn't make him do anything,' Beorn says sharply, and then to Oslac: 'Who are you really?'

Merewyn says, 'Beorn, this is nonsense.'

'Shut up. Shut up, both of you, and let me speak. Answer me, wretch. Tell me why it is that our friend the priest is now dead.'

'He's dead?' Tova echoes.

Merewyn gasps. 'No.'

Beorn swallows. His voice quakes ever so slightly as he says, 'He is. I tried to stop them. I did my best, but there were too many of them. They ran him through in front of my eyes, and I couldn't do anything, and now he's dead, and it's all because of him.'

He draws his seax and points it at Oslac, who flinches back.

'It wasn't supposed to happen this way,' the poet blurts. 'He wasn't meant to die!'

'How was it supposed to happen, then?'

Oslac is silent.

'Speak,' Beorn says. He kicks the younger man hard in the side.

The poet puts out a hand to defend himself, to no avail, and cries out.

'How much did they offer you?'

'What's he talking about, Oslac?' asks Tova.

The poet doesn't lift his eyes, but keeps watching the point of the seax, as if expecting the killing thrust to come at any point. Out of the collar of his tunic hangs the gold chain she spotted him fingering the other day. There's something attached to it, she sees.

'What's this?' Beorn reaches down and snatches at it, tearing it from the poet's neck before he can raise a hand. He examines it closely. 'They gave you this, didn't they?'

Oslac says nothing. Beorn tosses it to Tova. She isn't expecting it, but somehow she manages to catch it in clumsy, unfeeling fingers.

A thin disc of gold is suspended from the chain. Like a coin, only larger: if she put the tip of her forefinger to that of her thumb, it would just about fit through the hole. Embossed upon its face, she can make out in the moonlight, is a depiction of a rider at full gallop, with a sword in one hand and a pointed shield in the other. Writing around the edge.

'Look at the other side,' Beorn says.

She turns it over. Stretched across the middle of the disc is an animal. She squints, trying to work out what she's looking at. A long tail that doubles back on itself. Four legs, claws. A mane.

A lion, she thinks. The lion of Normandy. But why would he have—?

Oh.

Her cheeks flush hot. Angry that he has managed to trick them. Angry at him. Angry at herself for not seeing it.

'Oslac?' she asks uncertainly as she gives the chain to her lady to look at. 'Is it true?'

His voice, when he speaks, is cold. 'It's true.'

'You led the Normans to us?'

He nods.

'You deceived us,' Merewyn says. 'We trusted you!'

Beorn stands over him, stopping him from getting up. 'Who are you really?'

'Who am I?' he asks. 'I should be asking you that question.'

Tova frowns. 'What do you mean?'

'Ask him. Ask him what his real name is.'

She turns to the warrior, whose teeth are clenched. He looks as if he might kill Oslac at any moment. 'Beorn?'

Beorn doesn't answer. He's shaking his head, slowly. The blade pointed at the poet's throat trembles.

'You thought no one would work it out, didn't you?' Oslac says to him. 'Well, I did. For a long time I wasn't sure, but as soon as I was, I knew I couldn't—'

'This isn't about me,' Beorn says, cutting him off. 'This is about you and your lies.'

'My lies? What about yours?'

'I'm not the one who gave us away to our enemies. Everything I told you was the truth.'

'Not everything. You told us Cynehelm was dead.'

'He is. He died that day, in the fight.'

'What does this have to do with anything?' Merewyn asks.

But Oslac's attention is on Beorn, and him alone. 'Are you going to tell them, or should I?'

'I should just kill you now,' the warrior says.

'You mean like you slaughtered all those others? You killed them in their beds. You burned them alive inside their own feasting halls. Yes, I heard the tales, long before I heard them from you.'

'I'm warning you, whelp. Give me one reason why I shouldn't just bury this blade in your gut.'

'Do it. If that's what you want to do, I can't stop you. But it won't change anything. They'll still want to know. If they haven't already guessed it by now. They'll still want to hear it from your own mouth.'

'Hear what?' Merewyn asks.

But Tova knows. She has worked it out, even if her lady hasn't. She turns to face Beorn – the man whom she has known as Beorn, at any rate.

'You're Cynehelm,' she says. 'He wasn't your lord, was he? He was you.'

Cynehelm Caldheort. Cynehelm the Unfeeling. It's him. But why would he change his name? Why pretend to be someone else?

'Cynehelm is gone, girl,' Beorn says. 'He set out to kill Malger that morning and he didn't come back, and that's all there is to it. There's nothing left of him now.'

'I don't understand,' says Merewyn, glancing at Oslac. 'What does it matter?'

But Oslac isn't paying her any attention. 'You see now why I did it, don't you? I didn't mean for anyone else to be caught up in it. I didn't mean for Guthred to get hurt, or any of you. That's why, when I saw you this morning, Tova, I urged you to leave while you still had the chance. To leave and to run as fast and as far away from him as you could.'

'You tried to get me killed,' Beorn says.

'I only did what I had to do,' Oslac answers. 'What my heart and my head were telling me was right. I didn't mean for Guthred to die, I really didn't. You have to believe me.'

'I believe you're a worthless worm that doesn't deserve to live.'

Beorn brings the blade closer to Oslac's face, so close that the point is almost touching his skin.

'No!' Tova says.

The warrior stops. 'What?'

'We should let him speak. It's only right.'

'And suffer him to live another moment? Why should we, when he's already as good as admitted everything?'

'Because . . . because that's not what we do. That's not who we are. We don't kill for the sake of it. We don't murder out of hand. We're not them.'

'She's right,' Merewyn says. 'We had the chance to tell our tales, didn't we? Well, now it's his turn. And I for one want to hear what he has to say for himself.'

'And when he's finished telling, what then?'

'Then we can decide, all of us together. We can decide if he should die, or if we ought to let him go.'

Beorn doesn't speak for a long time; his seax remains at the poet's throat. Oslac watches it warily, taking shallow, quick breaths, expecting his death to arrive at any moment. He looks terrified, as well he should. Like a small child, defenceless. A wretched creature.

'All right,' Beorn says at last. 'Whatever it is you have to say, spew it out. This is your one chance, you understand? So make it quick. And you can give the lady your cloak too. She looks as though she's about to freeze.'

OSLAC

This is how it's going to be then, is it? You let me speak and then you judge me? Why should I bother? You're not going to show me any mercy. You, of all people, Cynehelm.

All right, all right. You want to know who I am? Well, I'll tell you. My name is Oslac, and that's the truth. Oslac, son of Osferth, son of Oswald. I won't bore you with tales of my childhood. As if you cared, anyway.

I was in my eighteenth summer when my father was killed. Not by the Normans, before you ask. By rebels. Fellow English folk. He was reeve of Suthperetune, the manor where I grew up. One of the king's manors, it was. He'd been the reeve there for as long as almost anyone could remember: he'd been there in King Eadward's time, long before the foreigners ever set foot on these shores, and he continued to serve after Wilelm took the crown. When all the nobles of the southern shires came together to offer their surrender to the new king after his victory at Hæstinges, Osferth was among them.

Go ahead. Call him a traitor if you like, but remember that it was either that or else exile or death. That was the choice he had to make.

'I know what I'd have chosen,' Beorn mutters.

'We're not asking you, though, are we?' Merewyn says. She gestures for Oslac to go on.

*

Almost a year after the foreigners first came across the sea was when it happened. One night some men raided the manor, our home, and burned it to the ground; four of them armed with swords burst into the chamber where my father slept and dragged him into the open and slew him in front of my eyes. They let me say my last farewell to him and then they made me watch while they ran him through. They left everyone else alive. He was the one they were after, simply because he'd chosen to make his peace with the Normans.

I was his only surviving child; there was no one else to share my sorrow with and there was nothing else left for me there, so I gathered the few belongings I had and took to the road with my harp and songs and tales I'd learned from him, thinking to make my living as a storyteller while I tracked down the men who had murdered him. I had no idea then what I planned to do if and when I did somehow manage to find them; my head was so full of anger and grief and I wasn't thinking that far ahead.

In the end it was easier than I expected. As I travelled the shire, I heard tales of similar attacks. All I had to do was follow the trail of blood they'd left in their wake. Within two weeks of my father's death, I'd tracked them to their camp on the edge of the marshes, in a nook of land that could be reached only by a single narrow path. There were fewer of them than I'd first thought – only eight men in all, it turned out. From speaking with various people on my wanderings, I'd already managed to find out the names of half of them. Mostly local folk, they were, who'd run away to take up arms when they heard that the invaders were seizing the land. I found a hiding place amid the reeds and I watched them for the better part of an afternoon, slipping away as the sun was setting. They'd seemed like terrifying, towering giants that night, but by day, I saw how unimposing they were, some so thin that they were almost wasting away; as young as me and some even younger.

These were the men who had murdered Osferth.

There were too many of them for me to do anything alone, much as I would have liked to kill them myself. So I did the next best thing. There was a castle a few miles away, built by a Norman who was determined to root out all the rebels in the shire so that he could win favour with the king. So that's where I went. To begin with I was refused an audience, but I persisted and eventually his men agreed to take me to his writing room, where he was composing a letter. Once there I told him what had happened to my father, the king's reeve, how I'd been seeking out his killers and how I'd been able to track them to their camp. He listened patiently and sent for food and wine to be brought to me, and as soon as I'd finished saying what I had to, he rode out with his retinue.

Three hours later he returned full of cheer, carrying a bloody sack with eight heads that he tipped out into the yard. He ordered his men to impale them on stakes for all to see, while he came and put his arm around my shoulder and placed a leather purse filled with silver in my hand. In broken English he told me that if I ever heard any more news of rebels hiding in the marshes and the hills then I should come to him with what I'd been able to learn, and there would be further rewards.

You're already judging me, I can see. But I tell you this: there's not a doubt in my mind that I did the right thing. Did I feel guilty? Never for a moment. I wasn't shocked when I saw those men's bruised and scarred faces, with eyes glazed and mouths hanging open. My heart didn't sink; I didn't feel as though my soul had been stained by sin. No, I was overjoyed.

My father was worth all those eight men put together, and

more besides. If it had been fifty men, it still wouldn't have been enough. They had no right to take his life.

And that's how it started.

Afterwards, it didn't even cross my mind to go home. I wanted to get as far away from there as I could, and to forget everything that had happened. That was my life for the next year: I'd travel from place to place, playing my harp and singing for a penny here, a warm bed or a hot meal and a flagon of mead there. I left Sumorsæte and made my way to Lundene, and from there north into Mercia. Most of the time I travelled alone, although sometimes I would meet a monk or a pedlar or someone driving their livestock to market, and I would walk with them and listen to what they had to say.

As much as I wanted to, though, I couldn't forget. Everywhere I went, I heard news of cattle thefts or church raids or burnings or roadside killings. Almost every alewife and dairymaid I spoke to had a story to tell of husbands and brothers and cousins who had gone away to join the wild men, whose numbers seemed to be swelling as the months passed.

No one, Norman or English, felt safe. And the less safe the foreigners felt, the less trusting they became of the common folk who worked on their lands. They levied ever higher rents, forcing them to work harder and for less reward. They meted out harsh penalties for the smallest crimes, whether it was stealing a cheese from a storehouse, or gathering more than your allowance of kindling from the woods. Any of the wild men they did manage to catch they disembowelled and strung up for all to see. They didn't do such things because they were wicked or callous, though. They weren't like that. Most of them, anyway. That's what I came to realise.

No, it's true. Do you think, deep down, they're any different to us, really? They're not fiends sent by the Devil to plague us. They're not God's instruments, harbingers of the end of days. They're people, just like us.

'I don't have to listen to this,' Beorn mutters.

'Why not?' Oslac says. 'It's true. Don't you see? Every Frenchman ambushed on the road or murdered in his bed only gave them another reason to fear us. To be suspicious of us. To hate us. To punish us. All that bloodshed, and what did it achieve? Nothing, except to spread suffering and resentment. Why do you think this is happening right now? Why do you think their armies are ravaging the country? It's revenge. If the rebellions hadn't happened, if Eadgar had never raised his standard—'

'You don't know what you're talking about.'

'King Wilelm wouldn't have marched all this way to lay waste this land, if you and everyone like you hadn't carried on the war even though your cause was long lost. If you'd only stopped for a moment to see the hurt it was bringing—'

'You're wrong. We saw how the Normans were treating folk; that was why we fought in the first place. Were we supposed to just let that happen? Were we supposed to give up and let them take this kingdom without a struggle?'

'They're never going to be driven from this land. Things aren't going to go back to the way they were before. Anyone who doesn't realise that is deluding himself.'

Beorn makes a noise of disgust as he turns away.

'As I saw it,' Oslac continues, 'there was only one way to avoid further misery, and that was to make our peace with the enemy. That's why I did it. That's why I went to them again, like I'd done that first time, except now it wasn't about vengeance. It was about doing the right thing. I gave them information I'd learned on my travels and in return they gave me silver. I told them where the wild men were gathering, how many of them there were and how well they were armed. Sometimes I'd seek out the rebels myself, and join one of the small bands that hid in the fens or the forests or the moors. I'd live with them for a week or two or sometimes longer, gain their confidence until I discovered where they planned to attack next, and then one night I'd slip away and report what I knew, so that when the time came for them to carry out their plans they found the Normans waiting for them.'

'You betrayed them?' Tova asks.

'Because I knew that things would only grow worse if I didn't.'

And they did grow worse, anyway.

Time after time over the next year I went to the Normans to pass on what I'd managed to glean about the wild men and their movements. It was now two years since the invasion, and for a while it seemed that things were getting better: that the will to keep fighting was waning, that at last men were beginning to accept that things could not go back to being the way they were.

Soon, I thought, the bloodshed would be over and we could all live our lives without fear once more.

But then Eadgar raised his army and sent his messengers throughout the kingdom, urging every Englishman who could hold a spear or a spade or a pick to take up arms against the Normans, and it started again, only this time it was worse than ever. More raids, more killings. Not just lords and reeves but also messengers and monks, traders and stonemasons, blacksmiths and hired men: anyone who was suspected of having consorted with the foreigners or taken their coin was a target.

If you weren't with them, the wild men seemed to think, then

369

you must be against them. There was no sense to it, no sense at all.

Those were miserable, desperate times. In some villages crops were left to spoil in the fields because so many ran off to join the rebellion. Meanwhile the Normans brought in more and more warriors to protect them from ambush and to guard their castles and their halls, unruly, boorish men, quick to anger, who made folk afraid wherever they went. People worried about what would happen when Eadgar and the Danes were defeated, and what that would mean for them, and if there would be further reprisals. If you think that across the kingdom all Englishmen were praying for the ætheling to lead his army to victory, you're wrong. They were praying simply that the fighting didn't come their way. The last thing they wanted was another war.

I had the confidence of the Normans by then; they saw they could rely on me and they sent me on ever more difficult tasks. The king was calling out his barons, marching north to head off the threat posed by Eadgar and his allies the heathens, who had captured Eoferwic. And so that autumn I was sent on ahead of the king's army, with instructions to make my way into the city and seek an audience with the Danes' leader, Jarl Osbjorn, and deliver a message—

Beorn fixes him with a sharp look. 'A message?'

'An offer,' Oslac says, 'from King Wilelm. For weeks I carried word back and forth between Osbjorn and the Normans as they tried to forge an agreement.'

The warrior advances upon him. 'You?'

'Yes, me. And I'd do it again, if I had to.'

'You brought down the rebellion. You handed this kingdom to King Wilelm.'

370

'I saved you from yourselves. I was doing what I could to bring an end to a hopeless war, if you'd only been able to see it.'

Besides, if you want to blame anyone, blame the Danes. You should have known from the start they weren't trustworthy allies. This isn't their land; they weren't about to give their blood to defend English homes and halls. All they wanted was enough booty to fill their holds and to sail home as rich men. And that's what we gave them.

We thought that would be it. We hoped that when Eadgar's army fell apart, that would be the end of the bloodshed. No more thoughtless murders, we thought. No more needless suffering.

But it wasn't.

As you know – as Beorn has told you – there were still some who refused to believe that it was over. They wrought ruin throughout the kingdom, striking suddenly from nowhere with fire and sword, spreading terror wherever they went. This time they were experienced warriors: men born to the sword, who had stood in shield walls, who had fought at Hæstinges and Dunholm and Eoferwic, for whom killing was the only trade they dealt in.

And it wasn't just Normans who died at their hands. It was English folk, too: men like my father, whose only misdeed was that they'd come to terms with the fact that things were different now. That a new king sat on the throne. All they wanted was to live their lives in peace, to keep their wives and their children from further hardship. To save themselves from yet more grief. But the rebels didn't care. They slew those folk anyway, without thought and without pity.

There was one whose name was known everywhere, whose cruelty was unsurpassed. He took pleasure in others' pain; he never offered mercy even when his victims pleaded for it. It was said that if ever you managed to cut him he would shed ice, not blood. There was no love in his heart, no compassion, no Christian kindness. Only hatred. It consumed him. People called him a godless fiend, a shadow-walker, a night-wraith. Long after everyone else had given up the struggle, still he kept up the slaughter, leaving only blood and ashes in his wake as he burned and pillaged from shire to shire.

He never stopped. He wasn't ever going to stop. He was going to keep on fighting and killing, killing and fighting, no matter how insignificant each of his victories were, or how hollow. No matter if all his friends and loyal companions deserted him. He didn't care. He had one goal, and he would pursue that goal above everything else, for ever and ever and ever, until his dying breath. Until the world's end.

His name was Cynehelm.

'Enough,' Beorn says and kicks Oslac again. 'Tell yourself such things if you have to, if they help you feel better about what you've done. But don't poison their minds with this filth.'

'It hurts to see yourself as others see you, doesn't it?'

'You're nothing but a craven. You hide behind your lies because you can't accept the truth.'

'You're the one who won't accept the truth. You refuse to see that everything you've fought for has been for nothing.'

'It hasn't been for nothing. And it's not over. Not until every Englishman thinks like you. Not while there are still people like me willing to defend what's ours and to make a stand for what's right.'

'There is no one else. Don't you understand? They're dead. All of them.'

'What are you talking about?'

'There aren't any others. You're the only one left still fighting. No one else. The rest of the rebels are all dead. Hagustaldesham is no more. They burned it, killed everyone, destroyed everything.'

Tova feels as though all the air has been knocked out of her. She can't breathe. Her stomach lurches. The darkness is about to swallow her.

No.

Beorn crouches beside Oslac, seizing him by the collar. 'What?'

Oslac spits in Beorn's face. At once the warrior's blade is back in his hand, at the poet's throat again.

'Speak, you worthless turd, or I'll cut you apart, piece by little piece.'

But this time Oslac doesn't flinch. No fear shows in his eyes as he stares back at the warrior.

'The Normans have already been there,' he says. 'King Wilelm himself went and he crushed the rebels, the few hundred of them that were left, the ones who hadn't already fled. There was a battle, but it didn't last long. There's nothing left now. They slew everyone they could find, destroyed the rebel camp, sacked the town and then razed it to the ground.'

'Who told you this?'

'Who do you think?'

But if Hagustaldesham is no more, Tova thinks, if the rebels have been destroyed, where else can they go? What are they supposed to do now?

She asks weakly, 'When did this happen?'

'Two days ago. So they said – the ones I was with. Some of them were there. They told me how they fell upon the town, surrounded the rebels and cut them down. Like pigs to the slaughter, they told me. Pigs in mail shirts, running and crashing about, squealing in panic—'

'What about Gospatric?' Beorn asks, cutting him off. 'What happened to him?'

'Gospatric? He surrendered to the king more than a week ago. Not in person. By way of messengers. He fled as soon as he heard the king was on his way to Hagustaldesham – slunk away in the dead of night, back to his stronghold in the distant north, leaving the rest to face the Normans by themselves.'

'He'd never do that. He'd rather die than bend his knee to the foreigners.'

'He saw what was about to happen. He did the sensible thing. The only thing.'

More than a week ago, Tova thinks. Before they ever left Heldeby. Before all of this.

'Did you know?' she asks. 'When we first met you, did you know then that Gospatric had already surrendered?'

Of course he did. Even then, on that very first night when they were all together, the five of them gathered in that barn, he was arguing against going to Hagustaldesham. She remembers.

'You did, didn't you?'

Oslac doesn't reply, but he doesn't have to. His silence says everything.

He knew. He'd already heard, or guessed, that the Normans were marching north to finish off the remnants of the rebellion. All the time he was travelling with them, he knew it was a lost cause. He knew they'd never reach Hagustaldesham before the enemy. He knew that Beorn was only leading them into ever greater danger.

He could have warned them, but he didn't. He chose not to. Right from the very beginning he was deceiving them.

'Why didn't you tell us?' she asks, but she knows the answer. He was interested only in Beorn. In Cynehelm. He never really cared about the rest of them.

'You realise, don't you,' says Merewyn quietly, huddled in her two borrowed cloaks, 'that if you'd just told us the truth from the start, then Guthred would still be alive?'

'I never meant him to die,' Oslac insists.

'But he did die,' Beorn says as he yanks the other man's collar, pulling him forward and forcing him on to his hands and knees.

The poet is whimpering like a wounded hound.

'He did die,' Beorn says again. 'As did all those others you sold to the Normans. All for a few miserable pieces of silver. How many Englishmen went to their deaths because of the things you did? Do you grieve for them too?'

'I did what I had to do.'

Beorn stands behind Oslac. He glances questioningly towards Merewyn. She nods slowly but deliberately.

His eyes meet Tova's. Her throat is dry and she swallows. She knows she has to decide. She doesn't want to. But she has to. All of them, together. That was what they agreed.

And she will be complicit. She will become like them.

She nods.

Beorn nods too. Then he clamps his free hand on Oslac's chin and wrenches his head up, exposing the poet's pale neck. He lowers his knife so that the edge rests against the skin.

Oslac's breath comes in short, sharp stutters. His teeth are clenched but he doesn't struggle. He knows it's no use. There is no escaping his fate now.

'You did what you had to do,' says Beorn. 'And so do we.'

*

375

They stumble on through the darkness. Through the trees. Through ditches and hollows thick with wet bracken. Through freezing streams. Tova keeps glancing over her shoulder, expecting to see the enemy bearing down on them, to hear them shouting to one another, to hear the sound of hooves, but there's no sign of them.

'Don't stop,' says Beorn.

'What about Wulfnoth and the others?' she asks.

'He's dead. I don't know about the rest of them. They ran. I didn't see where they went.'

She wants to go back to find Winter, to find Guthred's body so that they can pay their respects to him, but she knows they can't. Their packs too. Their provisions, their food, water, firewood, blankets.

Gone. All of it.

Guthred's scrip slaps against her thigh as she runs, or tries to. The strap digs into her shoulder. She hadn't appreciated its weight until now.

Beorn sees that she's struggling. 'Leave it.'

'I can't.'

'Yes, you can. It's not important. What do you plan to do with it, anyway?'

'It was important to him, so it's important to me. Don't you see? It's all we have of his. It's what he would have wanted.'

'Girl—'

Her mind is made up. 'I'm not leaving it.'

He shakes his head in frustration, but he doesn't bother arguing.

The snow is falling again, heavier this time, darting and swirling about them, by the time they find the small church nestling near the bottom of a wide vale, almost hidden from sight amidst the folds of the earth. It stings Tova's cheeks, but she grits her teeth as the three of them make their way carefully down the slope, fighting the gusting wind, trying not to slip on the wet grass, towards the squat dark building with the cross nailed to the gable.

They try the door. The lock is rusted, but one good strike from Beorn's axe and it gives way. The door is heavy; it grinds against the floor, but he presses against it with his shoulder and it opens.

He moves stiffly, she sees, and with a limp. Is he injured? Was he wounded during the fight? Why didn't she notice before? Why hasn't he said anything?

Inside it smells stale, as if no one has been here in weeks, or months, or maybe even years. At least the roof still holds. It's shelter, and that's what matters.

There are hangings on the walls: thick linen, nothing extravagant. Motheaten but otherwise in one piece. Beorn tears them down while Tova sits Merewyn down, then takes the altar cloth and wraps it around her lady's shoulders. She's shivering violently, drawing quick, shallow breaths. They need to get a fire going and get her out of her sodden dress, and soon.

Beorn goes in search of wood they can burn while Tova huddles close to her lady, rubbing her arms and her shoulders, doing her best to keep her warm.

Outside, the night wind howls.

SIXTH DAY

In the morning the hills, the fields, the trees are white. The whole world lies silent and empty beneath winter's blanket. And still it snows, sometimes lighter, sometimes so heavy that it's impossible to see even ten paces beyond the door of the church.

Beorn ventures out to fetch more wood. It looks like they're going to be stuck here, at least until tomorrow. Hopefully by then it'll have relented. In the meantime they'll have to stay put and keep warm as best they can.

They sit in silence on what used to be one of the wall hangings, in front of the meagre fire. Merewyn's cheek rests on her shoulder. Her eyes are closed but Tova thinks she's awake. She has stopped shivering, but her nose won't stop running. Every so often she'll break out in a fit of coughing that leaves her hoarse. Some honey mixed with warm water is what she needs to soothe her throat. That's what Eda would say.

Tova hefts the book in her lap. What's left of it, anyway. Already more than a third of the pages have gone. Beorn couldn't find much by way of dry wood in the dark last night, and they needed the parchment to help feed the flames, to keep them going. A good thing she didn't leave it behind, she thinks bitterly, although she doesn't think Beorn appreciates the irony.

She protested, of course, but he asked her impatiently if she wanted to die of cold, and in the end she had no choice. She made him wait, though, while she leafed through the pages, picking out those without pictures on either side, making sure he took those first. He said nothing as he ripped them from the binding, one by one, and twisted them and crumpled them into balls, and placed them atop the flames, then cupped his hands over them and blew gently.

At first nothing happened. Tova wondered if maybe the holy words couldn't be destroyed, that they were somehow protected by God. But then the edges began to curl, going first yellow and then brown and then black, and that blackness spread slowly across the surface, which shrivelled and hissed and smoked, until suddenly it all went up in a mass of writhing orange tongues: line after line of intricate ink curls dissolving into searing brightness, vanishing into smoke and ash.

One sheet, then another. Then another. Hours and days some poor monk spent hunched over his writing desk, copying out by candlelight, slaving through summer heat and frosty winter. Gone in moments.

What would Guthred say if he knew they were burning his precious book? Would he be consoled by the fact that the word of God was granting warmth and life? She hopes so.

Carefully now, trying not to make a sound so as not to disturb her lady, she opens the book's cover. The gold panels are dented, and a couple of the garnets are missing from its setting.

The first page shows the Christ figure with his halo. She doesn't like his dark eyes staring back at her, judging her, and so she turns past it quickly, past the writing that Guthred called the preface, until she comes to some large letters surrounded by flowers and angels decked in green and red robes and blowing trumpets.

'*In principio creavit Deus caelum et terram*,' her lady murmurs as she raises her head. 'In the beginning, God created the heavens and the earth.'

'Is that what it says?'

Merewyn nods. 'That's what it says.' She leans forward, turns the page and carries on reading, her brow furrowed in concentration as she traces her finger back and forth along the lines. '"And the earth was void and empty, and darkness was upon the face of the deep; and the spirit of God moved over the waters. And God said: may light be made. And light was made. And God saw that the light was good, and He separated the light from the darkness. He called the light Day and the darkness Night. And the evening and the morning were the first day."'

There are more pictures on the facing page, these ones less brightly coloured. A naked man with only leaves to preserve his modesty, who must be Adam, surrounded by all manner of animals: horses and dogs and stags and fish and birds, and what she supposes must be some kind of cow except that it has a long neck and spindly legs and two great humps upon its back.

She has never seen anything like it. The creature is so strange she can't help but laugh, for a moment forgetting where they are, and how hungry and cold she is. 'What's that supposed to be?'

'I think they call it a camel. Leofa, my tutor, told me about them once. He said you find them in Egypt and other faraway places in the east. They're a bit like horses, I think, but they can go for days, weeks even, without having to drink.'

'Weeks?'

'That's what he said. I think he must have been wrong, or else he was teasing me.'

'Will you read me some more?'

Merewyn sighs. 'I don't know. I haven't practised my Latin in so long. I'm not sure I can.'

'Please?'

Merewyn is asleep again by the time Beorn returns with armfuls of bracken and branches, some of it dry, some of it less so. He sets it all down in the corner, then comes and joins Tova by the fire. Still limping. A dusting of snow upon his lank hair, upon his shoulders and his sleeves.

He winces in pain as he sits down gingerly beside her, clutching at a spot just below his ribs.

'It happened during the fight,' he explains. 'A graze, that's all.'

'Let me see.'

'I've cleaned it out with snow as best I can. There's nothing more to be done. I'll live. Believe me, I've suffered far worse in my time. Don't worry for my sake.'

He doesn't look at her as he speaks, she notices.

'So what now?' she asks.

'We wait. That's all we can do. We can't go anywhere, although at the same time neither can the enemy. We're safe for today at least.'

'What are we supposed to do for food?'

'Try not to think about it. Just keep as warm as you can. That's what we did when we were camped in the woods near Stede-hamm. After a while you forget about your stomach growling.'

'And what if it keeps on snowing? What if we're stuck here until it thaws?'

'I don't know. You ask too many questions, girl.'

'Stop calling me that.'

'What?'

'Girl. Stop calling me "girl". I don't like it. I'm not a child any more. And my name is Tova. You know that.'

Beorn sits for a long time without saying anything. Just watches Merewyn buried under their cloaks, with the altar cloth and one of the torn-down wall hangings on top. 'How is she?'

'Mostly she's just been sleeping. I tried to get her to sit up, the last time she woke, but she was too tired. She keeps coughing and sneezing. I don't know what more to do for her.'

For a long while they listen to the sound of her breathing. In, out. In, out.

'Was Oslac telling the truth about Hagustaldesham, do you think?' Tova asks him eventually. 'When he said that the Normans had been and—'

'No. It was just another of his lies. He only said it to spite me, and to try to confuse us.'

'How can you be so sure?'

'Because.'

'Because what?'

'Just because.'

'What about Earl Gospatric? He seemed sure about him.'

Beorn takes a clutch of sticks and arranges them on the fire. 'Gospatric,' he mutters, shaking his head. 'He deserved better allies than us.'

'What do you mean?'

'Without him the rebellion would never have happened. It would have failed before it had even started. He raised our spirits. He made us believe. When the rest of us let despair get the better of us, he berated us all for our weak stomachs. He told us we should be ashamed to call ourselves Englishmen.'

'Not you, surely?' Tova asks. 'I thought you said you were one of his strongest supporters.'

Beorn cups his hands and blows through them, coaxing the flames higher. 'I told you before that the rebellion was finished by a rumour. That when Eadgar heard the Normans were only a few hours away and coming for him, he panicked and took flight. But that isn't the whole story.'

He carries on building the fire up with pieces of dead bracken. Tova senses there's more to come, but she knows better than to rush him, and so she sits patiently until she can feel a flicker of heat upon her cheeks. When at last it's burning steadily, he sits down next to her.

She hasn't been this close to him before. So close she can smell the sweat upon his skin, sharp and warm, mixed with blood and grime – weeks of it. How did she never notice before? Then she supposes that after so many days without washing, she must reek too.

To think that he used to be a thegn, like Skalpi, with land and a hall and a ship and a wife, fine clothes and food and mead. And now here he is.

'Soon after word came,' he explains in a low voice so as not to wake Merewyn, 'we were called to the ætheling's tent to offer him our counsel. All his leading nobles were there: Earl Gospatric, his cousin Waltheof, Siward, Mærleswein. Many others whose names I don't remember. And then there was me. Compared with them, I was no one: a thegn of low birth who'd earned his rank not by blood right but through hard toil. Maybe my reputation went before me. I don't know. Certainly I'd never gone bragging about the number of foemen I'd killed. I wasn't interested in anyone's praise. But I did have their respect.'

'You never mentioned that you were known to Eadgar.'

'That's because I wasn't. Not really.'

'But you were a part of his council of war.'

'It was Gospatric who wanted me there, as an example to the rest, I think. I'd stood in the front rank of the shield wall and rallied our spearmen and withstood the enemy's swords. Most of the others hadn't, at least not without their hearth warriors to protect them. Yes, they'd fought, but I alone had the scars to prove it. Now, will you let me speak and stop interrupting me, girl?'

'I told you to stop calling me that.'

'When the news came,' he says, going on as if he hasn't heard, 'Gospatric was all for standing our ground and meeting the enemy in battle. He said this was the moment we'd been waiting for. The moment of fate. Shouting him down were his cousin Waltheof and others, who tried to persuade Eadgar that we should flee, saying that if the enemy captured him they'd have his head. The ætheling's face was ashen. The boy feared for his life, and who could blame him? He was only seventeen years old. He knew little of war. Eventually he turned to me. It was the first time he'd ever spoken to me directly. Eadgar looked straight at me and asked me whether or not, if it came to a battle with King Wilelm and his army, I believed that we could win.'

'And what did you tell him?'

'Until I opened my mouth I thought I knew exactly what I'd say. That Gospatric was right. That we should go out and fight, and if our fate was to fall in the fray then at least we would have gone to our deaths with pride. But then I met Eadgar's gaze and saw how frightened and desperate the boy was. And something changed.'

'What?'

'As I stood there with all those people looking at me, I realised that I didn't want to risk my life for them any longer. I couldn't do it. I didn't believe any more. In the war and our cause, yes. Not in that bickering band of nobles. Even less in the boy they wanted to make their king. I didn't want to fight for them, and

I didn't want to die for them. It was as simple as that: I didn't want to die.'

His voice is almost a whisper. His head is bowed; his hair hangs like a curtain across his face.

She asks, 'What did you say?'

'I told him flatly that I didn't believe we could. At once Gospatric roared that I was a coward, that we were all cowards. He cursed me in front of everyone for turning my back on him. I couldn't even look at him because I knew he was right. As for everyone else, they saw one of the last and staunchest of the earl's allies abandoning him. That's how Eadgar saw it. After that, there was nothing more to say. The meeting was over, and that was it. The rest you know.'

'But all you did was what you were asked to do. You spoke your mind.'

'I gave in to fear. At the one time when it really mattered, I backed down from a fight.'

'The rebellion didn't fail because of you,' Tova says, trying to reassure him. 'The pyre was already built. The wood was dry. One spark was all it needed, from the sound of it. It could have gone up at any time. You said as much yourself.'

'I know,' he growls. 'That's not why I'm telling you this.'

'Why, then?'

He closes his eyes as he wrings his hands. 'Because I don't want you to think that any of those things that Oslac said about me were true. And because I want you to understand. Why afterwards I swore to carry on the war, even though it was hopeless. Why I became so determined to kill Malger, for all the good that it did. Why, when I heard about Hagustaldesham, I knew I needed to be there. It wasn't about seeking revenge on the Normans for what they'd done, or rather that was only a part of it. I've

388

never taken any pleasure, any thrill from killing. I happen to be good at it, but I've never enjoyed it. So that wasn't the reason. Those months I spent raiding and burning after the rebellion's collapse, I didn't do it out of hatred. I did it to make amends for my cravenness, the only way I knew how.'

'You wanted to atone. Like Guthred.'

'Like the priest, yes. I suppose we had more in common than I cared to admit. Not that any of it matters now. If Oslac was right then it's too late. If even Gospatric has given in to King Wilelm, then all is lost. England belongs to the foreigners. I've done everything I can, but it isn't enough.'

Tova gets to her feet. 'No,' she says, suddenly angry. 'You're wrong. Remember what you told Oslac last night? As long as there's someone left who's willing to carry on the fight, it isn't over.'

He shakes his head. 'I'm not sure if—'

'Don't you dare say it,' she says, cutting him off, using the same tone that Merewyn sometimes uses when speaking to her. 'Don't tell me you're not sure if you believe that any more. You do. Of course you do. You're Beorn.'

He stares at her. She wonders when the last time was that anyone dared speak to him like this. Too long, obviously. But she can't just sit here and watch while he sinks ever deeper into despair. She has to do something. It's up to her. There's no one else.

'Listen to me,' she says, just as he has said to them so many times these past few days. 'This is what we're going to do. They want to kill us, don't they? They want to ravage this land and everything in it. So we don't let them. We survive, and then we come back and rebuild everything they've destroyed. We live our lives. That's how we carry on the fight. That's how we win.'

He shouldn't need her to tell him these things. Hasn't he been the one always urging them on through everything? Single-minded. Determined. He's supposed to be telling her this, not the other way round. He can't give up hope. He, of everyone, should know better.

He looks up at her, those wolf eyes more like cub eyes. He could be a child being scolded by his mother.

She says, 'If we give in, if we tell ourselves they've won and that's the end and there's no point any more, then we become like Oslac. Is that what you want? He told himself he was doing a good thing when really he just didn't want to admit he was taking the easy path.'

'I've been fighting for too long,' Beorn says. 'I can't keep on doing it.'

Not so long ago she thought like he did. But not any longer. She's come too far and seen too much. She's not going to lie down and wait for death to take her. And she's not going to let him either.

'Don't just sit there,' she says. 'Get up.'

He looks sharply at her. 'Why?'

'Because I need you to teach me some more.'

For the better part of an hour while Merewyn sleeps, he shows her how to thrust and how to cut, how to move her feet so that she doesn't overreach and leave herself off balance and open to attack. He shows her different ways opponents might attack and how to anticipate them. The places she should aim for. How she can twist the blade in a wound to inflict more pain and kill a man all the more quickly.

He challenges her to come at him. Like before, she's worried about hurting him; he's already injured, moving stiffly. The last thing she wants to do is add a knife wound to his woes, but it's soon clear there's no danger of that. For all that she lunges and charges, he dances easily out of the way of her knife, again and again, circling around her, until they're both laughing and she's out of breath.

She sits back down next to the fire. Her cheeks are hot, and her heart is pounding, but with delight rather than fear. She feels exhausted and yet at the same time stronger and more alive than at any time she can remember in days. She'd almost forgotten what it felt like to smile.

Beorn tosses some more sticks on to the flames, then reaches inside a pouch at his belt and produces two lumps of cheese, each half the size of his fist.

'Here,' he says, offering them to her, closing her hands around them. 'I didn't want us to eat what little food we had all at once, so I was keeping these until we really needed them. Well, soon it'll be that time. And you need to keep your strength up. You and your lady both.'

'Don't you want any?'

'I'm not hungry.'

'Are you sure?'

He nods. 'There's something else I want you to have.'

He holds out the scabbard that contains his seax. She stares first at it and then at him. He doesn't mean it, surely?

'Take it,' he says.

'But it's yours.'

'I don't want it any more.'

Still uncertain, she places the cheese down beside her, then lifts the sheathed weapon from his outstretched hands. It's lighter than she might have expected, even though it's longer than her forearm. Plain leather, scuffed and worn. Unadorned

391

by jewels or gold fittings. The cross guard and handle are just as simple: no inlay or twisted threads of silver.

It's exactly his kind of blade, she thinks. Not showy. Made for a task and nothing more.

She takes hold of the corded grip and pulls gently. The blade slides out easily, without a noise. He must keep the lining well oiled. Now that she sees it up close she can make out the swirling patterns in the steel, like eddies in a stream when it's in spate.

'I had it made as a hunting knife,' he says, 'although I never did get a chance to use it for that.'

Holding the hilt carefully in both hands, she turns it over, admiring the way the edge catches the light. The balance is different with a longer blade, compared with the knife she's been practising with. Along one face, she notices, are inscribed some letters that she can't read.

She points to them. 'What does that say?'

'It says, "Cynehelm had me made." Since Cynehelm is no more, there's no point me holding on to it any longer.'

'Don't you need it?'

He rises, grimacing a little as he does so, and makes towards the door. 'I have my bow. My axe. They've always been enough.'

'Where are you going?'

'I've made a decision. It can't be far to Hagustaldesham. Half a day on foot through the snow. Maybe a bit more. If I go now, I can probably get there before dark.'

'You're leaving?'

'I'm going to get help.'

'But what about us?'

'Your lady won't be going anywhere quickly. Someone needs to stay with her and take care of her.'

'You can't just leave.'

'Either I go now, before it gets any later, and try to reach there by nightfall, or we wait as the snow comes down, and we freeze or we starve, whichever comes first.'

Tova shakes her head. 'You can't.'

'Would you rather go yourself?' He rests a hand on her shoulder. 'There's no other way. If there was, if I could think of one, I wouldn't be doing this. But there isn't, so I have to.'

'No. We need you.'

'I'll bring help, and we'll make it through this. All of us. You'll see. But you have to trust me.'

Trust me, he says. This man whom she still hardly knows. Their lives in his hands. Again. Without him they'd never have made it this far. Without him they'd be dead several times over.

He clasps her hands in his. His palms are rough and marked with a hundred cuts and scabs.

'Whatever you do,' he says, 'whatever happens, you have to keep the fire burning.'

She nods. 'Of course.'

He taps his chest, where his heart is. 'I mean the fire in here. Don't let it go out. Ever. If you do, that means they've won. What you said earlier, you were right. Whatever happens, you mustn't give up, you have to keep on going. For you and your lady. For the priest. For me.'

She has never heard him talk like this before, and it unnerves her. Her skin crawls. 'I don't understand.'

'You aren't like the rest of us. You don't have to carry the burdens we do. You're a good person.'

'Don't say that.'

'Why not?'

'Because it isn't true.'

Murderer. Isn't that what she is now? She's a killer too. Like

393

him. Like Merewyn. They made that choice together, the three of them. How can he possibly say she's a good person after that?

And then there are the things he doesn't know about. The things she hasn't told anyone.

'You're loyal,' he says. 'Forgiving. Honest. A better person than the rest of us. When times grew hard, we were weak. We gave in to greed, to anger, to fear. But you won't. I know you won't. You're strong. Stronger than most warriors I've known. You have the fire within you. As long as you keep it burning, there's still hope.'

He's beginning to frighten her now. All this talk only sounds to her like farewell. Why else would he be saying these things?

'Don't,' she says. 'Please.'

'Believe me. Everything will be all right.'

He tries to let go of her hands, but she won't let him. 'You're hurt. You'll never make it in this weather. What if you get lost? What if the Normans find you?'

'I can take care of myself. And I'll be coming back.'

'When?'

'Tomorrow. I promise. You know I don't make oaths lightly.'

'Beorn.'

'What?'

She allows his fingers to slip through her grasp. A part of her wants to throw her arms around him and thank him for everything he's done, but that would seem too final. Besides, he knows it already.

Instead she says, 'Be safe.'

'I will.'

He grabs the handle and jerks once, hard. The door creaks open and the snow bursts in. It eddies around his feet. A blast of chill air greets her. Outside the flakes fall thickly in waves and spirals that make her dizzy. There's so much of it. How is he going to find his way?

But she says nothing and keeps those worries to herself. He knows what he's doing, she tells herself. He's managed to endure this long, after all.

He ventures out into the storm. Takes one step, then another, then another, fighting against the wind. He doesn't look back; she doesn't expect him to. But just in case he does, she stands by the doorway, watching as he trudges on through the snow. The flurries envelop him, until all she can see of him is the outline of a figure, growing steadily fainter with each passing moment.

But still she watches, until, all too soon, he vanishes into the whiteness.

He's gone.

Less than a day away. That's how close they came.

Unless, if Oslac was right, they were never really close at all, and they've been chasing a dream.

They'll know soon. When Beorn comes back. If he finds help, or if he doesn't.

Either way, they'll know.

It's nearly dark by the time Merewyn wakes again. Tova hasn't ventured outside since Beorn left. For the last hour she's been watching the sliver of daylight around the door turn steadily dimmer and dimmer. Now it's nearly gone. She doesn't know if it's still snowing. The wind hasn't ceased; she can hear it screeching through the trees outside. She has dragged the altar across in front of the door to barricade it and stop it from blowing open, but it still rattles.

They sit close together, sharing in one another's warmth.

Tova's legs ache with the cold. She has never seen her lady so pale, so stiff, so fragile. Merewyn's dress is still drying on the makeshift frame beside the fire.

She takes out the book again, searching through the pages for more pictures of stories that she recognises. Before long she comes across one of a great, brightly coloured ship with golden dragon heads at each end, afloat upon the dark and turbulent seas and laden with livestock: with pigs and goats and horses and hounds and ducks, and again those strange humped animals that Merewyn said were called camels. Two of each creature, their heads peering over the sides.

A man, leaning from a window on the ship's upper deck, reaches his hand towards a dove. An olive branch in its beak.

You relented, Lord, she thinks, that time long ago. Please, have mercy upon us this time too.

'There's something I need to tell you,' Tova says. 'Something I've been keeping secret. Something I'm ashamed of.'

Beside her Merewyn stirs. 'What is it?'

'I've wanted to say for so long, but it was never the right time.'

'You can tell me, whatever it is.'

Tova takes a deep breath and then says, 'Do you remember the harvest before last, when the silver went missing from Skalpi's strongbox?'

'You know I do. Why?'

'It was me.'

'You?'

'It wasn't Gunnhild who took it. It was me. I meant to run away.'

'Run away?'

Tova swallows. 'We were always talking in the dairy about

what we might do if we ever earned our freedom. If we ever managed to escape. We'd all heard stories of slaves who'd done that, but always they ended up getting caught again. They were never able to hide for long; after a while they had to make themselves known somewhere if they didn't want to starve, and people were always on the lookout for runaways, eager to claim a reward. I thought that if I had money, I might be able to pay my way – maybe I'd flee to the sea and buy passage somewhere. I don't know that I ever truly had a plan, but that's why I did it. It was only a few pennies. I didn't think anyone would miss them.'

'You hated it that much?'

'Of course I hated it. We all did. You would too. All day you work hard for no reward, and the next and the next and the next, and all the time you're told that it's not enough. Every night you bed down on damp rushes or flat straw because no one ever bothers to give you fresh bedding. You're always last to eat, and if there's nothing left for you after all the servants have had theirs then you go hungry. You never have your own clothes, only what others give you, and often they're full of holes or wearing out and you have to mend them as best you can. No one cares for you or thinks about you at all, except when they need something done.'

'Oh Tova,' Merewyn says. 'I never knew.'

'It's all right. There's no reason you should have. Anyway, you did the best thing anyone ever could for me. You gave me my freedom. It wasn't you. Ælfric was the one who was supposed to look after us and make sure we were properly fed and clothed. He was always looking for more from us, and we had no choice but to give it. If you disobeyed or refused to work you were beaten, and at the same time you were supposed to be grateful for whatever you were given, however little it was.'

'But once you had the money, why didn't you flee?'

'I don't know. Until I had the coins in my hand I never had any doubts, but as soon as I did, I began asking myself how far I expected to get before they caught me or some other fate befell me. I wondered how I'd manage to survive on my own, and what kind of life that would be. And, on top of everything else, I didn't know where to go. In the end, I was too frightened to do anything.'

'So you changed your mind, but you still kept the silver.'

'I meant to return it, really I did. I knew that someone would notice it was missing sooner or later. But there was never a good time. I kept it hidden inside a small cloth pouch that I stuffed inside my mattress. I thought no one would find it there, but before I could take it back they searched our quarters.'

'How did it find its way under Gunnhild's bed, then?'

'That was Orm's doing.'

'Orm?'

'They tore our room apart. Him and Ælfric, I mean. He found the pouch, but he didn't say anything until they came to Gunnhild's bed. Only then did he pretend to find it. That's why she didn't know anything about it.'

'How do you know this?'

'Because he told me afterwards. A few days later.'

'Why would Orm do anything to help you?'

'Why do you think? Because he wanted something.'

'Oh Tova.'

'I'd noticed the way he looked at me, but then I thought he looked at all the girls that way. For a long time I didn't think anything of it. I didn't think he'd ever do anything, if only out of fear of his father. After his mother was driven out, though, he changed, became more withdrawn. Some of the ceorls didn't like the looks he gave their daughters, the way he'd watch them when they were at work in the fields. They went to Skalpi to protest, and he managed to put a stop it for a while, but only for a while.

'Anyway, I was as confused as Gunnhild was when they accused her. I'd been fearing the worst. I knew it was a mistake, but I had no idea how it had happened. Not until a couple of days later, in the kitchen, when Orm told me what he'd done. That he'd lied for me and that he'd done it to protect me. He told me I ought to thank him, and that if I didn't do the things he wanted then he'd tell everyone the truth. When I still refused, he hit me and told me that I was worthless and no better than a slug. He said that if he liked he could kill me and nobody would care because I was only a slave. That's when you came in. After that I kept expecting him to carry out his threat.'

'But he never did.'

'No, he didn't.'

'You should have said something.'

'I was too afraid.'

'But we sent Gunnhild away. Her daughter as well. We sold them to a trader who was going to take them across the sea.'

'I know,' Tova says, feeling very small. She wonders what has happened to them and where they are now. Are they even still alive? If only she could say sorry, but she can't.

Forgive me, Ase, Gunnhild, both of you, she pleads silently. Wherever you are, forgive me.

'You let us think it was her,' Merewyn says. 'You knew it was wrong and yet you said nothing.'

'I was frightened!'

Merewyn shakes her head as if she cannot quite bring herself to believe it. 'I begged Skalpi to be merciful, begged him not to be too hard on her. God be thanked he listened to me, but he didn't have to. If he'd wanted he could have had Gunnhild hanged. Would you have kept silent then, knowing she was paying with her life for something you'd done?'

'I–I don't know,' Tova says. She really doesn't. She thinks she would, but she isn't sure.

'Why are you telling me this now, anyway?'

'Because . . .' says Tova, but the rest of the words stick in her throat and she can't get them out. She can't make herself say it.

Remember what Beorn promised, she thinks. He hasn't let you down yet and he won't let you down now. She must believe it. She must.

'Because it might be the last chance I get,' she says. 'If I didn't tell you now, it might be too late. And I didn't want to die without telling someone.'

'Don't talk like that,' Merewyn snaps, but Tova notices the tremor in her voice as she says it.

'There's another reason. Before he went, Beorn said these things to me. He told me to keep the fire burning and that I should never give up hope, no matter what happened. He kept saying it, and then he told me I was a good person. That's what he believed. But it isn't true. It isn't true at all. I'm a thief and a liar, just like Guthred. I'm no better than anyone else.'

It's a long time before Merewyn says anything. 'What you did, you did out of desperation. There's no shame in that.'

'But Gunnhild, she was like a mother to me. And Ase, she was my best friend.'

'Did they hate it as much as you did?'

Tova nods.

'Maybe, then, it was a good thing you did for them.'

'How could it be a good thing?'

'Well, they could have ended up somewhere better than

Heldeby. Somewhere without an Ælfric always watching them. Somewhere with fresh straw and blankets to sleep on, and clothes that weren't falling apart. Somewhere safe from the Normans. From all this. Who knows? They might even have earned their freedom by now.'

She's trying to make Tova feel better, but it's not working. 'You don't know that.'

'It's possible, though, isn't it?'

'I suppose.'

'We can't change the things we've done. We can't make them right, not completely. But you'll get the chance to see Ase and Gunnhild again. Perhaps not in this life, that's all. In the next. You'll be able to tell them then. You'll be able to say sorry for everything. And they'll understand.'

'Do you really believe that?'

Merewyn hesitates before, in a small voice, she says, 'I have to. The thought that this world is all there is . . . Well, there has to be something more, hasn't there? A place where there's no pain, no hunger, no bloodshed. A place without evil.'

Tova has seen and heard enough evil, enough pain, in this past week to last her the rest of her life, even if she were to live to Thorvald's age. No matter what happens after this is over, she thinks, it'll seem like paradise.

Her lady is shivering again as she leans towards Tova. 'I hope Beorn comes back soon.'

'So do I,' Tova says, but she cannot keep the doubt from her mind. It throbs away inside her. Like a headache she can't ignore.

What if the flurries turn heavier and he loses his way in the storm and cannot find his way? What if, in the gloom, he falls down a ravine that he doesn't see until it's too late? What if he can't find help and keeps on wandering, more and more desperate, until the freezing night or hunger or his injured leg brings him down? What if he runs into another band of Normans? How well will he be able to fight? How well will he be able to run?

What if he's already dead?

They would never know.

They could be sitting here, waiting for days, and not have any idea. At some point they'd have to accept he wasn't coming back, but when? How long can they make the firewood last? How long before the snow relents?

She asks, 'What if he doesn't?'

Merewyn's reply, when it comes, is drowsy. 'Doesn't what?'

'Come back.'

'He said he would, didn't he? And so he will. He hasn't broken a promise to us yet. He won't now.'

'But if he doesn't?'

The question hangs between them, unanswered.

She supposes that Beorn, better than anyone, knows how to survive. That's what he does. It's what he's good at.

Tova slides deeper under the folded wall hanging that serves her as a blanket, like a badger burrowing down into the earth, where she can hide, safe and snug, until winter has passed. The floor is hard, and she shifts, trying to find a more comfortable position, but there is none, and so she concentrates instead on staying as still as she can, curled as tightly as possible, her knees drawn up in front of her chest, her arms folded and her gloved hands tucked into her armpits, but nothing she does seems to work.

Outside the wind keens, rising to a screech before stuttering and breaking down into a weary moan. A death song. A lament for the fallen. No light now save the glow of the fire, which has dwindled to almost nothing.

Keep it burning, she thinks. Don't let it go out.

Her limbs are stiff and protest as she tries to move, but she wills herself to get up, bracing herself as she sheds her portion of the hanging. She gets to her feet slowly. This is what it must be like to be old, she thinks.

'What are you doing?' Merewyn mumbles sleepily.

'Trying to keep the fire going, that's all.'

From the corner where the wood is stacked she retrieves some of the smaller twigs, which she lays on top of the glowing embers, and more that she'll keep for later, along with a few larger pieces. She doesn't want to build it up too much or too quickly, or they'll burn through everything they have before the night is done.

Her lady's eyelids are drooping again, but she jolts awake as Tova slips back under the covers next to her.

'It's all right,' Tova says. 'You should sleep. I'll be here. I'll stay awake.'

'No,' her lady says. 'It's your turn.'

'You need it more than I do.'

Merewyn sighs. 'I'm so tired.' Her voice is muffled as she buries her face in Tova's shoulder.

'Me too. I hardly remember when I last slept. Properly slept, I mean. In a bed, not curled in a cold corner of some damp hovel, miles from anywhere, with one eye open all the time.'

How she longs to lie down and surrender herself, to let sleep enfold her. Every inch of her body that isn't numb with cold is numb from all this journeying, all this running, all this fighting, all this fleeing from one place to the next and then the next. Her arms and shoulders are aching and her neck is barely strong enough to keep her head up. Each time she closes her eyes for even an instant, she feels her lids tugging down, down, down, like they're made of lead. Each time it's a struggle to lift them again.

403

No.

She mustn't succumb.

Tomorrow. All she has to do is stay awake through this night, until tomorrow. Beorn will come back, and there'll be others with him. They'll bring food and blankets and warm clothes, and all will be well. They'll leave here and they'll find a safe place where they can weather the storm until the Normans have turned back south, as eventually they must. If they keep on burning, keep on slaughtering, it won't be long before there's nothing left. Nothing more to raze to the ground. No one else to kill or drive from their homes.

And then what? Yes, they could go back and try to rebuild, like she told Beorn. But if everything they used to know is gone, lost for ever to the enemy and to the flames, is there any point?

A land of ash and bone. That's all there'll be. No halls or houses. No clothes save for the ones they're wearing. No pigs or goats or cattle. Not a horse between them. No silver or gold. Nothing.

'So we'll leave,' she murmurs. 'We won't go back.'

Merewyn stirs. 'What's that?' she says sleepily.

Tova hesitates. She swallows, not quite willing to believe what she's about to suggest.

Don't fight the waves, she thinks. Ride them. Wasn't that what he said? To survive, sometimes you have to change.

'Let's not go back to Heldeby,' she says. 'Let's keep on going north towards the lands of the Scots. We can take the book – what's left of it anyway – to the monks at Lindisfarena. And then, after that, we could leave England altogether. Find a ship, go across the sea. To Yrland, maybe, or the land of the Danes. Some place where we can make new lives for ourselves.'

She has heard of folk fleeing all the way to Miklagard, where the eastern emperor rules, to seek sanctuary there, but they needn't go that far. It could be anywhere, as long as the Normans can't come at them. That's all that matters.

To leave England altogether . . .

The thought terrifies her even as it thrills her. They couldn't, could they? Tova has only ever seen the sea once; she has no idea what it would be like to take to the water, or how they'd even go about finding a shipmaster who could take them, or how long it would take them to reach these places. A week? A month? Longer?

'What do you think?' she asks. 'Merewyn?'

Tova glances down at her. Her lady's eyes are closed, her mouth a little open, her breathing light and steady.

She'll ask her again when she wakes. There'll be plenty of time to make those decisions later. First they have to make it through this night.

Trying not to move too suddenly, she lays Merewyn down on the bracken and the leaves where she'll be more comfortable. Her lady hardly stirs. She must be utterly spent. Tova lies down next to her, curled tight and hugging her arms close to her chest, making sure as she does that the covers are wrapped close around them both. Their feet are pointed towards the fire. The flames dance and flicker, swell and subside, like there's a spirit inside each one that guides it and gives it radiance and causes it to flare up, to play and leap, to glow hot and then cool, cool and then hot again. A moving, breathing thing, as delicate and as changeable as any other creature.

She watches them, twisting and intertwining in their many colours, safe in the knowledge that as long as she does so, they will not go out.

SEVENTH DAY

Cold. It binds her and clutches at her chest. She can hardly breathe: the air, when she can catch it, is thin and sharp and takes her by surprise, each time like being stabbed from the inside. She shifts, searching for warmth, but there's none to be found. Her neck is stiff and her mouth and throat are dry. She coughs, once, twice; blinks, trying to shove away sleep's grasping embrace, but her lids are heavy and to move them at all takes all her strength.

She eyes the door, with the light spilling in from underneath, bright and harsh and painful to look at for long. It must be morning. There's an ache in her head, as if a shard of ice has become lodged in her skull and is driving ever deeper, making it difficult even to think.

She never imagined she could be this cold.

Where is she? Trying to remember is like wading through pitch. She recalls the fight, but dimly, like it was a long time ago, and she isn't sure that she has all the events in the right order. She remembers fleeing, and the snow beginning to fall. Beorn going to find help, and the two of them staying behind. He told them to wait for him, to stay inside where it was warm, to make sure they kept the fire going—

The fire.

Her heart racing, she tries to raise herself, but she has become tangled in their makeshift blankets and she has to fight her way out from underneath. But even before she does, she knows.

'No,' she says, her breath misting. She throws back the cloth and sits up. 'No, no, no.'

It's gone out.

Not a flicker, nor a wisp of smoke. Only ash, white as snow and just as lifeless. She scrambles on unfeeling hands and clumsy knees towards it, searching for any spark amid the embers, however small, from which she can coax it back into being. She tries blowing upon the remnants, gently at first and then harder, hoping to make something happen, but nothing will.

How long is it since it burned out? When did she fall asleep? Hours ago, it must have been, for it wasn't long after dark when she and her lady were talking—

Merewyn.

She turns and sees her huddled beneath the covers, her cheeks milky pale in the wan light. Unmoving.

Oh God, please no, Tova thinks. Oh God, oh God, oh God.

She rushes to her lady's side, places her hand on her arm, shaking her gently and saying her name, over and over and over and each time more urgently.

Beorn trusted her to take care of them both. He trusted her to not let the fire die. She promised him she would. She promised herself.

The one thing she had to do was not fall asleep.

'Wake up.' She feels the tears welling. 'Please, wake up. I'm sorry. I didn't mean to.'

But Merewyn doesn't stir or even seem to hear her at all. Her face is tranquil, like those of the angels painted on the walls of

410

the church at home, ascending to the eternal kingdom. Like the faces of the saints that she saw in Guthred's book.

Please, let her live.

She fumbles beneath the covers for her lady's hand and clasps it in her own. It hasn't gone stiff as she had feared, but it's cool to the touch. Merewyn is no longer shivering, Tova sees, and she knows that's a bad sign, because that's what happened to her mother near the end. First she grew still, and then she stopped breathing, and then—

No. She can't give up hope. Not now. Not yet.

She leans forward, pressing her ear close to Merewyn's lips, desperate for some sign that she is still breathing. Nothing. With every heartbeat she feels what hope she had melting away. Despair clutches at Tova's stomach. Her heart is thumping so loudly that she's worried she won't be able to hear her lady's breath when it comes.

But then there it is: the feeblest brush of warm air against her cheek. It wouldn't make a candle flicker, but it's enough. She's alive, if only barely.

Tova could cry with relief, but she holds it back. She can't waste even one moment. She has to keep Merewyn warm, but how? Should she try to get the fire going again? How long will that take?

Beorn would know what to do. She wishes he were here.

But he isn't, she chides herself. No amount of wishing is going to make him appear. If she's to help her lady, she must do it on her own.

Think.

She lies down next to Merewyn, pressing herself close, hugging her lady like she might a little child, while at the same time murmuring reassuring words in her ear, hoping that Merewyn might still be able to hear her. She can't remember ever seeing

411

her look so fragile, so young and so small. Behind those pale eyelids and that serene expression, is she as afraid as Tova?

She keeps talking to her, talking about the past, about Heldeby before the war, before Orm, while Skalpi was still alive. The happy times they shared, when they were less like lady and servant and more like sisters. All the while hoping that Merewyn will hear her and come back to her.

She asks, 'You remember, don't you, that day last spring when we rode together to the market at Skardaborg?'

It was the first time Tova had ever seen the sea. How she marvelled at the way it fragmented the light into a thousand tiny suns, and at the ships with their striped sails skipping across its surface. Men clambering ashore to drag the hulls up over the sand. Nets filled with writhing, silvery fish. Wicker cages into which were crammed strange many-legged creatures that Merewyn called crabs. More people than Tova had ever seen in one place before, dressed in bright clothes, speaking in many tongues. Blue-eyed fair-haired folk who'd sailed from the northern lands, the lands of Skalpi's ancestors, barking orders to their crewmen on the wharves, calling out prices and holding up their wares for all to see.

And then there were the stalls, with their canopies to shield them from the weather. While Merewyn bought cinnamon and pepper from the spicer, Tova went exploring, thrilled and nervous at the same time, picking her way through the thronged streets, past the fleshmongers and wine merchants. Past the carvers with their tables stacked with wooden bowls and spoons, some plain and others painted with intricate patterns. Past the pedlars with their scraps of cloth laid out on the ground and on them trinkets and charms, bracelets and necklaces of pewter and amber, pendants of jet and cheaper wooden amulets inscribed with runes. A thin-faced merchant with rolls of fine linen and dyed wool, and ribbons that he said came all the way from the eastern empire: lengths of silk as long as her arm, in green as dark as holly, and other colours as well – black and red and white – but it was the green that Tova thought most beautiful. They shone and shimmered in the light like butterfly wings.

'I wanted one of those ribbons so badly,' Tova says. 'I wanted one like I'd never wanted anything before. I suppose I was thinking I could wear it in my hair on special days. For Christmas, maybe, or whenever we had a feast.'

The trader, though, wanted five pennies for each one, and that wasn't just all the money Tova had with her, it was all the money she had in the world. She tried to bargain with him, but he said with a sneer that if she couldn't afford his prices then she should take her grubby fingers away and waste someone else's time. Tova replied indignantly that her fingers weren't grubby, but he wasn't listening. He came out from behind his stall and tried to shoo her away like a calf that had strayed into the wrong field, but Merewyn came and told the man curtly that the ribbon was meant for her. She'd sent her maidservant to buy it on her behalf, she said, but having seen how he treated his customers, she'd changed her mind.

She bade him good day and turned to leave. At once the merchant, red-faced, called after her, stumbling over his words, saying he hadn't known, that he'd been rash and presumptuous, and that if the lady would reconsider he would ask only four pennies for the ribbon. Merewyn offered three and the trader hesitated, but she made to walk away again, and the man gave in. He watched avidly as she counted out the coins from the pouch she kept inside her sleeve.

'You turned to me and asked me which one I thought was best,' Tova says. 'I was so surprised I didn't know what to say, but I pointed to the green one. You picked it up, and he said that was a wise choice, but then you handed it to me and said it was a gift and I should look after it. I was so grateful I think I just nodded. He was furious, do you remember? He thought we'd set out to trick him, and made a fuss, or tried to, but the other traders just turned their backs.

'And I looked after it, just like you said,' she whispers. 'That night, when you came and said we had to leave, I couldn't go without it.'

She rolls up her sleeve, where the ribbon is tied around her wrist, dirty now but still intact, as if to show Merewyn, but her lady does not wake. Tova holds her tighter so that she doesn't slip away. There has to be something more she can do, but what?

And it's because she doesn't know what else to do that she carries on talking and whispering those words of encouragement, for her own comfort as much as for her lady's.

'We're going to be all right,' she says. 'Soon we'll be safe.'

She speaks the words again and again, trying to keep her thoughts from dwelling on the cold seeping ever deeper into her flesh, on the dampness in the air and in her clothes, the hunger that clutches at her stomach and causes it to twist and wrench. There's a small voice inside her saying she should save her breath, but then there's another reminding her that if she does that there will only be silence. Nothing but the wind whistling through the branches outside, and that's what she can't bear. Because then she'll be forced to admit that she is truly alone.

Just her, out here on her own, at the end of the world.

'Wake up,' she murmurs again. Her eyes are squeezed shut. She hopes that when she opens them all this will turn out to have been a dream, some horrible, horrible dream.

'Wake up, wake up,' she urges, no longer sure if she's talking to her lady or to herself.

'Tova?'

She blinks away the moisture from her eyes. 'Merewyn?'

Hope. She feels it flooding back, like the streams after the snow has melted, rushing together, their strength renewed after the long stillness.

'Tova,' her lady says again. More than a whisper but less than a murmur, the sounds drawn out and tentative, as if she's not quite sure of their shape. Like an old person might speak. Her eyes are closed still, her brow furrowed slightly.

'I'm here.' Tova rests her hand gently on her lady's forehead. Her fingers feel deadened, devoid of blood and warmth, but Merewyn's skin is no warmer.

'So cold,' Merewyn says, slurring her words, and gives a small tremble, a tremble that becomes a shudder. Tova takes this for a good sign. Better to be shivering than still.

'It's all right,' Tova says, nestling as close as she can. 'We'll keep each other warm.'

She knows she mustn't let her drift back into sleep. She can't risk losing her again.

But she also needs to get the fire lit, and if she's going to keep it fed then they'll need more wood too. What they have left should last them through the day, but probably not the night as well. They'll need to be prepared.

Before she can start to get settled where she is, she slides out from beside Merewyn. She'll have to be quick; she doesn't want to leave her lady for too long. She stumbles on frozen feet across to the door, fumbling at the handle and readying herself for the chill blast that is to come. And it does. It slaps her across the face, and again, stinging her cheeks and her eyes and the exposed skin at her neck. She winces as she steps out.

Into a world so bright that to begin with she can't look at it.

415

She lifts her hand to her eyes to guard against the glare. Snow everywhere: across the fields and the distant hills and upon the branches of the trees in the thicket down in the hollow; wind-blown against the church wall, so deep that the water butt standing next to it is almost buried. It lies a foot deep on the thatch and on the ground. The clouds hang low and heavy with the promise of more to come. She closes the door behind her and crunches and squeaks her way across it, her shoes sinking in.

It's hopeless, she thinks. She'll never find anything dry under all this.

Folding her arms across her chest and with her hands tucked into her armpits, she sets off down the slope towards the thicket, as quickly as she can manage, which isn't very quick at all. It's hard to walk; her legs are tired and tiring further with every stride.

Keep the fire burning.

Don't give in.

The wind is like an invisible hand that seizes her body and squeezes it tight, wringing the breath from her chest. Each gust flings up flurries of snow that billow and tumble and assault her. She ducks her head and stumbles on.

Halfway down the slope her foot strikes something hard buried beneath the white. She cries out as she falls, only to find her mouth full of snow as she meets the ground, and she is tumbling forwards, sideways, the sky and the snow a blur of white and grey, and she doesn't know which way is up. Eventually she comes to a stop. She spits out what's in her mouth and swears, loudly, violently, like she would never do in Merewyn's presence.

She rises to her knees and flings her fists at the snow again and again, but it doesn't give her the satisfaction she hoped for. It isn't dense and packed hard, but fine and powdery. She wills it to fight back, to resist her, but it refuses. She hits it again, and keeps on hitting it, screaming and yelling as she does so, letting out all the anger that has been building for days and weeks and months. At the Normans. At the world. At life. At God.

When she's finished she lies there, on her back, staring up at the grey sky, breathless and empty and strangely calm. The wind whips about her and the cloud swirls and scurries overhead.

She could stay here for ever. Just lie here until it's all over. That would be the easiest thing. She wouldn't even have to try.

No.

Slowly she picks herself up, drags herself to her feet. Fire shoots up her ankle as she places her weight on it. She must have twisted it. But nothing is broken, nothing is cut. She tries to brush off the worst of the snow, not out of any pretence at maintaining her dignity but because she doesn't want it to melt and make her clothes wet. It comes away in clumps, although some refuses to be dislodged. Even when she shakes her skirt and her sleeves to loosen it, it clings stubbornly to her like a thousand tiny burrs.

She has to be more careful. The last thing she needs is to break her wrist or her ankle. If she does, that really would be the end for her, and for her lady as well.

She finishes dusting herself off and she turns—

And sees them.

Horsemen.

Three of them. No, four. Up there, on the hilltop to the east, strung out along the ridge. A quarter of a mile away? Less than that? When almost every direction looks the same, it's hard to be sure. She shields her eyes against the sun struggling through the clouds and against the snow glare.

Beorn? Is it him?

She can hardly believe it. Her heart is pounding almost out of her chest with excitement and relief. But they aren't coming this way. Instead they're riding along the crest, heading southwards. Have they even spotted her?

She waves her arms and is about to call out to catch their attention when she sees their spear points, their helmets, their shield bosses gleaming coldly under the leaden skies. The words stop in her throat just as she opens her mouth.

Fighting men. Mounted men. A war band. A raiding party.

No, it can't be. Is it?

She hears the voice inside telling her to flee. Back to the church, it says. Back to Merewyn. Now. If it's the enemy and they see her . . .

But her feet won't move. The cold has found its way into her bones, sunk deep into her flesh, and her limbs have seized up. She knew it had to happen eventually. For day after day she has pushed on through wind and rain and hail and snow, over field and fell, across moor and dale. Ever since leaving Heldeby they've been living in fear as they try to evade one danger or another, and she can't do it any more.

The men are riding on. They haven't seen her. She can only make out two of them now; the others have already disappeared over the rise.

And then she thinks, what if they aren't Normans? What if this is their one chance to be rescued, and she's letting it slip through her fingers? But how can she know? She can't. Not unless they come closer. But they aren't coming closer. They're getting further away.

She has to decide, one way or another. She has to decide quickly. To call out or to stay quiet and let them go? Will they even hear her from so far away, or will the wind take her words and scatter them? If she waits any longer, it'll be too late. The riders will have gone. Their chance will be gone.

Only one of the horsemen is still visible. The straggler. A shadow against the skyline.

Whatever she does, she must do it without regret, without fear. Whatever happens, she tells herself, it's fate. And suddenly she is no longer afraid. The wind is behind her. She fills her lungs with the chill, sharp air.

'Hey!' she yells, cutting the stillness. 'Hey!'

For a moment, nothing. And then the straggler stops. At the very crest of the hill he stops and he turns.

She yells again, waves both her hands.

Shortly he's joined by the other three riders. For the longest time they stay very still, watching her. What are they doing? Are they talking to one another? What are they saying?

She squints against the brightness as one of them produces what looks like a ram's horn. He puts it to his mouth, and a call blares out across the still land: once, twice, three times. Three long blasts. A signal? Does that mean there are more of them?

Oh God, she thinks. What have I done?

If she wanted to, if only her feet would move, she could still flee. She could make for the woods, where they'd never find her. But that would mean leaving Merewyn.

The horsemen start down the slope towards her. All four of them, kicking up thick swirls of snow dust that the wind takes and scatters. Their spear points shining coldly in the light.

She sheds her gloves, curls her numb fingers around the hilt of her knife. Not the one Beorn gave her. Her own. The one she brought with her all the way from home. The one she practised with, which he showed her how to use. Smaller, more easily concealed. She pulls it from its sheath and draws it inside her sleeve,

419

where they won't see it. Not, she hopes, until it's too late. If she is to die, then she might as well try to kill one or more of them first.

Stay strong, she tells herself.

She fixes her gaze upon the horsemen. Tries to, anyway. Everything is blurred. White stars creeping in at the corners of her sight. She blinks to try to get rid of them, but they won't go away.

Closer the riders come, and closer still. Her lungs are burning. Her cheeks are burning.

Attack, don't defend, she remembers. Be quick. Strike first. Kill quickly.

She grips the knife hilt as tightly as she can as they loom larger. It won't be long now.

She can hear them shouting, but not what they're saying. Are they calling to each other or to her?

She will not falter. She will not cry. She won't go to her fate timidly, but proudly. Like Guthred, throwing himself into the fray. Like Beorn, knowing what he had to do, venturing out alone into the cold. Even Oslac, when he realised there was no escape, faced his death with his head held high.

Like her forefathers, whom she has heard so many stories about. The heathens, when they came to these shores from across the sea. No better death than in battle against one's enemies. Wasn't that what they believed?

And so must she.

The world is swaying, spinning. The white stars are gone, replaced by dark blotches that open up like great holes in the sky, growing larger and larger. She hears a rushing, like floodwaters tumbling over a weir. All around her.

Breathe.

And again.

And again.

420

The dark spots recede. The world stops spinning around her. And there they are. Four of them. Riding through the snow towards her with their spears in hand. Round shields slung across their backs. Scabbards at their sides. Clad in boar skins and wolf pelts, and in trews bound tightly with bands. Just like the men at home wear when they go out to work in the fields.

Not Normans, then. Englishmen.

But warriors all the same. Two younger and two older. One freckled, the rest fair. One missing a hand, another an ear. One with a stove-in nose. And yet despite that somehow they all look alike. Gaunt, grim faces. Sunken eyes. Beards left to grow far too long. Hair that hasn't seen a comb in weeks, or shears in much, much longer. Bruised cheeks. Scarred lips.

They look just like Beorn, she thinks.

Survivors from the battle at Hagustaldesham? Or reavers like the ones the priest fell in with? Just because they're English, that doesn't mean they're friendly.

The cord wrapped around the knife hilt digs into her fingers and into her raw palm.

When they're about a dozen paces away they stop, dismount. One of the younger men approaches. The freckled one. Is he their leader?

She doesn't move. Inside her cloak and her dress her whole body is shaking. She can't bear it. Waiting, not knowing. She knows that she mustn't let it show. She has to stand her ground. She can't let them know she's afraid.

But she is.

I can't do it, she thinks. I'm not Beorn. I'm not Guthred or Oslac. I'm not brave like them. I don't want to die.

The freckled one approaches slowly, trudging knee-deep, heavy-footed, through the snow.

She tenses, watching his hand closely in case it goes to the hilt of his weapon. Instead both hands are away from his body, palms facing outward. The look on his face is one of concern.

He says uncertainly, 'Tova?'

The breath catches in her chest. She stares at him, open-mouthed. She's dreaming. She must be. Surely he didn't just say what she thought he did? It's not possible.

She swallows. 'H-how . . .' Her tongue is frozen and she can't seem to get it around the words. She tries again. 'How do you know my name?' Her voice sounds somehow distant. As if it belongs to somebody else.

The freckled one glances behind him at the rest of his band. His expression is anxious. But she's the one at their mercy, not the other way round. What does he have to be anxious about?

He says, 'A friend of yours told us. You don't know how glad we are to see you.'

A friend. That can only be—

'Beorn,' she whispers.

He did it. He made it through the snowstorm. He reached the rebel camp. He got help just like he said he would. Like he promised. She should never have doubted him. If he were here right now, she could throw her arms around him. She could kiss him.

'He told us you were out here,' the man goes on. 'He gave us directions as best he could, told us what landmarks to look out for. We brought clothes and blankets. Firewood too. Food. As much as we could gather. Everything he said you'd need. Look.'

He gestures to his companions with their horses. For the first time she notices the packs strapped to the saddles.

'We didn't know whether we'd be the first to find you, or whether the others would reach you first.'

'Others?'

422

'We're not the only ones looking for you. There's another search party in the next valley. We knew it wouldn't be easy to find you in the snow, so we decided to split up to cover more ground. But your friend said there were two of you. Tova and Merewyn, he said. Where is she? Is she with you still?'

Merewyn. Of course. Her lady is still waiting for her to come back. She glances back in the direction of the tiny church. From here it's hard to spot, all but buried in the snow as it is.

'This way,' she says. 'Hurry.'

It's true what Oslac said about Hagustaldesham. About Gospatric and about the rebellion. All of it, every bit. The town is gone. The rebels, the few who are left, all either killed or forced to flee.

It really is over.

That's what Lyfing, the one with the freckles, says. Despite being the youngest-looking of them, he seems to be in charge. They've managed to get the fire going again and they've wrapped Merewyn in dry clothes and thick cloaks while they heat beans and lentils and carrots and some kind of salted fish.

'He didn't come with you, then,' Tova says, her voice small, as he sits down beside her. 'To show you the way himself.'

Lyfing hesitates. He won't meet her eyes. But it's all right. He doesn't have to. She's worked it out already.

She knows.

He would have said something by now otherwise. Why Beorn isn't with them. Where he is. What's happened to him. He'd have told her not to worry. That he's well and waiting back wherever they've come from, and they'll see him soon.

'No,' Lyfing says. 'He didn't.'

'Tell me.'

'What do you want me to say?'

'Just what happened. That's all.'

She's had enough of people talking down to her, trying to keep her from the truth, shielding her from hurt as if she's a child and they must take care of her. As if they think she won't understand. As if she can't take care of herself.

'He stumbled into our camp late last night,' Lyfing says. 'Wet through. Shivering. Bleeding. Wounded badly. He could barely stand up. He was mumbling something; we could barely make out what at first, or get any sense out of him at all. He told us your names, what you looked like. Said we had to go out straight away to look for you. He was begging us. He said there was no time to lose. We did everything we could for him. It wasn't enough.'

This isn't how things were meant to end. Not after everything. He was supposed to come back to help them find safety. The three of them, together. He promised. He gave her his oath.

Why did she ever let him go out on his own, into the cold? She could see he was hurt, but still she let him do it. She should have known he wouldn't make it. She should have insisted he stay with them.

This isn't how it was supposed to be. Not Beorn. Not like this.

But it's how it is.

She closes her eyes, tries to swallow her sobs before they overcome her. There'll be time enough for that later.

She asks, 'What about the Normans?'

'Gone back south. We think, anyway. Now that there's nothing left to burn or sack, they've got no reason to stay.'

Merewyn sighs in her sleep. She was awake for a while earlier, when their rescuers arrived, but she could barely hold her head up long enough to take some food and drink some ale, let alone speak. At least now there is colour in her cheeks again, and her breathing is even.

Tova strokes her on the arm and then clasps her hand, and is relieved to find her skin is no longer icy to the touch.

'Will she be all right, do you think?' she asks.

Lyfing takes a long sigh and scratches at his eyebrow. 'I can only say this: I've walked fields of battle after the fighting and seen men who were struck down, barely able to move, their limbs broken, left for hours in the cold and the wet to bleed and bleed until help came. They lived. So will she.'

'Beorn didn't, though.'

'Beorn?'

'Our friend.'

'That was his name?'

She nods.

'He never told us,' Lyfing says. 'The strange thing is, I thought I recognised him. From before, you understand. While the war was still going on. I was sure he looked like someone I'd met. One of our best warriors. A man called Cynehelm. When I mentioned that name to him, though, he just stared blankly at me. Obviously I was mistaken. Memory can be a strange thing. It can play tricks on you.'

Tova opens her mouth, then closes it again just as quickly. There's no need, she thinks. It's not important.

'No,' he goes on, 'Beorn didn't live. But I think maybe he realised his time was growing short. That's the feeling I had, seeing him. That he'd given everything and there was nothing left. When he came in out of the snow, his skin so pale and with blood all over his face and his hands, he looked like death already. Your lady, though, I'd say she looks as though she still has something to live for. Sometimes that's all it takes. The will to keep going. That's why I think she'll live. She has to. For Eadmer's sake, as well as her own. When he heard the news that she was alive—'

That name.

'Eadmer?' she echoes. Merewyn's brother. The one she hasn't heard from in months, since before the rebellion.

Lyfing nods. 'I fought by his side at Hagustaldesham, stopped him from getting himself killed. He would have done too. He thought he'd lost everyone and everything dear to him. He often talked to me about his sister, and how they'd once been close but had grown apart, and how he thought it was his fault. He missed her more than he missed anyone. And to think that, if I hadn't pulled him from the fray when I did, he'd never have known.'

Tova strokes Merewyn on the arm and then clasps her hand. 'Did you hear that?' she whispers, even though her lady doesn't stir. 'Eadmer's alive. He's alive and we're going to see him. Everything will be all right. It will, just like you said.'

The other party arrives within the hour. Four more men, in the next valley when they heard the horn. The newcomers bring more supplies, though little cheer.

Eadmer isn't among them. He would have joined the search, Lyfing explains, but he was hurt during the fighting.

'Lost his hand,' he says. 'His sword hand it was too, although he could have lost much more than that. When it was agreed we'd send out people to look for you, of course he wanted to come with us, but he's still weak, and we told him it would be better if he waited back at the camp.'

'The camp?' Tova asks. 'Where's that?'

'A short way to the north of here. The other side of Hagust-aldesham, a few miles up the valley, near where the river bends. It's where we fled after the battle, everyone who managed to get away. It's where we'll find him.'

EIGHTH DAY

They spend that night in the church, and then in the morning, as soon as Merewyn is strong enough, they leave it behind. The wind is still from the north; Lyfing thinks they might be due another heavy snowfall soon, and he doesn't want to be trapped out in the wilds if that's the case, and so they set out, eight men and Tova and her lady, fighting the wind and the occasional flurry.

Merewyn's strength is returning, though slowly. Her nose is running and her forehead is hot and she says her throat is sore and her feet are unsteady, but she's determined to stay awake. Her eyes are red and bloodshot, but she insists she's fine and tells Tova there's no need to keep fussing.

'Thank you, though,' she adds and smiles tiredly from atop the gelding loaned to her by one of Lyfing's men. 'For everything.'

In the distance, just beyond the hills, rise thin, grey, inter-twining curls. Hagustaldesham. No one speaks of it; the men avert their eyes and concentrate on the way ahead.

They stop by a stream to let the horses drink. Tova overhears the men discussing in low voices what they should do and where they should go in the days to come, and whether it's safe yet to send scouts back south, to see what's left of their homes. But the feeling seems to be that it's pointless until the thaw at least,

429

and until they can be sure there aren't any bands of Normans still prowling.

'How long will that be?' Tova asks Lyfing.

He doesn't answer.

The camp is only half a day's ride away through the snow, he tells them, but the sun is already low, touching the treetops to the west, gilding the fields with its light, when she spots the fires burning bright down by the riverbank.

Around the fires are dozens of tents and crude shelters. Paddocks for the horses. Pens for sheep and cattle and pigs. Everywhere piles of broken timber for firewood and stacks of barrels. Paths and tracks where the snow has been cleared for carts. Most folk are huddled by the fires, trying to keep warm, but some are hauling sacks and carrying pails, while others chop wood, skin haunches of meat and lead oxen and horses to drink at the water's edge.

There must be a hundred people, at least. Maybe twice that. More than ever lived at Heldeby, anyway. The last time Tova saw so many in one place was at Skardaborg. Some so old and frail and unsteady on their feet it seems a wonder they've made it this far. And not just men but women too, she notices as they grow closer. And children: running, shouting, chasing one another around the campfires, cupping snow in their mittened hands and hurling it at one another, shrieking and squealing in protest and delight, the sound of their voices and their laughter something Tova thought she might never hear again.

She wonders if they understand. If they have any idea, really, what's been happening.

Lyfing calls out as they descend towards the camp. He gestures to one of his companions and again the horn is sounded. Three sharp blasts. Women rise from tending the fires; men put down their tools and turn to see what's happening.

Shouldering his way through the gathering crowd of warriors and wives comes a young man. A boy, really – he can't be any older than herself, Tova thinks. Tall, gangling and fair. Wide eyes stare out from underneath a tangled mass of hair. His tunic is stained, his face smeared with grime. One of his sleeves is rolled up to the elbow, and the end of his arm is bound and tied with cloth.

He sees them. He sees Merewyn. He lets out a cry and pelts towards them, up the slope, twice slipping in the mud and the snow and ending up on his front, but he manages to pick himself up despite his missing hand.

Tova is at Merewyn's side, lending her hand in support as, shakily but as hurriedly as she can, she dismounts.

Eadmer is there already, waiting for her, his face streaming with tears, rubbing his eyes as if he can't quite believe what they're telling him, and Merewyn is weeping too as she flings her arms around him.

They stand without saying a word, brother and sister holding one another, as the sun disappears behind the hills.

Tova wanted to see Beorn before they buried him, so that she might have the chance to say farewell properly. But she's too late.

Lyfing says he can show her the place where he lies, if she'd like. She tells him she'd like that very much. He takes her to a spot perhaps a hundred paces from the edge of the camp, on a slight rise where the snow has been cleared, in the shelter of a birch copse.

A carved wooden cross, no taller than her hand is wide, is the only thing to mark the spot – one of dozens that stand there.

431

'He'd have hated that,' she tells Lyfing as she kneels down and takes a handful of the damp earth.

'He didn't believe?'

'No, he believed. But in something else, that's all.'

For a while Lyfing is silent. Pensive. He doesn't kneel down beside her, but stays standing out of respect.

'We can take it away, I suppose,' he says. 'Though the priests won't like the thought of a heathen being buried in consecrated ground.'

'Then we don't tell them.'

Lyfing nods. 'We can do that. If it's what he would have wanted.'

She thinks it is. Of course in ages past, she remembers from the songs, the heathens wouldn't have laid him in the earth like this. They'd have built a pyre and let the flames take his body, and the roaring blaze would have drowned out the mourners' weeping even as the smoke billowed and stung men's eyes. Afterwards they'd have heaped earth over the ashes to make a grave mound, raising it until it stood taller than a person, and filling it with silver ingots and arm rings of twisted gold so that in the next life he could reward his followers as richly as they deserved. Twelve mail-clad warriors would have ridden three times around it, beating their shields and shouting praise for his deeds and challenging any man to deny them, raising such a noise that the gods themselves would be compelled to take notice.

But she knows he'd have hated that too.

To be remembered is all he would have wanted. Not for his deeds to be recounted in song or recorded in ink by monks in their books, but simply for someone to know his story, to know who he was. Who he really was. Someone to know what he'd done, and to go on and live happy and well so that all his striving didn't turn out to have been for nothing.

That's what he would have wanted. And so that's what she'll do.

Most of the people in the camp are survivors from nearby villages and manors, it seems. A few have fled from further south to seek refuge at Hagustaldesham, but none have come from as far afield as Merewyn and herself. When they hear how far they've travelled, they besiege her with questions. How did the two of them manage to survive, out there on their own, with the Normans everywhere? How did they find their way? Did they ever come face-to-face with the enemy? Was there ever a time when they gave up hope?

'No,' she says. 'We never did. Because the truth is we were never alone.'

And they sit in silence and listen, never taking their eyes off her. They hand her a bowl of thick, steaming broth, and she sips it and tells them everything, from beginning to end, or as much of it as she can remember. She leaves out certain parts: some of the things she isn't proud of, as well as those she knows Merewyn would rather she didn't reveal. She talks about Beorn and how he saved them from the Normans, and about Guthred and Oslac as well, though only as fellow travellers whom they happened to meet and who guided and helped them and who fell along the way. Of their misdeeds and secret shames, she says nothing. These people don't need to know those things, and, besides, what does any of it matter now? Ashes on the wind. That's all it is.

After she's finished, the grown-ups disappear off to their own fires and their tents, leaving just the children, a dozen of them, clustered around her. Maybe their fathers and mothers are elsewhere, or maybe they have no families to return to. They've noticed the scabbard belted to her waist, the one containing

Beorn's seax. One of them, a girl of ten, maybe eleven, with a round face and cheeks flushed pink and brightly painted wooden beads on a cord around her neck, asks nervously why she carries a weapon like that. Did she steal it? Who from?

'I didn't steal it,' Tova says. 'It was a gift.'

She draws it from its sheath and shows it to them, turning it over slowly so that it gleams in the firelight. They marvel at the coils and whorls and waves in the steel. Like smoke, says one boy. Like dragon's breath, says another.

The pink-cheeked girl asks, 'Did you fight the Normans? Did you kill any of them?'

'Don't be stupid,' one of the older boys sneers. 'Girls can't fight.'

'Why not?'

'Because they can't. Everyone knows.'

She turns to Tova and asks, 'Girls can fight, can't they?'

'Listen,' Tova says. 'There's nothing glorious about fighting, about war. It isn't anything like you think. It isn't like in the poems. It's what you do when you don't have any other choice. That's all. You do it because you know that if you don't, people you care about will get hurt.'

The same boy asks, 'What about the warrior, the one named Beorn? The one you said killed five Normans all by himself. I want to hear more about him.'

Yes, the others clamour all at once. Tell us more about the warrior.

'But there's nothing more to say.'

They all groan at once. The disappointment on their faces. Go on, they plead with her. Tell us about him.

Tova sighs, exasperated. Have they been paying any attention at all?

434

'No,' she says firmly. 'I'm not going to tell you about him. But if you're quiet, I'll tell you another story.'

Once, she says, not so long ago, not so very far from here, there was a green land, a peaceable land, where the barley grew tall and strong, and the wide meadows were bright with knapweed and cowslips and forget-me-nots.

Then, you could wander the woods in search of blackberries without worrying about reavers lurking amid the hazel and the hawthorn. Afterwards you could go down to the beck and sit under the alders and dip your toes in the clear water while you watched for trout and grayling. If you were lucky, you might catch a flash of blue as a kingfisher darted between the weir and the reeds.

And people travelled the roads without fear, and lords and reeves never asked for more than was their due, and rumours of far-off wars were no more than that. Folk toiled and some prospered while others struggled, but that was the way of the world, and we always tried to help one another whenever we could. Yes, sometimes there was hardship and sometimes there was hunger, but rarely was there famine. And, yes, there could be discord and strife, but hardly ever did it spill over into bloodshed. Pleas were heard in the proper manner; justice was dealt, and usually it was regarded as fair, and never were the punishments harsher than they needed to be.

In those days there were great halls of oak, and sometimes in those halls, on special days, there'd be feasts, and everybody would come together, the whole village: thirty, forty, fifty people. We'd gorge ourselves on as many sweetmeats and honeyed pastries as we could, until we were sure our stomachs would burst, but it didn't matter how much we ate because there'd always be plenty for everyone, whether you were the lord's wife or a humble dairy slave. On the hearth fire a hog, newly slaughtered, would be roasting. You could hear the hiss of fat as it dripped into the flames.

And there'd be people playing harps and flutes and drums, and streamers of white and green and yellow nailed to the roof beams, and the lintel above the great doors would be hung with boughs of yew and holly. And after we'd all had our fill, the revels would spill out into the yard. Under the light of the stars, folk would link arms, folk who often didn't see eye to eye the rest of the year round, but they'd dance with one another all the same and fall about with laughter when they got the steps wrong, and even hoary old Thorvald the priest would join in, blushing as the women pulled him into the circle. Long-held grudges would be set aside and new ties of friendship would be forged, while down by the willows a slight girl with a ribbon of green silk in her hair would share her first shy, drunken kiss.

And the mead and the ale would carry on flowing, and still more platters would be brought out to the table, heaped with freshly baked treats too hot to hold in one's hand. And the hall would be filled with the songs of old, and the hearth fire would blaze brightly all through that long night.

There was joy in this land once, she says. There was joy and there was light.

And there will be again.

ACKNOWLEDGEMENTS

Every novel is a journey into the unknown, a pilgrimage towards a destination only vaguely envisioned and along a route never before travelled. I'd like to take the opportunity to express my gratitude to all those who have joined me on the road to offer their guidance and spur me on towards my goal.

Above all, thanks to my editors at Heron Books, Jon Watt and Stefanie Bierwerth, for their faith in my writing and for guiding *The Harrowing* on its path to publication. I'm particularly grateful to Jon for having glimpsed the potential in this hugely ambitious project at what then was still a relatively early point in its development, for all his insights and considered suggestions along the way, and for his dedication in helping to hone this novel and to make it the very best work of fiction that it can possibly be. Thanks also to my copy-editor, Hugh Davis, and to Kathryn Taussig and everyone on the team at Quercus, whose hard work has been instrumental in bringing this book to publication and making it a success.

I'm immensely grateful to fellow writers Beverly Stark, Liz Pile, Lyndall Henning, Kayt Lackie, Joanne Sefton and Jonathan Carr, who were all kind enough to give feedback on sections of the novel at various stages of its composition. I'm indebted to them for the time and energy they've devoted to reading and discussing my work over the past few years, and I consider it a tremendous privilege to be a part of such a talented and enthusiastic writing community.

My interest in the Middle Ages, and the Norman Conquest in particular, was first nurtured by my dissertation supervisor and director of studies, Professor Elisabeth van Houts, while I was reading History at Emmanuel College, Cambridge. *The Harrowing* is the product of more than a decade's accumulated research into Anglo-Saxon and early Norman England, but those supervisions were crucial in broadening my appreciation for this fascinating period of British history, and without that early inspiration and encouragement, I would not be where I am today. This book is dedicated to her.

Last but by no means least, I'd like to offer my thanks as ever to my family and friends for their unfailing support throughout the writing process. Without them, this novel would not have been possible.